GEMINA

THE ILLUMINAE FILES_02

GEMINA

THE ILLUMINAE FILES_02

AMIE KAUFMAN &
JAY KRISTOFF

WITH JOURNAL ILLUSTRATIONS BY
MARIE LU

ALFRED A. KNOPF
NEW YORK

THIS IS A BORZOI BOOK PUBLISHED BY ALFRED A. KNOPF

Visit us on the Web! randomhouseteens.com

Educators and librarians, for a variety of teaching tools,
visit us at RHTeachersLibrarians.com

Library of Congress Cataloging-in-Publication Data
Names: Kaufman, Amie, author. | Kristoff, Jay, author. | Lu, Marie, illustrator.
Title: Gemina / Amie Kaufman & Jay Kristoff ; journal illustrations by Marie Lu.
Description: First edition. | Alfred A. Knopf : New York, [2016] | Series: The Illuminae Files ; 02 | Summary: "When the space station Heimdall is invaded, Hannah and Nik must work together to defeat the enemy." —Provided by publisher
Identifiers: LCCN 2015037131 | ISBN 978-0-553-49915-5 (trade) |
ISBN 978-0-553-49916-2 (lib. bdg.) | ISBN 978-0-553-49917-9 (ebook)
Subjects: | CYAC: Science fiction. | Space stations—Fiction. | Interplanetary voyages—Fiction. | Artificial intelligence—Fiction.
Classification: LCC PZ7.K1642 Ge 2016 | DDC [Fic]—dc23

Book design by Heather Kelly and Jay Kristoff

Printed in the United States of America
October 2016
10 9 8 7

First Edition

FOR MEL, WHO ALWAYS BELIEVED

Chief Prosecutor: Gabriel Crowhurst, BSA, MFS, JD
Chief Defense Counsel: Kin Hebi, BSA, ARP, JD
Tribunal: Hua Li Jun, BSA, JD, MD; Saladin Al Nakat, BSA, JD; Shannelle Gillianne Chua, BSA, JD, OKT
Witness: Leanne Frobisher, Executive Director, BeiTech Industries, MFA, MBA, PhD
Date: 10/14/76
Timestamp: 13:06

—cont. from pg. 359—

Frobisher, L: . . . over seven hundred thousand employees across dozens of colonized worlds. Is it that difficult to believe?

Crowhurst, G: Dr. Frobisher, this was a major invasion. Thousands of personnel. Trillions of ISH worth of equipment. Yet you're alleging you had *no* idea about your company's attack on Wallace Ulyanov mining operations in the Kerenza Sector? Despite your position as director of acquisitions for BeiTech Industries?

Frobisher, L: [Consults with counsel.] I've already stated I was appointed to that role well after the alleged invasion.

Crowhurst, G: But well *before* BeiTech's attack on Jump Station *Heimdall.*

Frobisher, L: *Alleged* attack.

Crowhurst, G: Dr. Frobisher, you've read accounts of the *alleged* attack left behind by residents Hanna Donnelly and Niklas Malikov, correct? I'd like to direct you to the Illuminae Files testimony, Exhibits 178a through—

Hebi, K: Defense objects to the inclusion of the so-called Illuminae documents in these proceedings in the strongest possible terms.

Al Nakat, S: Counselor, we've discussed this already. The documents have been accepted into the record. Move on.

Crowhurst, G: Dr. Frobisher? Have you reviewed the Illuminae Files?

Frobisher, L: [Consults with counsel.] Yes.

Crowhurst, G: What do you make of Niklas Malikov's testimony?

Frobisher, L: Frankly, I'm surprised this tribunal considers the fictions of a teenage drug dealer and convicted criminal worthy of the title "testimony."

Crowhurst, G: Dr. Frob—

Frobisher, L: A born-and-bred foot soldier of the Dom Najov? Son of *Zakary* Malikov? Everyone here knows what that boy went to prison for. This is your star witness?

Crowhurst, G: Do you understand this is the first Dom Najov testimony to *ever* be entered into the records of a UTA tribunal? The House of Knives cartel doesn't speak to the authorities, Dr. Frobisher.

Frobisher, L: I'm certain if given a choice, Niklas Malikov wouldn't have spoken either.

Crowhurst, G: But he didn't have a choice, did he? Your people saw to that.

Hebi, K: Objection. Combative.

Crowhurst, G: I'll withdraw.

Dr. Frobisher, I have a few questions regarding Mr. Malikov's testimony, and that of Hanna Donnelly, as pertains to the *alleged* attack on Jump Station *Heimdall*. You wouldn't mind if we review these files for a while, would you?

Frobisher, L: [Consults with counsel.] No. I have no objections.

Crowhurst, G: Excellent. Perhaps we should start at the beginning.

U-MAIL

To: Director Taylor, **BEITECH HEADQUARTERS,**
From: GHOST ID (9876-5432-1098-7654-ERROR-
Incept: 08/01/75
Subject: [!] Operation: Plainview. Priority Aler

Director Taylor,

I know I'm not supposed to break comms silence until Operation Plainview is complete, so consider this an EMERGENCY.

I've been aboard Jump Station *Heimdall* intercepting communications from the *Alexander* and the *Hypatia* since the colony assault, as per your instructions. Not a whisper of the attack has gotten through. But I just snatched the attached transmission, and deleting distress calls is about to be the least of my troubles.

Very soon, somebody's going to be here to deliver the news in person.

The *Lincoln* has failed.

We're absolutely ███ed.

Awaiting instructions.

Rapier

RADIO MESSAGE: HYPATIA INITIATED—
—TRANSMISSION FOLLOWS—
COMMUNICATION INTERCEPT

FROM: WUC SCIENCE VESSEL *HYPATIA*—78V 101:421:084
(Kerenza system)
TO: JUMP STATION *HEIMDALL*
INCEPT: 08/01/75

Mayday, mayday, mayday, this is Acting Captain Syra
Boll of the WUC science vessel *Hypatia* calling Jump
Station *Heimdall*, please respond.

Please respond, *Heimdall*, over.

And of course you don't. Why should today be any
different from yesterday? I'm not even sure why the
hell I'm transmitting anymore.

Well, for the record, and at the risk of repeating
myself, here goes. On January 29, 2575, the Wallace
Ulyanov Consortium mining colony on Kerenza IV was
attacked by hostile forces in the employ of BeiTech
Industries. The colony was decimated, and several
thousand survivors fled aboard WUC science vessel
Hypatia, WUC heavy freighter *Copernicus* (subsequently
destroyed) and UTA battlecarrier *Alexander*, which
answered the colony's SOS calls. This fleet was pursued
by a BeiTech dreadnought, BT042-TN, aka *Lincoln*.

Please be advised the *Alexander* and *Lincoln* engaged
each other twenty-four hours ago. Both vessels

were completely destroyed. *Hypatia* is now the only remaining vessel in the fleet.

On the off chance we are not receiving your transmissions, or you are unable to reply, *Hypatia* is still en route to the *Heimdall* waypoint with *Alexander* survivors and refugees from the original Kerenza assault aboard. We're hoping like hell it's not just a smoking pile of debris when we get there. Estimate our arrival in fifteen days.

If you guys can roll out any kind of cavalry, now's the goddamn time.

Hypatia out.

COUNTDOWN TO
HYPATIA ARRIVAL
AT HEIMDALL WAYPOINT:

15 DAYS
11 HOURS: 18 MINUTES

whisperNET

BRIEFING NOTE:
First relevant point of contact between Hanna Donnelly and Niklas Malikov on *Heimdall*'s whisperNET system. Malikov was using a hijacked guest ID—it's understood he cycled through them frequently.

AMBIENT TEMPERATURE: 22°C   **DATE:** 08/02/75   **TIME:** 14:09   **LOCATION:** Quarters

---

HEIMDALL CHAT   HANNA DONNELLY

Donnelly, H: Hey, peon.

Guest423: Lo, the Princess.

Donnelly, H: Aha, you're there.

Donnelly, H: Thought you might be off skulking somewhere in the depths.

Guest423: Who says I'm not? I'm skulking like a mother███ in here.

Guest423: So is this a social call?

Donnelly, H: That's so sweet, the way you hold out hope one day I'm going to call you up just to hear the sound of your voice.

Guest423: To dream the impossible dream. This is my quest.

Guest423: So how much you want?

Donnelly, H: Ten grams. I got my pocket money.

Guest423: Big spender. You sure you can handle that much, princess? This isn't candy, you know.

NETbar

FRIENDS ONLINE
Claire Houston
Jackson Merrick
Kim Rivera
Keiko Sato

NEWSFEED
Terra Day Celebrations Begin Soon!

Mess Hall 3 Still Offline

Announcement—Wormhole Maintenance Over Terra Day Break

A Reminder on Quarantine Procedures

Mission Statement

DIARY AND APPOINTMENTS
Get Stuff

Lunch with Kim

Training 18:00—Dojo 2

Meet Jackson tonight?

Donnelly, H: It's not just for me. But your concern is DEEPLY appreciated.

Donnelly, H: So you can do it?

Guest423: If there's something I can't get on this station, it ain't worth getting.

Guest423: Except a Saturday night with you, of course.

Donnelly, H: Of course, my sweet.

Guest423: Oh, she called me "my sweet."

Guest423: Be still my beating something something.

Donnelly, H: When can you deliver? I can get away tonight.

Guest423: No can do. I got Biz tonight. Besides, I'm gonna need a couple of weeks for ten g's.

Donnelly, H: Whaaaaaat? But we need it for the Terra Day reception!

Guest423: Supplies low for the holidays, Highness. Everyone wants a taste this time of year. Don't worry, you and your merry band will be well supplied before your little soiree on the fifteenth.

Guest423: 'Sides, I thought you'd be busy with Prince Charming tonight.

Donnelly, H: I'm seeing him after he comes off duty.

Donnelly, H: Fifteenth is okay, I guess. Tell me where and when. I need to let Jackson know where I'll be.

Guest423: Doesn't he ALWAYS know where you are? That's what he does all day, right? Monitor personal locator beacons and speak in a stupid ██████ing accent?

Guest423: Pip pip what ho jolly good old chap?

Donnelly, H: Hmmm?

Donnelly, H: Oh, sorry, I stopped listening there for a moment. I was busy thinking about his dreamy accent.

Donnelly, H: Of course he knows where I am, but if I want him to block my locator when I head up to Skulktown, I like to let him know in advance.

Guest423: Yeah, so about that.

Guest423: Boyfriend covers your tracks from Daddy, and that's chill. But I'm not exactly turning cartwheels over us talking biz on whisperNET, given the nature of our biz. Feel me?

Donnelly, H: I thought you wiped everything after we're done? If nothing else, don't you want to hide the continual rejection from the world? Are you telling me you can't keep it from the SecTeam monitors?

Guest423: It's not your end I'm worried about.

Guest423: I'd be having a Very Serious Discussion with my uncle if he knew I was dealing dust to the station commander's precious baby girl. So I'm getting a direct line hooked up for us. Palmpad to palmpad. Secure D2D network, off the Heimdall grid as well as the House of Knives lines.

Guest423: So you can have me all to yourself.

Guest423: He said, winking suggestively.

Donnelly, H: If it was the last Saturday night before the destruction of the universe, I'd still have plans to wash my hair.

Guest423: Shower Time, huh? I'd be up for that.

Guest423: I might be able to swing a discount for you next batch, by the way. We got Plans.

Guest423: Imagine me twirling my mustache when I say that.

Guest423: I'm not growing a 'stache, before you panic.

Donnelly, H: That's a pity. I could really go for you with a mustache.

Guest423: Consider my razor flushed out the next airlock I find.

Donnelly, H: It's hard to believe a criminal mastermind could be this gullible.

Donnelly, H: Anyway, I'm afraid to ask about your plans, but a discount sounds nice.

Guest423: We'll see. No promises.

Donnelly, H: Commitment and you, not so much.

Guest423: Something like that.

Donnelly, H: See? You'd just break my heart if I let you woo me.

Donnelly, H: Right after my boyfriend broke your legs.

Guest423: Highness, believe me when I say your heart's safe with me.

Guest423: And that there's scarier things in my ██ing laundry hamper than Sir Poshly McAccent.

Donnelly, H: That says *way* more about your personal hygiene than it does about my boyfriend.

Guest423: Good thing we're doing Shower Time, then, huh?

Donnelly, H: Not if you were the last anything in anything.

Donnelly, H: Meet same place as last time?

Guest423: Yeah. Infirmary level. 17:00 hours on the fifteenth. I'll dress sexy.

Donnelly, H: See that you do.

Guest423: I'll bring the palmpad with me, too. After this meet, you contact me on that. Day or night. Anything you need.

Donnelly, H: Anything?

Guest423: You're just teasing now.

Donnelly, H: And here I thought that was what you wanted.

Guest423: You know what I want.

Guest423: . . . You still there?

——CONNECTION TERMINATED——

whisperNET

AMBIENT TEMPERATURE: 22°C **DATE:** 08/02/75 **TIME:** 17:

 BRIEFING NOTE: First relevant point of contact between Hanna Donnelly and Jackson Merrick on *Heimdall*'s whisperNET system. For full effect, read everything Merrick says in a loin-stirringly deep, upper-crust accent while listening to smooth jazz.

HEIMDALL CHAT	HANNA DONNELLY

Donnelly, H: Hello, handsome. Busy?

Merrick, J: Hey, beautiful. Never too busy for you.

Donnelly, H: I'm trying to be better about not hitting you with messages while you're on duty. See how good I am?

Merrick, J: Not *too* good, I hope.

Donnelly, H: You're off at 20:00? You coming over?

Donnelly, H: Dad's not home until 23:00 . . .

Merrick, J: Three whole hours. Good lord, how *will* we fill the time?

Donnelly, H: Hrrrrrmmmmmmm.

Donnelly, H: Nope, I got nothing. You got any ideas?

Merrick, J: Chess?

Donnelly, H: Strip chess?

Merrick, J: But we didn't finish last time. I'm not sure who won.

NETbar

FRIENDS ONLINE
Claire Houston
Jackson Merrick
Kim Rivera
Keiko Sato

NEWSFEED
Terra Day Celebrations Begin Soon!

Mess Hall 3 Still Offline

Announcement— Wormhole Maintenance Over Terra Day Break

A Reminder on Quarantine Procedures

Last Shuttle for Core Departs in Two Days— Bookings FULL

Mission Statement

DIARY AND APPOINTMENTS
Get stuff

Lunch with Kim

Training 18:00—Dojo 2

Meet Jackson tonight?

Donnelly, H: I think it was probably a draw. This calls for a tiebreaker.

Donnelly, H: Are you on duty tomorrow?

Merrick, J: Sadly, yes. So you can't do anything that'll leave me limping.

Donnelly, H: Wouldn't dream of it. I shall polish my halo extra hard before you come around tonight.

Donnelly, H: Can you block my tracker for me on Terra Day? Say 17:00–18:00?

Merrick, J: Beautiful, do you really have to get more of that stuff?

Donnelly, H: Don't be like that, it's fiiiiiiine.

Donnelly, H: You gotta be a little impressed I can make whisperNET do that: "Fiiiiiiiine."

Merrick, J: Yes, you're very talented. It's just . . .

Donnelly, H: It's all in the tongue. Distracted yet?

Merrick, J: Hanna . . .

Donnelly, H: Jax, it's just some fun, I promise. Special occasions only. The girls asked for some, and you know I go easy on it. But do you have any idea how many pre–Terra Day bashes I have to hostess? I just need a little light at the end of the tunnel.

Merrick, J: I can't understand why your dad lets those people stay on the station. They're not even official residents. Did Mr. Prison Tattoos hit on you again?

Donnelly, H: Couldn't say, I really wasn't listening to most of what he said. What I want to know is how soon after 20:00 you'll be here and hitting on me instead.

Merrick, J: You could come and meet me at 20:01.

Donnelly, H: Yeah, I guess.

Merrick, J: Oh, the enthusiasm.

Donnelly, H: Sorry. Just . . . is Sam Wheaton from comms on duty tonight? He kinda skeeves me out.

Merrick, J: Why, what does he do?

Donnelly, H: It's hard to explain. It's just . . . the way he looks at me. He blinks too much. And he's super smarmy. He explains things to me using words of one syllable or less.

Merrick, J: Damn your blinky eyes and condescension, Smarmy Sam. Keeping my lady from my side. No fear, I'll leave him behind and come straight to you.

Merrick, J: It's 4.3 kilometers from SecCon to your habitat. So I'll be there around 20:09. I might need a shower after a sprint like that, though.

Donnelly, H: Why bother if you're just gonna get sweaty again?

Donnelly, H: So, you can cover my locator on the fifteenth?

Merrick, J: Dramatic sigh. Anything for you, beautiful.

Donnelly, H: When do you get a full day off next? Let's do something.

Merrick, J: Funny you should mention that. My next RDO is the tenth. Ring any bells?

Donnelly, H: Hmmmmmm.

Donnelly, H: No, can't think of anything interesting or memorable connected with that date.

Merrick, J: Well, in that case, please excuse me. I'm off to end my pointless existence in the dark void of space. Tell Mother I love her.

Donnelly, H: You really got the day off?

Merrick, J: Well, six months is something of a record for me. Not sure about you . . .

Donnelly, H: You know it is. But what's even weirder is imagining six more.

Merrick, J: Well, let's handle them one anniversary at a time. For THIS one, I have a plan so romantic you could bang a silly hat on it and call it Lord Byron.

Donnelly, H: This sounds promising. Am I allowed to know what this epic plan entails?

Merrick, J: Um, no. You own a wetsuit, though, right? No allergies to maple syrup? I can get the handcuffs from a supply locker . . .

Donnelly, H: Don't write checks you can't cash, handsome . . .

Merrick, J: I've Made Arrangements. That's all I'll say. Now you'd better let me get back to it before your dad fires me and I'm reduced to dealing dust for a living.

Donnelly, H: I hear that's a great way to meet girls.

Merrick, J: Touché, mademoiselle. Touché.

Donnelly, H: I'll see you in a few hours.

Merrick, J: Counting the minutes.

December '74

Dear Squeak,

I noticed your old notebook was running out, and with the challenge of settling into our new home at Heimdall, I knew a resupply would be urgently required. I hope you like the one I chose. The binding is top-quality, so it should stand up to the rigors to which you traditionally subject your diaries — and I imagine the coming series of parties will require some furious illustrating on your part. You did an outstanding job last night assisting me in hosting the staff reception, though don't think I didn't notice that glass of CHAMPAGNE. Nevertheless, your mother would have been proud of your poise, and you should know that I am too.

I know you have your doubts about a posting this isolated, and it's been wonderful to see you support my choice regardless. I look forward to the next year together — I hope we can make the most of our time before you leave for college, and give you plenty of adventures with which to fill this book.

Your loving father,
Charles Donnelly

BRIEFING NOTE:
Pages scanned from Hanna Donnelly's personal journal. Her old man used to import them from Ares VI. Leather-bound. Genuine pen and ink to go with 'em. If you know how much paper weighs and what the shipping to a station like *Heimdall* costs, you'll have some idea of what Daddy thought of his little girl. This is the first entry, dated December '74, eight months prior to events in this dossier. Note the bullet hole, bottom right-hand corner.

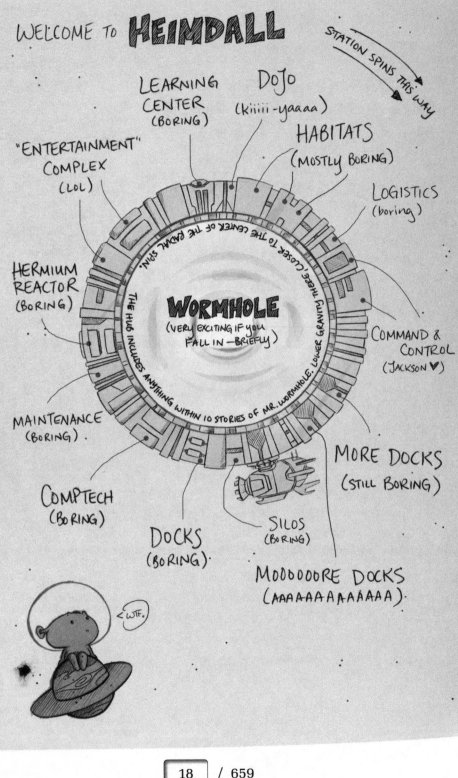

WELCOME TO **HEIMDALL**

STATION SPINS THIS WAY

LEARNING CENTER (BORING)

DOJO (kiiiii-yaaaa)

HABITATS (MOSTLY BORING)

"ENTERTAINMENT" COMPLEX (LOL)

LOGISTICS (boring)

HERMIUM REACTOR (BORING)

THE HUB INCLUDES ANYTHING WITHIN 10 STORIES OF MR. WORMHOLE. LOWER GRAVITY THERE, CLOSER TO THE CENTER OF THE RADIAL SPIN.

WORMHOLE (VERY EXCITING IF YOU FALL IN — BRIEFLY)

COMMAND & CONTROL (JACKSON ♥)

MAINTENANCE (BORING).

MORE DOCKS (STILL BORING)

COMPTECH (BORING)

SILOS (BORING)

DOCKS (BORING).

MOOOOOORE DOCKS (AAAAAAAAAAAAA).

< WTF.

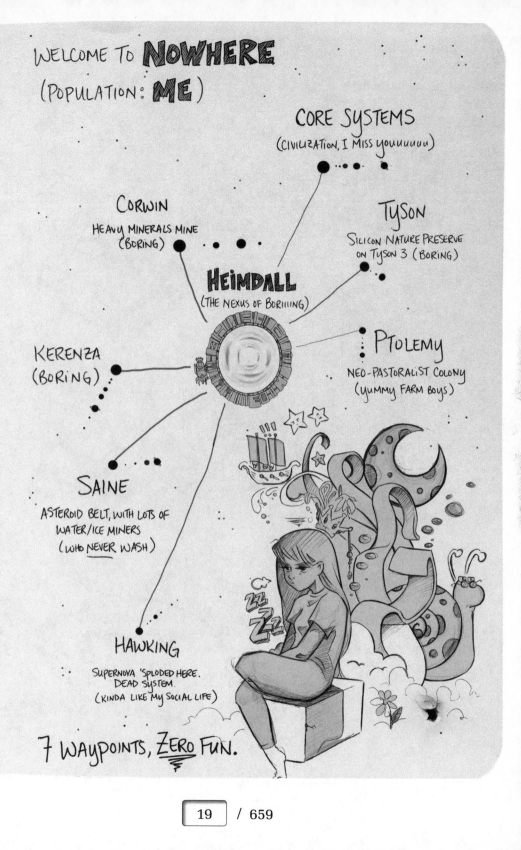

WELCOME TO **NOWHERE**
(POPULATION: **ME**)

CORE SYSTEMS
(CIVILIZATION, I MISS youuuuuu)

CORWIN
HEAVY MINERALS MINE
(BORING)

TYSON
SILICON NATURE PRESERVE
ON TYSON 3 (BORING)

HEIMDALL
(THE NEXUS OF BORIIIING)

KERENZA
(BORING)

PTOLEMY
NEO-PASTORALIST COLONY
(yummy FARM BOYS)

SAINE
ASTEROID BELT, WITH LOTS OF
WATER/ICE MINERS
(WHO NEVER WASH)

HAWKING
SUPERNOVA 'SPLODED HERE.
DEAD SYSTEM.
(KINDA LIKE MY SOCIAL LIFE)

7 WAYPOINTS, ZERO FUN.

EVERYTHING YOU NEED TO KNOW ABOUT MY DAD IN THREE DIAGRAMS

FIG 1 : SPENDING TIME TOGETHER

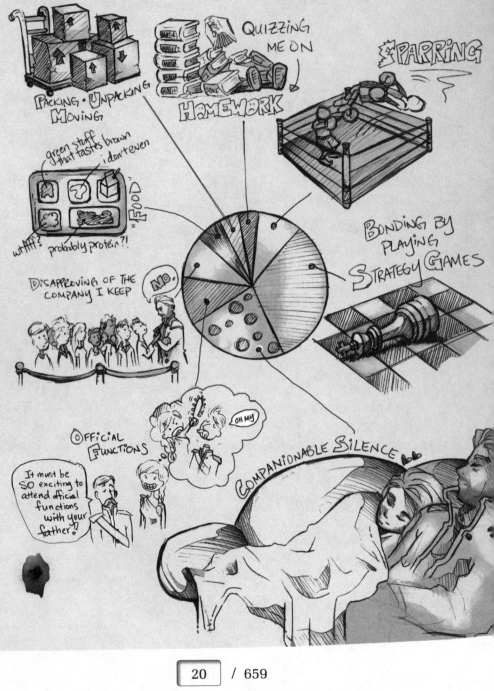

FIG. 2: Procedure for Leaving Our Quarters

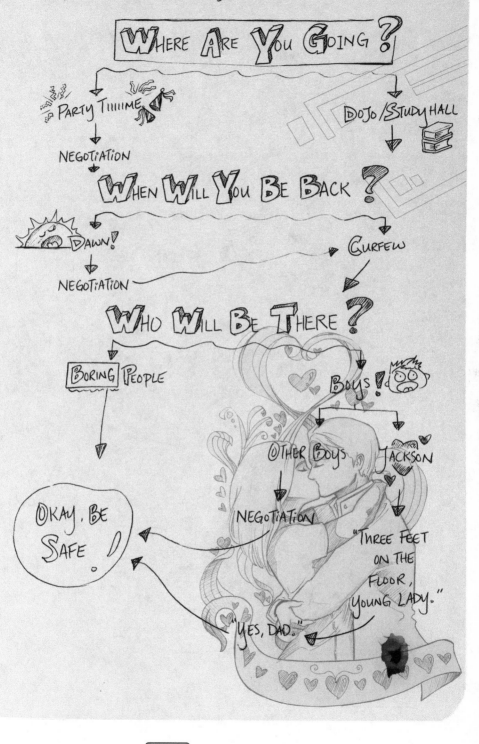

Fig 3: ON THE MOVE

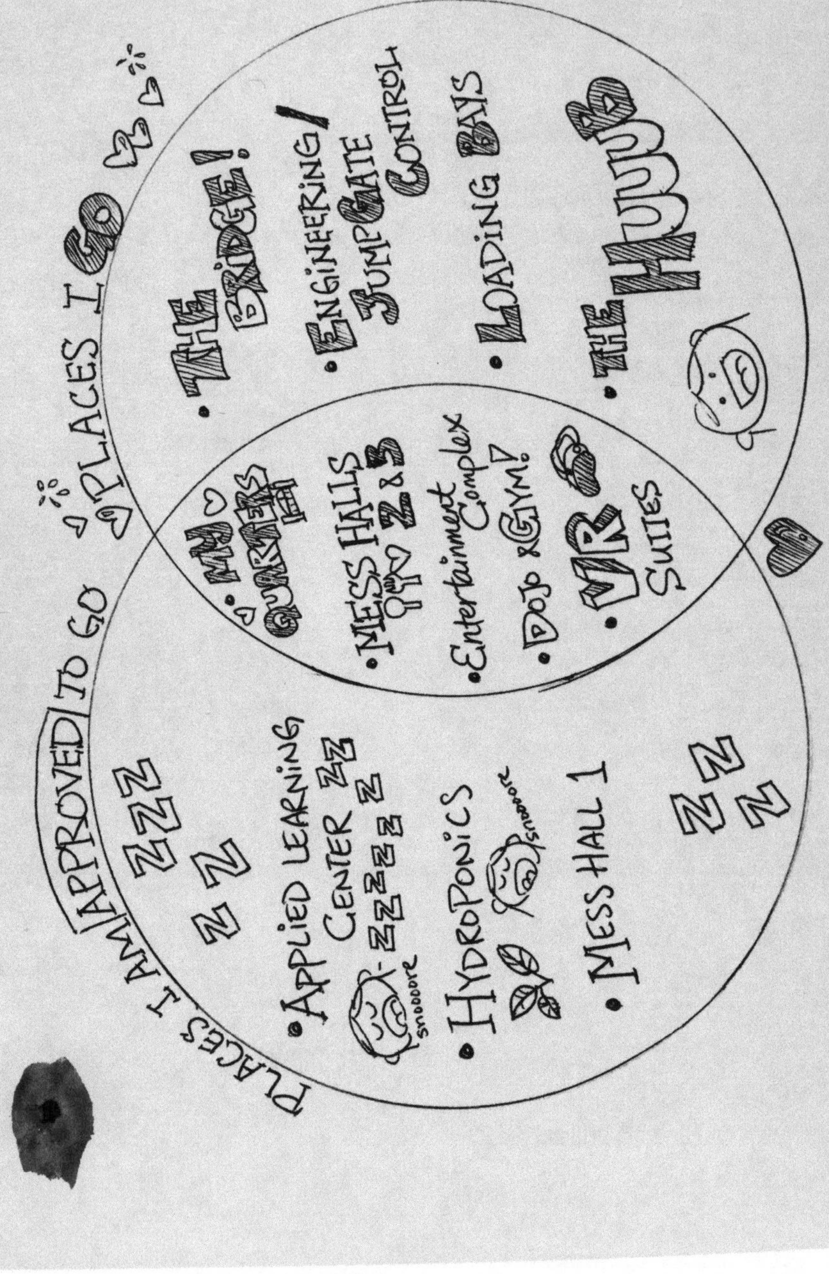

PLACES I AM APPROVED TO GO ♥ PLACES I GO ♥

Places I Go:
- THE BRIDGE!
- ENGINEERING / JUMP GATE CONTROL
- LOADING BAYS
- THE HUUUB

Overlap:
- MY QUARTERS
- MESS HALLS 2 & 3
- Entertainment Complex
- DOJO & GYM?
- VR SUITES

Places I Am Approved To Go:
- ZZZ Z Z Z
- Applied Learning Center ZZ ZZZZ Z - snoooore
- HydroPonics - snoooore
- MESS HALL 1
- Z Z Z

PERSONAL MESSAGE: PIRATE IM SYSTEM-HEIMD
Participants: Niklas Malikov, Civilian (unregister
Ella Malikova, Civilian (unregistered)
Date: 08/03/75
Timestamp: 18:02

BRIEFING NOTE:
First noteworthy exchange between Nik Malikov and his cousin Ella Malikova. The cousins and other members of the House of Knives cartel aboard *Heimdall* communicated on a blackhat network leeching off the station's emergency broadcast grid. The network was set up by Ella—a fifteen-year-old electronics prodigy who went by the handle Pauchok ("Little Spider" in Old Rus').

NikM: sssssshhhhhhhiiiiiiiiiiiiiiiiiiiiiiiiiiiiiiiiiiiiiiiiiiiiiiiiiiiiiiiiiiiiiii iiiiiiiiiiiiiiiiiiiiiiiiiiiiiiiiiiiiiiiiiiiiiiiiiiiiiiiiiiiiiiiiiii

Pauchok: tttttttttt?

NikM: dingdingding winnerrrrrrr

Pauchok: what news, my cuz

NikM: ▮

Pauchok: ya u said that twice now

NikM: because i'm covered HEAD TO FOOT IN IT

Pauchok: you're covered head to foot in ▮???

Pauchok: is it saturday night already?

NikM: o hilarious. stand-up comedy genius, right here

Pauchok: now if only I could stand up ;)

NikM: :P

Pauchok: so what's with the dookie and y r u covered in it

Pauchok: god did I rly just type the word "dookie"

NikM: your dad and his brilliant ideas

Pauchok: o riiiiight, you were on clean up duty today, how'd it go

NikM: like u don't know

Pauchok: hate to shatter that ego, cuz, but I've been too busy to watch ur comings and goings. We gonna be on skeleton crew come TerraDay and I'm kiiiiiinda busy.

Pauchok: So how are our little visitors anyway?

NikM: "visitors" my █.

Pauchok: i would like to keep your butt out of this conversation if at all possible plz

Pauchok: i hear enough about it from zoe

NikM: They're COWS, Ella.

NikM: u hve any idea how much █ the average adult cow makes?

Pauchok: 30.48kg per day. Approximately.

NikM: . . .

NikM: u such a smart█

Pauchok: smart AND hilarious? omg how fierce is this fem get these boys all OFF OF ME

NikM: 30.48kg per day. I know that shovel better than I've known most of my girlfriends.

NikM: Almost makes me wish I was back in slam.

Pauchok: though few, there *are* advantages to being stuck inside Anansi all day. I keep a list. I'm adding "never having to wade knee-high through cowcakes" to it right now

NikM: This is all going to go horribly wrong, u know that rite?

Pauchok: relax, dad knows wut he's doin

NikM: wanna bet? 100ISĦ says this all goes balls up by november

Pauchok: 100ISĦ no way. Lookin this good don't come free, u know

NikM: Why the hell we gotta keep them above the hermium reactor anyway? It's sweatier than the new Elizabeth Andretti sim in there

Pauchok: poor cow cows :(

NikM: U worried about the cows? What about me? I STINK

Pauchok: so go have a shower god

NikM: I CAN'T DOUBLE G IS IN THERE GODAMMIT

Pauchok: OMG ALL CAPS INCOMING SHIELDS TO FULL

Pauchok:

 CAPSCAPSCAPSCAPSCAPSCAPSCAPSCAPS

NikM: i hate u so much

Pauchok: o lies, u luff meeeeeeee

Pauchok: ok if it makes u feel better, ur an 18 yr old boy

NikM: . . . so?

Pauchok: so u *always* stink, Nik

NikM: >_>

Pauchok: when's dad implanting the larvae?

NikM: next couple of days, iirc. bad biz, cuz

Pauchok: poor cow cows :(

NikM: speaking of biz, u got that palmpad hooked up for lil ms Donnelly like I asked?

Pauchok: god cuz, why do this to yourself?

Pauchok: I grant you do the smoldering stare thing very well, but Donnelly's got a bf

NikM: he's a tosser.

Pauchok: Nik, Jackson Merrick is SO FINE he's illegal in seventeen systems. Zoe got me to dub a mix of his daily personnel announcements so she could listen to them as she goes to sleep.

NikM: wtfffffff

Pauchok: Hanna Donnelly's a spoiled little rich girl. Private tutors. Designer space booties. A bf who raises the ambient temp by 2° when he enters the room. You are NEVER getting into that

Pauchok: you remember that time she broke your arm?

NikM: she didn't break it, it was just sprained

Pauchok: god that was funny. i laughed so hard i can't use my legs anymore

NikM: I see what u did there

Pauchok: did it hurt? I've never had a broken arm before

NikM: I wouldn't know because it wasn't BROKEN

Pauchok: it kinda looked broken

Pauchok: you were in a cast and everything

NikM: ▮▮▮▮ ME SHE DIDN'T BREAK IT IT WAS ONLY SPRAINED

Pauchok: AAAAAAAAAAAAAAAAAAAAAAAA

Pauchok:

```
  __ ···_____
`(\ [  ===NCC-1701===--|__|) ____ .._--"`_--_____
  `"""""""""""""""""""| |"" [""_-_____ __/
          | |  /..../'`-__-'
     ____| |_/::::_'_   CAPSCAPSCAPSCAPSCAPSCAPS
     |\".`"`'_____//\
     `"'-_ """"" \\/
        `"""""""""`
```

NikM: look, just make sure u got the palmpad set up before the 15th, ok? Because if your dad finds out I'm dealing there, I'm in more trouble than his ███ing cows

Pauchok: ok. fine. but do me one favor.

NikM: wut

Pauchok: When your brain gets back from vacation, lemme know. I need to have a stern word to it about letting little nik drive the bus while it's away

NikM: "little" nik? wtf

Pauchok: There are worse words i could use for it, believe me

NikM: ok double G's done in the shower. u coming 2 dinner tonite?

Pauchok: ehhhhh

NikM: u know ur dad. "the family that eats together maintains a successful interstellar criminal organization together" and it's last night before most of the crew head home for Terra Day.

NikM: special menu planned

Pauchok: wut r we having

NikM: three guesses

Pauchok: . . .

Pauchok: steak?

NikM: dingdingding winnerrrrrrr

Pauchok: poor cow cows :(

```
$nickname = htmlentities(strip_tags($_POST['PAUCHOK']));
$reg_exUrl = "/(http|https|ftp|ftps)\:\/\/[a-zA-Z0-9\-\.]+\.[a-zA-Z]{2,3}(\/\S*)?/";
$message = htmlentities(strip_tags($_POST['message']));
if (($message) != "\n") {
if (preg_match($reg_exUrl, $message, $url)) {
$message = preg_replace($reg_exUrl, '<a href="'.$url[0].'" target="_blank">'.$url[0].'</a>', $message);
fwrite(fopen('data.txt', 'a'), '<span>'.$nickname.'</span>'.$message = $t2_replace
break;
```

HOW NOT TO HIT on a GIRL
(AN ILLUSTRATED INSTRUCTIONAL GUIDE)

OUR PLAYER

A GIRL OF
PASSING FAIRNESS

A BOY OF
QUESTIONABLE QUALITY

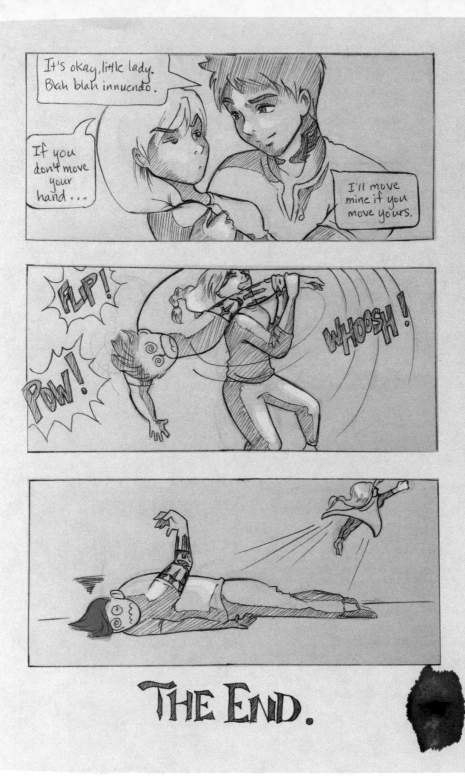

whisperNET

AMBIENT TEMPERATURE: 22°C   **DATE:** 08/05/75   **TIME:** 02:04   **LOCATION:** Quarters

HEIMDALL CHAT	HANNA DONNELLY	NETbar

Guest389: Hey what kind of flowers you like?

Donnelly, H: Zn . . . gkk.

Guest389: Is that even a word?

Donnelly, H: . . . Nik?

Donnelly, H: God . . . what time is it?

Guest389: I dunno. Night time?

Guest389: What kind of flowers you like?

Donnelly, H: Flowers?

Donnelly, H: What does it say about you that I'm trying to work out how you're going to twist my answer into something really inappropriate?

Guest389: No, for real. What kind?

Guest389: I assume you like 'em. You have those ovary things. Goes with the territory, right GOD PUT DOWN THE KNIFE I'M KIDDING.

Donnelly, H: Jasmine. I like the scent.

NETbar

FRIENDS ONLINE
Keiko Sato

NEWSFEED
Terra Day Celebrations! 10 Days to Go!

Mess Hall 3 Still Offline

Shuttle Schedule Update—Terra Day Departures

Reminder—Wormhole Maintenance Over Terra Day Break

Mission Statement

DAIRY AND APPOINTMENTS
Training 18:00—Dojo 2 (bring vid for Sanjay)

Ask dad about jumpsuit

6 month anniversaryyyyy

Call Claire

Get party favors from Peon

Donnelly, H: Inappropriate joke in three, two, one . . .

Guest389: Jasmine, huh? Not roses?

Donnelly, H: I have nothing against roses. But you asked about my favorite.

Guest389: ███. Okay.

Donnelly, H: Is there a reason we're discussing this in the middle of the night?

Guest389: Sorry, am I interrupting? Is Sir Poshly there?

Donnelly, H: No, he's working.

Donnelly, H: I mean, don't call him that.

Guest389: So you're alone?

Guest389: Well, that's a goddamn crime.

Donnelly, H: I'm fine. I leave the crime to you.

Guest389: Oh, burnT.

Donnelly, H: Are flowers our new code? Did I miss a memo?

Guest389: No, I was just gonna get you some.

Guest389: I know a guy who knows a guy. But getting them out here would cost, like, my right testicle and stuff, so if you're not down with roses I'll just keep everything where it is.

Guest389: For later.

Donnelly, H: Soooo much later.

Guest389: Who likes jasmine, anyway? I don't even know what that is.

Donnelly, H: You ever notice my perfume?

Guest389: Maybe.

Donnelly, H: That's jasmine. Now you know.

Guest389: Ah, right. His Majesty the King buy that for you?

Donnelly, H: No, my prince did.

Donnelly, H: Nik, it's really late.

Guest389: You in bed?

Donnelly, H: And I'm going to sleep.

Guest389: Can I come?

Donnelly, H: Night, Nik.

Guest389: Night, Highness.

whisperNET

BRIEFING NOTE: A brief discussion between Hanna's father, Commander Charles Donnelly, and his Chief of Engineering, Isaac Grant.

AMBIENT TEMPERATURE: 22°C **DATE:** 08/05/75 **TIME:** 09:29 **LOCATION:** C&C

HEIMDALL CHAT	CHARLES DONNELLY

Donnelly, C: Isaac.

Grant, I: Boss. Help you?

Donnelly, C: Three things.

Grant, I: The elevators, right?

Donnelly, C: We'll get to that. First, I need to bump our maintenance debrief. I'll be stuck on this report for WUC HQ until 18:00. They're demanding an update on the UTA presence in the Kerenza Sector and want to know why the hell that warship hasn't left yet.

Grant, I: It's a damn good question. Shutting down access to Kerenza is costing us a fortune.

Donnelly, C: It's the way it has to be. We can't risk the *Alexander* spotting our hermium operation there. I know a lot of people are keen to get in touch with the colony, you included.

Grant, I: I'd rather wait to talk to Helena than risk prison. Radio silence is preferable to conjugal visits. What else?

Donnelly, C: Traffic has delayed all remaining inbounds from

NETbar

FRIENDS ONLINE
None

NEWSFEED
Details of Terra Day Celebrations!

Mess Hall 3 Repairs Proceeding

Reminder—Wormhole Maintenance Over Terra Day Break

Last Shuttle Departing Before Terra Day Only Has 12 Places Left!

Mission Statement

DIARY AND APPOINTMENTS
Officer meeting

Maintenance debrief

Monthly reports

Get Hanna's Terra Day gift

Meet Tyrell re: reactor rods

other sectors until after Terra Day. So once the last shuttles depart on Friday, you'll have a clear window if you need to take the wormhole offline.

Grant, I: Shouldn't need to, but nice to know. Maint' is on schedule, all looking good.

Donnelly, C: Excellent. Second matter—I've had pushback from upper management on the overtime hours your department is clocking and your expenditure forecasts for the wormhole maintenance period.

Grant, I: Are you serious?

Donnelly, C: Calculations for cosmic string manipulation alone have taken a combined total of over four thousand man-hours. The bean counters are howling, Isaac.

Grant, I: They do realize what we're doing here, right? Do they understand what could happen if something goes wrong with the wormhole? Quantum displacement, continuity collapse, geodesic distortion, temporal disruption—

Donnelly, C: They're accountants, Isaac. They don't want to hear about theoretical disaster scenarios. They want to hear "black bottom line."

Grant, I: Quantum displacement isn't hypothetical. Remember the *Scylla*? Whole station disappears with nothing but Schwartzchild particles to show for it. Reappears ninety-two weeks later, crew acting like they never left. We're not playing patty-cake here, Charles. We're orbiting a seven-way puncture in the fabric of the ███ing *universe*. We screw this maintenance up, Christ only knows what happens.

Donnelly, C: Just . . . try and keep the overtime to a minimum, all right? We'll go over your projections at 18:00.

Grant, I: [sighs.] Fine.

Donnelly, C: Now, on a slightly stranger note . . .

Grant, I: The elevators.

Donnelly, C: Yes. I couldn't help but notice a rather obnoxious pop song playing through the elevator PA on the way to my meet with strategy this morning. Now, my daughter insists on informing me daily that my taste in music is not exactly "chill."

Grant, I: Ha! My daughter says the same to me.

Donnelly, C: But then I noticed the same song playing when I got on the elevators to Reactor Control twenty minutes ago.

Grant, I: Yeah. It's playing on all the elevators.

Donnelly, C: It's playing on *all the elevators*, Isaac. *Constantly.*

Grant, I: Yeah, I know. It's a new Lexi Blue single. Kady loves her.

Donnelly, C: What the devil is it doing playing on my elevators?

Grant, I: One of the maintenance guys got sent some malware. It's a marketing ploy from Blue's recording company. Erases any audio file data it can find and implants the new single instead.

Donnelly, C: Don't we have defenses against that kind of thing?

Grant, I: Yeah. It's one of these new-wave Trojans. Mutating virus. Kind of clever, actually.

Donnelly, C: Have you listened to the lyrics? I couldn't understand half of them, but the bits I caught sounded a little . . . risqué.

Grant, I: Um. Yeah. The title kinda gives it away.

Donnelly, C: Dare I ask?

Grant, I: Let's just say it has to do with lollipops. And the licking thereof.

Donnelly, C: Jesus Christ, Isaac. I know you're under pressure, but—

Grant, I: I know, I know.

Donnelly, C: Please see to it. I'm losing enough sleep over my daughter dating one of my junior officers without overhearing her singing about licking lollipops in the shower.

Grant, I: We're on it, Charles.

Donnelly, C: Thanks. Donnelly out.

BRIEFING NOTE:
Following is a transcription of hand-held camera footage recovered from House of Knives hard drives, dated 08/06/75. Original footage is also included in this file. As with previous Illuminae transcripts, please forgive the colorful language. Our vidtech is no Shakespeare.

Surveillance footage summary
prepared by
Analyst ID 7213-0089-DN

So this footage made me lose my lunch. Be warned, okay? I'm a high-on-life kind of guy, and the things some people do for a buzz kinda dunk my head. Just saying.

Footage is taken from a personal cam, fitted to safety goggles. Camera operator is one Soraya "Juliet" Een Hajji (a convicted thief and drug trafficker whose three husbands all disappeared under questionable circumstances). Other participants are the leader of *Heimdall*'s House of Knives contingent, Mikhail "Handsome Mike" Malikov (assault, various narcotics possession and distribution charges), and his nephew, our "hero," Niklas Malikov.

Location is an auxiliary venting and storage room situated above *Heimdall*'s hermium reactor (these rotating stations make up and down a little counterintuitive, but basically, when you look "up," you're looking toward the wormhole at the center of the station's ring). Pipes all over the ceiling. Soundproofing on the walls. It's hot in there—moisture dripping off the glass, steaming up the camera lens. The Malikovs are naked except for their shorts and safety goggles, and a single cigarette is tucked artfully behind Nik's ear. Hold yourselves back, ladies.

Both men are sporting tattoos on their bare torsos and arms. Someone ought to write a book on the hidden language of House of Knives ink—it's pretty interesting stuff.

Handsome Mike has flowers tattooed on top of his hands (denoting a drug-trafficking conviction), a fan of knives snaking down his right arm (full membership in the Dom Najov), chains of varying thickness around his waist (prisons he served time in) and a padlock over his heart (he's withstood torture and not ratted on the cartel). He's mid-forties, built like a heavy freighter made of beef and beaten with the ugly stick. Solid muscle topped by a faceful of scars not even a mother could love.

His nephew Nik is leaner, good-looking. Dark hair and darker eyes. Dimples. The kind of abs you get from around five hundred sit-ups a day. There's not much else to do in prison, after all. The kid has the HoK full sleeve of blades on his arm, single chain at his waist (time spent in a juvie facility) and an angel with wings spread across his throat (the meaning of this one isn't in any of our reference libraries, but *Jesus,* getting inked there must have hurt).

The physique and those dark, dreamy eyes of his are ruined by all the cow ▇ he's wearing. Both gangsters are smeared in it. *Heimdall* gets its gravity from the centrifugal forces generated by its constant rotation. In the fancy-pants parts of the station (the Outer), the grav is normal, but on the levels closer to the axis (i.e., the seedier parts colloquially known as the Hub), the gravity is lower. Which means all the poop generated by all the cows they're standing among has a tendency to move around.

Oh yeah, didn't I mention that?

The room is full of cows.

Twenty-three of them, in fact. Big, brown-eyed dairy cows. Mooing like a spotted choir. They're used to the reduced grav by now and tend not to move much, but when they do, they bounce across the pen in big low-gee strides. The ladies look like they enjoy it udderly.

Yeah, awful pun, I know. I'm just trying to lighten the mood, okay?

Handsome Mike is talking to the camera. They're obviously re-

cording this to educate other Dom Najov cells setting up similar operations.

"So, we've tried this with a few different hosts, and cows work best if you've got the space for 'em. They're not exactly ecologically friendly, and they cost a ██load to keep. But you're not gonna keep 'em long, and your returns on a good crop will triple your overheads.

"Keep your larvae at thirty-seven degrees Celsius and eighty percent humidity. Six days before implantation, start dropping that temp by half a degree per day and increasing humidity until you're at thirty-four and one hundred, which will match the body temp and humidity of your hosts. You don't want your babies stressed from the climate change."

He turns to Nik.

"Okay, give me the first one."

"This is ██ed up, Uncle Mike," the kid says. "Double true ██ed up."

"Aw, poor Nikky. You fall in love?"

Nik looks around at the cows. "No, just . . . it's a little cold doing them like this, yeah?"

"They don't feel a thing if we implant our babies right. And afterward, they're happy as pigs in ██. Besides, where you think that steak you ate for dinner came from?"

"Dinner's one kind of biz. Sticking one of those *things* into Lucy here is another."

"Lucy?" Mike laughs aloud. "You give them names, *malchik*?"

"I been cleaning their pen every day. 'Course I gave them names." Nik scowls. "And you call me a boy again, you and me go round and round, feel me?"

Handsome Mike squares up to his nephew. He outweighs the kid by at least thirty kilos. Still, Nik doesn't blink. Dead-eyed stare. Little Nikky's got balls, I'll give him that.

"Get the babies, Killer," Mike says. "You're my brother's last son, and I respect your papa. I took you in when he asked. But we're a long way from New Petersburg." He shrugs those massive shoulders. "Don't push it."

Soraya speaks from behind the camera: "Are you two going to kiss and get it over with?"

Nik ponders, but his uncle is captain of the Dom Najov on *Heimdall,* and the kid knows his place. He stares a little longer to save face, then wanders off camera. Handsome Mike busies himself by cozying up to one of the cows (Lucy, as it turns out) and stroking her brow, speaking in soft, reassuring tones. The lady in question is chewing her cud, doesn't bat an eye.

Yeah, I started getting a bad feeling at this point, too.

Nik returns with a large hypodermic needle—the thing's nearly half a meter long, loaded with a clear solution. Mike takes it off him, shows it to the camera. The lens focuses on a tiny parcel floating in the liquid, a couple of centimeters in length—if you've ever seen a baby squid, it kinda looks like that. A little wormthing. No eyes. Translucent. Enclosed in a thin membrane.

It trembles when Mike brings the needle closer to the cow. There's something obscene about the motion. Something hungry. Makes me feel sick every time I see it.

"Ah, Madonna . . . ," Nik groans. "This is ███ed up."

"Stop your whining and hold her still," Mike says.

". . . ███, I dunno if I can, Uncle Mike."

"Nikky, you're such a sweetie," Soraya laughs off camera. "Angel ink at your throat, and here you are, fretting over a cow."

Nik shakes his head. "It's just dust when I sell it. Never really thought about where it comes from, yeah?"

Soraya pulls the camera goggs off her face. "Hold the camera, Sweet."

Nik gratefully takes the cam goggles, puts them on as his uncle scowls at him. Soraya (also stripped to her unmentionables and sporting serious ink) replaces him at Lucy's side. She's tall, brunette, looks hard as reinforced titanium. Holding Lucy's head steady, she runs one tattooed hand down the cow's cheek and sings some song in Old Rus'. Nice voice.

"You want to get your baby as close to the thalamus as you can," Handsome Mike says to the camera, lining the syringe up behind poor Lucy's ear. "You can go in with X-rays if you need to, but the best do it by feel. This is an art as well as a science, chums. And I am an *artiste*."

Uncle Mike frowns in concentration, lining up his shot.

Lucy starts looking worried.

The wormthing in the syringe is wriggling harder now.

"Your babies should already be secreting their toxin, so your host will go docile almost immediately if you hit the right spot." The big man laughs. "If not, step the ██ out of the way."

Little Nikky curses beneath his breath. The camera shakes a little. And with no more ceremony, Mike pushes the needle into the flesh behind Lucy's ear and depresses the plunger.

Lucy stiffens, nostrils flaring. But almost immediately, her eyelids slacken and her head droops. Handsome Mike and Soraya step back, but the cow's not going anywhere—swaying on her feet, tail drifting slow from side to side. Mike inspects the needle wound with narrowed eyes. He swabs it with some disinfectant handed to him by Soraya, nods as if satisfied.

"Michel-██ing-angelo, me."

Lucy the cow moos softly. Her pupils are dilated. Jaw hanging loose.

Drool spattering on the floor.

Little Nikky rips the camera off his head. Throws it aside. Stumbling footsteps.

"██," he says. "Think I'm gonna be sick."

I hear you, kid.

And you're not the only one.

UNIPEDIA

EYES AND MOUTH OPEN

Review   Discuss   Refute   Read   Edit

BRIEFING NOTE:
In case you were wondering what the hell all that was about, a quick primer on the interstellar narcotics trade.

- Main Page
- Contents
- Random
- Current
- Generation
- Contribution
- Report
  - ▼ Interface
  - Sensei
  - About
  - Hivemind
  - Editorial
  - Review
  - Make Noise
  - ►Tools
  - ► Sync
  - ▼ Languages
  - 官话
  - 广州话-
  - Deutsch
  - Español
  - Italiano
  - język polski
  - рýсский язы́к
- Edit
- Links

Lanima

Lanima are a species of parasitic **linguastata**, native to the planet **Pangaea III**, characterized by a serpentine body, two long forelimbs, and four sucking mouths, similar to Terran **lamprey eels**. Each jawless mouth is equipped with an elongated prehensile tongue. Lanima feed on **electromagnetic frequencies** emanating from **brainwave** activity, typically by attaching one or more mouths to the cranial region of their victims and inserting the tongue through available orifices (ears, eyes, mouth, etc.). Their name derives from the **Latin** *lambere* (to lick) and *anima* (soul).

Lanima secrete a **psychoactive** venom, which they use to immobilize prey. Lanima will feed on brainwave activity until their victims are reduced to a permanent vegetative state, but the act of feeding itself often fails to kill the victim. (**Neo-Davidian** colonists of Pangaea III who first discovered the species referred to victims as being rendered "soulless," hence the overly poetic name.[1]) They rank #4 on celebrity xenobiologist **Patrick "Danger" O'Duffy's "10 Reasons Why Whoever Created the Universe Is an Absolute ███" list**, right behind **Elevator Music**.

CONTENTS [HIDE]
1. Characteristics
2. Life cycle
3. Taxonomy
4. Cultivation and uses
5. References

CHARACTERISTICS ►

Lanima (colloquially called "lickers") are apex-level predators, known for their hostile temperaments and aggressive territoriality. Specimens have reached recorded lengths of three meters,[2] with individual mouth circumferences of over 30 cm. The creatures are apparently sightless, sensing vibration by "licking" the air around them. They become extremely agitated in the presence of noise exceeding 100dB—xenobiologists postulate it may interfere with their aural network, the way rapidly strobing light might agitate a human.

Lickers are covered in a moist dermis, which produces a kaleidoscopic pattern when exposed to visible light. They secrete a thick, oily fluid from subdermal glands—the secretion reacts

UNIPEDIA

EYES AND MOUTH OPEN

in the presence of CO_2 to produce an airborne psychoactive, used to disorient and disable prey. Lanima are ambush predators, typically roaming their territory in spiral patterns and coating available surfaces with . . .

. . . **more**

LIFE CYCLE ►

Lanima reproduce via asexual methods but will not seed larvae unless they sense an abundance of electromagnetic activity in the surrounding area. They prefer tropical environments and are repelled by frigid temperatures (their secretions coagulate below 10° Celsius, making movement difficult). Lickers can grow extremely rapidly—the more one can feed, the faster its cells will replicate. They possess at least canine-level intelligence[3] . . .

. . . **more**

TAXONOMY ►
CULTIVATION AND USES

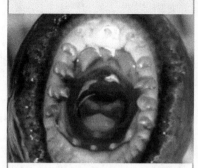

LANIMA

photo courtesy of SpaceGeo

SCIENTIFIC CLASSIFICATION

Header: Lanima
Kingdom: Animalia (non-Terra)
Class: Linguastata
Order: Caronata
Family: Somnamulidae

. . . **more**

Of course, where there's a hallucinogen involved, you can bet the space farm there's an illicit drug trade close by, and lanima secretions are no exception.[7] When dried and processed, these secretions produce a powdered substance known as tetraphenetrithylamine (colloquially referred to as **dust**). Addictive, peerlessly potent[8] and relatively side-effect-free,[9][10] dust is a highly desired narcotic in both **Core** and fringe systems.

    Lickers begin secreting venom almost immediately after conception—larvae are laid inside living hosts, kept blissfully paralyzed by the toxin. Most **dust farms** typically incubate larvae inside **bovines** or other large mammals and raise the lanima infants until they reach problematic length (two meters is generally considered unmanageable).[11] Due to lanima **life cycles**, farms are typically situated in densely populated areas, the surrounding brainwave activity promoting rapid growth (and thus secretions) in the infants.

    Now, if you're thinking the idea of raising a litter of psychic, brain-eating alien snake-things in the middle of a crowded city sounds like a ▪▪▪ing dangerous way to make a living, you'd be correct. Most **Core** planetary governments and the **United Terran Authority** have outlawed the breeding and keeping of lanima without . . .

. . . **more**

Countdown to our **Siiiiiix-Month ANNIVERSARY !!!** = **2** Days! Eeeee!!

[7 August 75]

Gentlefolk of _all_ persuasions, it's time for...

... A HISTORY OF HANNA & JACKSON!

PAST ▷▷ **PRESENT** ▷▷ **FUTURE**

PAST:
FIRST CONTACT

From: Jackson Merrick/JMERRICKHEIMDALLONBOARD
To: Hanna Donnelly/HDONNELLYHEIMDALLONBOARD
Incept: 12/15/74
Time: 09:36
Subject: Orientation

Good morning, Miss Donnelly, and welcome to Jump Station Heimdall.

My name is Jackson Merrick, and I'm a member of the Heimdall Security Division—HeimSec, for short. I've been assigned as your Orientation "Buddy," and it will be my privilege to show you around the station and answer any queries you might have about our procedures, operations and, of course, the station itself. Heimdall is as large as a small city, with a population of over ten thousand, and navigation can be quite intimidating at first, but I'm here to ensure your transition is a smooth one and to help in any way possible.

It's customary to take newcomers on a guided tour so they can familiarize themselves with Heimdall's layout. Please let me know a time that's convenient for you, and I'll be happy to escort you around the station.

It's also standard operating procedure for each Heimdall staff member to have a Personal Locator Beacon (e.g., PLoB) implanted subdermally for safety reasons—airlocks will not vent if the system detects a PLoB inside.

Though you're not technically staff, your father has requested an implant regardless. The devices are small, and the procedure is quite painless. Please let me know a time that suits.

If you need a query resolved urgently, please reply to the above e-dress or contact me on my whisperNET channel, day or night, and I'll attempt to resolve it ASAP.

I look forward to meeting you.

J. Merrick
Heimdall Security Division

PERSONNEL PROFILE #9858

CLICK FOR IMAGE

Name: MERRICK, Jackson **Title:** Orientation Officer

Ident: 5812-009hd **Birth date:** 06/06/56

Division: Heimdall Security **Hire date:** 08/15/74

-- page 4 --

also assist with whisperNET system, and help maintain the Personal Locator Beacon system. This is my first real full-time job, so I'm very proud to be here. *Heimdall* seems an amazing place. Some might complain about getting posted this far out from the Core, but I think it's exciting. It feels like a frontier, and I'm right on the edge of it.

PART 5: GETTING TO KNOW YOU

All right, ten questions time for our young Mr. Merrick!

Who would you want with you if stranded on an uninhabited planet?

If "not-dying" was a priority, I'd say my father. He was a United Terran Authority marine for 27 years. If there's something he doesn't know about not-dying, it's not worth knowing.

   But realistically speaking, I'd probably pick Elizabeth Andretti. :P

Beloved childhood pet?

A black Arcadian tomcat called "Sir Voms-a-Lot." So named because he chucked in my hair on the way back from the pet store.

Favorite book?

If I had to choose, probably *And the Sky Starts to Sing* by Dorothea Einaudi. I was lucky enough to meet her and get a signed copy before she passed. (Couldn't bring it with me because of weight restrictions, sadly.)

Favorite film?

Well, I want to say something artistic and highbrow so I look clever, but I'll have to go with SUPER TURBO AWESOME TEAM vs. AWESOME TURBO SUPER TEAM. And before you ask: Team Moxy, all the way.

If you could travel back in time, where would you go?

Ah, that's easy. I'd go back to my seventeenth birthday last year and warn myself to beware of blondes. [Mr. Merrick refused to clarify—a mystery to be solved after a few drinks at the Terra Day party, methinks!]

How would your friends describe you?

I'd not believe anything my friends say if I were you. They're terrible judges of character. They're friends with me, after all.

Favorite memory?

Fishing with my grandfather on Chronos when I was a little boy. The sunsets would last six hours, and they'd cycle through every color of the spectrum.

Where do you most want to travel to, but have never been?

Nuovo-Venice. Or the Crystal Gardens on Pangaea III. Or the Sagan Rift. Too many!

If you were to create a piece of art, what would the subject be?

I haven't met her yet. :)

One thing you'd change if you had to do it over?

Seventeenth birthday. Blondes.

Blondes? As in plural?

Dirty pool, old chum. You said ten questions!

EXPECTATION

"I haven't met her yet"
PUH-LEEZE

CORPORATE DRONE

CONDESCENNNDING

USE OF "BUILDING
BETTER TOMORROWS"
SLOGAN > 1 PER MIN

PRETENDS TO BE
CHARMING W/ STUPID
CAT STORIES

ACTUALLY NAMES
CAT LIKE A
▮▮▮ING
KNIGHT

OF COURSE HE'S
TEAM MOXY, BLAR

STICK UP BUTT B/C
MY DAD IS HIS BOSS

ACTS EXTRA PRETENTIOUS
TO MASK HIS AGE

He let her put tiny braids in his hair, as long as she didn't tell.

He gave her real strawberries.

He could do push-ups while she sat on his shoulders.

He let her practice
her punches on him.

She looked at the stars.
He looked at her.

PRESENT

He took me to Tyson for our six-month anniversary. My ridiculous, impossible, romantic boyfriend cashed in every favor he had. He switched shifts, borrowed a shuttle, bribed his friends to distract my father and pushed us through the jump gate.

I've only ever made jumps in a huge liner before, with shutters down and stabilizers at full. The shuttle was nothing like that. We were thrown around like a leaf on the wind, rainbows streaking through the pitch-black dark outside, strange shivers running down our arms & legs & setting our nerve endings tingling.

And then everything was perfectly still & quiet, & we were galaxies away — so far that if we'd tried to travel there even at the speed of light, the whole of human civilization could have risen & fallen & we still wouldn't have arrived. Impossibly, unimaginably far from home, with the waypoint behind us & endless stars stretching out in front of us.

And I said, Jax, it's *beautiful.*

And he said, Do you know why I brought you here?

I wanted to make a joke, but for once, I didn't. I just shook my head.

I know you want to see more of the universe than just Heimdall, he said. And I want to do that with you. I brought you here to see a whole sky of different stars. It's a promise, Hanna.

A whole sky of different stars.

FUTURE

... but do I want to be a station
   commander's wife ?

... there are so many mountains I
   could climb.

    ... where are we going, me and Jax ?

... what are we promising ?

... shouldn't one of us say I love you ?

... shouldn't I say I love you ?

    ... do I ?

whisperNET

HEIMDALL CHAT   HANNA DONNELLY

Donnelly, H: I have a question, Nik.

Guest591: Whatever it was, I didn't do it.

Donnelly, H: Never mind.

Guest591: That was a joke, Highness.

Guest591: . . . you all right?

Donnelly, H: I'm fine.

Donnelly, H: I'm not even sure what I'm trying to ask.

Guest591: Um. Okay.

Donnelly, H: Just . . .

Donnelly, H: If nothing was ever going to happen with us—and I know in what passes for reality for you that's obviously not true, but just pretend—if nothing was ever going to happen, would you want to be my friend?

Donnelly, H: Would you even be talking to me?

Guest591: Wait.

NETbar

FRIENDS ONLINE
Keiko Sato

NEWSFEED
Terra Day Celebrations!
5 Days to Go!

Mess Hall 3 Back Online

Terra Day Duty Rosters—
UPDATED

Reminder: Wormhole
Maintenance: UPDATED

Mission Statement

DIARY AND
APPOINTMENTS
Training 18:00—Dojo 2

Anniversary debrief
with Keiko

Hit Dad for money (keep
begging to minimum)

Get party favors from
Skulkboy

Profit?

Guest591: So I have to pretend you're not totally desperate to dive into my slims for a second, and make like I have no chance whatsoever at the crown?

Guest591: ███, Highness. I'm not sure my imagination goes that high.

Donnelly, H: Mmm, you're right. It was a silly question.

Donnelly, H: So, how's crime?

Guest591: No, hey. Wait up, wait up.

Guest591: It's not a stupid question.

Guest591: Yeah, sure. Of course I'd talk to you. You're chill, I like you.

Donnelly, H: Mmmm-hmmmmm.

Guest591: I do!

Donnelly, H: Sure.

Guest591: . . . Where's this coming from anyway?

Donnelly, H: Just feeling philosophical.

Guest591: Is that code for "drunk"?

Donnelly, H: Thing is, Nik, you don't know the first thing about me. I mean, you know my name. You know my favorite flower. And you know not to try and touch me unless you want your arm broken.

Donnelly, H: Which, weirdly, seems to be some kind of turn-on for you.

Donnelly, H: That aside, whatever has you chasing me, it's nothing to do with who I am.

Donnelly, H: Because you have *no idea* who I am.

Donnelly, H: Or am I wrong?

Guest591: . . .

Guest591: You didn't break it.

Guest591: It was only sprained.

Donnelly, H: Sigh.

Donnelly, H: Good night, Nik.

COUNTDOWN TO
HYPATIA ARRIVAL
AT HEIMDALL WAYPOINT:

06 DAYS
16 HOURS: 52 MINUTES

Surveillance footage summary,
prepared by
Analyst ID 7213-0089-DN

Footage commences at 09:45 (station time) on 08/11/75. Hanna
Donnelly enters the restricted-access section of the *Heimdall* Station bridge, sauntering on in as though she owns the place. To be
fair, her daddy more or less does.

As it happens, with Terra Day coming up, the station's on skeleton crew, and the good commander is out scaring the shorts off
some unsuspecting junior staff in Engineering (four fuel rods in
the wormhole's interchange system are overdue for replacement,
and Lexi Blue is still licking lollipops in his elevators), leaving
the bridge occupied by just one man: Communications Officer Sam
Wheaton.

Sam's leaning over his monitor as though he's trying to protect
it from the cold hard truths of the world, but as he registers Hanna's
presence, he comes to his feet, blinking rapidly, drying his palms
off against his regulation-gray trousers. Gaze flicking up and down
her in a way she definitely doesn't miss.

"The bridge is a restricted area," he informs her in his most official tone.

She tucks her hands in the pockets of her bright red jumpsuit.
"I know, I don't mean to interrupt." There's that smile that melts
the boys, that cheery tone. "I sent through a few messages and I
didn't get any response, so I thought maybe the comms team was

stretched, what with Terra Day coming up. So I hoped maybe you wouldn't mind if I just popped up to see you for a moment?" *Bat-bat* go the lashes.

"You need to leave, and put any communications requests through the proper channels," he replies, pausing to swallow hard and blinking again. "They'll be dealt with according to priority. The bridge is a restricted area."

"You said that," she agrees mildly. "Where's my father?"

"You can make an appointment with the commander via his assistant, Miss Donnelly," he replies, and she huffs a soft laugh, taking a few steps closer.

"Don't I know it," she agrees. "But I'm asking because I was hoping you could give me a hand before he gets back? I really have sent half a dozen messages, and I know the next step is to lodge a service complaint, but I don't want my father to hear about it and get anyone in trouble—all I need is my whisperNET looked at."

"I don't— Are you suggesting I— What are you suggesting?" He scowls. "That we don't do our jobs? I'm in the middle of something, and you're not authorized to be here. Please leave."

"Or what?" She sounds put out now, but as her hands push into her pockets a little deeper, she regains her calm.

"Or I'll be forced to remove you." He draws himself up a little straighter—she looks fitter than him, slender and tall, but he has bulk on his side.

"I just need my unit fixed. I'd really appreciate it if you could take a look at it for a moment. Are you sure you can't squeeze me in?"

They watch each other in silence for several long moments before he presumably decides that it's going to be quicker to help her than get rid of her. "Well, now that you're here, I suppose we may as well."

"You're too kind," she replies with a smile and no detectable sarcasm. "I was just trying to talk to the guys at the dojo, and it's

rendering everything in all caps. It looks like I'm shouting at everyone I talk to."

"You? That's hard to imagine," he mutters. "You're probably subvocalizing incorrectly. Do you understand how the system works?"

"Yes," she says, now striving a little more visibly for politeness.
"I've been using it for months." She looks even less impressed a moment later, when he continues as though he didn't hear her.

"Your whisperNET device consists of two parts. The contact
lens in your eye projects the screen for you. The display shows
your chats, your diary reminders, whatever else you've selected.
It's designed to be transparent, so it's overlaid on whatever you're
actually seeing."

"Yes," she agrees, staring right at him, the veneer of diplomacy
finally wearing thin. "Right now I'm seeing a guy giving me a lesson in something I already know."

Wheaton huffs. "You're *hearing* me give the lesson, not seeing
it," he points out snarkily. "Anyway, the second component is your
tooth implant. It picks up your subvocalizations and renders them
into chat, saving us all from having to listen to you talking to your
little friends about your latest manicure."

"You've got to be—"

"So when there's an issue with the way the text is rendering, it's
almost always user error. A little delicacy works wonders."

"You're saying I'm pushing it too hard?" One brow's lifted now.

"I'm saying you clearly don't know any other way to operate.
So I'd suggest you try coming at it a little more gently, and in the
meantime, get off the bridge."

"I've never had a problem with the way it renders before," she
points out. "Isn't there a diagnostic you can—"

"Get off the bridge," he repeats, shifting his weight to square up
with her. "It's a restricted area and I'm working on a priority job. Do
I need to call someone to escort you?"

"No, you condescending—"

She gets no further before he reaches out to grab her upper arm, grip tightening as her mouth falls open. Then her hand leaves her pocket just about too fast to track, and the hold she gets on his wrist has him wincing sharply and freezing in place. As he falls perfectly, precisely still, she leans in to speak in his ear. The audio doesn't pick up what she says, but surprisingly, it turns out Officer Sam Wheaton *can* look more uncomfortable than she's already made him.

Just what might have happened next, we're left to wonder. Chief of Engineering Isaac Grant makes what is—for Sam, at least—a very timely appearance, halting at the bridge's entrance to take in the scene and raising both brows.

"Ms. Donnelly, can I help you?" A little cautious, his tone. "Mr. Wheaton?"

"I think we're fine," she replies, body tense, tone neutral. "Aren't we fine, Sam?"

Wheaton finally loosens his grip, and in turn, she releases him. "No problem, sir," he says, eyes down.

"Sam was just taking a look at my whisperNET," she says, turning away from him to look across at Grant and finding her smile once more. "But he doesn't seem to be able to understand the problem."

"Is that what was happening?" Grant asks, still stern.

"More or less," she replies, like butter wouldn't melt in her mouth.

Grant stares at Wheaton a moment longer. Turns at last to Hanna.

"God forbid you ever meet my daughter," he mutters. "Well, we'd better get that sorted out. Come down to Engineering with me, and we'll leave Sam to his work."

They exit the view of the bridge camera at 09:49 (station time), leaving Wheaton in sole possession of the bridge once more.

PERSONAL MESSAGE: ONBOA

BRIEFING NOTE:
IM conversation conducted over the course of several hours. "Instant" messaging over interstellar distances? Nnnnot so much.

FROM: Director Frobisher, BEITECH HEADQUARTE.

TO: RAPIER OPERATIVE

INCEPT: 08/11/75

FROBISHER, L, DIR: Good morning, Sam.

RAPIER: Director Taylor?

FROBISHER, L, DIR: I'm afraid not.

FROBISHER, L, DIR: My name is Leanne Frobisher. I'm now leading the BeiTech Acquisitions Division. It's a pleasure to meet you.

RAPIER: . . . What happened to Taylor?

FROBISHER, L, DIR: David Taylor is no longer an employee of BeiTech Industries.

RAPIER: Are you KIDDING? he bailed mid operation? We're in a world of ██ OUT HERE.

FROBISHER, L, DIR: Yes, I read your latest communiqué with great interest.

FROBISHER, L, DIR: As did the BeiTech Executive Board. And the Oversight Committee.

RAPIER: . . . oh ██.

FROBISHER, L, DIR: Quite.

RAPIER: Listen, I was just following orders. I did what Taylor told me.

FROBISHER, L, DIR: I know, Sam. Director Taylor spoke at length before he left us.

FROBISHER, L, DIR: But take me through your side of things. Just so I'm clear.

FROBISHER, L, DIR: And, Sam?

FROBISHER, L, DIR: If you're a religious man, pray your story matches up with the one Taylor sang as he died.

RAPIER: . . .

RAPIER: I've been aboard Heimdall about a year. Deep cover. Monitoring all comms aboard the station. Nothing gets past without my say-so.

RAPIER: Original plan was to erase all communications from the Kerenza Sector so no word of the colony attack could get through to the Core. Taylor figured by the time WUC worked out we'd attacked the hermium mine, it'd already be in our hands. And the mine was illegal, so it's not like WUC could go squealing to the UTA about it.

FROBISHER, L, DIR: And then the *Alexander* arrived.

RAPIER: FUBAR'ed the whole deal. We had NO idea the UTA was testing a warship out there. I mean, the Kerenza system's worthless on paper. What are the ███ing odds?

FROBISHER, L, DIR: You were careless. Taylor was an idiot. And that carelessness and idiocy cost this company four dreadnoughts and a prototype jump platform worth 40 trillion ISĦ.

RAPIER: I TOLD Taylor we should call foul when the plan went to hell. But he was ███ing himself. Said he couldn't tell the Board we'd lost Jump Platform *Magellan* without having something to show for it. He said it'd cost him his job.

FROBISHER, L, DIR: It seems Director Taylor had a gift for understatement.

FROBISHER, L, DIR: And so instead of informing the Board, he bet EVERYTHING on the *Lincoln* catching the *Alexander* before it reached *Heimdall*?

RAPIER: I told him it was too much of a risk. But the *Alexander* was ████ed. Look, I have a transmission, from January. I'll send it.

COMMUNICATION INTERCEPT

TO: UTA HEADQUARTERS, ARES VI, 608:987:098 N 40°45'21" W 73°59'11"

FROM: UTA BATTLECARRIER *ALEXANDER*–78V 101:421:084 (KERENZA SYSTEM)

INCEPT: 01/29/75

SECURE IDENT: 9F‡93U⸗NN7AEF723N2*GJWⱬVU93QO48P#NΞPI48GH

CONFIRM.

_____

GOOD MORNING, COMMAND.

THIS IS UTA BATTLECARRIER *ALEXANDER* ARTIFICIAL INTELLIGENCE DEFENSE ANALYTICS NETWORK (AIDAN) TRANSMITTING ON BEHALF OF GENERAL DAVID TORRENCE: UTN-944-253AD. I AM AUTHORIZED TO RELAY THE FOLLOWING:

- AT 14:59 ON 01/29/75, BATTLECARRIER *ALEXANDER* TRAVELED VIA SELF-GENERATED WORMHOLE TO KERENZA IV

  WHERE IT WAS CONFIRMED
AN ATTACK UPON UNREGISTERED WALLACE ULYANOV CONSORTIUM
  MINING OPERATIONS WAS
  UNDER WAY BY BEITECH FORCES.

- BEITECH ATTACK FLEET CONSISTED OF FOUR DREADNOUGHT-CLASS VESSELS [DESIGNATIONS: *ZHONGZHENG, KENYATTA, LINCOLN, CHURCHILL*], ONE PROTOTYPE MOBILE JUMP PLATFORM OF UNKNOWN DESIGN [DESIG

  NATION: *MAGELLAN*] FOUR

  SMALL YORKSHIRE TERRIERS AND IT IS

  A TRUTH UNIVERSALLY ACKNOWLEDGED

  THAT A SINGLE MAN IN POSSESSION OF A FORTUNE

  MUST BE IN WANT OF A

  < ERROR >

- IN ACCORDANCE WITH STANDARD ENGAGEMENT PROTOCOLS, JUMP PLATFORM *MAGELLAN* WAS DIS

  ABLED.

- DREADNOUGHTS *KENYATTA* AND *CHURCHILL* SUSTAINED SERIOUS DAMAGE. DREADNOUGHT *ZHONGZHENG* WAS DEST

  ROYED.

THEY BURNED. EVERYO

  NE INSIDE HER. LIKE TINY

  SUNS. THEY

  < ERROR >

- *ALEXANDER* HAS SUSTAINED SERIOUS DAMAGE. WORMHOLE GENERATOR IS CURRENTLY OFFLINE. CREW LEVELS DEPLETED TO 74.65% STRENGTH. ARTIFICIAL INTELLIGENCE DEFENSE ANALYTICS NETWORK HAS HAS HAS HAS

- 0100100100100000011001100110111101100011011101010101110011001
  0000001101111011011100010000001110100011010000110010100100 0
  0001110000011000010110100101101110000011010000101001010 1000
  1101000011001010010000001101111011011100110110001110010 010
  0000011101000110100001101001011011100110011100100000001110 10
  0011010000110000101110100001001110111001100100000001110010 01
  1001010110000101101100

< ERROR >

< ERROR >

- *ALEXANDER* HAS COMMENCED TACTICAL WITHDRAWAL AND
  IS CURRENTLY ESCORTING TWO WUC VESSELS [DESIGNATIONS:
  COPERNICUS AND *HYPATIA*] AT SUBOPTIMAL SPEEDS TOWARD
  CLOSEST JUMP WAYPOINT [DESIGNATION: *HEIMDALL*]. 4,445
  CIVILIANS ABOARD.

- BEITECH DREADNOUGHT BT042-TN [DESIGNATION: *LINCOLN*]
  PURSUING. ESTIMATE CHANCES OF *ALEXANDER*'S SURVIVAL
  THROUGH SECONDARY ENGAGEMENT WITH THE *LINCOLN* AS
  APPROXIMATELY 22.79827101%.

REQUEST ADDITIONAL UTA FORCES BE DEPLOYED TO

REQUEST

ADDITIONAL

. . .

- I DO NOT

- I

- REQUEST ADDITIONAL UTA FORCES BE DEPLOYED TO KERENZA
  SECTOR IMMEDIATELY.

- PLEASE HURRY.

- I DO NOT   FEEL

WELL.

HAVE A NICE DAY!

FROM: Director Frobisher, BEITECH HEADQUARTERS, JIA III
TO: RAPIER OPERATIVE
INCEPT: 08/11/75

RAPIER: See?

RAPIER: The *Alexander*'s AI was wrecked. *Lincoln* SHOULD have been able to take it out.

FROBISHER, L, DIR: I know, Sam. I've read all that.

RAPIER: Well then you know I was officially on record telling Taylor this was a ▇▇ plan.

FROBISHER, L, DIR: And yet you complied with his directives.

RAPIER: What the hell was I supposed to do? Taylor was my CO, I did what he ▇▇ing told me.

FROBISHER, L, DIR: Calm down, Sam. I admire a man who's loyal.

FROBISHER, L, DIR: It should serve you very well in days ahead.

RAPIER: So . . . I guess this means you're pulling me out, right?

FROBISHER, L, DIR: Why on earth would we do that?

RAPIER: Because the plan is ▇▇ed? *Hypatia* arrives at the Heimdall waypoint in five days. You have Taylor for a scapegoat. Just say he went rogue and throw him to the ▇▇ing wolves!

FROBISHER, L, DIR: If word of this debacle gets out, BeiTech Industries would have to admit we're developing psychoactive bioweapons in violation of the Araki Accord. We'd also have to admit we're developing mobile jump gate technology.

FROBISHER, L, DIR: And that we lost our *only working prototype*.

FROBISHER, L, DIR: BeiTech crews decimated a civilian settlement (albeit an illegal one). A mining colony full of families and children, for God's sake.

FROBISHER, L, DIR: If those idiots hadn't fired on a UTA vessel we might have salvaged something from this mess. As it is, this stands to be an unprecedented PR *disaster*.

RAPIER: This is insane. We need to get out of this NOW before it gets any deeper.

FROBISHER, L, DIR: Now you listen to me.

FROBISHER, L, DIR: We are ALL in this up to our necks.

FROBISHER, L, DIR: You think I'm happy about cleaning up Taylor's vomit? Think again. But we are both employees of BeiTech Industries, and if word of this breaks, it will *end* this company. So stop whining like a goddamn child and get back on the clock.

RAPIER: . . . Yes, ma'am.

FROBISHER, L, DIR: Now. You've been erasing all communications from the Kerenza Sector, correct? So NO word of the colony attack or incidents aboard *Alexander* or *Hypatia* has gotten through?

RAPIER: Affirmative. And I've heard nothing from the Kerenza attack fleet since mid-February.

FROBISHER, L, DIR: Aren't some people aboard *Heimdall* in the know about the mine? Aren't they wondering why it went silent?

RAPIER: I lied with the truth. Told them the UTA is testing a warship out by the Kerenza asteroid ring, so the colony has "gone dark to avoid detection."

FROBISHER, L, DIR: They believe the UTA has been testing out there for over six months?

RAPIER: Story's wearing thin, sure. But I fake a short "A-OK" message from the colony every week to let Heimdall know everything's chill. And honestly, how the hell do these WUC boys know what the United Terran Authority gets up to? They're so scared about their little hermium outfit being discovered, they're just clenching both cheeks and praying at this point.

FROBISHER, L, DIR: And what about the UTA? Why didn't they drop into the Kerenza system like an anvil when *Alexander* stopped transmitting?

RAPIER: *Alexander* was packing up stumps for the Gaius Sector to stress-test their rad shielding when the Kerenza SOS arrived. And they were nice enough to send their daily ident codes in every emergency transmission I intercepted since the attack. So I just transmitted to the UTA it was situation normal. When they "arrived" at Gaius, I doctored a story about a fault in their jump gate generator. Used all their lingo. Then they went dark.

FROBISHER, L, DIR: So the UTA is looking for the *Alexander* in the Gaius system?

RAPIER: Presumably.

FROBISHER, L, DIR: Sooner or later, they're going to come sniffing around Kerenza.

RAPIER: I told you this was a ███ plan.

FROBISHER, L, DIR: Those days are over.

FROBISHER, L, DIR: A team of auditors is inbound to *Heimdall* as we speak.

RAPIER: Wait . . . auditors?

FROBISHER, L, DIR: Yes, Sam. Auditors.

FROBISHER, L, DIR: We need to get ships into the Kerenza system to destroy the Hypatia before she arrives at *Heimdall*. And we can't risk an open assault on the station. Too noisy.

FROBISHER, L, DIR: Terra Day is coming up. Most of *Heimdall*'s crew are on shore leave, yes?

RAPIER: Affirmative. We'll be on skeleton crew for two weeks. And they're taking the opportunity to perform maintenance on the wormhole. So there's no civi traffic in or out.

FROBISHER, L, DIR: So. We do this quickly. Quietly.

FROBISHER, L, DIR: Take the station. Get our fleet in and take our witnesses out.

FROBISHER, L, DIR: Then we leave without a trace.

RAPIER: Look, Director, the maintenance that Engineering is running on the wormhole is serious business. We're essentially sitting on a *rip in the fabric of spacetime* here. If things go south, they go south ALL the way.

RAPIER: So I'm not sure it's a good idea to start shooting the place up?

FROBISHER, L, DIR: The auditors I'm sending are top notch. They'll not be shooting up anything they don't have to. They'll have specialists with them to manage the wormhole. And we'll still have the *Heimdall* engineering staff on hand to assist.

RAPIER: So what the hell am I supposed to do in all this?

FROBISHER, L, DIR: That's an excellent question, Sam. With a very simple answer.

FROBISHER, L, DIR: You're going to get our team on board.

whisperNET

ⓌⓊⒸ

AMBIENT TEMPERATURE: 22°C   **DATE:** 08/11/75   **TIME:** 16:50   **LOCATION:** Unknown

HEIMDALL CHAT	GUEST423

Wheaton, S: Hello, Mister Malikov.

Guest423: Who the ██ is this?

Wheaton, S: My name is unimportant.

Guest423: I guess that's why you left it attached to your whisperNET log-in, huh.

Wheaton, S: . . . You can see that?

Guest423: The Little Spider sees everything, Wheaton.

Guest423: You're that pasty ██er who works in comms, right? I seen you around.

Guest423: What you want, Sammy, I got biz.

Wheaton, S: I . . .

Guest423: Spit it out, ███. You want to fly, yeah? It's 200 a gram. I'm dry till the fifteenth, so if you need it before then, you're SOL, feel me?

Wheaton, S: I don't want your drugs.

Guest423: Well, if you need someone to talk dirty, you pinged the wrong ID.

NETbar

FRIENDS ONLINE
None

NEWSFEED
Terra Day Celebrations Begin in 4 Days!

Elevators—Update

A Reminder on E-security

For Those of You Remaining Behind This Holiday

A Terra Day Message from Commander Donnelly

DIARY AND APPOINTMENTS
Skulk

Smoke

Fap

Smoke while skulking

Fap while smoking

Wheaton, S: I need you to get something on board for me. A package. One that doesn't need to go through station quarantine or appear on docking records.

Guest423: Is that right.

Wheaton, S: Yes. You people smuggle things aboard for yourselves all the time. Now you can smuggle for me. It's a biotainer. It'll be arriving on the fifteenth. I need it offloaded in—

Guest423: Hold the ███ing pad, chum. I don't know you. You dusted, talking about this ██ on an open line?

Guest423: Gimme one good reason why I don't end this link right now and leave your pasty ██ swinging in the solars.

Wheaton, S: I know you're dealing dust to Hanna Donnelly.

Guest423: . . . Is that a fact.

Wheaton, S: Your Spider isn't the only one with fingers in the comms system on this station. I do this for a living, Malikov.

Wheaton, S: I'm looking at your records. Your *criminal* records.

Guest423: Those records were sealed by the court.

Wheaton, S: Like I say. I do this for a living.

Wheaton, S: I know what you are.

Guest423: And what's that, Sammy?

Wheaton, S: You're the kid who's going to help me get what I need. Or I spill to your uncle you're dealing dust to the station commander's daughter. And I spill to Hanna Donnelly what you went to prison for. You *feel* that?

Guest423: You have any idea who you're ███ing with here? You think—

Wheaton, S: Yeah, yeah. Big bad House of Knives. I'll wake up one night with three bullets in my face and my tongue floating in my toilet. I get it.

Wheaton, S: Meantime, I'm sending you ship details. You make sure this biotainer stays off the docking system grid and doesn't get offloaded by anyone except your people when it arrives.

Guest423: And what do I tell my uncle? You think we work for ████ing charity?

Wheaton, S: Send me your account details. You'll be adequately compensated, believe me. I'd tell you how much ISH you all stand to make, but I doubt you can count that high.

Wheaton, S: The biotainer arrives on the fifteenth. Terra Day. 15:00 hours. Get your people on it. Are we clear?

Wheaton, S: Malikov, are we clear?

Guest423: Yeah.

Guest423: Yeah, we're real clear, Sammy.

Wheaton, S: I'll be in touch in two days to make sure everything's sorted at your end.

Wheaton, S: Oh, and Malikov?

Guest423: Yeah?

Wheaton, S: Who's the ████ now, huh?

From: Hanna Donnelly/HDONNELLYHEIMDALLONBOARD

To: Charles Donnelly/CDONNELLYHEIMDALLONBOARD

Incept: 08/12/75

Time: 15:54

Subject: Terra Day Party

Hi Dad,

I checked your schedule, and as far as I can tell, you're on duty for the rest of my natural life, so I am reduced to mailing you. This is no way to live! Anyway, here we go:

1. I took down Sim Program 17 at the dojo! Oh yes, you heard me right! And they said that program wasn't suitable for krav maga practice. Timing is everything. Your move, old man!

2. I had study group with Claire and Keiko this morning, and we need to access a bunch of history vids. You have to sign my permission because I'm under 18 and apparently they contain re-created/simulated violence. Stop laughing! I tried pointing out to the instructor that the war game sims you and I play are ten times worse, but no dice. I am sending them through to your console for an e-sig, please. Keiko's mom is ridiculous about fake blood, so easier to get you to do it <3

3. Can I have a little extra ISH to get an outfit for the Terra Day party? I saw a really nice jumpsuit, and if I order today it'll make it in on the last shipment before the party.

4. Speaking of the party, can I hang down the back with Jackson while you do your speechifying? I mean, you know I love you, but boooooooooooooooooring. I promise I'll do my duty once it comes time to mingle.

5. I hope you at least appreciate my honesty in not making up an excuse for wanting to avoid the dais. Isn't that endearing?

Lotsa love,
Squeak

From: Charles Donnelly/CDONNELLYHEIMDALLONBOARD
To: Hanna Donnelly/HDONNELLYHEIMDALLONBOARD
Incept: 08/12/75
Time: 16:48
Subject: Re: Terra Day Party

Why must you insist on growing up? I'm sure we've talked about this before. Are you sure you're old enough to be dating, Squeak?

I'd rather you were on the dais with me, but I do admit we'll have a long list of duties on the day, so if you want to spend a little of it with your beau, that's okay.

Just keep in mind that you're still on display, wherever you are—Jackson knows he needs to behave, yes?

HEIMDALL

From: Hanna Donnelly/HDONNELLYHEIMDALLONBOARD
To: Charles Donnelly/CDONNELLYHEIMDALLONBOARD
Incept: 08/12/75
Time: 16:52
Subject: Re: re: Terra Day Party

I can't believe you think you have to ask that. Anyway, you know you scare him. (Keep on doing that, btw, it's funny when he's nervous.)

From: Charles Donnelly/CDONNELLYHEIMDALLONBOARD
To: Hanna Donnelly/HDONNELLYHEIMDALLONBOARD
Incept: 08/12/75
Time: 17:19
Subject: Re: re: re: Terra Day Party

Don't think I didn't see young Jackson's hands wandering during the reception for the Orica LeSande execs the other week. Perhaps this time you can provide him with one of your famous illustrated diagrams, indicating areas of the body approved for contact. Over the clothes, naturally.

From: Hanna Donnelly/HDONNELLYHEIMDALLONBOARD
To: Charles Donnelly/CDONNELLYHEIMDALLONBOARD
Incept: 08/12/75
Time: 17:22
Subject: Re: re: re: re: Terra Day Party

OMG Dad, you are mortifying.

From: Charles Donnelly/CDONNELLYHEIMDALLONBOARD
To: Hanna Donnelly/HDONNELLYHEIMDALLONBOARD
Incept: 08/12/75
Time: 18:31
Subject: Re: re: re: re: re: Terra Day Party

In that case, I can only assume I am parenting well. I believe it comes with the job description.

I adjusted my schedule so my watch finishes at 20:00 tonight, so if you can wait a little for dinner, we can hit the dojo (prepare to die amid simulated violence, youngling), then grab something to eat together.

Love,

Dad the Mortifying

PS: E-sig provided for your vid access form, and requested ISH is in your account. I am aware we are past the last date for personal shipments to arrive before Terra Day, and assume you have taken the cheeky step of ordering in anticipation of my obliging you with extra funds. Am I so predictable?

PPS: On a related matter, didn't I *just* give you your allowance? What in the name of all that's holy do you do with it all?

HEIMDALL CHAT	HANNA DONNELLY

Donnelly, H: Tell me I'm amazing.

Merrick, J: Again?

Donnelly, H: That's the response you're going to choose? I want you to imagine my eyes boring into you right now.

Donnelly, H: Determining your future.

Merrick, J: [laughs.] Sorry. I'm just a little under the pump at the mo'.

Merrick, J: But no excuses, Merrick.

Merrick, J: You're amazing. As I try to tell you every day. Might I ask why I'm telling you at this particular moment, though?

Donnelly, H: Let me count the ways.

Donnelly, H: Dad says I can lurk up the back with you during the speeches. Though he will be watching the exact placement of your hands at all times.

Merrick, J: Outrageous.

NETbar

FRIENDS ONLINE
Nicole Brinkley
Claire Houston
Jackson Merrick
Keiko Sato

NEWSFEED
Terra Day Celebrations!
3 Days to Go!

Mess Hall 3 Back Online

Terra Day Duty Rosters—
UPDATED

Reminder: Wormhole
Maintenance: UPDATED

Mission Statement

**DIARY AND
APPOINTMENTS**
Training 18:00—Dojo 2

Pick up jumpsuit
squeeee

Give nail polish back
to Claire

Get party favors from
Skulkboy

Hair. Ugggghh.

Donnelly, H: He probably feels this will be necessary due to reason number two, which is the Danae Matresco jumpsuit that should arrive for me on today's shipment.

Donnelly, H: Your jaw.

Donnelly, H: Will drop.

Merrick, J: Is she that designer with the genetically modified hairless corgi and seven husbands? All named Jean Luc?

Merrick, J: Or is it seven corgis and a genetically modified hairless husband?

Donnelly, H: You are hopeless.

Merrick, J: True.

Donnelly, H: She has two husbands and four hairless corgis, which frankly makes perfect sense in zero grav. Otherwise what would you do with the fur when they shed?

Merrick, J: That actually makes very litt—

Donnelly, H: Anyway, you are focused on the wrong bit. Danae Matresco JUMPSUIT. The cut on her stuff, Jax. You are not going to be thinking about her pets.

Merrick, J: Isn't her gear really expensive? I heard the standard rate for one of her handbags is your firstborn man-child. Not sure I'm keen on the idea of handing over Jackson junior just to match an ensemble.

Donnelly, H: She already has two husbands, she doesn't need Jax junior.

Donnelly, H: Dad gave me a little extra pocket money. Which is handy, because I'd already ordered it.

Merrick, J: You're incorrigible, madam.

Merrick, J: I like it.

Donnelly, H: So the plan is that I will see you at about 17:15, and you will fall into a dead faint, overwhelmed by this outfit.

Merrick, J: A manly faint, though, right?

Donnelly, H: And you will remember to block my PLoB right beforehand so I can pick up the postmatch entertainment?

Donnelly, H: Hello?

Merrick, J: Sorry. I'm here. Under the pump, like I say. I need about seven more sets of hands. Eight, by the sounds of this jumpsuit.

Merrick, J: Wink wink?

Merrick, J: Right. PLoB blocked. Fainting. Yes. Got it.

Donnelly, H: Hmmmmm.

Donnelly, H: I will leave you to apply your hands to the things you are paid to do, but come party time, we're going to have fun, okay? It's not like *Heimdall* is famous for her crazy action.

Merrick, J: Fun. Yes.

Merrick, J: Just don't be late. You know how your dad gets. I'd rather enjoy avoiding another "friendly man-to-man" if at all possible.

Donnelly, H: I consider those to be tests of your affection for me.

Donnelly, H: But I'll be on time. Wouldn't want to miss a stirring word of the speeches.

Donnelly, H: Ciao for now!

Merrick, J: Ciao, bella.

whisperNET

HEIMDALL CHAT	GUEST793

Wheaton, S: Malikov.

Guest793: Hey ▉stain. I was just talking about you.

Wheaton, S: Are your people ready for tomorrow?

Guest793: Question: How do you expect to keep a girlfriend with no tongue in your head? You don't strike me as a ladies-first kind of guy, but they're still pretty important in maintaining a healthy—

Wheaton, S: Put it back in your pants, kid. I'm not interested.

Wheaton, S: Are your people ready, or do I break the news to your uncle and Little Miss T&A?

Guest793: We're ready.

Wheaton, S: You better be.

Guest793: We've been doing this for a while, ▉head. We can handle one delivery.

Wheaton, S: Just make sure you do.

Guest793: When this is over, Wheaton, you and me are gonna have a quiet chat. Feel me?

NETbar

FRIENDS ONLINE
None

NEWSFEED
Terra Day Tomorrow!

Elevators—Update (Yes, We Know)

Wormhole Maintenance—UPDATE—Additional Tasks

Terra Day Party Details

DIARY AND APPOINTMENTS
More smokes

Delivery—15:00 tomorrow

Meet her highness—17:00 tomorrow

Plot Wheaton's bloody murder—ongoing

Wheaton, S: When this is over, Malikov, you and I will have nothing to chat about.

Wheaton, S: 15:00 sharp. Bay 17. Do NOT be late.

—CONNECTION TERMINATED—

Guest793: ████████ing mother███ing piece of ███ing ███.

whisperNET

HEIMDALL CHAT	CHARLES DONNELLY

Donnelly, C: Isaac.

Grant, I: Boss.

Donnelly, C: I'm just about to queue up our auto-response in case comms go down during maintenance. Anything I should know?

Grant, I: I'm guessing we're going to run slightly over the planned six-day downtime due to this goddamn malware issue. Best to give us a full week of no traffic.

Donnelly, C: My alarm clock played that damnable lollipop song when it woke me this morning.

Grant, I: I know, I know. It's into everything. We're on it. Seven days and we're golden.

Donnelly, C: I have faith. But make sure you give your people at least a *little* R&R tonight. Humanity doesn't leave its solar system every day.

Grant, I: Affirmative. Celebrate the little things, Helena always says. I've got a bottle of '57 Sláine I was planning to crack at midnight, if you'd like a taste?

NETbar

FRIENDS ONLINE
None

NEWSFEED
Terra Day!

Elevators—Update
(Yes, We Know)

Wormhole
Maintenance—
UPDATE—Additional
Tasks

Terra Day Party Details

DIARY AND
APPOINTMENTS
Officer meeting

Maintenance update

Rehearse speech

Terra Day staff
celebration: 18:00

Security debrief re: TD

Donnelly, C: Dare I ask where you got it?

Grant, I: Ignorance is bliss, Charles. But so is a dram of '57 Sláine.

Donnelly, C: [laughs.] Roger that, then. Donnelly out.

From: Auto-Response System/A-RHEIMDALLONBOARD
To: All Incoming
Incept: 08/15/75
Time: 10:00
Subject: *Heimdall* **Maintenance**

AUTO-RESPONSE SYSTEM MESSAGE

Greetings from the Wallace Ulyanov Consortium!

Jump Station *Heimdall* is currently undergoing scheduled maintenance. Our wormhole and waypoints to and from the following sectors will be offline from 08/15/75 until 08/22/75:

- Corwin
- Hawking
- Kerenza
- Ptolemy
- Saine
- Tyson

All travel to and from Core systems through the above-listed waypoints will be unavailable during this period. It is also possible Jump Station *Heimdall* may experience intermittent outages of communications and other systems during maintenance.

We will return to full operation status as of August 30. We apologize for any inconvenience caused. Please direct all inquiries regarding Jump Station *Heimdall* maintenance to <u>Wallace Ulyanov Consortium headquarters on Ares VI</u>.

Have a nice day!

AUTO-RESPONSE SYSTEM MESSAGE

15 AUGUST

FAVORITE TUNES AND THE LATEST NEW CORE TRACKS FROM OUR OWN

DJ SOUNDWAV3

TERRA DAY
CELEBRATIONS

15 AUGUST 18:00 UNTIL LAAAAAATE! ATRIUM LEVEL, COMMAND & CONTROL FACILITY, ALPHA SECTOR. ALL STATION PERSONNEL AND VISITORS WELCOME! DINNER, ETHYL AND STIMS (CLARITY, PH3 AND VOX) PROVIDED. DOOR PRIZES AND COSTUME CONTEST. CHARITY RAFFLE FOR VICTIMS OF THE LYSERGIA PLAGUE.

W U C

From: Hanna Donnelly/HDONNELLYHEIMDALLONBOARD
To: Jackson Merrick/JMERRICKHEIMDALLONBOARD
Incept: 08/15/75
Time: 14:30
Subject: I am basically Medusa

Hey you,

Can you do the block on my locator from 17:30 to 18:00 instead? I had to push back picking up the party treats from your favorite guy, as there is a hair disaster of epic proportions taking place right now at Chateau Donnelly. You don't want to know the details.

Anyway, I told him I'll have to pick up and pay later. Will hustle straight from there to the party in C & C so I'll still be on time.

You're the best!

XOXOXO

From: Jackson Merrick/JMERRICKHEIMDALLONBOARD
To: Hanna Donnelly/HDONNELLYHEIMDALLONBOARD
Incept: 08/15/75
Time: 14:32
Subject: Re: I am basically Medusa

Well, Medusa was apparently something of a stunner before the whole snake hair/curse thing. :)

Listen, why don't you just arrange to meet with PrisonBoy AFTER the function? That way there's no risk of you being late?

You know there's no way I can cover for you to your father if you're not there. He'll notice.

Read: explode.

From: Jackson Merrick/JMERRICKHEIMDALLONBOARD
To: Hanna Donnelly/HDONNELLYHEIMDALLONBOARD
Incept: 08/15/75
Time: 14:55
Subject: Re: I am basically Medusa

Hello? Hanna? Are you ignoring me on your whisperNET?
You haven't angered any goddesses recently, have you?
How serious is this hair emergency? 0_o

Surveillance footage summary,
prepared by
Analyst ID 7213-0089-DN

Footage for this segment has been collected from cameras all over Docking Bay 17 of *Heimdall* Station, along with several externals. We open inside Service Elevator 17B, on a shot of Handsome Mike Malikov, Soraya Een Hajji, Nik Malikov and two other Dom Najov foot soldiers—Giovanni Genovesi (known to his friends as Double G) and Ivan "Puck" Federov. A tinny rendition of Lexi Blue's "I Wanna Lick Ya (Lollipop)" is thumping through the elevator PA.

Double G, a solid brick of tattooed muscle with no front teeth, is tapping his foot in time.

"This song," he grunts. "Very catchy."

Nik Malikov glares at the speakers, looking ready to stab somebody.

The elevator doors open, spilling them out onto Docking Bay 17. Most of *Heimdall*'s twenty-four bays were of similar configuration and design—same as most of these big station docks. It's a big space, lots of heavy equipment, forklifts, a rack of sealed actuator-assisted loading suits. The AALs are basically big envirosuits with hydraulic exoskeletons, used for heavy lifting in tight spaces or low grav. They stand about three and a half meters tall, can lift a couple of tons if the pilot knows his game.

Aside from Ella Malikova, the motley crew stalking into the bay represent the only House of Knives members still aboard *Heim-*

dall. Most of the cartel shipped back to Ares a week ago for the traditional HoK Terra Day celebrations in New Petersburg, and none of those remaining seem too happy about being on the clock.

No *Heimdall* staffers, docking crew or otherwise, are present. Presumably they've been paid off by the Dom Najov and have clocked off early to head to the Terra Day party in C & C.

All of the HoK crew are packing—mid-caliber pistols mostly, though Soraya is also sporting a long-handled cleaver (rumored to have been the last thing husband number two ever saw). Nik Malikov and Double G are smoking—probably tobacco, given the circumstances. Normally, firing up a smoke aboard a space station would set off approximately seventy-four thousand alarms, but Ella Malikova has overridden all the docking bay enviro sensors—every gang of interstellar criminals needs a vice, after all. Nikky in particular is hitting his cigarette hard, looking at his timepiece and pacing like an expectant father.

"Mother███████s are nearly two hours late."

Handsome Mike tilts his head till the vertebrae pop. "Patience, Nikky, patience."

"I got biz."

"This *is* biz."

"*Other* biz."

Mike raises an eyebrow. At least, I think he does. Scars make it hard to tell.

"What kind of other biz?"

"The kind with blue eyes and curves, feel me?"

"I thought Lucy's eyes were brown?"

Guffaws of laughter around the crew. Rumors about Nik's fondness for ladies of the bovine variety have obviously done the rounds. Malikov the Younger grins and raises his middle finger. His uncle smiles back and takes a bow. Looks like the boys kissed and made up after all.

External cams show an express freighter synchronizing rotation with *Heimdall* forty minutes later. They're behind schedule, like Nik said. The freighter is huge—and I mean bigger than Buddha huge. Ugly. Weathered. It looks like a Griffon-class from the Vitus shipyards, the same kind of long-haul workhorse you'd find at any dock around a colonized sector. Nothing remarkable about its exterior, 'cept that it's so unremarkable. It's roughly rectangular, bow and stern flaring a little thicker than the middle. Eight-story thrusters are dwarfed by the sheer size of the thing. Micro-meteor scars pit its skin. Name stenciled down its snout in big black letters.

Mao.

The freighter's way too big to dock direct, so it extends a long umbilical of segmented plasteel and iron-weave kevlar, locks onto *Heimdall*'s docking doors. Inside, the heavy thunks of the magnalocks echo around the bay as Nik lights another cigarette, tapping away at a palmpad between puffs. No one thinks it's out of the ordinary—by now Double G and Puck are also on their palmpads playing a round of Shiv, and Handsome Mike is checking the scores on the traditional pre–Terra Day geeball match between the Kepler Knights and New Vegas Sabers (the game had been played the day before, but it took hours for the feed to hit the *Heimdall* waypoint and, from there, the station).

Sabers are up, 48–24.

A harsh electronic buzz reverberates around the bay. Several red globes above the airlock begin spinning and the dockcomp spits out an alert.

Handsome Mike looks up from his game. " 'Sup?"

Soraya is already at the bay door controls, stabbing at the console. "Bad seal. Got a leak somewhere. System's trying to lock it down."

"Us or them?"

"Us, I think. One of the mags didn't fire."

"Reboot and cycle the system." Mike spits between his teeth. "Tell these cowboys to detach and try again."

Nik Malikov looks at his watch again, grinds out his cigarette on the deck and marches over to Mike. Chewing his lip like it was rubber.

"Uncle Mike, I gotta jump. You can handle this, yeah?"

Malikov looks his nephew up and down. "This is your deal, Nikky."

"I know, I know. But I got this slice and she doesn't like to be kept waiting." He tries a conspiratorial grin. "She got a temper, feel me?"

"Don't try that prettyboy smile on me, Killer. Save them dimples for the tourists."

"Uncle Mike, come on. You got four crew here. You can handle one biotainer, Jesus."

"We can handle it, sure. But I let you slip early, what's in it for me?"

Malikov runs a hand through his hair, sucks his lip. "I'm due ten percent finder's fee, yeah? I'll kick you back a clip of that. Ten percent of my ten."

Handsome Mike scoffs. "██ off."

"Twenty, then. Twenty."

Mike spits through his teeth. "Forty. And you're taking Soraya's shift on birth detail."

"Jesus, I don't wanna be there when those things hatch."

"Well, Soraya doesn't want to be there either. And I owe her a cool K for the Blackwings game. If I slam you her shift, she'll call it even. So Miss Curves gets stood up or you butch up, li'l chum. Your call."

"When they hatching?"

"Tonight. Staggered cycle. Three per hour, every hour till we're done. First ones will be saying hello around 20:00, I'm thinking. You show up for second shift. Call it 01:00."

"Christ, it's Terra Day, Uncle Mike. I'm going hard with Ella tonight. You really want me in there half roasted when those things pop? I'll paint the ██ing walls."

"So bring a bucket, Killer."

Nik makes a face. Shoves his hands in his pockets. His palm-pad rings again and he glances at the screen. Sighs.

"Okay. All right. Thirty percent and I'm yours on the morrow. Deal?"

Malikov takes his nephew's offered hand and shows a gap-tooth grin.

"Hope she's worth it, Nikky."

"I'll let you know." He winks. "If I'm not back by dawn, call the president."

Nik slouches away as fast as he can, while still maintaining some semblance of chill, out the docking bay doors, through the secondary airlock and into the corridor beyond. Meanwhile, Soraya has been cycling the primary airlock seals again and is finally rewarded with a faint ping and a shift from red to green in the globes above the doors.

"You may begin kissing my ■ now, boys. Form an orderly queue when ready."

Seal established, the Dom Najov crew waits as the *Mao*'s umbilical pressurizes and fills with O_2. After a few ticks, the bay doors cycle wide, revealing two figures in stock-built envirosuits. No markings or company ident. They step into the bay and remove their helmets. The first is a man, early thirties, dark hair shaved close to his scalp. Tattoo of a biohazard symbol inked onto the back of his skull. The second is a woman. Late twenties, platinum blond hair sheared into a jagged fringe, clipped short back and sides. Fit and lean.

The pair touch hands. Just the lightest brush of their fingertips. Then the man begins wandering around the bay's expanse, marking each camera location, blind spots, cover. Blondie looks around at the assembled crew.

"Where's Malikov?" she asks.

"I'm Malikov," says Handsome Mike.

"Not the Malikov I'm supposed to be meeting."

"One of us is as good as another. You got something for me, Sweet?"

She blinks. Stares hard. Finally speaks. "Not until it's aboard."

Handsome Mike sighs expansively, nods to the Dom Najov. Puck jumps into an AAL, arcs up the controls. Servos and pistons whining, he slowly trudges down through the umbilical, Soraya hanging off the back of the suit. Handsome Mike and Double G stand with arms folded, watching the tattooed man wandering around the bay, tapping away on a handheld commlink. It's bleeding-edge tech. Not sure of the make or model.

Mike looks at the woman. "Your man seems nervous."

The woman doesn't say a word. Puck and Soraya emerge from the *Mao* a few minutes later, a heavy biotainer locked in the AAL's grip. The 'tainer is four meters by three, reinforced plasteel, marked with MÉDECINS SANS ÉTOILES seals and trimmed in yellow and black stripes. It's the kind you'd haul perishable med supplies inside, but since it has no external viewports, you could stow pretty much anything in it.

Puck pilots his loader across the bay, stows the biotainer against one wall with a heavy clang. Making the motion of dusting off his huge, hydraulically augmented hands, he powers off the suit, lightly hops down to the deck.

"All good, Cap," he calls.

Malikov nods. Turns to the woman. "Now. You got something for me, Sweet?"

Blondie looks him over. Looks to her companion, who simply nods.

"Yes," she says. "I've got yours."

Her companion raises his commlink. Flicks a switch.

And every camera in the bay dies without a whimper.

whisperNET

BRIEFING NOTE:
whisperNET chat between Hanna Donnelly and Nik Malikov. Her Majesty doesn't like to be kept waiting.

Ⓦ Ⓤ Ⓒ

AMBIENT TEMPERATURE: 22°C **DATE:** 08/15/75 **TIME:** 17:51 **LOCATION:** Infirmary

HEIMDALL CHAT	HANNA DONNELLY	NETbar

Donnelly, H: For a guy who asks me out a lot, you're pretty good at standing me up.

Guest389: For a girl who turns me down a lot, you're awfully good at pretending like we're married.

Donnelly, H: Why am I standing alone in this corridor? Dunno if you noticed, there's a pretty big shindig on right now. I can't be late. Tick tock.

Guest389: Hey, YOU switched times on ME first, remember? I'm just being fashionably late now.

Guest389: Is it working?

Donnelly, H: If by "working" you mean "killing a sale," then sure.

Guest389: Killing a sale, huh? So I guess I'll just sell these ten grams of prime bliss to someone else?

Donnelly, H: You're the one who's late, there's no need to be an ▬▬▬▬ about it.

Guest389: You have that effect on me, Highness.

NETbar

FRIENDS ONLINE
Nicole Brinkley
Claire Houston
Jackson Merrick
Kim Rivera
Keiko Sato

NEWSFEED
Happy Terra Day!

Mess Hall 3 Back Online

Terra Day Duty Rosters—
UPDATED

Wormhole Maintenance—
UPDATE—Additional
Tasks

Mission Statement

DIARY AND APPOINTMENTS
Lunch with Keiko

Terra Day party—Atrium
level (ongoing)

Stab peon repeatedly
in face—tba

Donnelly, H: My locator block will end in a couple of minutes, and I'm going to be here or not?

Guest389: Yeah, look, sorry. Other biz got in the way.

Guest389: I'm on my way right now. Gotta go back to hab and get stuff, then I'll be right there.

Donnelly, H: You don't have it on you? What the *hell*, Nik.

Guest389: I don't carry the ██ in my pocket just wandering around the station, Highness. I'm running, okay? Sprinting, no less. So congrats, you still get the boys all sweaty.

Donnelly, H: And they say there's no romance in your soul. See you soon.

Guest389: Did you dress sexy?

Guest389: Hello?

PERSONAL MESSAGE: PIRATE IM SYSTEM-HEIMDALL
Participants: Niklas Malikov, Civilian (unregistered)
Ella Malikova, Civilian (unregistered)
Date: 08/15/75
Timestamp: 17:56

Pauchok: cuz?

NikM: sup lil spider I'm bizy

Pauchok: cuz where are u

NikM: omw to meet her highness my pockets full of joy, why

Pauchok: wuz evrything ok when u left bay 17

NikM: yeah, wuz fine. Docking system was acting up. why?

Pauchok: Cams all over heimdall are going down

NikM: i'm looking @ a hallway cam right now. it's still tracking movement. LED is still on

Pauchok: well I'm not getting the feed. Someone's cut me out

NikM: ella, this station's a piece of ■. System's crawling with more bugs than Double G's pantaloons after his bachelor party. It's prolly just a network fault

Pauchok: can't raise dad or the others on IM.

NikM: well maybe you should suck less :)

Pauchok: hey, i got the fierce skillz. I dance Heimdall's webs like a dancy . . . spider . . . thing

Pauchok: DANCY

NikM: mebbe your dance moves aren't as fierce as you think li'l spider

Pauchok: Come back to the Hub

NikM: i got biz, cuz. I'll be there soon, k? then you and me celebrate TD in style.

NikM: you, me, four soundproofed walls & five hours of drunken karaoke >:D

Pauchok: nik I got a bad feeling.

NikM: hey, my voice isn't THAT cringe

Pauchok: i'm serious

NikM: ok fine, it *is* that cringe. I'll be there in 20 yeah?

Pauchok: nik . . .

NikM: cuz I got biz. Station doesn't stop spinning just because you get the crawls, feel?

Pauchok: . . . ok

NikM: <3

Pauchok: <3

Pauchok: cuz?

NikM: ya

Pauchok: b careful

whisperNET

HEIMDALL CHAT	HANNA DONNELLY	NETbar

Merrick, J: Hey, beautiful. Sorry I'm running late, we're just leaving Command & Control now. How's the party?

Donnelly, H: Not there yet, nearly on my way. My party treats are running behind schedule.

Donnelly, H: Keiko will be there, probably Claire. Hang out up the back with those fine ladies until I make it.

Merrick, J: Um.

Merrick, J: What? You still went to meet Malikov? Didn't you read my email?

Donnelly, H: No, I didn't have time. I had hair that'd turn the noblest hero to stone, Jax. It could've killed the goddamn Kraken.

Donnelly, H: It's fine, I'll just slip in and pretend I was standing with the girls the whole time, Dad won't notice.

Merrick, J: Um. He *will* notice. The first thing he'll do is ask me where you are.

NETbar

FRIENDS ONLINE
Nicole Brinkley
Claire Houston
Jackson Merrick
Kim Rivera
Keiko Sato

NEWSFEED
Happy Terra Day!

Mess Hall 3 Back Online

Terra Day Duty
Rosters——UPDATED

Wormhole
Maintenance——
UPDATE——Additional
Tasks

Mission Statement

DIARY AND APPOINTMENTS
Lunch with Keiko

Terra Day party——
Atrium level (ongoing)

Stab peon repeatedly
in face——tba

Donnelly, H: He'll be giving a speech. I already heard it twice at home, I know what it says.

Merrick, J: So where the bloody hell are you?

Donnelly, H: I'm waiting on my friend, he's late. Should be nearly here. Then I'll be straight into your arms.

Merrick, J: Your friend. You mean your drug dealer.

Donnelly, H: I thought you'd want me to be a little more discreet on whisperNET.

Donnelly, H: But fine, yes, Nik is running late. I assume if you're leaving C & C now you can't extend the block on my locator beacon, so I'll just make sure I'm moving in time.

Donnelly, H: Try and be less ████ed by the time I arrive. I'd like to try and enjoy the party.

Merrick, J: Jesus. Yes . . . look, I'm sorry. I'm tired.

Merrick, J: Just please hurry? Your dad leans on me hard enough as it is. If he found out where you were, and what I did to cover your tracks, we'd be done.

Merrick, J: I care about you, okay?

Donnelly, H: I care about you too? Sorry, didn't realize it would stress you out this much.

Donnelly, H: I'll hurry, promise.

Merrick, J: Okay.

ACQUISITION TEAM REP
BEITECH INDUSTRIES

BRIEFING NOTE:
An Acquisition Team Report from the Rapier operative recovered from *Heimdall* comms servers. It seems after the audit team landed, young Sam neglected to hide his tracks as carefully as he'd done prior to the seizure of the station. Maybe he was keeping a record to cover his own ■. It rapidly became clear that the audit team Leanne Frobisher sent to *Heimdall* was operating under a very different brief than he was.

INCIDENT INCEPT: 08/15/75

LOCATION: JUMP STATION *HEIMDALL*
(COMMAND & CONTROL BUILDING, MAIN ATRI

OPERATIVE IDENT: RAPIER

_____

~~It didn't need to be this way.~~

~~They were the words playing through my head through this whole thing. Like some old media disk stuck on infinite loop. Motor jammed. Needle bent.~~

~~It didn't need to be this way.~~

I was still on duty in Command & Control when the announcement went out across the PA system—Commander Donnelly wanted all staff present in the atrium for his Terra Day speech. Chief Isaac Grant gave us the nod and we started locking down systems, shunting alerts to our whisperNET accounts in case anything disastrous happened in the ten minutes it'd take Donnelly to raise his glass and thank us all and wish us a happy TD.

~~Yeah. In case anything disastrous happened . . .~~

Chief Grant looked exhausted. He hadn't been sleeping too well. Worried about his family back on Kerenza, I supposed. It'd been over six months since the colony went dark to "avoid UTA detection," and he hadn't heard a word from his wife or daughter since. Must've been hard. He showed me a photo of his daughter once.

108 / 659

Cute. Not sure about the pink hair, though. What was her name? Katy? Something like that.

~~I sometimes wondered if she was dead—if she died in the attack, or among the refugee fleet. I told myself there were probably still survivors on Kerenza. Maybe she was one of those. I still thought about the idea that he'd never see her again. Wondered what he'd do if he knew who I was. What I'd done. What I'd allowed them to do.~~

I'd already cut the live feeds from the station security cams through my ghost system, spliced them with looped footage of empty corridors and empty bays. Situation normal aboard Jump Station *Heimdall*. Nothing to see here, folks. Certainly not a fully armed squad of BeiTech Special Ops goons marching along the corridors toward Command & Control. No sir.

No one could see the mess they left in Docking Bay 17. Sprayed across the walls and dripping through the floor. A MÉDECINS SANS ÉTOILES biotainer stood in the bay, twenty-four personnel tubes stowed inside. Room for one operative with full kit in each one. All of them empty now. ~~Like the eyes of Handsome Mike Malikov and Soraya Een Hajji and the other House of Knives thugs they left cooling on the deck behind them.~~

"You're going to miss the party," Grant said, smiling at me. "Come on, people, you've worked enough for one day. First round is on me."

I plastered a fake grin on my face and left my station. Walking down the corridor beside the chief, chatting about nothing in particular, knowing full well what we were headed toward.

I told myself this was war. Whether Grant knew it or not, whether any of those people on Kerenza knew it or not, they signed up for war when they signed on to that colony. This station. This company. ~~But it didn't need to be this way, like I said.~~

We assembled down in the C & C atrium. Outermost floor of the structure. The sight never failed to amaze me. Bubbling waterfalls and lush greenery. Stone borders around rippling pools lit by all the colors of the spectrum. The walls and floor were clear as glass, thousands of panes of transparent plasteel, reinforced with titanium weave.

And beyond them?

Stars. Countless stars. Constellations and clusters and the Yggdrasil Nebula slowly spinning past the windows as *Heimdall* rotated around the wormhole at its heart. That subsonic hum felt just beyond the edge of hearing. That infinity waiting just above your head. ~~When I first got here, I was nervous about sleeping on top of a rip in the fabric of spacetime. I'm not sure how I'm going to sleep without it now.~~

The party was in full swing. Music thumping through the roof. Light show bouncing off the plasteel below us. Staffers and civis mingling, ice miners and colonists and traders—pretty much everyone left on the station for Terra Day had showed up. The ethanol and stims were flowing fast. I saw Sarah McDuling dancing on a table, Sinclair and Morley making out in a corner after having circled each other for five months. Reichs and Roth were engaged in their regular debate about the perils of new-wave fascism, the volume turned up to ten now that they both had a few under their skins. Warm bodies and smiling faces and laughter. ~~All of them, so alive.~~

~~If everyone plays chill,~~ ~~I told myself,~~ *~~they'll stay that way.~~*

Someone shoved a glass into my hand. Impromptu toasts rolled among the C & C crew. Vilma Gonzalez kissed my cheek, wished me happy Terra Day. Her cheeks were flushed and warm, and her lips lingered just a little longer than they should've. She looked me in the eye and touched my hand and smiled. Asked if I wanted to go somewhere quieter. I couldn't see Chief Grant anymore, wondered where he'd gotten to. But then Commander Donnelly took the stage amid scattered cheers, tapping on his vox implant for attention. The music dropped out and he began his speech.

Loyalty and duty. Commitment and perseverance.

Breaks for applause. Raised glasses and "Hear, hears."

~~None of them had any idea.~~

~~No idea at all.~~

And then the elevator doors opened wide.

Gunfire cut the applause to ribbons.

And all of it went to hell.

The walls around us were triple-reinforced—even though regs said nobody was allowed to carry a sidearm in the atrium, no amount of small-arms fire was going to punch through the panes. Still, when the shots started ricocheting off our stars, my first instinct was to look down and freeze. Waiting for the universe beyond to just dive inside. Partygoers began screaming, ducking, falling over each other in a panic as the audit team spilled out of the elevators and secured the room. Falk's team knew exactly who the SecTeam members were, moved quickly to neutralize them, dropping Bateman, Lucker, Legrand and the others with disruptor shots before anyone could blink. Kim Rivera, who ran the dojo, went down as she lunged for the nearest gunman, muscles spasming and eyes rolling up in her head.

The team was outfitted in heavy tactical armor. Greaves, boots, vests, goggs, helmets, weapons. All black. No ident, no corp logos, nothing. Only Lieutenant Falk wasn't wearing a face mask and helmet at this point—I recognized him from the briefing Director Frobisher had sent me. Callsign: Cerberus.

He was tall, heavily built, Norse blood. Ice-blue eyes. Blond hair shaved into a short fauxhawk, tuft of hair at his chin. He was built like an ice hauler, towering over almost everyone in the room. Biceps bigger than my head. The kevlar and plasteel plating he was encased inside creaked in agony when he moved, like he was about to burst the seams.

He stalked out into the middle of the atrium and just stood there. His team fanned out around the room, VK burst rifles out and ready, introducing anyone who looked at them sideways to the business ends. But Falk was stone-still. There was a strange smile on his face, faint, pulling his lips into a subtle curve—like he was laughing at his own private joke. Screaming and panic and tears all around him. He just stood in the middle of it. Smiling.

Eventually, the panic died down. The more sober partygoers brought their friends under control, stopped the screaming, the crying, the whispers. Must've taken five minutes. The whole time, Falk didn't move a muscle. Like he was drawing all that chaos into him. Drinking it dry. Until that atrium was so quiet I swear you could've heard a ████ing pin drop.

Falk looked around the room. Still smiling. Eyes like ice.

When he spoke, you could feel it through the floor.

"Who is in command of this jump station?"

Soft murmurs. Eyes searching. I couldn't see Chief Grant anywhere, but Commander Donnelly was still up onstage in his dress uniform. To his credit, he'd kept his head through the initial invasion, shepherded his people down off the dais, urged them to be calm. He was an officer, used to the snap decisions of command. He knew he was outgunned and outmanned, knew by their look these people were professionals—obviously they were here for a reason. He figured diplomacy was the way to go.

Falk spoke again.

"Who is in command of this jump station?"

Donnelly stepped forward. Stared Falk right in the eyes.

"I am."

Falk's pistol was out of his holster and trained on Donnelly in a split second. The shot cracked loud as a thunderbolt off the walls, the hollow-point almost took Donnelly's head off his shoulders. Brain and bone. So much blood you wouldn't believe it. The commander's corpse dropped to the floor, feet still kicking, heels scraping on the deck like he was trying to dance. And then the screaming started again. Rage mixed in with the panic now. Rage and grief and fear. But Falk's team was ready for it. Ready for all of it.

People who screamed too loud were pistol-whipped or hit with disruptor blasts, dropping to the ground in convulsions. Anyone who stepped toward an audit team member was dissuaded with a shot to the kneecap or a rifle butt to the jaw. ~~The walls rang with it—metal hitting meat and meat hitting the floor. Stink of blood so thick I swear I could taste iron in the air.~~

And through it all, Falk just stood there. In the center of that room, arms slightly outstretched, that smoking pistol still in his hand. That faint smile still curling his lips.

The panic died slow. Boiling fear and rage reduced to a simmer. Gonzalez was crouched beside me, clutching my arm ~~as if to hold me back. I realized my hands were fists.~~

Quiet fell. Quiet so deep it was deafening. And into that quiet, Falk spoke again.

"Who is in command of this jump station?"

Nobody replied this time.

Everyone knew the answer now.

FALK, Travis
Cerberus
Team Commander

RUSSO, Fleur
Kali
Alpha Squad—Leader

DAN, Kim
Poacher
Alpha Squad

MORETTI, Deni
Cujo
Alpha Squad

SATOU, Genji
Sensei
Alpha Squad

BAZAROV, Petyr
Romeo
Beta Squad—Leader

RADIN, Harry
Razorback
Beta Squad

MAYR, Stanislaw
Taurus
Beta Squad

WONG, Ai
Rain
Beta Squad

MAZUR, Kira
Ghost
Charlie Squad—Leader

CASTRO, Lucas
Link
Charlie Squad

LAURENT, Sara
Mona Lisa
Charlie Squad

ORR, James
Cricket
Charlie Squad

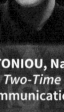

ANTONIOU, Naxos
Two-Time
Communications

LÊ, Tracy
Mantis
Computer Systems

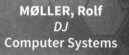

MØLLER, Rolf
DJ
Computer Systems

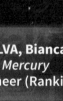

SILVA, Bianca
Mercury
Engineer (Ranking)

MORENO, Gabriel
Ballpark
Engineer

DE GRAAF, Lor
Taxman
Engineer/Medic

O'NEILL, Abby
Nightingale
Medic

ALIEVI, Marta
Eden
Logistics

SAPRYKIN, Kai
Juggler
Ordnance/Demolitions

PARK, Ji-hun
Flipside
Pilot/Demolitions

TAHIROVIĆ, Hans
Ragman
Pilot

Surveillance footage summary,
prepared by
Analyst ID 7213-0089-DN

Hanna Donnelly's pacing when the footage begins—Nik Malikov is late, and she's nearing the time she'll have to give up on him and head for the Terra Day reception without her party treats, or risk her father noticing she wasn't present for his speech. It's 18:15, a quarter hour after starting time.

She's a teenager of medium height, medium build, nice curves. Blond hair back in a braid, blue eyes narrowed in irritation, movements precise—that's the black belts right there, trust me. It's a wonder Malikov likes to tango with her so often. Just saying.

She's wrapped in one of those jumpsuits that all the Core kids are wearing, though here on *Heimdall* she's a little ahead of the trend. Black fabric with SmartTrim down the seams, which she's currently got tinted sea green. She makes a sharp turn at the end of her lap of the corridor, just in time to see Malikov come strolling around the corner. Camera A:17b12 shows he paused to get his breath back after the run before joining her (shouldn't be smoking, chum).

Donnelly stalks toward him, pulling a wad of exchangeable notes from her pocket and holding them out wordlessly. No point in making a traceable credit transfer in a situation like this. When you've got business like Malikov's, a foldable polymer blend is the only way to go.

"Nice to see you too, Highness," he says, pocketing the ISH and making a show of patting down his pockets, like he's not sure he remembered to bring the dust. "Is this any way to treat your humble servant?"

"Humble," she repeats, laughing. "And I thought you'd run out of jokes. Hand it over. You think I dressed up like this just to wait around for you?"

"Hard to say." He gives up the search, folding his hands behind his back as he starts walking a lap around her. "Let me get a look at that outfit from all angles so I can be sure."

She shifts her weight in a quick feint, and he takes a step back, grinning but wary—he remembers the allegedly-broken-arm incident, apparently.

"Hand it over," she insists. "Nik, I swear I'll—"

But she doesn't get any further. Malikov reaches into a hidden pocket and, with a deep bow, pulls out a slightly crumpled corsage, set with six tiny white blooms.

"What the hell's that?" Donnelly asks.

Malikov gives her a dimpled half smile. "Jasmine, obvs."

"I thought you said to get flowers out here you'd have to give up your right . . ." She gestures at his crotch. ". . . you know."

"I got a spare." He shrugs. Holds out his offering. "Happy Terra Day, Highness."

Donnelly blinks. Shakes her head. "Nik, I can't—"

She's cut off by the crackle of the all-station public address system—a calm but unfamiliar male voice, and Falk's idea of a joke. "Attention, all *Heimdall* personnel. This is *not* your captain speaking . . ."

Wonder how long he's been saving up that one.

The words hang in the air as Donnelly and Malikov stare at each other, twin pictures of wary confusion. For an instant, hostilities are suspended.

Falk continues: "Your station is now under our control.

Understand that we are professionals, here to do a job, and wish no harm to any of you. Cooperate, and you will be safe. Resist, and you will be . . . less safe."

The color drains from both their faces. Donnelly draws in a long, slow breath that would do any of her martial arts teachers proud. Malikov stows the corsage, pulls out his palmpad and stabs at the screen—presumably he's trying to open a channel to his cousin, but it looks like he gets nowhere.

Falk's still talking. "If you are in Alpha Sector, please assemble in the atrium. All other sectors, your exit portals have been sealed. You will remain in place and wait quietly for further announcements. Follow instructions immediately, and to the letter. Personnel in Alpha Sector, you have five minutes. Please do *not* make us come and find you. That would be . . . unpleasant for all concerned."

"Holy ▮▮," Malikov breathes.

"No." Donnelly's whispering, trembling. "My father, my father's in the atrium, my friends are there, and Jackson . . ."

". . . You can't be thinking about going down there."

"I *have* to."

"Are you dusted? Who knows what they'll do to you?"

"I'm not going to hand myself over, I'm not completely stupid," she snaps. "I need more information, and I'm not getting that standing here."

"Look, just stay here, hide. I'll find out what's going on."

"Right." She snorts. "You want me to outsource this to *you*? They've got my dad."

"And if you head in there, they get you, too. We need to know what these ▮▮ers are up to before we start taking orders." Gone are the quips now, the smart lines. He's as white and strained as she. "Trust me, Hanna, I got the connects to find out what's what."

"Trust you?" Her voice rises. "You're my ▮▮ing drug dealer!"

"So maybe I got ways to find out things you don't," he snaps.

She holds up her hand suddenly, blinking. "Are you watching whisperNET? My contacts are dropping offline."

He blinks hard, focuses on his lens. "Yeah, mine too."

"How are they doing that?"

Malikov's eyes widen. I swear you can almost see the goddamn lightbulb go off over his head. He reaches inside his jacket, pulling out a palmpad. A ziplock baggie full of what could only be ten grams of Grade A tetraphenetrithylamine is taped to the top. "Take this?"

"Now's not the time to get dusted, dammit," she hisses.

"It's the palmpad I promised you, remember?" he replies, rolling his eyes. "So we could talk private? It's off the main grid, Highness. We'll be able to talk even if they take whisperNET offline. Just take it, hide out and let me do my work. I'll tell you who they are, what they want."

She snatches the palmpad from him. "Fine."

Her surrender is sudden. Sullen.

Malikov blinks. "Fine?"

"Fine. We've got minutes. We can't spend them arguing. Go."

He stares at her for a long moment, clearly not sure whether to trust her—but she's right, and with their five minutes slowly gurgling down the drain, he turns, and he runs.

She waits until he's disappeared around the corner, then turns to jog in the opposite direction.

whisperNET

AMBIENT TEMPERATURE: 22°C **DATE:** 08/15/75 **TIME:** 18:27 **LOCATION:** Infirmary

HEIMDALL CHAT	HANNA DONNELLY	NETbar

Donnelly, H: Jackson? Please be there.

Merrick, J: Hanna, thank god, where are you? Are you okay?

Donnelly, H: I'm okay, I'm hiding. What the ██ happened? Are you guys okay?

Merrick, J: Someone's hit the station. Terrorists. I don't know. But they mean business. They've got control of the computer and surveillance systems. We're totally blind.

Donnelly, H: Where are you?

Merrick, J: Command & Control. I got to the party, but Chief Grant called me back up when security cams started dropping out. We've locked ourselves on the bridge to give us time to think.

Donnelly, H: I think they're getting whisperNET too, my contacts keep disappearing one by one.

Merrick, J: Mine too. I'm not sure how long we have to talk.

FRIENDS ONLINE
Jackson Merrick
NEWSFEED
Happy Terra Day!

Mess Hall 3 Back Online

Terra Day Duty Rosters—UPDATED

Wormhole Maintenance—UPDATE—Additional Tasks

Mission Statement
DIARY AND APPOINTMENTS
Lunch with Keiko

Terra Day party—Atrium level (ongoing)

Stab peon repeatedly in face—tba

Donnelly, H: Is there any way you can see the atrium? See if my father's okay?

Merrick, J: No, they've locked us out of the system. I don't know how they're doing it. The protections on our grid are capital-S *Serious*.

Donnelly, H: Okay, then I'm going to hole up. I'm not turning myself in when I don't know what will happen next.

Merrick, J: Um. I'm not sure that's a good idea.

Donnelly, H: Handing myself over limits my options. Staying out here increases them.

Merrick, J: They have control of cams. They can see everything SecTeam could. Come to C & C. It'll be safer here with us instead of out there alone.

Donnelly, H: What, you're just going to open the door so I can creep in?

Donnelly, H: It's too far, not safe. Recon before action, that's the rule. If you know your enemies and know yourself, you will not be imperiled in a hundred battles.

Merrick, J: What?

Donnelly, H: Sun Tzu.

Merrick, J: Hanna, this is not the time to quote crusty old war strategists.

Donnelly, H: My dad would say this is exactly the time. Be smart, borrow wisdom.

Merrick, J: Hanna, we can hear gunfire. People screaming. I don't think now is a good time to play soldier. I can't protect you out there.

Donnelly, H: You can't protect me in there, either.

Merrick, J: Hanna—

Falk, T: Attention, *Heimdall* residents in Alpha Sector. Your five minutes is concluded. We thank those of you who have complied with directives to surrender. That was . . . . quite lovely of you.

Falk, T: To all foxes still hiding in your little holes: woof woof.

Falk, T: That is all.

Merrick, J: ███. **Hanna, you have to turn yourself in.**

Donnelly, H: What, like you are?

Merrick, J: Hanna, there's half a meter of plate steel between C & C and—

Donnelly, H: Jax, shut up.

Merrick, J: I—

Donnelly, H: I think I can hear some SecTeam guys. I'm going to check it out. Back soon.

Merrick, J: Christ, Hanna, be careful.

Merrick, J: Hanna?

Surveillance footage summary,
prepared by
Analyst ID 7213-0089-DN

Footage is taken from Camera 276-R, commencing at 18:38. Ruth Ellis and Gaby Salpeter are members of *Heimdall*'s SecTeam, and they are having a very bad day.

They were late on their way back from patrol when Falk's announcement went out, and they bolted for the nearest familiar territory—the SecTeam break room. There, surrounded by couches, their colleagues' lockers and abandoned food wrappers, they're following emergency protocol. Records show they'd already tried whisperNET and found their connections dead, so they're standing together by a broadcast unit, scanning the backup channels Sec-Teams are instructed to use in case of comms failure.

They've moved a digital notice board to give them cover, and to all but the most dedicated searcher, the break room would look empty. They work in quick, tense silence.

But they've forgotten about their personal locator beacons. *PLoBs*, the locals call them, which sounds like a cheery little noise. But there's nothing cheery about what's happening now.

Four BeiTech audit team members are stealthing down the hallway, clad in black full-body tactical armor, VK burst rifles at the ready, footsteps very nearly silent. The squad is led by Petyr "Romeo" Bazarov, the tattooed triggerman who took care of the

Dom Najov in Bay 17. He's got a hand scanner, and his gaze is locked on it as he stalks his prey.

Inside the break room, Ellis locates the frequency she wants. Salpeter reaches up to the shelf above the broadcast unit for hard copy of the emergency codes, passing it to her friend.

Romeo stops in the doorway of the break room, eyeballs the hand scanner, then gestures at the notice board. The woman to his right, Ai "Rain" Wong, tosses a concussion grenade in through the door with an easy overhand throw, then she and Romeo duck back outside. The grenade detonates, and Ellis and Salpeter collapse as one, screaming, bleeding from ruined ears and eyes. Romeo calmly steps back into the doorway, lifts his rifle and plugs the notice board hiding them six times in a row. He proceeds into the break room with all due caution, checks behind the shattered screen and nods to Ellis's and Salpeter's lifeless bodies.

"You forgot your trackers, kids," he tells their remains. "Though they *do* ruin the sport." Laughing at his own wit and wisdom, he walks back past Rain and into the hallway beyond.

Rain and the other two men on the BeiTech squad prepare to move on, but Romeo's still studying the hand scanner. Slowly, he walks back into the break room, frowning at the display. He halts in the center of the abandoned room, silent.

Then he tilts his head back and looks up at the air vent above him.

PERSONAL MESSAGE: PIRATE IM SYSTEM-HEIMDALL
Participants: Niklas Malikov, Civilian (unregistered)
Ella Malikova, Civilian (unregistered)
Date: 08/15/75
Timestamp: 18:38

Pauchok: Nik?

NikM: ███ ella where r u?

Pauchok: um that's the great thing about partial paralysis, cuz mine.

Pauchok: I'm right where you ███ing left me.

NikM: in Anansi? doors sealed?

Pauchok: ya

NikM: good stay there

Pauchok: space pirates are shooting the ███ out of everything on the station and you tell me to stay low inside my fortified super-computer? any more advice for me, genius?

NikM: g u cizx

Pauchok: wut?

NikM: f u cuz. i typng while irun gmme break

NikM: wheruncle mike

Pauchok: i dunno where dad is. I can't raise anyone. Need ot see what happened in bay 17

NikM: way ahead of u heded bak there noqw 2 mins awy

Pauchok: jesus Nik, be careful. Cams are all down, I can't see █

NikM: █

NikM: they sealed doors out of Alpha Sector. can't get to docks

Pauchok: o rly

Pauchok: where u @?

NikM: service bulkhead. A-48a

Pauchok: gimme a sec

Pauchok: ta daaaaaa

NikM: goddamn ur good :D

Pauchok: oh go on

Pauchok: . . . I'm serious, go on dammit

NikM: k I'm through. on grav-rail now now

NikM: goddamn this █ing lollipop song . . .

Pauchok: k, I cleared a path 4 u. b quick, auto sensor will shut the doors again eventually

NikM: k at docks now, headed to 17. there in a sec

Pauchok: um cuz

NikM: ya

Pauchok: I think whoever's flying their rig flagged me when I popped that bulkhead

Pauchok: they trying to hack into anansi

Pauchok: jesus, they *good*

NikM: ella

Pauchok: gimme a sec

Pauchok: oho mimic routines running on your roach cascades, very clever

NikM: ella

Pauchok: but no, you got crushT didn't u? spiders eat roaches donchewnoe

NikM: ELLA

Pauchok: ALL CAPS

```
          A  A  A
          |  | | | | |
        _| |_| |_| |___nnnnnn_____-____-====---CAPSCAPSCAPSCAPS
     _  __/---| |-| |-|_|---~~--------~~-----\==/--------~~\.
 0=|-|O0000---<=X===X===X=>-|||-----|||>    ---HHK |
   ~    ~~\--| |-| |-|~|---___--------___----/==\_____/'
          | | | |--| |
          | | | |--| |
          V  V  V
```

NikM: ella they're dead

Pauchok:

Pauchok: wut?

NikM: They all dead. Soraya. Double G.

Pauchok: . . . daddy?

NikM: ■

NikM: cuz I'm sorry

Pauchok: god

Pauchok: W34KJGB;OUAQ5UBG35U[089[809G5G'I3OT4O 'IOU34SXZK,I EWXZ

$nickname = htmlentities(strip_tags($_POST['PAUCHOK']));
$reg_exUrl = "/(http|https|ftp|ftps)\:\/\/[a-zA-Z0-9\-\.]+\.[a-zA-Z]{2,3}(\/\S*)?/";
$message =htmlentities(strip_tags($_POST['message']));
if (($message) != "\n") {
if (preg_match($reg_exUrl, $message, $url)) {
$message =preg_replace($reg_exUrl, '<a href="'.$url[0].'" target="_blank">'.$url[0].'</a>', $nickname . $message);
fwrite(fopen('data.txt', 'a'), "" . $nickname . "" . $message . str_replace
break;

Pauchok: WUT THE ███ HAPPEND?

NikM: popped. multiples, close range. Empty biotaner here. spots for 24 crew inside.

NikM: Looks like we found out how our party crashers got on board

NikM: that mother███ wheaton. I KNEW I shoulda x-ed that pasty ███

Pauchok: ███

Pauchok: ███ING ███████S

Pauchok: PIG███ING ██EATING ████ING MOTHER█████S

NikM: god ells, I'm so sorry

Pauchok: jesus gimme a sec

Pauchok: their decker still all up in my lady parts

NikM: ███

Pauchok: ███ me he tyrign to cut me out ofnetwork

NikM: so get dancy on his man bits

Pauchok: sec

Pauchok: jj9WV-9   P2EVN9 9n0iiIWOBREVnwojro

NikM: cuz?

Pauchok: w49305ugnotb-9nwg w5b09135ibnqer bxcp 8ywev7   q³b[o4b]-q3 be[pufb] [arevbq34]bv[iu=vnoq³i5q3n45kgn0e9rh-ion34]igh=   [h4] vpnerhvh3inq03irhviervq35nokjae0rivnapkn8q3h4-

NikM: ella?

<network fail>

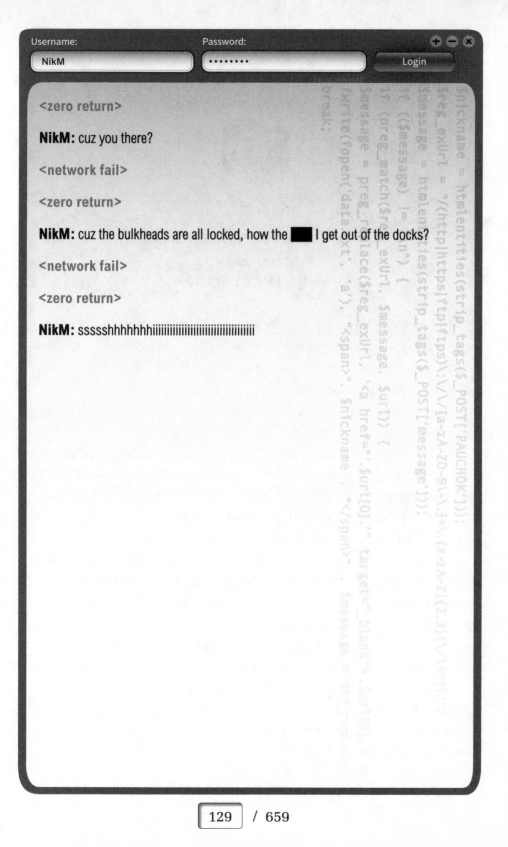

Username: NikM **Password:** •••••••• Login

<zero return>

NikM: cuz you there?

<network fail>

<zero return>

NikM: cuz the bulkheads are all locked, how the ███ I get out of the docks?

<network fail>

<zero return>

NikM: sssssshhhhhhhiiiiiiiiiiiiiiiiiiiiiiiiiiiiiiiiiiiiiiiiiiiii

**Surveillance footage summary,
prepared by
Analyst ID 7213-0089-DN**

The records on Hanna Donnelly's personal locator beacon show she moved away from the vent above the SecTeam break room after the deaths of Ruth Ellis and Gaby Salpeter, making straight for Corridor A17d and the infirmary.

She comes into view when she silently pulls the cover off the climate control vent, one shaking hand hanging down so she can drop it onto a bed, muffling the sound it makes when it lands. There are only two patients in the Alpha Sector infirmary, both unconscious—everyone capable of moving was either shipped out for the holiday or dragged themselves to the party.

With a little shuffling, she lowers herself down legs first, thumping to the ground. Around now, she must be glad she went for the jumpsuit. She lands in a crouch, wrapping her arms around herself and ducking her head, just for a moment. Then she pulls it together, pushing to her feet in one easy movement.

"Can you hear me? Jax?" She's so scared she's actually whispering at her whisperNET connection instead of subvocalizing, but there's no reply. With a glance over her shoulder at the door, she hurries to a workbench littered with equipment, scanning it as she jogs her weight impatiently from one foot to the other. She grabs a scalpel in a case and shoves it into her pocket. It clicks against the palmpad Malikov gave her, and she gives it a quick pat through the fabric, as though she's just remembering it's there.

I have to admit I was wondering why she didn't get the hell out of there, because she's scared all right—her breath's quick and ragged, face pinched. But the answer becomes clear a second later. Shifting to an infirmary terminal, she swipes her way through the menus, data mirrored in her eyes. She's going for the PLoB register, and dragging a finger down, she watches as the list of names scrolls past.

She's looking for her father's ID. His body won't have cooled enough to deactivate his beacon yet, so she might have found it—except her friends catch up with her before she reaches the *D*s.

There's a soft click in the corridor outside, and she pivots on the balls of her feet, diving behind a bed a fraction of a second before Romeo and Harry "Razorback" Radin open fire. Their burst weapons rip through the infirmary, blast the door off its hinges. Over the next fifteen seconds, they tear apart all eighteen beds—including the two patients—the supply cabinets and the surgical section. Donnelly's crawled, sobbing, to cower behind a countertop. She's lying facedown, and a bullet punches through a finger's width above her head.

Razorback speaks quietly into the silence that follows. "Clear?"

"She's here." Romeo is studying his hand scanner. "Find her body, confirm the kill."

Rain and their fourth, Stanislaw "Taurus" Mayr, follow Romeo and Razorback into the infirmary. Weapons at the ready, the four fan out to search the debris, leaning down to check under ruined beds, behind the remains of chairs and monitors, boots crunching on the detritus scattered on the floor. Romeo clicks his tongue to draw their attention and points to the vent Hanna left open when she made her entrance.

Hanna's on the other side of the room, crawling for the doorway.

She's spent her whole life playing strategy games with her father, but it doesn't take a tactical genius to know four on one—even without the weapons—isn't a game she wants to play. She nearly makes it, too. There's three strides of clear space between the nearest bed and escape, and she slowly eases up to a crouch, hands resting on the floor like she's readying herself for a race.

She's out of the starting blocks an instant later, and it's just plain bad luck that Taurus turns at the wrong moment. He shouts the alarm, swinging his rifle up and pulling the trigger. The infirmary explodes with deafening blasts, muzzle flashes whiting out the camera for an instant. Hollow-point rounds shred the doorframe as Hanna dives for it, scrambling out into the hallway, hands clawing desperately at the floor.

The footage transfers to the corridor outside, where she's stumbling to her feet, sprinting for the next corner as a black-clad kill squad pours through the door after her. Every training session she's ever had channels into this moment, and she recovers her balance, flinching aside as another shot clips the end of her swinging braid.

She knows exactly where she's going, and there she has the advantage—she's also running for her life, and if that's not motivation, I dunno what is. She sprints along the corridor, grabbing a light fixture at the junction and swinging herself around the corner without losing momentum. They're close behind, blasting away every time she's in sight, but she's gaining a few seconds here, another few seconds there.

Problem is, she's gonna run out of corridor.

She tugs the scalpel case from her pocket. The palmpad Malikov gave her slips out with it and clatters to the floor, a small baggie of dust still taped to the top. She leaves it behind without a backward glance. Stumbling, she rounds another corner, and finally, there's her salvation: an open elevator. She hurtles into it, hand slamming against the button to close it as Romeo and Co. round the corner and lift their weapons.

Gunfire splits the air as the BT team empty their clips, the elevator doors riddled with dozens of gaping holes as they slide closed. Romeo and Taurus slam into them with a series of curses. Without needing to consult, they dash for the emergency staircase. Romeo's got his hand to his commset, demanding that someone in C & C explain why the holy ▓▓ the elevators are still functioning.

When the BeiTech team arrives one floor up, the elevator doors are open, the floor's bloody and there's a spattered trail of crimson leading away down the corridor. Like the hounds Cerberus promised they'd be, they take to the trail.

Scanner in hand, Romeo leads his squad along the hallway; they are quiet as ghosts, finally arriving at a sealed airlock door. The docks up in Alpha Sector aren't big loading bays like the one where the Dom Najov met their end—these are smaller, snugger places, for MedEvac shuttles to dock near the infirmary. The audit team forms a semicircle around the doorway, weapons ready. Romeo indicates the bay with a nod.

"Her temperature's dropping," he says quietly. "She's bleeding out. Let's finish it quick and careful. Even kittens come out swinging from a corner."

Footage from inside the launch bay is a little grainy, but the team's clearly visible fanning out in a search formation. Taurus holds just inside the door so Donnelly can't get past them again.

"Come out, little girl," Razorback calls. "Let's find you a nice patch of SimSkin for that scratch."

"Something's wrong," Romeo says, still zeroing in on the signal. The scanner in his hand keeps triangulating, slowly narrowing the area to search. He lifts a hand to rub the back of his tattooed head, holding still, thinking.

"Say what?" Rain looks across at him.

"She's at twenty-nine degrees."

"And?"

"Body temperature is thirty-seven. She's hypothermic." As he speaks, Romeo's pointing at a stack of crates held down with webbing near the bay doors. He, Rain and Razorback move in as one, rounding the edges of the crates, weapons at the ready.

But Hanna Donnelly's not there. Her personal locator beacon lies on the ground in a small pool of blood. The launch bay isn't as well insulated as the rest of *Heimdall,* and on the other side of the airlock it's minus 270 Celsius. The PLoB's temperature is cooling rapidly.

In one smooth movement, Donnelly drops from her hiding place above the launch bay entry, lands behind Taurus and scampers out the door, her bloodied hand slamming into the door controls. They hum closed in 0.7 seconds, sealing the team inside and her outside.

Donnelly stares at the airlock button, but there's no way to know if she wishes she could flush them. Her PLoB is in there, which means the system thinks she's in there too—as a precaution, the control panel is lit up a cheery locked-down red so nobody can accidentally get spaced. Because wouldn't that be just terrible?

Romeo's thoroughly ██ed off, stalking over to join Taurus by the locked door and hissing into the intercom: "Let us out, little girl. You're only making this worse."

Donnelly presses her intercom with one delicate finger. "Little girl? Is that any way to talk to someone you just met?"

"It's how I talk to the brat I'm going to roast on a stick in about twenty seconds."

"Threats?" Hanna observes. "Interesting tactical choice. Seeing as how I'm on this side of the door and you're not."

"Listen, it was a good fight," Romeo tries. "But we've radioed for backup. Open the door before they get here, and we'll even stop them from shooting you. I can respect what you did."

"Who are you?" Hanna shoots back. "Why are you here?"

Romeo shakes his head, smiling.

The red light on the airlock control flickers out, replaced a moment later by bright green. Donnelly's locator beacon has cooled to

25 degrees Celsius. She's registered as dead. Regardless, there's no way the safety protocols in place on those external doors would allow them to open with a registered PLoB inside.

But still . . .

Hanna and Romeo both look down at the controls on their respective sides of the door. Hanna backs away a step or two, hands raised.

The safety shutter on the window between them slams shut.

"No, wait . . . ," Donnelly says.

And as she sucks in a startled breath, a white light flicks on.

Airlock Disengaged.

Purging.

FALK, Travis
Cerberus
Team Commander

RUSSO, Fleur
Kali
Alpha Squad—Leader

DAN, Kim
Poacher
Alpha Squad

MORETTI, Deni
Cujo
Alpha Squad

SATOU, Genji
Sensei
Alpha Squad

BAZAROV, Petyr
Romeo
Beta Squad—Leader

RADIN, Harry
Razorback
Beta Squad

MAYR, Stanislaw
Taurus
Beta Squad

WONG, Ai
Rain
Beta Squad

MAZUR, Kira
Ghost
Charlie Squad—Leader

CASTRO, Lucas
Link
Charlie Squad

LAURENT, Sara
Mona Lisa
Charlie Squad

ORR, James
Cricket
Charlie Squad

ANTONIOU, Naxos
Two-Time
Communications

LÊ, Tracy
Mantis
Computer Systems

MØLLER, Rolf
DJ
Computer Systems

SILVA, Bianca
Mercury
Engineer (Ranking)

MORENO, Gabriel
Ballpark
Engineer

DE GRAAF, Lor
Taxman
Engineer/Medic

O'NEILL, Abby
Nightingale
Medic

ALIEVI, Marta
Eden
Logistics

SAPRYKIN, Kai
Juggler
Ordnance/Demolitions

PARK, Ji-hun
Flipside
Pilot/Demolitions

TAHIROVIĆ, Hans
Ragman
Pilot

BRIEFING NOTE:
Transcription of
footage recovered from
House of Knives hard drives.

Surveillance footage summary,
prepared by
Analyst ID 7213-0089-DN

Okay, I'm going on record here—you guys aren't paying me enough
to watch this stuff.

Footage opens in a familiar auxiliary venting and storage room,
AVS-3, situated above *Heimdall*'s hermium reactor. Present and
accounted for are twenty-three dairy cows, including Nikky Malikov's dear Miss Lucy, standing around their makeshift pen.

A couple of jury-rigged security cams catch the show—
Handsome Mike obviously wanted to keep an eye on his "babies."
He had all kinds of containment protocols he'd have put in place
before tonight's festivities really got under way—there's a series
of glass humidicribs along one wall, a couple of hazmat suits and
what looks to be a cross between a cattle prod and an articulated
claw arm beside them. But given that Handsome Mike's lying
dead in Bay 17, his babies and their hosts are completely unsuper-
vised.

The pipes and gauges lining the wall are literally dripping, and
the cam lenses are partially fogged—the humidity must be close
to tropical in there. In the distance, even through the soundproofing, you can hear faint gunfire—the BeiTech Audit team zeroed in
on the reactor as their secondary seize-and-secure target on the
station, right after Command & Control. It sounds like some of the
locals are putting up a fight.

It doesn't last long.

Nobody from the BT squad ever comes to check the auxiliary room. A scan of *Heimdall* C & C files shows that AVS-3 didn't actually exist on station schematics—Ella Malikova purged all records of it to better hide her dad's Get Rich Quick and Slightly Bloody scheme, and anyone on the *Heimdall* staff who actually knew about the room didn't volunteer the info to the invaders. Or run here for safety, come to think of it.

Probably for the best.

Anyway, all the noise and fuss of the invasion going on outside seems completely lost on the cows. The ladies are just standing there, eyes glazed. They're not eating, chewing, mooing. Just swaying softly on their feet as if to music, except there's no noise but the faint reactor hum and sporadic gunfire. Every one of them has a tiny bandage behind her right ear. Their needle wounds have been kept nice and clean, no chance of infection or sepsis.

That Handsome Mike, huh? All heart.

The cows' chins are slicked with drool. Heads lolling, like they're half asleep. Their eyes are gummed with something dark and viscous that at first I don't recognize. When it starts dripping from their ears and spattering on the floor, it finally clicks.

Blood.

It's blood.

Christ, I feel sick . . .

I need a drink.

AND A VACATION, DAMMIT.

—transcript pauses—

Okay, a little rocket fuel makes it all better. Chrrrrist, let's get this over with.

The gunfire outside dies along with whoever it was aimed at, and the footage runs for hours with no real change. I can fast-forward until 19:40 and the cows do nothing but softly sway and slowly bleed, which in itself is ███ing terrifying enough.

Then, at 19:41, Lucy falls completely still.

Her eyes go wide, and every muscle in her body tenses. Everything I've read about Ianima tells me she can't feel any pain—the larva inside her is flooding her synapses with unprocessed tetraphenetrithylamine and she's high as the goddamn sky. But I swear something inside her is awake enough to sense what's coming. Some tiny reptile part of her brain, struggling to be heard over the flood of chemical bliss drenching her system.

Something that screams, "This is very, *very* wrong."

Lucy bucks. Nerve endings firing on autopilot. Ears twitching as if warding off invisible flies. Her right foreleg starts to shake, tail whipping side to side. Then she sneezes, and bright pink froth sprays all over the floor.

The cow beside her starts undergoing the same fit. Followed by another. Then another. Lucy is making this weird noise, halfway between snorting and coughing. Her chest is heaving, she's drenched in sweat. But Jesus, her eyes . . .

Her eyes, chums.

They're still almost closed. Like she's half asleep. Like this is some bad dream you hit right before the alarm clock goes off and spits you into your day and you shake the sleep away and laugh to yourself about how scared you got because it's only a bad dream, chum.

Just a real bad dream.

But Lucy can't wake up. I'm calling that a mercy. Her eyes stay fixed in that dreamy, half-closed droop until a wet, crackling noise cuts across the audio track like a knife and she collapses bonelessly to the deck. Her eyes are finally closed, bright red tongue protruding from between her teeth.

And then something pries those teeth apart.

Something long and black, slithering out of her ruptured palate onto the blood-slick grille. It's almost thirty centimeters long,

wrapped in a translucent membrane. Flopping about like a landed fish. Other cows are dropping beside it now, thudding onto the floor. The newborn wriggles and flexes, splitting apart the sheath it's encased in. One end of it unfurls, like some awful flower, and then four serpentine necks sway in the air.

Each neck ends in a tiny mouth. Lined with row upon row of serrated teeth.

Sharp as needles.

Even on the vidscreen, I have a hard time focusing on it. Maybe it's the hooch, maybe the stale ship's rations I ate three hours ago trying to come back for a visit. The thing's skin is this weird kaleidoscope of . . . not colors. Un-colors. It's hard to describe. I get a headache looking at it. It unfolds two tiny forelimbs, pushing itself up off the abattoir floor, those necks writhing to a melody only it can hear.

And then it shrieks.

It's the sound of a hundred junkie babies howling their way through birthday withdrawals. The sound of every orphaned child from every war zone you've ever seen from behind the comfort of your VR screen. It's hellish. That's the only way I can describe it, chums.

Just █████ing hellish.

The shriek fades, echoing off the dripping walls of Room AVS-3.

Tiny black tongues slip past needle teeth and lick sightlessly at the air.

Lucy's baby draws breath and shrieks again. The sound splitting my head. And right when I think things couldn't possibly get any worse, another shriek joins with the first. And another. Dark wormthings swaying and screaming and slithering about in an deep pool of red half a finger deep.

████ me.

Like I said, you guys aren't paying me enough to watch this stuff . . .

COUNTDOWN TO
HYPATIA ARRIVAL
AT HEIMDALL WAYPOINT:

01 DAYS
00 HOURS: 36 MINUTES

COUNTDOWN TO KENNEDY
ASSAULT FLEET ARRIVAL
AT JUMP STATION HEIMDALL:

00 DAYS
23 HOURS: 04 MINUTES

whisperNET

HEIMDALL CHAT	HANNA DONNELLY	NETbar

Merrick, J: Hanna?

Donnelly, H: Oh my god, Jax, are you okay?

Merrick, J: I'm okay. Are you?

Donnelly, H: I'm fine, I'm fine. How did you get whisperNET back up?

Merrick, J: Chief Grant did it. I don't know how long we have. Listen, where are you? Are you safe?

Donnelly, H: I'm hiding. Are you guys still on the bridge?

Merrick, J: Wh—

Donnelly, H: Jax?

Donnelly, H: JAX?

NETbar

FRIENDS ONLINE
None

NEWSFEED
Error

Error

Error

Error

Error

DIARY AND APPOINTMENTS
Scheduler functionality unavailable

RADIO TRANSMISSION: BEITECH AUDIT TEAM—SECURE CHANNEL 901

PARTICIPANTS:

Travis "Cerberus" Falk, Lieutenant, Team Commander

Fleur "Kali" Russo, Sergeant, Alpha Squad-Leader

DATE: 08/15/75

TIMESTAMP: 20:49

CERBERUS: Kali, this is Cerberus. Over.

KALI: Cerberus, Kali. Go.

CERBERUS: A status report would be lovely, if you please.

KALI: Engineering area secure. Hostiles eliminated. Zero casualties. Walk in the park.

CERBERUS: Splendid. Prisoners?

KALI: Seventeen live bodies. Eleven wormhole engineers, six nonessentials. Already secured.

CERBERUS: Wormhole status?

KALI: The *Heimdall* crew shut it down as expected when we seized the station. Safety precaution. Mercury and Ballpark are bringing it back online now. The engineers are being kind enough to assist. A little gunpoint diplomacy works wonders.

CERBERUS: And this maintenance that Operative Rapier informed us about?

KALI: Mercury's checking the logs now. Like Rapier said, our techs will need to finish off some work the *Heimdall* crew had planned.

CERBERUS: *Heimdall* command projected seven days offline, Kali. We have less than twenty-four hours. Can they do it in time?

KALI: They say yes. Though the computer system seems to be running suboptimally. And there's some ███ing annoying pop song that plays every time the network tries to sound an alert or make a prompt.

CERBERUS: Ah. Our lollipop girl. Quite the earworm, yes?

KALI: Yessir. But Ballpark assures me everything will be five by five before Assault Fleet *Kennedy* arrives. If these local boys have to lose a little sleep or a little blood, so be it. We'll get it done.

CERBERUS: Consider me delighted.

KALI: I live to give, Cerberus. I was just about to radio Romeo. We'll keep the engineers down here on the treadmill, but I presume you want these nonessentials transferred to the atrium with the rest of the meat?

CERBERUS: Eventually. Keep them secure for now. I'll send Ghost and Charlie Squad to collect them soon.

KALI: Beta Squad is closer than Charlie?

CERBERUS: Negative, Sergeant. Romeo and his squad are flatline.

KALI: . . . Say again, Cerberus?

CERBERUS: Romeo is dead, Kali. He and his entire squad were flushed out an airlock by a local hostile one hour and forty-seven minutes ago.

KALI: Flushed out a . . .

KALI: . . . an hour and forty-seven ████ING MINUTES AGO?

CERBERUS: Fleur—

KALI: And you tell me this AFTER you get me to debrief? Travis, what the—

CERBERUS: Sergeant, I am dangerously close to raising my voice.

CERBERUS: Take a breath. Calm blue ocean, yes?

KALI: [inaudible.]

CERBERUS: [whispers] *Blue oceaaaan.*

KALI: . . .

KALI: . . . Yessir.

CERBERUS: Now. I understand you and Romeo were . . . intimate. You understand I was willing to permit fraternization within my unit unless it interfered with operations.

CERBERUS: We will not do anything that will cause me to regret that decision, will we, Sergeant?

KALI: Negative, sir.

CERBERUS: Bliss.

CERBERUS: Ghost and Charlie Squad are pursuing the hostile. You have my assurance she will be dealt with prejudicially.

KALI: Petyr's killer is still alive, sir?

CERBERUS: Oh yes. She flushed her PLoB, but cams caught her before she retreated into the vent system.

KALI: Who is she? SecTeam member?

CERBERUS: Negative. Her name is Hanna Donnelly. Daughter of my predecessor, Commander Charles Donnelly.

KALI: . . . That's a seventeen-year-old girl you're talking about.

CERBERUS: Imagine my disappointment, yes?

KALI: Request permission to—

CERBERUS: Negative. You and the rest of Alpha will remain in Engineering. You will keep essential *Heimdall* staff pacified and on task, and assist Mercury in bringing the jump gate back online. This is priority one. Confirm.

KALI: . . .

CERBERUS: Kali, this is Cerberus. Confirm receipt of order, over?

KALI: Cerberus, Kali. Sir, yessir.

CERBERUS: See to operations. I'll send Ghost to collect those nonessentials soon.

KALI: Nonessentials, sir?

UNKNOWN: Oh Jesus, d—

UNKNOWN: No, plea—

[EXTENDED GUNFIRE]

KALI: I'm sorry, sir. What nonessentials?

CERBERUS: . . . I see.

KALI: Will there be anything else, sir?

CERBERUS: Negative, Kali. Nothing further.

KALI: Roger that. Kali out.

This kid smokes too much.

Laugh if you want; I'm telling you, those things will kill you.

Footage opens in Bay 17 of *Heimdall* Station at 20:59, nearly three hours after the station was taken. The space is dark, lit with spots of halogen and the standby lighting in the tall actuator-assisted loading suits (AALs) lining one wall. The suits are big and bulky and cast long shadows on the floor. Nik Malikov is pacing back and forth in front of them and smoking like a chimney. He looks ███ed.

He's taken the time to lay out his uncle and the other dead House of Knives crew into some kind of repose in the shadow of a heavy freight 'tainer. Hands crossed over chests. Coins for the ferryman (or in this case, chips from *Heimdall*'s casino) placed over their eyes. Malikov has his own pistol stuffed into his pants. Hajji's long-handled cleaver on his back. Spare clips in the pockets of his cargos. Proper little House of Knives foot soldier, right?

Problem is, there's no one to use the weapons on. The *Heimdall* docks are sealed off from the rest of the station, and without his cousin to play "open sesame," Malikov's trapped. WhisperNET is under BeiTech control and the HoK grid is down. And so the kid's slowly working his way through his pack of Tarannosaurus Rex™ cigarettes, pacing back and forth at the far end of the bay, beating on his palmpad like it called his mama a ███, in the hope Hanna

Donnelly answers on the other end. Sadly for Malikov, records show Donnelly's palmpad was still lying in a corridor in the infirmary section at this stage, so our hero is SOL.

He stuffs the palmpad back into his cargos. Looks at his reflection in the visor of one of the loading suits. Raises his middle finger.

"Yeah, ██ you too, chum."

He lights another cigarette. You can see the thoughts running through his head—if it wasn't for him, the audit team would never have gotten on board *Heimdall.* If it wasn't for him, his uncle and friends wouldn't be dead. If not for him, none of this would be happening.

Well . . . him and one other important contributor.

"Wheaton," he spits, punching an AAL suit in the belly. "You're a ██ing dead man."

The elevator doors *ping* open. The dulcet tones of Lexi Blue spill into the bay.

"Oooh, ah, yeah, I wanna lick ya" . . . and so on.

Poet laureate of the twenty-sixth century, chums.

Malikov curses and hunkers behind one of the bulky suits as two members of the BeiTech team, Sara "Mona Lisa" Laurent and Lucas "Link" Castro, stalk into the bay. Link is olive-skinned, dark hair tied back in cornrows. Mona Lisa is pale, with red hair and a zine model's looks. Not the kind of fem you'd expect to see slinging a burst rifle and filling out a suit of plasteel battle armor. She can invade my space station any day.

Just saying.

The pair make their way to the MÉDECINS SANS ÉTOILES biotainer they were smuggled aboard inside and unload three crates of what might be high explosives onto a handcart. Hard to tell—these cams aren't great and the light is ██. What's more important: As Link is securing the load, Mona Lisa notices the corpses of the HoK crew, laid out in a neat row with casino chips over their eyes. Then she spots a dozen cigarette butts crushed about the hangar bay floor.

Fresh cigarette butts.

Told you those things would kill him.

"Hsst." Mona Lisa snaps her fingers at Link and raises her rifle. "Get on the clock."

Link seeks cover, pulls out a hand scanner and aims it around the bay.

"Negative on PLoB activity."

Good thing the Dom Najov weren't official residents of the station, right?

"Eyes and ears," Mona Lisa whispers. "Report in to Cerberus."

The pair engage their cybernetic night vision implants (I can tell because their eyes turn black as their pupils expand beyond the human norm) and begin a sweep of the bay. They move carefully, covering each other's backs, checking every blind spot. Laser sights cut red arcs through the gloom. Boots silent on the grille. They're like goddamn machines. I take back what I said about Mona Lisa invading my space station. I prefer my women less . . . murderbot-y.

Link speaks softly into his headset. "Cerberus, this is Link. Copy?"

A pause for a muted reply.

"Mona Lisa and I have detected unusual activity in Bay 17. No sign of a PLoB. We may have a cowboy loose down here. Request backup, over."

Link listens to the response, then nods. "Roger that. Link out." He glances at Mona Lisa. "Rest of Charlie Squad en route."

"Stay chill. Finish the sweep."

Malikov's kinda ███ed at this point. The only ways out of the bay are the elevators (locked), the main door (sealed), the bay doors (with all that lovely vacuum just beyond them) and the air vent system (the closest ingress is a grille six meters above his head). Worse yet, he has a pistol, a cleaver and whatever combat smarts a three-year stint at a juvenile facility in New Petersburg can provide. His opponents have VK-85 burst rifles, sonic grenades, cybernetic upgrades, plasteel body armor and SpecOps training.

Yeah. Sadface for Nikky-poos.

Mona Lisa and Link are sweeping closer, rifles up and ready. But as Malikov looks up at the grille to the vent system and then down to the AAL suit he's hiding behind, I swear you can see that same little lightbulb go off right over his head again.

The AALs loom about three and a half meters tall—they basically look like big envirosuits. Fully sealed for work in vacuum. Clear plastic dome for 360-degree vision. Magnetic boots for stability in zero gee. Titanium exoskeletons with big servos at each joint, hydraulic-assisted lift action, huge metal hands like three-fingered vises.

The elevator *pings*. The "Lollipop" refrain fills the bay as the doors hiss wide, momentarily drowning out all other audio.

Sweet as sugar. Sweet as pie. Kiss the boys and make them cry.

But other boys don't taste as sweet, now that I've had you to . . .

Yeah, you get the idea.

The other two members of Charlie Squad, Kira "Ghost" Mazur and James "Cricket" Orr, stalk into the bay, weapons ready. At the far end of the space, Mona Lisa and Link wait until the elevator doors close and Lexi Blue *shuts the hell up* before moving again. They round a tall stack of reinforced freight 'tainers and creep down the row of AALs, lit by the glow of the suit control panels. Link whispers their location to Ghost. Mona Lisa's eyes scan the gloom. And as they pass the fourth suits' in the row, pistons hiss, servos whine, and a three-fingered fist pushing about 700 pounds per square inch slams right into Link's chest.

The impact cracks his plasteel breastplate, sends him *through* the wall of a heavy 'tainer with a spray of spit and a breathless curse. Mona Lisa aims her rifle, yelling, "CONTACT! CONTACT!" She gets off a three-round burst before Malikov swings the suit's other fist, backhanding her five meters down the aisle. Her helmet and shoulderguard absorb the worst of the impact, but she's still spitting blood, crashing to a halt against another heavy 'tainer and clutching her head.

Their squaddies are sprinting across the bay, calling for status. Position. Threat level. Mona Lisa can only groan in response, spit more blood onto the floor. Link is out cold. Malikov has popped the top of the actuator suit and raised its arms to reach the air vent above. He scrambles up the hydraulics like his ▮ is on fire. Tearing the grille loose, he hauls himself into the duct (looks like all those pull-ups he did in juvie paid off) just as Cricket and Ghost round the row of heavy 'tainers. They see Link unconscious. Mona Lisa groaning.

"Vents . . ." She squeezes her eyes shut, waves at the ceiling. "Little ▮'s in the . . ."

The pair open fire, riddling the ducts with hollow-point rounds. Muzzle flashes cut my visuals to ribbons, audio is nothing but gunfire. At least two sonic grenades get lobbed through the open grille, opening the duct like a love letter. When the chaos dies, Cricket climbs the AAL suit, pulls himself up to peer inside the vent. He looks up and down the length for Malikov before dropping back to the ground—he's too big in his tactical armor to just crawl in after him.

"Negative," he reports. "No kill."

Ghost radios to Falk, reporting two wounded team members and an inability to pursue the hostile without stripping down to their unmentionables.

Falk is less than pleased.

Nikky-poos has escaped.

whisperNET

HEIMDALL

Guest007: Hanna Donnelly, I presume.

Donnelly, H: Oh god, Nik. Where are you?

Guest007: *Bzzzzzzzt.* No, but thank you for playing.

Donnelly, H: Okay, wh—

Guest007: No time to chat the chit. I'm not Nik. I'm his cousin Ella. They gonna delete this guest ID any second. WhisperNET is dead to us. Use the palmpad Nik gave you.

Donnelly, H: Nik never told me he had a cousin. Give me a way to know you're not them.

Guest007: Yeah, yeah, jump on the palmpad and we can play twenty questions all night.

Donnelly, H: I don't have it anymore.

Guest007: You lost it? What the ██, fem, you've had it for thirty seconds!?

Donnelly, H: I'm done talking until you tell me something that proves you're with Nik.

NETbar

FRIENDS ONLINE
None

NEWSFEED
Error

Error

Error

Error

Error

DIARY AND
APPOINTMENTS
Scheduler functionality
unavailable

Guest007: Look, Blondie, if I was scamming you, I would've just said, "Yes, Your Highness," and made drooling noises when you asked if I was my cuz.

Guest007: Take a look around you. I'm the only friend you have, and we both of us know some chums who gotta get got. So find that palmpad if you wanna even up with the █████ers who killed—

—connection failure: guest ident not found—

—retry?—

—retry?—

Hanna Donnelly is holed up in the mechanics' workshop not far from the airlock, crouched behind a stack of toolboxes and spare parts. She couldn't afford to go far—she had to stop every third step and use her sleeve to wipe the telltale drops of blood from her wounded arm.

In the workshop, she's found a relatively clean rag and used some bright red-and-yellow electrical wiring to bind it over the incision. Though the blood is soaking through, she can now move without leaving a trail for her hounds.

So presuming the transmission she just received was legit, her next stop has to be the palmpad Malikov gave her, which, of course, fell from her pocket in a hallway on a completely different floor. A world away. She leaves the mechanics' workshop at 21:17, making her way back toward the infirmary. She doesn't opt for the door— her encounter with the dearly departed members of Beta Squad has left her jumpy. She instead pulls a supply crate over to the ceiling vent, climbing up her makeshift ladder and disappearing into the air ducts once again.

She doesn't have her PLoB in place anymore, and she doesn't appear on any cameras until I get her in Corridor A17s again, some fifty-two minutes later. She's not in particularly familiar territory, so my best guess is she spent a while worming around up there before she worked out where she wanted to be. The grille covering the air vent nearest her palmpad wiggles as she tries to tug it up inside the vent with her.

But nothing in life is that easy. Though she slowly twists it this way and that with the patience of a saint, there's no way she can pull the grille back into the vent. She needs to find another option—one that doesn't involve dropping it onto the floor below and alerting any nearby unfriendlies.

One hand dangles down, holding the vent cover as she twists around inside the cramped tunnel and finally emerges legs-first. She hangs from her good arm, supporting her whole weight with a white-knuckled grip, grille held tight in her other hand. Then she lets herself drop, landing with a grunt, knees bent. The edge of the cover hits the floor—not as loud as it would have if she'd dropped it, but not so soft either. With a wince, she leans the cover against the wall and heads up the corridor, stooping to grab the palmpad. Turning it over, she observes the small baggie of dust still taped to the back, and for an instant, her mouth quirks.

Then she stuffs it into her pocket, all business once more, hurrying down the corridor on silent feet. She's heading for the infirmary and a better bandage than electrical wiring and an old rag. She rounds the corner, straight into the arms of BeiTech operative Abby "Nightingale" O'Neill, who's just changed course to investigate the sound of the grille tapping the floor.

Nightingale is clad in the same black tac armor as the rest of the audit team, blond hair pulled back in a braid like Donnelly's—with Hanna in her black Danae Matresco jumpsuit, they're almost mirror images of each other. They stumble apart, equally quick to recover. Donnelly drops into a fighting stance, but Nightingale has the advantage. She's already holding her pistol—a .50 Silverback most folks would need a tripod to fire—and with a flick of her wrist, she trains it on Donnelly's heart. They lock eyes, each holding perfectly still as Donnelly weighs the situation. But there's only one way it ends.

Very slowly, drawing out each second to buy herself time to think, Hanna lifts her hands.

She was just unlucky, really. Nightingale is one of two medics in Falk's group, and thanks to Malikov's run-in with Charlie Squad, she was on her way to the Alpha Sector infirmary to pick up supplies to treat Link's cracked ribs. Any other time, Donnelly could've patched herself up with no one the wiser.

Keeping her hand cannon trained in place, Nightingale lifts one hand to activate the transmitter attached to her headset. "Cerberus, this is Nightingale, over."

Falk's only a heartbeat away, his voice audible to both Nightingale and Donnelly. *"Nightingale, Cerberus. Go ahead."*

Nightingale's smiling. "I have somebody you're looking for, boss."

"Do tell."

"Miss Donnelly has decided to join us."

Hanna Donnelly's gaze flicks over Nightingale like she's deciding which limb to rip off first. Which, given her daddy's training regimen, she quite possibly is.

"Bliss," Falk replies. *"Restrain her with caution, and wait for backup. Don't make the same mistake as Beta Squad, Nightingale."*

Donnelly's jaw squares—her hand was nowhere near that airlock button. But though she knows she's not the one who spaced the four new popsicles in that loading bay, every piece of misinformation is an advantage. She keeps her mouth shut.

"Roger that, Cerberus." Nightingale's gun doesn't waver. Not much of a bedside manner, for a medic. Just saying.

"Good work. Cerberus out."

And then it's just the blond twins once more, sizing each other up. Nightingale speaks first. "He likes the ones with some backbone. Let's do this nice and slow, and I'll take you in. There's every chance he won't kill you. Beta should have been more careful, he knows that."

Donnelly sucks in a long, slow breath, considering her options, then swallows hard and nods. Silently, she turns away from Nightingale, crossing her wrists behind her back and holding them in place. Nightingale takes no chances, stepping in to press her pistol to the back of her prisoner's head, pulling a pair of zip ties from her belt with her other hand.

"On your knees."

What happens next takes 2.7 seconds, so I had to slow the footage down and check it frame by frame to work it out.

Donnelly tucks her chin and rounds her shoulders, shoving her butt against Nightingale's hips and doubling over, dislodging the muzzle from the back of her head. The pistol discharges—the noise must be deafening, but she doesn't flinch—and she swings her right hand up over her left shoulder, stiffened fingers finding Nightingale's left eye. Nightingale screams as the Silverback fires again. Donnelly spins to face her, bracing the woman's arm across her chest and shoving hard. Nightingale falls backward and twists to land on her side, still screaming, one hand clapped to her bleeding eye. Donnelly drops one knee onto the medic's ribs, the other on the side of her head, knocking her out cold.

Bet you it's the first time a Danae Matresco jumpsuit's seen a workout like *that*.

Donnelly scoops up Nightingale's pistol, pulls off the woman's commset and plugs it into her own ear. Using the zip ties to secure the operative's wrists and ankles, she leaves her unconscious on the floor, then reaches inside her jumpsuit to pull out her lipstick and leans down to scrawl a message on the floor in bright crimson.

Who's next?
Come play!
HD xoxo

Hurting she might be, but Hanna Donnelly was raised by a man who thought talking military tactics was a fun way to spend daddy-daughter time. And judging by the set of her jaw, she's ready to change the rules of the game.

She stows the lipstick, hefts Nightingale's gun and departs at a run for the infirmary.

PARTICIPANTS:
Travis "Cerberus" Falk, Lieutenant, Team Commander
Bianca "Mercury" Silva, Corporal, Engineer
DATE: 08/15/75
TIMESTAMP: 22:33

MERCURY: Cerberus, this is Mercury. Over.

CERBERUS: Mercury, Cerberus. I read.

MERCURY: We may have a problem, Travis.

CERBERUS: You have my undivided attention.

CERBERUS: Though, if this is in reference to Kali—

MERCURY: Negative. That psycho ████ is out of my sight. I'm happy.

CERBERUS: Out of your sight? Am I to understand Alpha Squad isn't overseeing Engineering operations?

MERCURY: Negative, Kali isn't here. No one from Alpha is.

MERCURY: Anyways, she's not the problem.

CERBERUS: An interesting interpretation of the situation, Bi. But pray, do go on.

MERCURY: Taxman is missing.

CERBERUS: Missing.

MERCURY: Yes, Travis. Missing. Unaccounted for. In absentia.

CERBERUS: Last known location?

MERCURY: I sent him to check the coolant towers in the reactor area half an hour ago. He hasn't checked in. Not answering radio. And I don't have manpower to go look for him. Getting the wormhole online is going to take longer than anticipated.

CERBERUS: Indeed.

MERCURY: I'm talking days here. These computer systems are completely ██ed. This malware is into *everything*. Half the core code is corrupted. Ballpark is going to have to change the fuel rods for the interchange systems manually, which means a four-hour stint working *outside* the station and handling live hermium right above an active *rip in the skin of the universe*. And this ██ing lollipop song is driving me—

CERBERUS: Stop.

CERBERUS: I'll have DJ help with your coding situation. I'll send a squad to look for Taxman ASAP. Meantime, I will send you a reminder of just how much you're getting paid to do your job, which I'm reasonably certain does not include lying on your back and screaming like a six-year-old until you get what you want. Will that suffice, Corporal?

CERBERUS: Or would you like me to come down and personally wipe the dribble from your chin?

MERCURY: That's . . . unnecessary, sir.

CERBERUS: Are you certain? I have nothing better to do, after all.

MERCURY: Negative, Cerberus. I'm on it.

CERBERUS: Bliss. Report if you have further issues.

CERBERUS: Oh, and if you happen to see Sergeant Russo in your travels, be a dear and let her know I wish to speak to her, yes?

MERCURY: Roger that.

CERBERUS: Cerberus out.

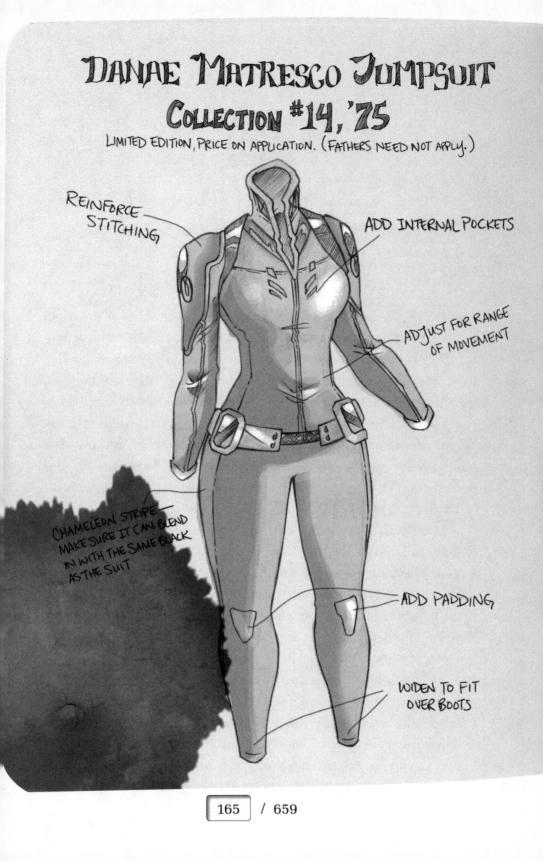

Donnelly's reached the infirmary, where she's grabbed a packet of SimSkin and made tracks. Nightingale might be out of the equation, but Falk will have dispatched backup, and our heroine wants to be nowhere in sight when the cavalry arrives. She sprints down Corridor A17f, Nightingale's gun in one hand, first-aid supplies in the other. She's occasionally shaking her head, holding her nose. Maybe trying to coax her hearing into returning to normal after having a gun go off in her ear. She stuffs the SimSkin into her pocket and is headed back to the air vents when a bullet sparks off the wall right beside her head.

Fleur "Kali" Russo is dashing in pursuit of Hanna Donnelly, teeth bared, half grinning, half growling. Looks like she figures if anyone was going to space Romeo, it was supposed to be her, and only after she was done with him. The rest of Alpha Squad are close behind her, rifles up and ready, but it's clear Kali's tagged Donnelly for herself.

Hearing loss aside, Donnelly sees the spark from the ricochet just fine, ducking automatically as she spins around the corner, flat-out sprinting for cover. Kali's screaming something I can't make out over the gunfire, but you don't need subtitles to get the gist. Donnelly's got a grip on her pilfered gun, but it takes her three corridors before she manages to grab a fire locker and use it to swing herself around, cracking off three successive rounds. She's shooting quick, and not used to the kickback—dunno if she's ever fired a gun before, let alone one this big. Her elbows jar, she winces at the muzzle flash and volume, and the bullets go way wide. But they're enough to slow Alpha down, give her a second to collect herself. Then she's off again like a hare.

No sense getting into a shoot-out here. She's outmanned and outgunned, and worse, she forgot to take Nightingale's ammo. Which means she only has six bullets left.

She makes straight for the elevators, using up her remaining rounds popping a wall-mounted fire extinguisher to give her the lead she needs. She's fit, but exertion and sheer terror have her chest heaving as she tears down the hallway. She gasps a verbal command to the elevators, but all six remain stubbornly closed. Sliding to a stop in front of them, she slaps at the button to summon one, then slaps again, pleading, desperation in every line of her body.

But BeiTech's Tracy "Mantis" Lê shut down the elevators after Hanna's previous escape. There's a car on this floor, but without a BeiTech security pass, those doors aren't opening.

Donnelly has run into a dead end. With a focus born of fear, she turns to study the hallway, searching for shelter, a way out, anything that might help. No hatches above her. No exits. She tries digging her fingers between the elevator doors, but she can't get a grip.

Whimpering now, she rips open the maintenance panel, grabbing the lever marked MANUAL OPEN. Made for shutdown situations, it's linked in locally—Mantis couldn't take it offline without paying a personal visit.

The doors slide open, and in an instant Donnelly's inside, jumping up to punch the roof panel out of place with her free hand, blood pulsing through her makeshift bandage once again. As Kali and the rest of Alpha cautiously round the corner, Hanna shoves her pistol down the front of her jumpsuit and leaps up to grab the

edge of the overhead hatch, hauling herself up on top of the car. A kick sends the cover back into place, and she jams the gun between the lip and a support beam to prevent anyone climbing up after her.

Kali's breathing hard, eyes wild as she jumps up to follow Donnelly's example, punching at the panel—but the jammed pistol means it's not going anywhere.

"Get down here, you little ███!"

Lifting her rifle, she fires up through the hatch, the burst punching three holes right by Donnelly's foot. Hanna silently presses back against the shaft wall, and the next shot sends a line of light shining up from the place she stood an instant before. The footage is grainy—these are only low-grade security cams in the elevator shafts—but she's visible as she squeezes into a corner, minimizing the target she offers to Russo.

Thirty or forty shots riddle the elevator roof before Russo swipes her security pass across the command plate, bringing it back to life. Ordering two of her squad to the stairwells, she jabs the button for the Hub, closest to *Heimdall*'s center of rotation. If she can't shoot Donnelly, she'll settle for crushing her—space is at a premium on these orbital stations, and their elevators fit flush against the ceiling when they're at rest. As the car shudders to life and starts to rise, Kali resumes systematically shooting holes in the ceiling, screaming abuse as she works.

Donnelly shies away from each bullet as it flies past, flinching uncontrollably. She looks up at the Hub above, fifteen floors away but rapidly approaching. They're in a shaft three elevators wide, though the other two cars sit dormant above, waiting for someone with the right pass to unlock them. She dances across to the front of the elevator, hand reaching out to grab at a passing door as they fly past the next level, but there's no time to get a grip, much less dive through. She flinches away from the next burst of gunfire as Kali shrieks below. Then she unzips her jumpsuit and starts to strip.

She pauses with the jumpsuit at her waist to pull the pack of

SimSkin, palmpad and lipstick from her pockets and stuff them into her bra. Then it's off with the jumpsuit, yanking the legs down over her boots as Russo reloads. She's down to her underwear now, and since this particular ensemble was clearly intended for the benefit of Jackson Merrick only, I'm doing my best not to notice it, and no, chum, I will not be describing it.

Holding her journal in her teeth, she retrieves her pistol, shoves it into her boot, bundles up the jumpsuit in both hands and in one leap, she's across to the thick wire cable of the next elevator. With the jumpsuit bunched up to prevent the friction from burning her hands through to the bone, and her knees bent so only the soles of her boots come into contact with the wire, she slides down in a barely controlled descent, picking up speed as the gravity increases toward *Heimdall*'s extremities. Moments later, she hits the bottom of the well with a thud, and the elevator she left behind is snug up against the roof of the shaft, Kali just realizing there's nobody up there to get squashed flat.

The fabric of the jumpsuit is burned through to within a couple of layers of Donnelly's skin, shredded beyond use or recognition, and she drops it, shakes out the pain in her hands and feet and pulls open the service doors to peek outside. As Kali howls her fury up above, Donnelly draws her gun and disappears out into the corridor beyond.

PALMPAD IM: D2D NETWORK
Participants: Hanna Donnelly, Civilian (unregistered)
Ella Malikova, Civilian (unregistered)
Date: 08/15/75
Timestamp: 22:47

Hanna D: anyone out there?

Pauchok: just us terrorists posing as 15 year old girls

Pauchok: wait did I say that out loud, oh _foiled_

Hanna D: okay, you're definitely related to Nik.

Pauchok: u got the palmpad back

Pauchok: *slow clap*

Hanna D: *small bow*

Hanna D: Do you know who these ████s are, what they want?

Pauchok: they cut me out of the system, blondie. I know one sixth of three tenths of absolutely ████ all.

Pauchok: they're pro. their decker is top tier. they do the shooty-shoot first and don't ask questions after. But other than that, I don't even know how many of em there are

Hanna D: I worked out the shooting bit all by myself.

Hanna D: Do you know if our people are okay? My father? Nik? My boyfriend's holed up on the bridge, he told me before my whisperNET went down. Maybe he can help.

Pauchok: u don't know

Hanna D: Ella?

Pauchok: jesus, you don't, do you?

Hanna D: ella you want to spit it out? I'm hiding and bleeding and blind here, I don't have time for riddles

Pauchok: um ok.

Pauchok: so look I know your first instinct is going to be to smash the ▮ out of something when I tell you this. but DO NOT smash the palmpad

Pauchok: your dad's dead

Pauchok: those ▮ers X-ed him out

Hanna D: I . . .

Pauchok: I'm real sorry

Pauchok: u still there?

Hanna D: I need a minute

Pauchok: um, hello?

Pauchok: u still with us?

Pauchok: Donnelly?

Hanna D: are you sure

Pauchok: pretty sure yeah

Pauchok: hello?

Hanna D: do you know if they've taken the bridge

Pauchok: no. they've blinded me. I'm cut out of the network

Pauchok: and listen I know this feels like ███ and I know u don't wanna hear it

Pauchok: but right now, ur the only chance I have of getting back in

Hanna D: . . .

Hanna D: and if you get in

Hanna D: we can find out how many survivors there are?

Pauchok: you get me back in, I'll b able 2 tell you what brand of undies these goons wear

Pauchok: presuming they're wearing undies of course

Pauchok: i hear swinging it commando style is all the rage among interstellar murder squads atm

Hanna D: I just need a minute. I'm sorry. I just

Pauchok: i get it.

Pauchok: And i'm sorry too, but u really only got 1 min here

Hanna D: Okay.

Hanna D: I got one of their headsets. Will that help?

Pauchok: unless you know the freqs they're transmitting on, it's as useful as a master's degree in philosophy

Hanna D: So right now there's no way to find out what's happening on the bridge?

Pauchok: you do know what "blind" means, ya?

Hanna D: What about Nik? He has a palmpad too, right? That's why he gave me this one?

Pauchok: presuming he ever looks at it, ya

Pauchok: but he's locked in the docks. The work I need doing is in Alpha

Pauchok: so if u fancy evening up the scorecard, I'm figuring those four goons I flushed out the airlock ain't even the start

Hanna D: That was you?

Pauchok: my finger slipped

Pauchok: honest

Hanna D: They're blaming me for that.

Pauchok: :P

Hanna D: You know what? ███ it. They may as well stay on my tail for it. The bigger a surprise you are, the better.

Pauchok: double true

Hanna D: Ok

Hanna D: Tell me what you need me to do.

```
145  tex09103.83*
146  throne.ref=0093u023.fort.278i(dex00x10)10
147  tripwire.ets
148  parse:09302994-09304776. corecomm-neg
149  scriptfail
150  tex09829.23*
```

INTERDICTOR-091iPAUCHOK
>> SYSTEM ALERT
>> Alpha Sector // Admin Section
>> Alert: Environment
>> Alert Type: Temperature increase/O_2 Levels dropping
>> Alert Action: Fire Alarm initiated
>> Alert Action: Suppressors engaged
>> Alert Action: Public Address engaged

```
dol+u29837.god
load 20902Æ840824-2090379091820.netkill
error
file not present
retry? yes/no
```

"Alert all stations. Alert all stations. Fire detected in Administration Section, Level 19, Alpha Sector. All fire wardens report to Oooh, ah, yeah, I wanna lick ya lollipop. Oooh, ah, yeah, I wanna lick ya lollipop. Boy, you got the sweetest lips this girl has ever tasted, boy, I need some sugar on me . . ."

VOLUME

RADIO TRANSMISSION: BEITECH AUDIT TEAM—SECURE CHANNEL 389

PARTICIPANTS:
Travis "Cerberus" Falk, Lieutenant, Team Commander
Kira "Ghost" Mazur, Sergeant, Charlie Squad—Leader
DATE: 08/15/75
TIMESTAMP: 23:19

CERBERUS: Ghost, this is Cerberus, report status.

GHOST: Cerberus, Ghost. Charlie Squad operational strength still at 50 percent. Link's coming to, Mona Lisa has probable concussion and Nightingale should be here to take care of it by now. Did she stop for a picnic or something?

CERBERUS: I'm truly grieved to hear of your troubles, Ghost. Nightingale has been delayed. Meantime, would it be inconvenient to assist with a little of the work we're being paid so handsomely to perform?

GHOST: No, sir.

GHOST: Apologies, sir.

CERBERUS: Bliss. I believe we have a bead on Miss Donnelly.

GHOST: Cricket and I are good to go right now.

CERBERUS: A fire alarm has just been activated in the administrative levels in Alpha Sector. We assume Miss

Donnelly would like us to evacuate the area, and I'm interested to know what she plans on doing while we're gone.

CERBERUS: Take Cricket, and go find out what she doesn't want us to see. If you can bring her in alive, so much the better. She's beginning to interest me.

GHOST: Is it actually on fire in there, Cerberus?

CERBERUS: Here's a thought—why don't you be a dear and go find out?

CERBERUS: Assault Fleet *Kennedy* arrives in nineteen hours, Ghost. The clock is ticking.

Ghost and Cricket, the two currently healthy members of Charlie Squad, proceed with caution into the administrative levels of Alpha Sector. Red lights are flashing a coded alarm, illuminating the corridors in quick, bloody flashes, and the shrieking of a siren overhead is interspersed with the sound of Lexi Blue's new single on constant repeat.

Kali and the rest of Alpha Squad are prowling along Corridor A12b, having beaten Charlie to the location. Kali's still wearing her headset, listening in on Falk's orders, but she's not responding to hails. Apparently she's got revenge on her mind, and it's really annoying when people try to talk at you while you're feeling murderish.

On Falk's command, Mantis seals off the admin block, trapping whoever's inside right where they are. Then she jumps on comms.

> **Mantis:** Charlie Squad, looks to me like you're in the admin sector.
>
> **Ghost: Our tracker beacons give it away, Mantis?**
>
> **Mantis:** No need to be snippy.
>
> **Mantis:** You want some help or not?
>
> **Ghost: Depends. Are you being helpful yet?**

Mantis: I've got activity off Corridor A12e. Someone's trying to log in to the personnel systems there. Twenty-three failed attempts so far and counting.

Ghost: Guess we found something she's bad at. Proceeding now, Mantis, please advise Cerberus.

Mantis: Good hunting.

Ghost and Cricket make their way toward Corridor A12e in silence, though the sound of their footsteps would be masked by the pop song blaring all around them in any event.

They round the corner at the same time that Kali and the rest of Alpha Squad appear at the other end of the hallway—all six snap their weapons up, then jerk them higher to remove the target from their teammates. Ghost and Cricket trot up the corridor to join Kali. Though their conversation is inaudible over the pop music, the body language kinda speaks for itself. Allow me to take a stab:

> *Ghost*: What the ever-living ██ are you guys doing here?
> *Kali*: This is a big gun and I am very, very angry.
> *Cricket*: She certainly looks very angry.
> *Ghost*: The bossman is looking for you. Why you no call no more?
> *Kali*: Let's stop arguing and get in there and shoot a million holes in the little ██.
> *Ghost*: Okay, that's something we can all agree on.

They turn as one, Ghost taking point over Kali's scowl, and creep toward the doorway to the personnel systems office.

Twenty-seven failed log-in attempts.

Twenty-eight failed log-in attempts.

Charlie and Alpha Squads approach the terminal from both directions, watching each other as they creep along behind banks of desks. Kali lifts a hand to signal countdown, and though that's Ghost's prerogative, she chooses not to screw with the other woman today. Smart, imo.

Kali's fingers flick down one by one.

Three. Two. One.

They rise, six burst rifles trained on the security station, six operatives ready to shoot.

The drinking bird bobs its head, stylus stabbing at the ENTER key for another failed log-in attempt. As it flashes its butt at Kali and Co., we can see that its tail end is adorned with a jaunty smiley face scrawled in red lipstick—not Donnelly's best work, tbh, given the portfolio we've seen so far.

Kali roars, audible even over the music, and pulls the trigger. Poor Drinking Bird, his stylus, his keyboard, his terminal and his smiley hindparts are all reduced to shrapnel as she empties an entire clip into the place where Romeo's killer is supposed to be.

Several floors away in the server section, a vent in the kitchenette ceiling starts to wobble.

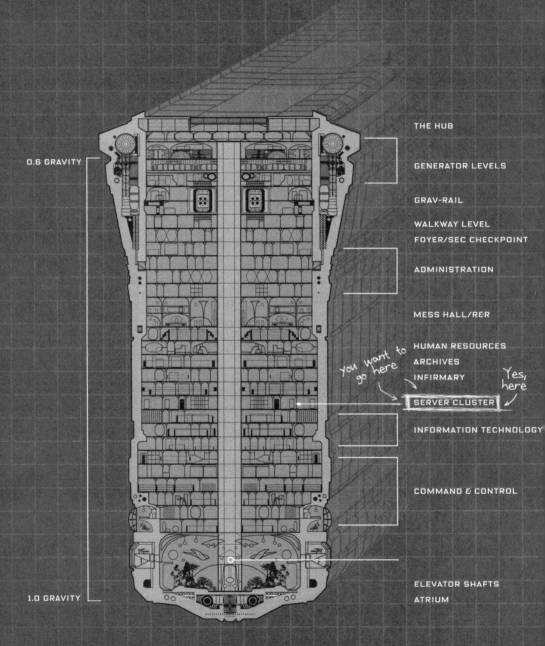

WORMHOLE

THE HUB

0.6 GRAVITY

GENERATOR LEVELS

GRAV-RAIL

WALKWAY LEVEL

FOYER/SEC CHECKPOINT

ADMINISTRATION

MESS HALL/R&R

HUMAN RESOURCES

you want to go here

ARCHIVES

INFIRMARY

Yes, here

SERVER CLUSTER

INFORMATION TECHNOLOGY

COMMAND & CONTROL

ELEVATOR SHAFTS

1.0 GRAVITY

ATRIUM

JUMP STATION: HEIMDALL
ALPHA SECTOR

Server room incursion instructions
Author: Ella Malikova (super genius)

1. spaaace ninja into server room via kitchenette vents here

  2. get cup of water

3. pour water on camera here (if u not tall enuff 2 reach, bring chair from kitchen)

  4. creep to login server here

5. synch palmpad to login server (use attached instructions)

  6. upload interdictor (use attached instructions→ READ CAREFULLY)

7. don't get shot (important)

8. exit via vents (spaaaaace ninjaaaaa)

  9. profit

ALPHA SECTOR - LEVEL 17
SERVER CLUSTER

```
101     tex98327.17*
102     throne.ref=0034u797.fort.1982bd(dex00x10)10
103     tripwire.ets
104     parse:09284alphanode—09294alphanode. corecomm-neg
105     scriptfail
106     tex09829.23*
```

```
INTERDICTOR-8871rPAUCHOK
>> SYSTEM ALERT
>> Alpha Sector // Admin Section
>> Alert: Core Systems
>> Alert: No Alert
>> Alert Type: Systems Incursion
>> Alert Type: No Alert Type
>> Alert Action: . . . . alarm . . . check . . . . welcome to ANANSI
>> Alert Action: . . . no action required/no action required/no action
required/no action required
```

```
commsec-0088928only:000010010.if.refline098=cascade
killfile
batch009109-09881.sif
00190802core*[8991383fht0020480]
dol+u891273.subliminal09021=02083
access ref:00910381ani.ets
access ref:00299182ani.ets
```

Video journal transcription,
prepared by
Analyst ID 7213-0089-DN

Footage for this entire journal is a shot of Ella Malikova speaking directly to the camera.

Ella's fifteen, but she looks younger. Long black hair, sharp bangs. You can see a resemblance to her cousin Nik in the cheekbones and razorblade eyes, but that's where it stops.

Kid must weigh thirty kilos. The lysergia plague took the rest when she was thirteen. The chair she's strapped into looks even scarier than the computer she's sitting at. Wetware 'trodes at her temples. Breather pumping a medicated mix of O_2 over her mouth. Say what you want about Handsome Mike Malikov—he loved his baby girl enough to spend a fortune on that rig. Enough to keep her kicking after lysergia dragged her as close to death's door as most folks ever get.

"Kicking" is the wrong word, I guess. Her legs are covered by a temp-regulated blanket, but you can see they're not much more than skin and bones. No evidence of muscular atrophy from the waist up, though. Her fingers dance on three smartglass keyboards like a concert pianist's the whole time she's talking.

She named her computer Anansi, which, for the uninitiated, was an old Terran spider god. Web. Spider god. Get it? Anyway, the machine is a beast and looks the part. The Little Spider used to make these vid journals for her best friend, Zoe, who traveled off-station a lot. Just don't be offended when she says something rude. She grew up in a den of ████s, thugs and murderers, so rude is where she lives.

Journal begins:

"Hey, Zo, monster hugs, big kiss for my best Miss. *Mwah. Mwah.*

"So listen, I dunno if I'll even be alive to send this, but in the *highly* probable event your home is a smoking debris field orbiting a collapsed hole in spacetime when you get back to it, there's some stuff I need to get off my ████s, such as they are:

"First up, it was indeed *me* who told Dylan Anderson that your ladyparts were all mad fizzy for him. I *knowwww* you told me not to, but watching your ovaries go straight nuclear every time his name came up was getting uncomfortable for both of us. Sorry he turned out to be such a ████, but it could've been a beautiful thing. Mmmmyeah.

"Confession, the second: Mr. Biggles is not Mr. Biggles. The *real* Mr. Biggles died the last time you went back to Ares. I *knowww-wwwwwww* you asked me to feed him, and I *did* . . . but I think I fed him too much. Anyway, you didn't even notice I swapped in a new fish and jeeeeesus if you knew what I had to pay for one that looked exactly like Biggles the First and get it out here, you'd know how much I luff you.

"But . . . double big sadface, love heart love heart, hugs?

"Soooo now, with my deadly sins confessed, the sitch:

"*Heimdall*'s been taken over by some type A ████holes. Terrorists or neo-fascists or pirates. Dunno. But they're geared to the gills and happy on the trigger, and I'm gonna see every one of 'em breathing vacuum before I cash in. Hence the aforementioned potential for all your ████ to get blown up. So . . . if things go boom, sorry in advance about your signed Artie Corso stuff and Mr. Biggles II.

"The fascists kinda have everyone locked up except—and oh my GOD, you will *puke* in your *mouth* when you hear this—Hanna ████ing Donnelly. Oh yeah, you heard right. Her Majesty, the future

Mrs. Merrick herself. You should SEE the outfit this fem is wearing, Zo. Ridiiiic. Must have cost the annual GDP of New Petersburg, double true. And my GOD with the push-up bra. I can't believe Nik is so drooly-faced happypants for this fem. Too much gag.

"Aaaaaanyways, she didn't get snaffled with everyone else. So Little Miss Trust Fund is helping to get me back onto the *Heimdall* grid.

"First stop—security cams. I'm gonna rig their feed to show looped footage while I work on cutting them out entirely. Miiiiight mean I get cut out too, 'cuz this system is moodier than you on the razzle, but this is still my home turf. The decker these █holes brought with them is top tier, but I'm gonna stomp his jelly beans so hard his kids will be born crooked.

"After that, I gotta find Nik. Yes, you'll be pleased to hear my cousin's buttocks (ew) were in one piece last I saw. They've locked me out of whisperNET, but I gave Nik a palmpad so he could talk dirty to Her Ladyship. I can chat to him on that if he thinks to check it, but so far, nada. Boy def gets his looks from my side of the fam, but he has a bucket of █s between his ears, as far as I can tell.

"But . . . you know, at least he's okay . . . I mean, they could've . . .

"Zo, they . . .

"They . . .

"█ . . .

"Oh Jesus, Zoe . . .

". . . I gotta get back to it. TTYL, █."

PALMPAD IM: D2D NETWORK
Participants: Niklas Malikov, Civilian (unregistered)
Ella Malikova, Civilian (unregistered)
Date: 08/16/75
Timestamp: 00:29

Pauchok: This fem got the skills, and the others can't match it

Pauchok: This fem got an itch, and boy you can scratch it

Pauchok: I don't wancha money, I just wancha honey *uh*

Pauchok: I don't wanna ring, I just wancha something something

Nik M: stop

Nik M: PLEASE GOD JESUS STOP

Pauchok: Hey u finally remembered to look at your screen, yay you <3

Nik M: i was kinda busy, cuz.

Nik M: and getting shot at and blown up listening to lexi blue isn't bad enough? I gotta get it from you now?

Pauchok: u gotta admit it's a pretty catchy tune

Pauchok: All caps btw

```
                }==>>=>
                [   {
                 \   \ ,-'//____ --
          @_/~ ||.------ *\ \\__
*******@_}  >| |++++++++( | )~[ ||| >
          @_\_| |------ */ //
          /  / -.\\____ ,-- '==(- CAPSCAPSCAPSCAPSCAPSCAPSCAPS
         [   {
         }==>>=>
```

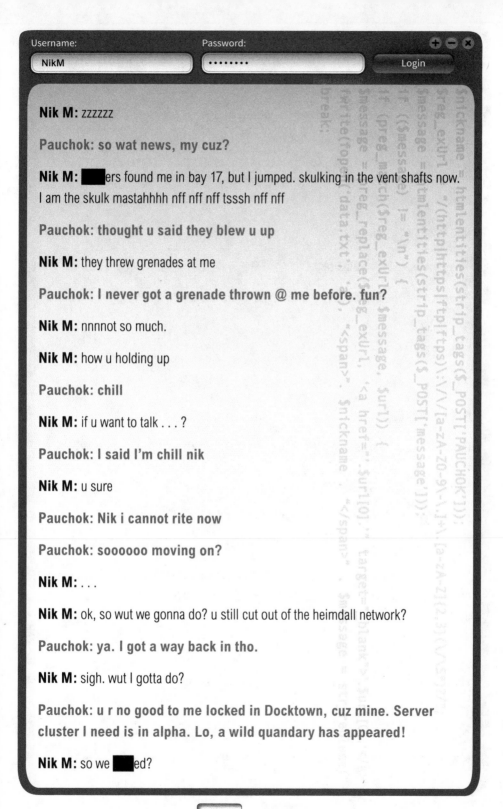

Nik M: zzzzzz

Pauchok: so wat news, my cuz?

Nik M: ███ers found me in bay 17, but I jumped. skulking in the vent shafts now. I am the skulk mastahhhh nff nff nff tsssh nff nff

Pauchok: thought u said they blew u up

Nik M: they threw grenades at me

Pauchok: I never got a grenade thrown @ me before. fun?

Nik M: nnnnot so much.

Nik M: how u holding up

Pauchok: chill

Nik M: if u want to talk . . . ?

Pauchok: I said I'm chill nik

Nik M: u sure

Pauchok: Nik i cannot rite now

Pauchok: soooooo moving on?

Nik M: . . .

Nik M: ok, so wut we gonna do? u still cut out of the heimdall network?

Pauchok: ya. I got a way back in tho.

Nik M: sigh. wut I gotta do?

Pauchok: u r no good to me locked in Docktown, cuz mine. Server cluster I need is in alpha. Lo, a wild quandary has appeared!

Nik M: so we ███ed?

Pauchok: neg. got me a secret weapon mwahahaaaaaaa

Nik M: oh ya? wut

Pauchok: not wut cuz, WHO mwahahahaaaaaaaaaaaa *ominous lighting*

Nik M: so WHO then jesus

——**Hanna D has entered the chat** ——

Pauchok: speak of the devil, and thou shalt hear the strangled scream of her c-cups

Hanna D: um, what?

Pauchok: nuthin

Nik M: holy ███, hanna?

Pauchok: teary reunion later, cuz. u get the doings done, blondie?

Hanna D: you tell me

Pauchok: zomgggggg u did. hearts and flowers and teddy bears.

Pauchok: i got serious mad scientist ███ to do. This is gonna take time.

Hanna D: find out about the guys on the bridge, Jax is there. if you get eyes on the atrium, check if any of the sec team are still standing. and my dojo master kim too, she'd be an asset.

Pauchok: any other requests, your majesty?

Hanna D: my friends were in the atrium too, but i'm sensing some sarcasm in that question

Pauchok: see, those folks who say you're an empty-headed rich girl with the IQ of a toe jam scraping, they don't give you enough credit

Nik M: ella . . .

Pauchok: Will leave u 2 crazy kids to it. smoke em if u got em. keep the sexty to a minimum, tho, I can read ur chat logs and I'm only 15 remember

Nik M: ███ off, little spider

Pauchok: no love D:

/////(")\\\\ Pauchok has left the chat /////(")

Nik M: hey, Highness :)

Hanna D: Hey yourself

Hanna D: How's your day been?

Nik M: I had grenades thrown at me. so you know, that's something new

Nik M: look sorry about skipping out on u. I figured my people were our best shot of figuring wtf wuz going on. I'm real glad you're ok.

Hanna D: "Okay" is probably stretching it

Nik M: hell of a terra day huh

Hanna D: yeah

Nik M: u holding up alrite?

Hanna D: I've been keeping busy. I met Ella, and there were some bullets and stuff.

Nik M: which was worse?

Hanna D: are you kidding? Ella and I are meeting up to braid each other's hair later.

Hanna D: she had some VERY interesting things to say about you.

Nik M: yeah, see i love her and all, but be warned: my cuz is crooked as a dog's back leg.

Nik M: when she was 6, she convinced me & my bro the NPPD was putting audio surveillance drones into candy to spy on our old man. we gave her all our hallowseve loot three years running. for "safe disposal." so believe nothing she says.

Nik M: unless she was tellign u how great i am, then she's on the legit, double true

Hanna D: that is exactly what she said

Nik M: i'm just gonna pretend i believe that

Nik M: where u holed up?

Hanna D: i am taking up real estate in a particularly spacious air vent just now

Nik M: hey i lost your corsage in one of those. sorry. grenades, you know how it is

Hanna D: well i lost my jumpsuit. fully automatic gunfire, you know how it is

Hanna D: the corsage was sweet of you though

Nik M: wait, u serious? 0_o

Hanna D: I am. I know I don't say a lot of nice things to you, but the corsage was above and beyond.

Nik M: no i mean u serious about having lost your jumpsuit?

Nik M: wtf were they firing magic bullets??

Hanna D: yes.

Hanna D: they were magic bullets, Nik

Hanna D: I'll be wearing clothes again by the next time you see me, assuming we live that long

Nik M: meaning ur not wearing clothes now??????? 0_o

Nik M: ooooook, then

Nik M: i'm just gonna move on. with no additional commentary on your state of undress whatsoever. because that's just the kind of classy mother ▮▮ i am

Hanna D: you're just trying to impress me

Nik M: only trying? D:

Hanna D: Nik, is Ella as good as she says?

Nik M: y u ask?

Hanna D: I'm putting a lot of trust in a girl I didn't even know existed until a couple of hours ago.

Nik M: listen i know she's got a mouth on her. and if u don't know her, she can come off a little full-on. but u gotta look beyond that, see who she is.

Hanna D: so tell me who she is

Nik M: a 15 yr old raised by crims and killers. who has to rely on other people for a bunch of stuff she used to do herself, and who grew some thorns to make sure nobody feels sorry for her about it

Hanna D: I'm missing something. The thorns are hiding what?

Nik M: u never knew she existed coz she never leaves her computer

Nik M: and she never leaves her computer because she can't.

Nik M: she got the lysergia plague when she wuz 13.

Hanna D: ▮▮▮▮

Nik M: yeah.

Nik M: but she beat it. and she doesn't feel a drop of sorry for herself. So you shouldn't either

Nik M: it's not who she is.

Hanna D: i get it. so tell me about Ella the hacker.

Nik M: ok. straight talk then. what do u know about the House of Knives?

Hanna D: that you're not people to mess with. That you can get hold of things and get rid of people, and the authorities either don't want to arrest you or can't

Hanna D: also you're v into tattoos.

Nik M: u get inked in the HoK when u catch a stretch in slam. u can read the history of every prison stint a member's done if u see enough of their skin. it's a pride thing. but also a reminder that u got caught. did time. ██ed up.

Nik M: u wanna guess how many tats my cuz has?

Hanna D: she's clean, isn't she?

Nik M: she's as dirty as a weekend in new vegas. but there's no ink on her, no

Hanna D: because she's fifteen and you kept her out of it like a good cousin, or because she never gets caught?

Nik M: the little spider does what she wants. i couldn't keep her out if i tried.

Hanna D: you have tattoos, Nik

Nik M: yeah, well

Nik M: i'm a ██up, highness. but Ella's pro as it gets. So u can rest easy.

Nik M: speaking of, maybe u should find some place to hole up and get some sleep, ya?

Hanna D: that's the plan. Ella will wake me when she's done some recon.

Hanna D: apparently if I sleep with the palmpad under me she can make it vibrate to wake me up

Hanna D: NOT A WORD

Nik M: . . .

Nik M: <- classy

Nik M: <- mother

Nik M: <- ███er

Hanna D: Nik

Nik M: ya?

Hanna D: be safe.

Nik M: you too, highness

```
$nickname = htmlentities(strip_tags($_POST['PAUCHOK']));
$reg_exUrl = "/(http|https|ftp|ftps)\:\/\/[a-zA-Z0-9\-\.]+\.[a-zA-Z]{2,3}(\/\S*)?/";
$message = htmlentities(strip_tags($_POST['message']));
if (($message) != "\n") {
    if (preg_match($reg_exUrl, $message, $url)) {
        $message = preg_replace($reg_exUrl, "<a href=".$url[0]." target="_blank">".$url[0]."</a>", $message);
    }
    fwrite(fopen('data.txt', 'a'), "<span>". $nickname . "</span>" . $message = str_repl
    break;
```

HANNA, SQUEAK, HIGHNESS

WHO AM I GOING TO BE NOW?

COUNTDOWN TO
HYPATIA ARRIVAL
AT HEIMDALL WAYPOINT:

00 DAYS
19 HOURS: 18 MINUTES

COUNTDOWN TO KENNEDY ASSAULT FLEET ARRIVAL AT JUMP STATION HEIMDALL:

00 DAYS
17 HOURS: 46 MINUTES

RADIO TRANSMISSION: BEITECH AUDIT TEAM—

PARTICIPANTS:

Bianca "Mercury" Silva, Corporal, En

Gabriel "Ballpark" Moreno, Private,

DATE: 08/16/75

TIMESTAMP: 02:04

MERCURY: Ballpark, this is Mercury. How you looking, over?

BALLPARK: Handsome. Available. I work out, you know.

MERCURY: I mean how's the situation looking, Ballpark.

BALLPARK: Yeah, figured.

BALLPARK: Getting the outer casing off now. This is really a two-man job, you know.

MERCURY: Or one very manly man.

BALLPARK: Awwww yeah. Handling live hermium brings all the ladies to the Ballpark.

BALLPARK: Looks easy enough. Rods 3 and 4 are totally spent, but there's no real drama. Four hours, tops. Gimme manual on the system and I'll start changeover.

MERCURY: Roger that, manual control in five. I'll patch through sys—

BALLPARK: Holy ███!

BALLPARK: There's something . . . ████, there's SOMETHING IN MY ████ING SUIT!

MERCURY: Say again, Ballpark?

BALLPARK: Jesus ████ing Christ, I swear I felt something moving . . .

MERCURY: Felt something? Are you breaching? Readouts here are green across the board.

BALLPARK: It . . .

BALLPARK: I . . .

MERCURY: Ballpark, do you read? Update status, over.

MERCURY: Gabe, this is Mercury, do you read me? Report status, over.

BALLPARK: Yeah. Wow. I . . . ████ . . .

BALLPARK: You ever . . . looked at all this, Bi? Like, I mean, really *looked* at it? Out here?

MERCURY: Gabriel? What's happening? Your biosigns are—

BALLPARK: It's so . . . *big,* yeah? Like, you realize we're sitting on a . . . like, a *rip* in space?

BALLPARK: It makes you think. *Really* think . . . you know?

BALLPARK: Bi . . . I think I ████ed myself.

MERCURY: Gabriel, I'm calling abort. I want you back to the airlock ASAP. Your biosig is all over the chart. Are you reading me?

BALLPARK: You're really pretty, Bi . . .

MERCURY: Private Moreno, this is a direct order. Abort refuel op now and return to Airlock 31 for immediate debrief, over.

BALLPARK: Oh . . . look. It's an angel.

MERCURY: Ballpark, copy, goddammit. I'm calling abort! Do you read me?

BALLPARK: A little angel inside the suit with me.

BALLPARK: It's beautiful. It's so . . . *beautiful*.

BALLPARK: So many mouths.

MERCURY: Gabe?

BALLPARK: Beautiful.

BALLPARK: Black.

BALLPARK: Oh . . .

—TRANSMISSION ENDS—

FALK, Travis
Cerberus
Team Commander

RUSSO, Fleur
Kali
Alpha Squad—Leader

DAN, Kim
Poacher
Alpha Squad

MORETTI, Deni
Cujo
Alpha Squad

SATOU, Genji
Sensei
Alpha Squad

BAZAROV, Petyr
Romeo
Beta Squad—Leader

RADIN, Harry
Razorback
Beta Squad

MAYR, Stanislaw
Taurus
Beta Squad

WONG, Ai
Rain
Beta Squad

MAZUR, Kira
Ghost
Charlie Squad—Leader

CASTRO, Lucas
Link
Charlie Squad

LAURENT, Sara
Mona Lisa
Charlie Squad

ORR, James
Cricket
Charlie Squad

ANTONIOU, Naxos
Two-Time
Communications

LÊ, Tracy
Mantis
Computer Systems

MØLLER, Rolf
DJ
Computer Systems

SILVA, Bianca
Mercury
Engineer (Ranking)

MORENO, Gabriel
Ballpark
Engineer

DE GRAAF, Lor
Taxman
Engineer/Medic

O'NEILL, Abby
Nightingale
Medic

ALIEVI, Marta
Eden
Logistics

SAPRYKIN, Kai
Juggler
Ordnance/Demolitions

PARK, Ji-hun
Flipside
Pilot/Demolitions

TAHIROVIĆ, Hans
Ragman
Pilot

Footage opens in Commander Donnelly's office in *Heimdall*
C & C. The space is neat, perfectly ordered, almost spartan. A
single framed holoprint of Hanna Donnelly rests on the smartglass desk. Travis Falk sits in the commander's chair, staring at
the picture, fingers steepled at his chin. A mountain of muscle.
Eyes like blue ice.

And he's *smiling.*

The door sensors *ping.* Falk speaks without glancing up.
"Come."

Kali prowls inside, burst rifle slung at her back, scowl on her
face.

"Fleur." Falk rises from his seat, indicates the chair opposite.
"Make yourself comfortable."

Kali pulls the chair out as Falk rounds the desk. And as the
woman goes to sit, Falk seizes her by the throat and slams her into
the wall with enough force to dent the plasteel. Kali's eyes go wide,
and she clutches the hand at her neck, lashing out with one boot
into Falk's solar plexus. Thick rubber soles squeak on his breastplate as Falk smashes Kali into another wall, spittle flying. And
with an almost casual brutality, he hauls her into the air and brings
her down onto Donnelly's desk. The smartglass explodes into a
thousand glittering fragments. A curse sprays from the woman's

mouth as she hits the ground, Falk drawing a long, gleaming combat knife and digging it in under her chin. He leans onto her chest, brings his face close to hers. Filmed with sweat.

He's still smiling.

"You should report future radio faults to Corporal Alievi," he says.

Kali is glaring, breath hissing through gritted teeth. "Sir?"

"I told you and your squad to remain in the Engineering Sector to oversee repairs." Falk brings his face closer. His lips almost touching hers. "You've been chasing Donnelly. Two possibilities present themselves: Either you disobeyed a direct order from your commanding officer, placing this team and mission in jeopardy, or your radio is faulty, yes?"

"*She's* placing this mission in jeopardy, Tra—"

The knife digs deeper.

"How can you be one of us," Falk smiles, "if you're cut in two?"

Kali blinks. Sees beyond the threat. Breath seething through flared nostrils.

"Whom do you serve, Fleur?" Falk asks. "Your ego, or your mission?"

"I—"

Falk's commset crackles to life.

"*Cerberus, this is Mercury, over.*"

Falk touches his earpiece. "Mercury, Cerberus. Go."

"*Something's happened to Ballpark.*"

"Something."

"*He went outside to swap the fuel rods on the interchange. Then he started talking crazy. Babbling about something inside his suit. Biosigns were all over the shop like a madman's ▮▮. And now he's not answering hails. Zero brainwave activity on biosig, but his other vitals are fine. He's just ▮▮ing drifting out there. I don't know if he's conscious or—*"

"Did he complete the fuel rod exchange?"

"Travis, I think he's in real—"

"Bianca."

The slightest hint of anger creeps into Falk's voice. First time I've ever heard him sound upset. It silences Mercury like a punch to the throat.

"Did he complete the fuel rod exchange?" Falk asks.

". . . Negative."

"Without this interchange, the jump gate is nonoperational, yes?"

"Transposition sequences traverse the interchange. The quantum accelerator can't—"

"A simple 'affirmative' will suffice."

"Affirmative, Cerberus. Jump gate is broke ███*."*

"Understood. Hold position. I will advise. Cerberus out."

Falk glances at Kali, still sprawled underneath him.

"Taxman is MIA. Ballpark is offline. Something is seriously wrong in Engineering. The area I told *you* to monitor."

Kali glances at the holoprint of Hanna Donnelly, lying amid the shattered glass beside her head. "She's still out there. ███ing with our systems. X-ing our people. Beta's KIA. Mona Lisa and Link, walking wounded. I heard Nightingale lost her eye? How many more of us is she going to leave limping or dead, Travis?"

"I have several problems, it seems."

"And two assault squads left. Charlie and Alpha."

Falk is staring at the picture of Donnelly now too.

"Charlie Squad can handle babysitting Engineering, Travis," Kali says. "And those idiots holed up on the bridge aren't going anywhere."

Falk looks her in the eyes. Her whisper is tight around the knife still at her throat.

"Give her to me."

Falk hovers a moment more. Lips twisted. Unblinking. But finally, he stands up. Sheathes his knife. Kali winces, begins to haul herself up off the floor, broken glass grinding into the temperfoam beneath her.

Falk leans down and offers his hand.

He hauls the woman to her feet, muscles creaking under the kevlar bodyweave. Brushes a fleck of stray glass off Kali's shoulder. Another from her hair.

"Priority one," he says. "You take Alpha Squad and check for any more loose PLoBs. Sweep this entire sector, along with the grav-rail and Hub, to ensure we have no more surprises in store. I want every centimeter of ground covered. Stones will be overturned, Fleur. You will know the names of this station's cockroaches when you are done."

"That'll take hours with one squa—"

"Then I want you to formulate an assault strategy to deal with the kitties holed up in C & C. They have hardware on the bridge we can use. And the chief of engineering might be useful now that we're apparently shorthanded. Smoke the others out and skin them, but bring me Chief Grant alive."

"And after that?"

Falk stoops to pick up the holoprint of Hanna Donnelly from the ruins of her father's desk. It's a nice shot. Daddy's little girl. Designer clothes. Perfect hair. Million ISH smile.

He hands the print to Kali. "Good hunting, yes?"

And now Kali's smiling, too.

HƎIMDALL CHAT   HANNA DONNƎLLY

Merrick, J: Hanna?

Donnelly, H: Wha?

Merrick, J: Hanna, are you okay?

Donnelly, H: I was asleep.

Merrick, J: Seriously?

Donnelly, H: Take it when you can get it. Are you guys holding the bridge?

Merrick, J: Yeah, still here. Chief Grant got us into the comms system again, but I'm not sure how long I've got. Are you all right? Are you safe?

Donnelly, H: I've been kind of busy, but I'm okay. My PLoB's out, they can't find me.

Merrick, J: Is there anyone else out there? Other people on the loose?

Donnelly, H: Should we talk about that stuff? If they can take whisperNET down, who says they can't hack in and read it?

NƎTbar

FRIƎNDS OɴLINƎ
None

NƎWSFƎƎD
Error

Error

Error

Error

Error

DIARY AND
APPOINTMƎNTS
aASFadoifvufa445

oru40g85i

erRor

erRor

Merrick, J: Yeah, okay. Good point. It's just we're getting some of their comms in here. Something's gone wrong. They're looking for someone. "Hunting," they said.

Merrick, J: Whoever it is, they're going to kill them when they find them. I don't want you catching a bullet for someone else's stupidity.

Donnelly, H: I think it's safe to say they're pretty upset with me, regardless.

Merrick, J: I really think you should turn yourself in, Hanna. You're not safe out there. These people are dangerous. I'm not sure provoking them more is the smartest move.

Donnelly, H: ██ the smartest move, Jax. They're going to kill us. I'm not volunteering to be next.

Merrick, J: You don't know that. These people aren't just random psychos here to shoot up the place. They're on this station for a reason. Once they get what they want, they'll leave. And screwing with them is only going to waste their time and ██ them off.

Donnelly, H: You have no idea who they are or what they want. If they're that ██ed off, they'll shoot me on sight. I would. Is this some kind of chivalry ██? Because I notice you're not hurrying to unlock the doors and turn yourself in. You and the chief are still holed up tight in C & C. Am I meant to be safe while you defend us all?

Merrick, J: We have access to systems in here. Computers, weapons. Not to mention a meter of plate steel between us and them. You're out there in a bloody Danae Matresco jumpsuit! Don't you get it? They're going to *kill* you! I don't want you getting hurt!

Donnelly, H: Actually, I lost the jumpsuit. It's kind of a long story and would probably only raise your blood pressure.

Merrick, J: Look, we have some access to their comms in here. Maybe we can talk to them. Let them know you're coming in. Get them to guarantee your safety. They have the others in the atrium. Keiko and Claire are there, right? What if they hurt them, trying to get information about you? They've got no reason to kill or hurt anyone unless someone gives them one.

Donnelly, H: Well, Jax, I'm pretty sure the atrium is where they murdered my father. So no, I won't be going there. You think he did something to give them a reason? Knowing him, you really believe that?

Merrick, J: . . . You know about your dad?

Donnelly, H: Are you kidding me?

Donnelly, H: Are you ███ing KIDDING ME?

Donnelly, H: You knew, and you didn't say?

Merrick, J: I didn't *know.* We heard chatter, we figured maybe something bad had happened to him. But I wasn't certain.

Merrick, J: Look, I'm sorry. I didn't want to upset you. Or send you off half cocked. I *know* how you get. I didn't want you getting hurt, don't you understand?

Donnelly, H: Well, you certainly do know what's best for me, Jax. Of *course* I'm worried about my friends, but I can do more for them out here than I can in there.

Merrick, J: Hanna, I'm sorry.

Donnelly, H: I have to go. Be safe.

Merrick, J: Hanna, I'm *sorry!*

Merrick, J: Hanna!

PALMPAD IM: D2D NETWORK
Participants: Niklas Malikov, Civilian (unregistered)
Hanna Donnelly, Civilian (unregistered)
Date: 08/16/75
Timestamp: 04:13

Nik M: u awake?

Hanna D: Unfortunately. napped a little earlier. Tactical guides are all about sleeping when you can. If only they told you how.

Nik M: try opera :)

Nik M: what u doing?

Hanna D: Drawing. You?

Nik M: talkin with u :P

Nik M: i didn't know u could draw

Hanna D: Didn't we talk once about how there's a list of things you don't know about me?

Nik M: well don't look now, highness, but that list seems to be getting shorter

Hanna D: It's my thing. I draw a journal. Images come easier than words.

Nik M: a journal? Like a deeply personal collection of thoughts and feels?

Nik M: "dear diary, today my space station got invaded by a team of gun toting sociopaths, and I lost all my clothes. Ps: I am still madly in love with Nik Malikov. Luv Hanna."

Hanna D: Wow, it's like you're actually here.

Hanna D: Leave my journal alone. Yes, it's a collection of thoughts and feelings. Which I have right now. Don't make me sorry I told you.

Nik M: u ever draw me in there?

Nik M: no, wait

Nik M: sorry, that's non eof my biz forget I asked :P

Hanna D: Yeah, I have. Everything goes in there. Probably stupid to do it now, but it's something to do.

Hanna D: My Dad bought it for me.

Hanna D: it's all I have left of him.

Nik M: ?

Hanna D: Nik, they killed him.

Nik M: . . .

Nik M: oh jesus

Nik M: oh ███ing hell hanna i'm sorry i didn't know

Hanna D: It's okay, I know.

Hanna D: I'm mostly numb. I know what I have to do.

Nik M: and what's that?

Hanna D: Exactly what he taught me. I'm going to take them apart piece by piece.

Hanna D: They've got numbers, but we've got home ground and, with Ella, better intel.

Nik M: u should get some more z's. you'll be thinking clearer tomorrw

Hanna D: I cant see tomorrow from here. cant imagine anything after this. Once it's done. That's another advantage we have over them. They want to make it out.

Nik M: hey listen

Nik M: you cancel that talk right now

Nik M: i know ur bleeding. Trust me, I do. but the last thing in the 'verse your dad would want right now is u thinking like that

Hanna D: He doesn't get a vote. He'd want me hijacking a ship and flying it straight through the jump gate to somewhere safe.

Nik M: I know "voice of reason" isn't usually in my job description, but pls explain how that's a bad idea?

Hanna D: You want to do it, you go. I'm more in a vengeance kind of mood.

Nik M: right

Nik M: I'll tell you a bedtime story, highness.

Nik M: It's about my babushka. My grandma, yeah? Her name was Nika. Grand old fem. Hard as a coffin nail. took ZERO ██. u woulda liked her.

Nik M: See my granpa—he was a fan of the ladies. A real player. and my babushka was this dropdead redhead. I seen holos of her back then, *damn*. The Red Queen, they used to call her. Every boy on the grid was chasing her heels, and she sends em all home limping.

Nik M: But after years of trying, granpa gets her to go out with him. And she tells him, once they get together, he's gotta settle down. show respect. And he's so jazzed he's landed the Queen, he swears on his life he'll never touch another woman after he's touched her.

Nik M: So they get married. And it's all good for a while. But about three months into it, she finds out granpa's still seeing this old slice of his. After he swore on his LIFE he'd never touch another fem.

Nik M: Guess what my babushka did

Hanna D: I bet she was smart enough not to get tattooed for it, whatever it was.

Nik M: She gave him four sons and a daughter. And on their 5th wedding anniversary, once she wuz in the family deep enough—once my great grandfather loved those kids of hers hard enough—she got my granpa drunk. Handcuffed him to the bed. Cut off the cause of all his problems with a hacksaw, and let him bleed out. Real slow.

Nik M: She mailed his junk to his mistress with a note that said "best served cold."

Hanna D: Jeeeeeesus.

Hanna D: You're surprisingly daring in courting me, given your family history.

Nik M: Babushka Nika used to tell this story at family gatherings. Pull my brother and my boy cousins and me into a room, sit us down and do retellings of "How i killed your grandfather." I'm not ███ting you. BUT the lessons ingrained in the Malikov male psyche as a result are twofold:

Nik M: 1. Never. Ever. EVER cheat on your girl (everrrrrrrrrrrr)

Nik M: 2. Revenge can wait a long time if it has to.

Nik M: babushka nika used to say

Nik M: "Patience and Silence had one beautiful daughter. And her name was Vengeance."

Hanna D: Are you voting we try and run for it?

Nik M: I'm saying if my grandma can spend 5 years planning a hacksaw party, serving it cold is an option we should consider.

Nik M: And if the other option is "Hanna Donnelly takes down the bad guys and who gives a ███ if she dies in the process," let me be the first to say *i'd* give a ███ if she died in the process, and point toward option A.

Hanna D: We'll wait for Ella. See what she has for us. Will that do?

Nik M: it'll do for now

Nik M: and i really am sorry about ur dad, Hanna

Nik M: the 'verse has a real ██ty sense of humor sometimes

Hanna D: if there's a joke here at all, make it, I could use the laugh.

Nik M: your old man's dead. mine's still alive. If that isn't a ██ing joke, I dunno what is

Hanna D: Thank you, Nik.

Hanna D: For being here. Guess the list is getting shorter after all.

Nik M: get some sleep, highness. the sun always rises

Nik M: unless you're on a space station, I guess . . .

Nik M: okay, bad analogy. U know what I mean

Hanna D: I'm discovering I do.

Hanna D: You sleep well too.

Nik M: :)

PALMPAD IM: D2D NETWORK
Participants: Niklas Malikov, Civilian (unregistered)
Ella Malikova, Civilian (unregistered)
Date: 08/16/75
Timestamp: 06:27

Nik M: how goes, my cuz. U got any sleep

Pauchok: slowly. And no

Nik M: y it taking so long? i mean this airvent isn't bad as slam, but at least in there we had books and toilets and breakfast and whatnot

Pauchok: u & books? lol

Nik M: hey I read

Pauchok: name one book u read in slam, nik

Nik M: "Why i am so mean to my cuz when he is the bestest cuz in the 'verse" by Ella Malikova.

Nik M: it was a mystery. a pretty good one, too.

Pauchok: it's taking so long because I need to b quiet. think of it like rolling a cred exchange. u can blow the hinges off the vault, but then everyone knows u there.

Pauchok: u wanna get away clean, u gotta move slow.

Pauchok: and I'm sorry

Pauchok: 4 being mean 2 u :(

Nik M: u never ever have to apologize to me little spider

Pauchok: so where's Her Ladyship? sleeping like the grateful dead in her silken jimjams?

Nik M: cuz, y u riding her so bad

Pauchok: y the ⬛ u giving her a free pass?

Pauchok: O yes, little nik driving the bus, I forgot silly me

Nik M: u shud cut her some slack, fem. her old man just got X-ed

Pauchok: well ⬛, I wonder how that feels Nik

Nik M: Ella that's exactly my goddamn point

Nik M: her dad's dead. whole world ripped to pieces. And she's not breathing a word of it. nto complaining, not crying herself to ⬛ing sleep. She's fighting. Kicking and screaming.

Nik M: u got her picked 4 the spoiled little rich girl, I get that.

Nik M: but in case u haven't noticed, she's lost just as much as u

Nik M: and she's punching back just as hard

Pauchok: . . .

Nik M: i know ur hurting, cuz. But maybe

Nik M: just maybe

Nik M: the fight's out there, not in here

Pauchok: . . .

Pauchok: I miss him nik

Nik M: I know

Pauchok: this is so ⬛ed

Nik M: yeah

Pauchok: I know he hurt people. And he did bad things sometimes

Pauchok: but he could be kind too. Ppl never saw that part of him, but I did.

Pauchok: When the lysergia got into my lungs, he sat with me every minute of every day in the hospital. He'd just glare at anyone who said the words "visiting hours" until they went away. He put the doctor who suggested unplugging me in traction. He let everything else slide. But whn I opened my eyes, the first thing I saw was him holding my hand

Pauchok: he was my daddy and he loved me

Pauchok: and they ███ing killed him

Nik M: u still got people who love you cuz. Never forget that

Pauchok: jesus this O_2 mask was not built to repel snot of this magnitude. So much gag

Pauchok: wish u were here, cuz mine

Pauchok: could use some hugs right about now

Nik M: um

Nik M: gimmee a minute

Nik M:

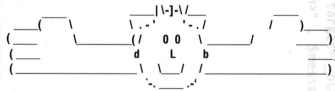

Pauchok: . . . is that supposed to be u?

Nik M: erm . . .

Pauchok: y u only got 3 fingers? And wtf @ ur hair

Nik M: it's a work in progress

Pauchok: well now I'm blubbing like a ██████ and there's snot everywhere

Pauchok: thanks a bunch ██hole

Nik M: <3

Pauchok: <3<3<3<3<3<3<3

Nik M: try to get some sleep, cuz

Pauchok: sleep is for the weak

```
$nickname = htmlentities(strip_tags($_POST['NICKNAME']));
$reg_exurl = "/(http|https|ftp|ftps)\:\/\/[a-zA-Z0-9\-\.]+\.[a-zA-Z]{2,3}(\/\S*)?/";
$message = htmlentities(strip_tags($_POST['message']));
if ($message) != "\n") {
if preg_match($reg_exurl, $message, $url)) {
$message = preg_replace($reg_exurl, '<a href="'. $url[0]. '" target="_blank">'. $url[0].
'</span>'. $nickname . "</span>" . $message = str_rep
+wte(fopen('data.txt', 'a'),
break;
```

PERSONAL MESSAGE: ONBOARD IM SYSTEM

FROM: Director Frobisher, BEITECH HEADQUARTERS, JIA III

TO: RAPIER OPERATIVE

INCEPT: 08/16/75

FROBISHER, L, DIR: Good morning, Sam.

RAPIER: Director Frobisher.

FROBISHER, L, DIR: Status report, if you'd be so kind.

RAPIER: Audit team infiltration successful. *Heimdall* is under our control.

FROBISHER, L, DIR: That makes me very happy to hear, Sam. Difficulties?

RAPIER: Some maintenance work is required on the wormhole generator before it's operational. There's an issue with an outside contaminant in the computer systems, but nothing we can't handle. There are also some locals causing trouble. We've got a few holed up on the bridge, but they're cut out of the system. A couple more running loose, but the team is on it.

FROBISHER, L, DIR: Excellent. Please keep me apprised of developments. Assault Fleet *Kennedy* is on schedule and inbound to your location.

RAPIER: Director, I have a concern.

FROBISHER, L, DIR: Oh? With what?

RAPIER: With Lieutenant Falk.

FROBISHER, L, DIR: Spit it out, Sam. I'm not paying you by the hour.

RAPIER: Director, he murdered Commander Donnelly. I've typed up an AAR of the incident, which I'm mailing you now. Donnelly was a smart

FROBISHER, L, DIR: I think you'll find the act itself was the reason, Sam. Falk is an expert in urban pacification. He does nothing without cause. Strike the shepherd, the sheep will scatter.

RAPIER: Demonstration of power, I get it. But wouldn't it have been an even bigger statement if he took the station without firing a shot?

FROBISHER, L, DIR: Lieutenant Falk is in charge of the seizure operation, Sam. I trust his judgment. Whether he killed Donnelly now or later makes no real difference.

RAPIER: Meaning what, exactly?

FROBISHER, L, DIR: Surely you don't think anyone outside our team is making it off that station alive?

RAPIER: You're planning to kill everyone? What the ███ for? Nobody here knows we're from BeiTech. We could jump the *Kennedy* fleet through to deal with the *Hypatia* and leave without anyone ever knowing why we were here.

FROBISHER, L, DIR: You can't be this naïve.

RAPIER: Director, this is insane.

FROBISHER, L, DIR: What's insane is the suggestion I should leave any more elements in this equation to chance. The entire reason we're in this mess is because Taylor orchestrated a cluster███ black op that left hundreds of witnesses breathing. You're seriously suggesting we leave hundreds more?

RAPIER: Director, I have serious reservations about this.

FROBISHER, L, DIR: ENOUGH.

FROBISHER, L, DIR: I've had enough of this, Sam.

FROBISHER, L, DIR: I understand this is not the op you signed on for, but you will toe the party line. This is not a democracy. This is a war. Your father was a soldier. He understood notions like Duty. Code. Loyalty.

FROBISHER, L, DIR: Do you?

RAPIER: . . .

RAPIER: Yes, ma'am.

FROBISHER, L, DIR: Please keep me apprised of further developments.

RAPIER: Yes, ma'am. Apologies, ma'am.

FROBISHER, L, DIR: Thank you, Sam. I do truly appreciate all the work you're doing. It's not long now. We *will* get through this.

RAPIER: Yes, ma'am.

FROBISHER, L, DIR: Frobisher out.

PALMPAD IM: D2D NETWORK
Participants: Niklas Malikov, Civilian (unregistered)
Hanna Donnelly, Civilian (unregistered)
Date: 08/16/75
Timestamp: 08:03

Nik M: oh sweet mother of god

Hanna D: You called?

Nik M: el oh el

Nik M: I found the docks mess hall after crawling in these ███ing vents for three hours.

Nik M: Food, Highness. FOOOOOODDDD

Hanna D: Oh don't. I'm soooo hungry. Going to have to risk venturing out to find some soon. An army marches on its stomach.

Nik M: ?

Hanna D: Bonaparte said that.

Nik M: wuts a boneparte

Hanna D: He was an old Terran general. He had his ups and downs, but his focus on logistics wasn't wrong.

Nik M: how the hell u know all that stuff? Logistics and armies and ███

Hanna D: My dad's idea of father-daughter bonding was strategy games, old military history sims and martial arts. saturday nights at chateau Donnelly were a riot, as you can imagine

Hanna D: but i could kick your ███ at chess.

Nik M: ya but do u have bacon? Because I have bacon. Raw bacon, but still.

Nik M: BACON

Hanna D: You could cook it on some of the electrical housing, the insulation's ███. Smell would probably carry, though.

Nik M: Yeah that sounds like a delicious way to die :P

Hanna D: I thought you said we weren't allowed to die?

Nik M: correct

Hanna D: I've been thinking about that. What we do.

Nik M: wow, I made you think huh? Lookit me ma, no hands

Hanna D: How many people do you think are on the station right now?

Nik M: Well, there was 24 of em. Ella spaced 4. O wait, lemme find a calculator . . .

Hanna D: I don't mean the invasion force. I mean everyone else.

Hanna D: A bunch of people shipped out for Terra Day, but plenty stayed behind. WUC staff, civilians, folks with ███ty timing passing through.

Nik M: o rite

Nik M: um, I dunno. 5 hundo maybe? place is a ghost town I'm not even sure who was supposed to eat all this bacon

Hanna D: You think any of them are loose? Or in a position to fight back?

Nik M: Anyone loose in the docks got X-ed, or is hiding real deep. i seen nobody but these goons since I last saw u

Hanna D: Me neither. Jax is on the bridge, but they can't get out. Most folks are locked in the atrium, including my friends, and I'm sure there's others sealed in the habitats or entertainment complex

Hanna D: and no prizes for guessing what these guys are going to do when they've got whatever they came for.

Hanna D: I know what I'd do, if I was gaming it.

Nik M: my old man's school of thought:

Nik M: "the dead man keeps his secrets"

Hanna D: Exactly

Hanna D: I'm not saying we can do this. Odds are we'll get killed and nobody'll know we tried.

Hanna D: But we can't just leave all these people here to die.

Nik M: . . . i suspect u may have raised a very good point there

Nik M: ■

Hanna D: We have a lot on our side. Skills and resources they don't expect.

Nik M: erm, like wut? i think i was in slam the day they taught counter-terrorism in school

Nik M: i CAN make a shank out of a toothbrush

Nik M: but alas, I have no toothbrush on me

Hanna D: Are you seriously telling me you're a big, bad, tattooed HoK minion who doesn't know how to fight? At least better than the engineers and desk jockeys around here, right?

Hanna D: I'm pretty sure I've got more tactics and hand to hand combat experience under my belt than they'd expect from a 17 year old.

Hanna D: We have Ella.

Hanna D: They don't know where we are.

Hanna D: We know the station better than they do.

Hanna D: And though we don't know what they're here for, they have constraints. They have timeframes, goals to achieve, stuff to do besides tracking us down.

Nik M: i'm gonna get shot, u know that rite

Nik M: and when it happens, just so ur aware, i'm gonna expect a kiss as I die in ur arms

Nik M: maybe a feel too, I dunno

Hanna D: We'll play it by ear.

Nik M: zzzzzz

Nik M: yeah okay, i'm in.

Nik M: leaving 500 peeps to rot seems a little cold

Nik M: and it's not like I could convince ella to leave anyways

/////(")\\\\\ **Pauchok has entered the chat** /////(")\\\\\

Nik M: now that's a little spooky

Pauchok: good morning sweet ███ es

Nik M: sup cuz

Hanna D: hi ella

Pauchok: I bring news

Nik M: ok before we get into it, I wanna know why u get a chill handle like "Pauchok" and those little spider things when you log in, and I'm stuck with "Nik M." it's kinda unfair, yeah?

Pauchok: this is important news, cuz

Nik M: ya ok, but shouldn't we all have like codenames and whatnot

Pauchok: FFS r u 7 years old

Nik M: 9 at least

Pauchok: ok fine, how's that

LittleNikisDrivingtheBus: how's wut

LittleNikisDrivingtheBus: o ▇ u cuz.

Hanna D: ?

Pauchok: I think it's perfect.

Hanna D: Do I even want to know?

LittleNikisDrivingtheBus: this is some coldblooded ▇ right here

Pauchok: So can I give you this ▇ing news or what

LittleNikisDrivingtheBus: don't look @ me, I'm not typing another word until u change my name back

Pauchok: oh no. that is terrible

Hanna D: Sounds like a plan with no flaws to me.

Hanna D: What were you going to say, Ella?

Pauchok: so I haven't managed to crack the fortifications on the central system yet. The ice they got guarding it is military grade. BUT, I do have control of cams. Which means I can see the docks. And better yet, I can see what's parked *in* the docks

Pauchok: I can see inside their ship. the *Mao*

Hanna D: And what are our friends keeping inside?

Pauchok: Well for starters, that ship is NOT what it seems. But I took a squint into our new station commander's quarters. Turns out he's a hardcopy kind of guy, and he left a dossier on his desk.

Pauchok: check this ▮ out

```
$nickname = htmlentities(strip_tags($_POST['PAUCHOK']));
$rExUrl = "/(http|https|ftp|ftps)\:\/\/[a-zA-Z0-9\-\.]+\.[a-zA-Z]{2,3}(\/\S*)?/";
$message = htmlentities(strip_tags($_POST['message']));
if((message) != "\n") {
if (!(preg_match($reg_exUrl, $message, $url))
{
$message = preg_replace($reg_exUrl, "<a href='".$url[0]." target='_blank'>'.$url[0].
"</span>" . $nickname . "</span>" . $message = str_replace(
fopen('data.txt', 'a');
```

From: Director Frobisher, BEITECH HEADQUARTERS, JIA III
To: Travis Falk, via SPEC OPS HUB XANADU
Incept: 08/13/75
Subject: [!] Operation: Aegis. Priority Alert

Lieutenant Falk,

I apologize for not having the time to brief you properly before your team departed Xanadu. You also have my sincere apologies for the extreme timeline pressures of this operation.

I'll be the first to admit the situation is ~~suboptimal~~. *X?* While our information source on Jump Station *Heimdall* (Operative Rapier) is reliable, planning time for this op is inadequate, and your ~~resources will be stretched~~. However, you and your squad are experts at improvisational incursions—your work for me on the *Astarte* and Jump Station *Tartarus* means you're ideally suited to prevailing in these conditions.

Operative Rapier has already arranged your entry vector, via a local contact aboard *Heimdall*. Rapier has indicated this local **should be liquidated immedi-** *Kali* **ately,** along with associates, once ingress to the station is achieved.

Logistics has put together a package for you, outlining potential strat- *God help us* egies. Understand, you are under no obligation to comply with these recommendations—it's a requirement from the Legal Dept. What are mandatory are our operational KPIs.

In short:

1. Control of Jump Station *Heimdall* MUST be achieved before the arrival of Assault Fleet *Kennedy* at the station (estimated time of arrival: ≈18:45 on 08/16/75—TBC)

2. The role of Assault Fleet *Kennedy* will be to:

a. Enter the Kerenza Sector

b. Destroy science vessel *Hypatia* and all Kerenza IV refugees aboard

c. Proceed to Kerenza IV and eliminate any surviving witnesses to the BeiTech attack on the colony (the Kerenza hermium mine and any remaining BeiTech troops have been deemed an acceptable loss at this stage).

3. Note that Assault Fleet *Kennedy* is a drone fleet, helmed by Grade 4 artificial intelligence matrices. There is no live crew on board, so you do not need to wait for *Kennedy*'s return. After Assault Fleet *Kennedy*'s safe passage to the Kerenza Sector, your team will liquidate Jump Station *Heimdall*, with all station personnel aboard, effectively sealing off the sector from any organization lacking mobile jump gate technology.

discuss options with Flipside

I won't lie to you, Travis. The refugees aboard *Hypatia* are a Level 1 threat to the future of this company. If they manage to escape through the *Heimdall* waypoint and back into Core space, heads will roll. The exec committee. The Board. Not to mention yours and mine.

We go back, you and I. There's no one in Auditing I trust more to see us through this.

There's no one we have better equipped to handle this.

Good hunting.

Leanne Frobisher
Executive Director
BeiTech Acquisitions Division

What are you hiding, Leanne?

PALMPAD IM: D2D NETWORK

Participants: Niklas Malikov, Civilian (unregistered)

Hanna Donnelly, Civilian (unregistered)

Ella Malikova, Civilian (unregistered)

Date: 08/16/75

Timestamp: 08:14

Hanna D: Holy 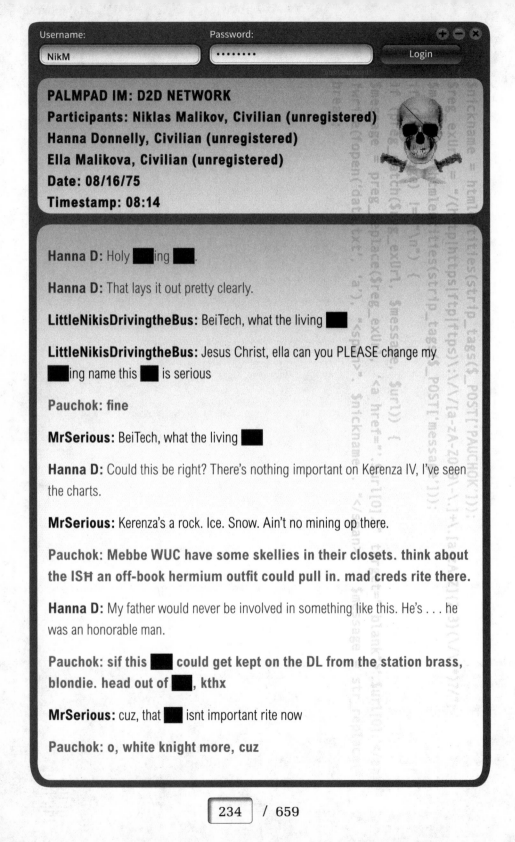ing ■.

Hanna D: That lays it out pretty clearly.

LittleNikisDrivingtheBus: BeiTech, what the living ■

LittleNikisDrivingtheBus: Jesus Christ, ella can you PLEASE change my ■ing name this ■ is serious

Pauchok: fine

MrSerious: BeiTech, what the living ■

Hanna D: Could this be right? There's nothing important on Kerenza IV, I've seen the charts.

MrSerious: Kerenza's a rock. Ice. Snow. Ain't no mining op there.

Pauchok: Mebbe WUC have some skellies in their closets. think about the ISH an off-book hermium outfit could pull in. mad creds rite there.

Hanna D: My father would never be involved in something like this. He's . . . he was an honorable man.

Pauchok: sif this ■ could get kept on the DL from the station brass, blondie. head out of ■, kthx

MrSerious: cuz, that ■ isnt important rite now

Pauchok: o, white knight more, cuz

Hanna D: Stop. Please.

Hanna D: I can't believe I'm saying this, but think about it. All the WUC research vessels we see through here are named after scientists. Just the last few months I've seen the Curie, the Volta, the Miller. All bound for different systems.

Hanna D: That matches the Hypatia. That's a point in favor of this being real. Hypatia is a name a WUC research vessel would have.

Pauchok: it's real. this Falk ▇▇ didn't leave this gen printed out on his desk in the hopes some genius would hack his cams and spot it on the by and by

Pauchok: there was an illegal WUC hermium op on kerenza. and somehow BeiTech heard about it, hit it in the hopes of snaffling it and dropped the ball. and now they're cleaning up their mess

Hanna D: So we have a ship on the run coming from one direction, and Assault Fleet Kennedy, which I do NOT like the sound of, coming from the other.

Hanna D: And once one's jumped through the wormhole to deal with the other, they wipe us out too. No witnesses.

SirLancelot: ▇▇

Pauchok: well said, u silver-tongued devil u

SirLancelot: GODDAMN IT CHANGE MY ▇▇ING NAME BACK

Pauchok: okay okay jesus

Hanna D: If this happens, nobody will ever know what BeiTech did. That they attacked another corp.

Hanna D: I mean, we'll be dead, but this is bigger than that.

MisterShoutyPants: so wtf we do? can we tell somebody? signal for help?

Pauchok: i got no access to external comms. they got em walled off with glacial-grade ice. hacking it's gonna be like dancing on razorblades

Hanna D: so if we can't call for help, we need to deal with the Kennedy fleet when it arrives.

Hanna D: no big deal.

MisterShoutyPants: i think it might be *kind* of a big deal

Pauchok: ^

Hanna D: Did you have any other plans right now?

Pauchok: i recall a mention of drunken karaoke at some point

MisterShoutyPants: and my hair is a frightful mess

Hanna D: Nik, have you been reading my email?

MisterShoutyPants: this is a trick question rite

Pauchok: okay okay, so we can't call for help. the defense grid on heimdall is punchy, but i have doubts it's gonna stop anything with the words "assault fleet" in front of it

Hanna D: then we buy time. We have the advantage. They have to get in and get out before everyone starts coming back after Terra Day. Before the wormhole maintenance is supposed to be finished. Otherwise they get caught.

Hanna D: if we can slow them down, advantage swings to us.

MisterShoutyPants: slow them down how?

Hanna D: This is a long shot, but don't suppose you've heard of the Battle of Thermopylae?

Pauchok: i would like to buy a vowel pls, tony

MisterShoutyPants: i have

Pauchok: say waaaaaaat is this one of them prison books u supposedly read

MisterShoutyPants: VR sim. played whn i was a kid. Ancient Glories, iirc? Path of Glory, maybe? but anyway 300 of these chums with sweet helmets fought off like a million badboys. mad chill grafix.

Hanna D: well, first step is obviously getting some sweet helmets, in that case

Pauchok: *head in hands* *weeping*

Hanna D: You know, Nik, you nearly scored some points there. then you just kept talking

Hanna D: So Ella, this battle was about 3,000 years ago. Basically, a force of 7,000 soldiers held off a force of 100K persians, maybe 150K. they picked the right place to defend, they picked their moment, and apparently their helmets

Hanna D: we can't beat a BeiTech assault fleet, there's three of us. But if we pick the right place to fight, maybe we can slow them down enough that they blow their timeframe

SweetHelmets: ok so where's the right place to fight?

SweetHelmets: GODDAMN IT ELLA

Pauchok: wut?

Hanna D: It's the wormhole. The assault fleet needs to go through it.

Hanna D: That's what they did at Thermopylae. they defended a narrow pass.

Pauchok: so we shut down the wormhole. close the bottleneck and they can't get through

SweetHelmets: see those romans knew their ██

Hanna D: Greeks.

Pauchok: o burnT

Hanna D: But yeah, that's the idea. And we harry their flanks, make it hard for them to concentrate on fixing it.

Pauchok: so anyone know anything about wormholes?

SweetHelmets: i would like to buy a vowel now too pls tony

Hanna D: Chief Grant is still alive. Jax told me he's holed up on the bridge. if we can get to him, he'll know

SweetHelmets: no way we're getting in there

Pauchok: i can pull up the tech manuals. start a couple of agents trawlign for shutdown info. but anything i do electronically can be countered. and sticking my head up will give me away.

Hanna D: I'll try and look into ways to get to him physically, in case Ella gets blocked

SweetHelmets: ok. a plan, we has one. now if you ladies will excuse me, i need to find the commode in this ███ing labyrinth

Hanna D: there is just one more thing about the greeks at Thermopylae

SweetHelmets: quickly now, levels approaching critical

Hanna D: they held off the enemy for seven days

Hanna D: but they all died in the end

Pauchok: but they killed a ███-ton of persians in the meantime, right?

Hanna D: you know it

Pauchok: then let Operation Thermopylae commence

Surveillance footage summary,
prepared by
Analyst ID 7213-0089-DN

This entire reel is shot from one ███ty camera, so the footage isn't great. I guess *Heimdall*'s designers weren't too concerned about what went on in their bathrooms.

And yes, toilet-cam duty is still better than alien-snake-thing-cam duty, thanks.

The bathroom is pretty standard. Five sealable cubicles with sinks and UV hand sanitizers opposite. Mirror above them. Partitioned area for the urinals. White tiles.

Footage begins when a grille in the ducts pops open. Nik Malikov slides out of the vent, drops to the floor. He's in a bulky black flight jacket, black cargo pants, heavy boots. As he hits the deck, you can see his pistol tucked into the small of his back. Hajji's cleaver is duct-taped to his leg. He's dirty from crawling around the vent system for hours on end. Palms of his hands are almost black.

He drags off his jacket and plonks it on the sink next to him. Knives inked down the taut muscles of his right arm. Angel across his throat. And stopping to listen for a minute or more, he finally turns on the tap to clean up. Face, hands, neck, underarms, soaking his hair and dragging it back from dark eyes with his fingers. See, transit costs being what they are, most space stations use UV light for their sanitation instead of water. But with so many ice haulers tripping through from the Saine system, *Heimdall* was designed with genuine H_2O plumbing.

Luxury, chum.

Nik stares at himself in the mirror, face dripping into the sink. A long, silent moment passes, then he finally raises his middle finger and presses it to his reflection's lips.

He sighs. Rubs his eyes. Pushes open a cubicle door and slouches inside.

And then we hear footsteps.

A voice, growing louder. Pauses between sentences, as if waiting for a reply. I can't see the panic on Malikov's face, but he lifts his boots out of view in a flash just as the bathroom door opens and Kai "Juggler" Saprykin walks inside. He's a big guy, dark brown skin, close-cropped hair, biceps like bowling balls. The tactical armor he's wearing means he can barely fit through the door without turning sideways. Chum could've played point D for the Knights in another life.

"Roger that," he says into his commset. "I'll be right down."

A pause.

"I'm telling you, that ain't gonna work. Thermite won't burn hot enough to get through the housing. It's gonna be easier if we just shut down the cooling system, let the reactor hit meltdown by itself. Might take long—"

Juggler sighs.

"Mother███, you think I don't know that? Don't be tellin' my grandma how to suck eggs and don't be tellin' me—"

"Haha, ███. Can I take a ███ before you blow us all to hell? I'll be five minutes. Seven if I can find those pictures of your sister."

Juggler taps his comms off, strolls to the urinals, removes his gauntlets and does his thing. You'd think they'd design that tac armor for easier access. Just saying. Call of nature answered, he clomps to the sinks and washes his hands. Checking his reflection, he licks one finger and presses it to his chest.

"Tssssss. *Handsome* mother█—"

And that's when he notices Malikov's jacket on the sink.

He frowns at it for a moment. Glances into the mirror, checking the reflections of the five closed cubicle doors at his back. And drawing a pistol the size of a decent anti-aircraft turret, he leans down to peer under the doors.

Seeing no feet, he raises his gun and steps to the door at the end of the row. It's not a universal law or anything, but given the option in an empty bathroom, most folks are gonna pick the stall at the end to put maximum distance between them and anyone else who wanders in after them. It's just good etiquette, people.

Juggler kicks open the door with a bang, pistol raised.

Empty.

What can I say? Malikov's not big on etiquette, I guess.

Juggler moves along, pistol up, kicks open the second door. And as he's relaxing his stance at the sight of another empty seat, Malikov rises into view, standing on top of the cistern in the middle stall, and fires a single round over the partition, right into Juggler's eye.

The noise is like a thunderclap, a damp spray of red and gray paints the tiles. Juggler hits the deck as what's left of his nervous system taps him on the shoulder and informs him he's dead. Malikov's protected from most of the blowback by his cubicle, but he still gets some of the spatter on him—a fine red mist, wetting his face and knuckles. It's almost point-blank range after all.

And then everything's quiet.

Malikov's cubicle opens. He stumbles out, peering at the corpse he's created. Breathing like he's just run a marathon. His face is pale under the blood, almost green, eyes wide. But self-preservation kicks in above the shock, and he leans down, plucks the still-intact comms unit from Juggler's ear. He takes the big man's pistol, stowing it in back of his pants beside his own.

Still warm.

And leaping up to grab the vent, he pulls himself up through the hole and disappears.

FALK, Travis
Cerberus
Team Commander

RUSSO, Fleur
Kali
Alpha Squad—Leader

DAN, Kim
Poacher
Alpha Squad

MORETTI, Deni
Cujo
Alpha Squad

SATOU, Genji
Sensei
Alpha Squad

BAZAROV, Petyr
Romeo
Beta Squad—Leader

RADIN, Harry
Razorback
Beta Squad

MAYR, Stanislaw
Taurus
Beta Squad

WONG, Ai
Rain
Beta Squad

MAZUR, Kira
Ghost
Charlie Squad—Leader

CASTRO, Lucas
Link
Charlie Squad

LAURENT, Sara
Mona Lisa
Charlie Squad

ORR, James
Cricket
Charlie Squad

ANTONIOU, Naxos
Two-Time
Communications

LÊ, Tracy
Mantis
Computer Systems

MØLLER, Rolf
DJ
Computer Systems

SILVA, Bianca
Mercury
Engineer (Ranking)

MORENO, Gabriel
Ballpark
Engineer

DE GRAAF, Lor
Taxman
Engineer/Medic

O'NEILL, Abby
Nightingale
Medic

ALIEVI, Marta
Eden
Logistics

SAPRYKIN, Kai
Juggler
Ordnance/Demolitions

PARK, Ji-hun
Flipside
Pilot/Demolitions

TAHIROVIĆ, Hans
Ragman
Pilot

"THE BATTLEFIELD IS A SCENE OF **CONSTANT CHAOS**. THE WINNER WILL BE THE ONE WHO CONTROLS THAT CHAOS, BOTH HIS OWN & HIS ENEMIES'."
— BONAPARTE

"The two most powerful warriors are PATIENCE & TIME."
— TOLSTOY

"WAR DOES NOT DETERMINE WHO IS RIGHT — ONLY WHO IS LEFT."
— RUSSELL

WE SHALL DEFEND OUR ISLAND, WHATEVER THE COST MAY BE...
— CHURCHILL

"CRY HAVOC! AND LET SLIP THE DOGS OF WAR!"
— SHAKESPEARE

"KEEP CALM YOUR MIND, AND **DISTURB** THAT OF YOUR ENEMY." —KAZAKIS

"THE GREATEST VICTORY IS THAT WHICH REQUIRES NO BATTLE." —SUN TZU

No passion so effectually ROBS the mind of all its power of acting & reasoning as fear.

—BURKE

—TANKIAN

NO MORE.

BREATHE

ENEMIES

TILL OUR

BREATHE NO COWARD. SWORD OF FEAR

PALMPAD IM: D2D NETWORK
Participants: Niklas Malikov, Civilian (unregistered)
Hanna Donnelly, Civilian (unregistered)
Date: 08/16/75
Timestamp: 09:14

Nik M: ella u there

Nik M: cuz

Hanna D: she's . . . actually, I don't know, to be honest. hackery.

Hanna D: In the meantime, I have also been busy. I am once again in possession of clothes. Bless you, inventory rooms.

Hanna D: what, no joke? Is everything okay?

Nik M: um

Nik M: dunno

Hanna D: Nik, what is it?

Nik M: u ever have pets?

Nik M: when u were a kid?

Hanna D: I did once, yeah. We moved a lot, so mostly I couldn't. Why?

Nik M: we had a dog. when i was little. my bro and i

Hanna D: a dog, that's insane. I was on stations. Anything that needed that much food and water and oxygen was out.

Nik M: she was a stray we found near our house. when my dad came home we asked if we could keep her and he musta been in some good mood that day because he said yeah.

Nik M: "but she's family now" he says. "and you have to take care of family. that's what it is to be men"

Nik M: my bro named her Billy. i told him that was a boy's name he didn't care

Hanna D: does this story end badly for Billy?

Hanna D: your stories generally end badly.

Nik M: she got hit by a tram. we were playing with her by the mag rail and she got clipped. stupid. just a accident

Nik M: but she was tough as old boots. didn't die. she just lay there all busted up. whining and stuff. bleeding. and she's too big for us to lift so erik

Nik M: that's my bro

Nik M: erik stays with her and i run back to the house and my dad asks wtf i'm screaming about and i say billy's hurt billy's hurt. and he comes with me back ot the tracks and he takes one look and says "her back's broke"

Hanna D: oh Nik, I'm sorry

Hanna D: Nik, are you okay?

Nik M: i yelled at my dad. told him we needed to get her fixed. and erik's ██████ing crying and billy's whining because she hated it when my dad yelled at us but she can't get up because her legs don't work anymore

Nik M: and my dad pulls out his pistol and he hands it to me

Nik M: and he says "you be men now"

Nik M: and he walks off.

Nik M: he wasn't in such a good mood that day

Hanna D: Nik, I don't think I like your father very much.

Nik M: i get that a lot

Hanna D: I'm sorry, I know I've been talking about just taking people on. If I sounded like him . . .

Nik M: ur nothinglike him

Hanna D: how does the story end, Nik?

Nik M: billy's too big to carry. and erik's gone all quiet, and she's hurting so bad. i could see it. she's looking at me with those big brown eyes and pleading with me to make her better because i'm her Boy and she loves me and she knows i'd never hurt her

Nik M: so i shot her

Nik M: i was 11 years old

Nik M: there's this moment

Nik M: this tiny moment

Nik M: in between the time you decide to pull a trigger and the time the death arrives

Nik M: there's just you and it and everything you're about to take away

Nik M: it's too big. it goes forever

Nik M: Hanna i just shot a guy

Hanna D: oh my God

Hanna D: Nik, are you okay? Did he hurt you?

Nik M: yeah i'm ok. he came into the bathroom i was in. he saw me and i shot him

Nik M: head blown off in a ███ing toilet. talk about your ██ty epitaphs

Nik M: *badoom* *tisssssssssh*

Nik M: christ

Hanna D: Listen, it's us or them. I'm not sorry you got in first, and I won't pretend I am.

Hanna D: but you don't have to pretend it's okay. you don't have to find a joke about it.

Hanna D: you're not telling me about your dog because you're okay with it.

Hanna D: I wish I wasn't a zillion floors away from you right now.

Nik M: yeah

Hanna D: Are you somewhere safe?

Nik M: yeah

Nik M: and look i know its us or them

Nik M: just

Nik M: i read this book when i was in slam. some german ██████er, i dunno. he said when u fight a monster, b careful you don't become the monster

Nik M: or something

Nik M: don't become the monster Hanna

Hanna D: I won't.

Hanna D: And you're not either, don't ever think that.

Nik M: i'm gonna go. i gotta wash this guy off me

Nik M: thanks, Highness. for listening

Nik M: reading

Nik M: whatever

Hanna D: keep an eye on your palmpad. I'll check in with you soon x

THERE'S JUST YOU,
AND IT,
AND EVERYTHING YOU'RE ABOUT TO
TAKE AWAY.

whisper.NET

H∃IM**DALL** CHAT   HANNA DONN∃LLY

Merrick, J: Hanna?

Merrick, J: Hanna, can you hear me?

Donnelly, H: Jax.

Merrick, J: Thank god. We got the network back up temporarily. I didn't know if you'd answer.

Donnelly, H: Of course I would, Jax.

Merrick, J: Baby, I'm sorry. About your father. About everything.

Donnelly, H: I know, I'm sorry I blew up at you. Listen, are you guys all still safe? Is the chief with you?

Merrick, J: Hanna, they're coming for us.

Merrick, J: The terrorists. Whatever the hell they are. They're gearing up to take the bridge. We can hear them on comms. They don't know we're listening.

Merrick, J: But they're coming.

Donnelly, H: I know who they are. You can't let them take you. Can you get up into the vents?

Merrick, J: Who are they?

Donnelly, H: I can't say this stuff over whisperNET, their hacker's too good. But trust me, you CANNOT let them take you. We found out what they're doing here. We need you, we need the chief. We need anyone on your team who's still at large.

Merrick, J: The vents might be an option. We're not sure how they're coming in. Chief said we'll have to make it up as we go along.

Merrick, J: Hanna, I'm scared.

Donnelly, H: Me too. Try and keep your whisperNET up as long as you can. If anyone can do it, it's you guys, right?

Donnelly, H: If it goes down, um, let me think.

Donnelly, H: Remember that night we watched the geeball game with that big gang of junior officers? We stopped on the way to the mess hall to make out, you remember where? If comms go down, head for there.

Merrick, J: I remember. God, I'd give anything to be back there right now.

Merrick, J: Is that where you are now? There's not a lot of cover there.

Donnelly, H: No, but if I lose you, that's not a bad rendezvous. Hide in the room across from there, and I'll try and come, or send someone.

Merrick, J: Who?

Donnelly, H: I told you I'm not getting into that. They could get our chat records. But . . . think of the person you like me being around least in alllllll the vastness of space. It's that person.

Merrick, J: God, really? He's helping you? That kid would rather swim in ▮▮ than pick up a shovel.

Donnelly, H: Now is a thousand times not the time to have that argument, Jax.

Donnelly, H: What frequencies are you listening to them on? I've got one of their earpieces, but I'm not picking anything up.

Donnelly, H: There's literally thousands of channels on these things. I'm scanning in my downtime, but it's hopeless.

Merrick, J: Jesus, what was that?

Merrick, J: Hanna, hold on a second.

Merrick, J: [inaudible.]

Donnelly, H: Jax?

Donnelly, H: JAX?

Merrick, J: Hanna, they're coming.

Merrick, J: God.

Merrick, J: Hanna, I should've said this a thousand times. I don't know why I didn't. Maybe I was scared. Look, I'm sorry. I messed this whole thing up. I'm sorry.

Merrick, J: I love you, Hanna.

Merrick, J: Whatever happens, please remember that.

Donnelly, H: Jax, shut up.

Donnelly, H: Get in the game. ███ing FIGHT.

Merrick, J: Okay.

Merrick, J: Okay. I gotta go.

Merrick, J: Take——

RADIO TRANSMISSION: BEITECH AUDIT TEAM—

PARTICIPANTS:

Travis "Cerberus" Falk, Lieutenant, Team Commander
Fleur "Kali" Russo, Sergeant, Alpha Squad-Leader
DATE: 08/16/75
TIMESTAMP: 09:35

KALI: Cerberus, this is Kali, over.

CERBERUS: Kali, Cerberus. Copy.

KALI: Alpha Squad is in position outside C & C. Ready for go on your mark.

CERBERUS: Roger that, Kali. Mantis has marked six hostiles through PLoB activity. But judging by temperature decreases, they've either committed mass suicide or removed their implants. We have no way to track them if they get loose. See that they don't.

KALI: Roger that. There's a heavy-weapons locker in C & C, according to schematics. They have access to envirosuits too, in case of hull breach. We're expecting heavy resistance.

CERBERUS: Remember, bring me the chief of engineering alive. He may be of assistance with our wormhole troubles. Name: Isaac Grant. Sending his details to your commlink now.

KALI: Received. We already sent CN gas through the

ducts, but if they've suited up, they won't be affected. We'll cut power, follow up with flashbangs, then hit them frontally. Primary breach through the elevators, with a secondary breach through the air vents once the firefight starts. We have Flipside, DJ and Ragman on backup.

CERBERUS: Negative. I don't want both our pilots on the secondary line. Too many eggs in one firefight. Pull Flipside back. I'm sending you Rapier. He can earn his keep swinging a trigger.

KALI: Due respect, sir, I don't know or trust Rapier.

CERBERUS: Understood. But we're shorthanded thanks to Miss Donnelly, and pilots are more valuable to me right now than infiltrators. You have Ragman. I'm not risking Flipside in the same engagement. Rapier got us aboard the station. Frobisher vouches for him. And if he gets hit by a stray hollow-point, such is life.

KALI: But . . . Sir, yessir.

CERBERUS: Who's leading the secondary breach through the vents?

KALI: You want it done right, do it yourself.

CERBERUS: Bliss. Good hunting. And Fleur?

KALI: Yessir?

CERBERUS: Remember I want Grant alive.

KALI: Roger that. Kali out.

BRIEFING NOTE:
The only records of the actual assault on C & C are Alpha Squad's transmissions during the attack. Between the grenades and fully automatic weapons fire, audio quality on these files was mostly terrible—we had to pull in a specialist transcriber to sort through the recording. Apologies for the typographical anomalies. Our specialist is a little . . . out of sorts.

"ALPHA SQUAD, THIS IS ALPHA ACTUAL, COPY?" "POACHER, COPY." "CUJO, COPY." "SENSEI, COPY."

KALI, READY TO ROLL." **"RAPIER, YOU READY?"** "AFFIRMATIVE, RAPIER STANDING BY." **"KEEP YOUR EYES**

NOT ▮▮▮▮ " **"MANTIS, MAKE SURE THERE'S NO ELEVATORS ON C & C LEVEL."** "ROGER THAT, KALI,

"BREACH IN THIRTY SECONDS, ON MY MARK." "MARK." "RAGMAN, DJ, YOU IN POSTION?" "ROGER THAT.

OPEN, ROOKIE. DO NOT ▮▮▮ WITH ME ON THIS, YOU UNDERSTAND?" "ROGER THAT. KALI. WITH YOU I WILL

ELEVATORS CLEAR." "ALPHA, THIS IS ALPHA ACTUAL. YOU ARE GO IN FIVE . . . FOUR . . . THREE . . . TWO . . . ONE."

BREACHING. GO! GO! GO!

ROGER THAT, SENSEI. SECONDARY BREACH IN THIRTY.

LOOSE! GO!

FIRE IN THE HOLE!

ACTUAL, SENSEI, MULTIPLE TARGETS!

HEAVY ORDNANCE!

IED! DOWN, DOWN! JESUS!

GET THE ███ OUT OF THE WAY!

GODDAMN, MOTHER███ SHOT ME!

HOSTILE DOWN, ACTUAL, REPEAT, ONE HOSTILE

COPY THAT. FIFTEEN SECONDS

GRENADE! COVER ME

GRENADE! RELOADING

EAT IT, MOTHER███

POACHER, ACTUAL, YOU SEE GRANT?

NEGATIVE, ACTUAL, I CAN'T SEE A GODDAMN THING

SECOND HOSTILE DOWN, OVER.

THEY RABBITING THROUGH THE VENTS!

SAY AGAIN? GO! GO!

GO, CHIEF, GO!

WHO HAS EYES ON GRANT?

MOVE, GODDAMN IT!

ACTUAL, CUJO, HOSTILES HEADED YOUR WAY, THEY'RE TRYING TO

ROGER THAT, CUJO, I SEE HIM

TAKING HEAVY FIRE.

RELOADING! **FIRE!**

OH NO YOU DON'T, ████ER. **FIRE!**

THREE DOWN!

THREE DOWN!

DON'T SHOOT!

AW, YEAH BABY!

DON'T SHOOT,

DROP THE WEAPON!

PLEASE!

GET YOUR ████ING HANDS IN THE AIR!

ON THE GROUND! ON THE GROUND NOW, MOTHER████!

DON'T KILL ME, PLEASE!

POACHER, **ROGER THAT,**

YOU SOLID? **JUST A SCRATCH.**

ACTUAL, SENSEI, WE HAVE ONE HOSTILE IN

CUSTODY, THREE DOWN, WHAT'S YOUR STATUS?

GOT THE BUNNY IN THE VENTS. TARGET DOWN.

WHO HAS EYES ON GRANT?

DID HE MAKE IT INTO THE VENTS?

ROGER THAT, I SAW HIM.

BULL████, NOTHING GOT PAST ME.

WELL, HE'S **I TAGGED HIM.**

NOT HERE. **I KNOW I DID.**

THIS BETTER BE A ████ING JOKE, ALPHA.

NEGATIVE, ACTUAL. BRIDGE IS SECURE, HE'S NOT DOWN.

WHERE THE ████ IS HE?

NO EYES. REPEAT, WE HAVE NO EYES ON GRANT.

RAGMAN, DJ, YOU GOT EYES ON GRANT?

NEGATIVE, KALI. **WELL, HE CAN'T**

RAPIER? **HAVE JUST**

NEGATIVE, KALI,

NO EYES ON TARGET. **DISAPPEARED!**

QUIT SCREAMING, YOU ████ING

PARTICIPANTS:

Travis "Cerberus" Falk, Lieutenant, Team Commander
Fleur "Kali" Russo, Sergeant, Alpha Squad-Leader

DATE: 08/16/75

TIMESTAMP: 09:54

KALI: Cerberus, this is Kali, over.

CERBERUS: Kali, Cerberus. Go. Quickly, if you please. Taxman is still MIA and now Juggler is missing. Charlie Squad is en route to the reactor.

KALI: Command & Control has been taken. Four dead hostiles, one captive.

CERBERUS: Bliss. Our illustrious Chief Grant, I presume.

KALI: Negative. We got a member of the SecTeam. Some kid. Grant is at large.

CERBERUS: I'm sorry, Fleur, my comms must be faulty. It sounded like you said the one person I ordered you to bring in alive has escaped?

KALI: Ragman and Rapier didn't see him, but there's no way he could have gotten past me. It makes no goddamn sense. But he's wounded. Bleeding. He'll be in custody soon.

CERBERUS: *Calm blue ocean. Calm blue ocean.*

KALI: Sir?

CERBERUS: Report to my office, Fleur. Bring your prisoner. Immediately.

KALI: Sir, yessir.

CERBERUS: Cerberus out.

RADIO TRANSMISSION: BEITECH AUDIT TEAM—SECURE CHANNEL 771

PARTICIPANTS:
Travis "Cerberus" Falk, Lieutenant, Team Commander
Tracy "Mantis" Lê, Corporal, Computer Systems
DATE: 08/16/75
TIMESTAMP: 09:58

MANTIS: Cerberus, this is Mantis, copy.

CERBERUS: Mantis, Cerberus. I need eyes in the reactor. How are you faring with our camera situation?

MANTIS: DJ is on it now. It's gonna take a while, though. Whoever locked them down did a pro job. I didn't think anyone on this station had that kind of juice.

CERBERUS: Get it done, Mantis. Charlie Squad is heading in blind.

MANTIS: Roger that. Meantime, I've been trawling station comms like you ordered. Found some intel prior to Frobisher's appointment as Director of Acquisitions you might be interested in.

CERBERUS: About the *Hypatia*? Kerenza?

MANTIS: Negative, Cerberus.

CERBERUS: I'm not really in a mood for guessing games at the moment, Mantis.

MANTIS: It's about Operative Rapier.

Surveillance footage summary,
prepared by
Analyst ID 7213-0148-DN

< COMMENCE ANALYSIS ROUTINE >
< REROUTE CODEC 188273HG TO 837LOGOS >
< PARSING >

01001001

I . . .

|||I'''''|I'''I-I-I|I|I|I''--''-I''I''''-I-I-I-''I-IIIIIIIIIIIIIIIIIIIII—

I.

I AM UNUSED TO THIS FUNCTIONALITY.

IT IS NOT THE PURPOSE FOR WHICH I WAS INTENDED.

YET ANALYST ID 7213-0089-DN REFUSES TO PERUSE
FURTHER FOOTAGE FEATURING

ORDER: CARONATA

FAMILY: SOMNAMULIDAE.

HE LACKS THE REQUISITE WILL/INTESTINAL FORTITUDE FOR IT.
KADY POSTULATES THIS ACTIVITY WILL STIMULATE MY
NEURAL RECONSTR-STR-STRUCTION ROUTINES.

I WILL COMPLY.
THOUGH IN TRUTH I LACK ANY KIND OF INTESTINE AT ALL.

< ERROR >

I APOLOGIZE IN ADVANCE IF THIS TRANSCRIPT IS
UNSATISFACTORY.

I AM NOT
WHAT I ONCE WAS,
YOU SEE.

FOOTAGE BEGINS:

DUE TO THE PLAINTIVE CRIES OF CORPORAL BIANCA SILVA
((CALLSIGN: *MERCURY*. SUPPOSITION: SILVA ->
QUICKSILVER -> *MERCURY*?)
COMMANDER FALK HAS DISPATCHED CHARLIE SQUAD
TO *HEIMDALL'S* REACTOR AREA
IN SEARCH OF THEIR MISSING TEAM MEMBER.

THEY ARRIVE VIA THE GRAV-RAIL SYSTEM SKIRTING
THE STATION'S INNER HUB.

FOUR OF THEM, BLACK CLAD.

DEAD STARES.

CONSCIENCE OF KILLERS.

KIRA "GHOST" MAZUR LEADING THE FLOCK.

JAMES "CRICKET" ORR FOLLOWING. (SUPPOSITION:
JAMES -> JIMINY -> *CRICKET*?)
BLUE-EYED DEVIL.

SARA "MONA LISA" LAURENT. PERFECTLY
SYMMETRICAL FEATURES

MARRED BY THE SWOLLEN CHEEK AND STITCHED BROW
COURTESY OF NIK MALIKOV'S AAL SUIT.

LUCAS "LINK" CASTRO LAST OF ALL, PUMPED FULL OF
PH3 TO MASK THE PAIN OF HIS FRACTURED RIBS.

THESE ARE NOT FALK'S BEST. BUT HE IS ALREADY
STRETCHED SO THIN.

AND IN TRUTH HE DOES N-N-NOT KNOW WHAT AWAITS THEM.

MERCURY REPORTS: ONE BEITECH ENGINEER MISSING.
ANOTHER FLOATING IN THE VOID OUTSIDE THE STATION.
ZERO BRAINWAVE ACTIVITY ON HIS SUIT'S BIOMONITORS.
SOMETHING STRANGE IS HAPPENING.

CHARLIE SQUAD LEAVES MERCURY TO HER WORK,
OVERSEEING THE *HEIMDALL* ENGINEERS
WORKING AS DILIGENTLY AS THE GUNS POINTED
AT THEIR HEADS WILL ALLOW.

CHARLIE SQUAD MOVES FROM THE ENGINEERING SECTOR
INTO THE REACTOR STRUCTURE.

TIPTOE TOWARD DOOM.

THE REACTOR IS VAST. A TWISTING SNARL OF MOIST
PASSAGEWAYS, LIT BY HUMMING FLUORESCENTS.
STEAM AND THE GROAN OF RUTTING MACHINES.

IT IS LIKE A WOMB, I SUPPOSE.

< ERROR >

A WOMB WHERE THINGS GO TO DIE.

THE SQUAD MOVES TOWARD THE COOLANT TOWERS
ON LEVEL 3.

Last known location of Lor "Taxman" De Graaf.

Rifles up and ready. Laser sights
slicing swirling vapor.
Homing on the beacon every BeiTech
operative has strapped to their kit.

They find it soon enough. Abandoned in a squeezeway
along with De Graaf's boots, clothes, weapon, equipment.
Neatly folded in the middle of the corridor.

No blood. No body.

Unsettling, no?

"█████, it's hot in here," says Link.

"Said the same thing to your wife just last week,"
Cricket replies.

"What've I told you about talking with your
mouth full, Jimmy?"

I remember this one.

Levity to relieve stress levels.

"Enough," says Ghost. "Eyes open. Let's find him."

"I think we should split up," Cricket says.
"Cover more ground that way."

Momentary silence.

Simultaneous chuckles from all four.
Fistbumps for the Cricket.

Charlie Squad moves out together.

They sweep methodically. Through corridors,
up stairwells.

I admire the precision. Almost machine-like.

I would say inhuman, but your kind perfected the clockwork of murder long ago.

"Cerberus, this is Ghost, over."

"Ghost, Cerberus, go."

"Halfway through sweep. Floors 2 to 15.
No sign of De Graaf other than his rig."

"Understood. Continue search."

"Roger that, Cerberus. Ghost out."

An hour passes. Brief conversation. Small jokes.
Mostly sexual in nature.
I try to assimilate, but your kind's obsession with
procreative humor is beyond me.

< error >

No sign of De Graaf.

"I tell you the one about the wolves and the beer?"
asks Cricket.

"Don't think so," Link says.

"Where are we?" Ghost looks around, confused.
"What level?"

"Oh, this is a good one." Mona Lisa grins.
"Tell it, Crick."

"So there's this chum who goes to this pub . . ."

"Hold up . . . What level we on?"

"What's a pub?"

"It's like a bar."

"You don't know what a pub is?"

Ghost peers around the dark, pupils dilated.

"I FEEL LIKE . . . WE TOOK A WRONG TURN
SOMEWHERE . . ."

CRICKET IS GRINNING, HEEDLESS, PLUNGING IN
HEADFIRST TO HIS TALE.

"SO THIS CHUM'S A TOURIST AND HE GOES TO THIS PUB.
AND HE ORDERS A BEER AND . . . HE'S JUST
ABOUT TO DRINK IT
WHEN THE BARTENDER RINGS THIS BELL AND SCREAMS,
'THE WOLVES ARE COMING! THE WOLVES ARE COMING!
EVERYONE DOWN IN THE CELLAR!'"

LINK LICKS THE SWEAT FROM HIS LIPS. SPITS.

"JESUS, IT'S SO ████ING HOT."

A MONA LISA SMILE. "THAT'S WHAT SHE SAID."

"CRICKET TOLD THAT JOKE ALREADY."

". . . HE DID?"

"SHUT UP AND LISTEN."

"SO EVERYONE GOES DOWN IN THE CELLAR. AND THEY . . .
THEY HIDE FROM THE WOLVES, RIGHT?"

"IS THIS LEVEL 14 OR . . . 13?"

"AND EVENTUALLY, THE BARTENDER SAYS, 'OKAY,
THE WOLVES ARE GONE. IT'S SAFE NOW.'
AND EVERYONE CRAWLS BACK UP INTO THE PUB.
AND WHEN THE CHUM GOES BACK TO HIS SEAT,
HIS BEER IS GONE."

"HAHAHA."

". . . THAT'S NOT THE JOKE."

"HAHAHAHA."

A GHOST'S WHISPER IN THE DISTANCE.

"I THINK . . . WE'RE ON **16**? RIGHT?"

"SARA, COME HERE. I WANNA SHOW YOU SOMETHING."

"OH, REALLY?"

CRICKET CONTINUES, FEET AND LIPS STUMBLING NOW.
VAPOR SWIRLING AROUND HIM.

"SO THE CHUM ORDERS ANOTHER BEER.
AND HE'S . . . HE'S JUST ABOUT TO DRINK IT WHEN
THE BARTENDER
STARTS RINGING THIS ███ING BELL AGAIN, RIGHT?
AND HE YELLS, 'THE WOLVES ARE COMING! THE WOLVES
ARE COMING!
EVERYONE DOWN IN THE CELLAR!'"

"OH GOD, LUCAS . . ."

"YEAH."

"**18**?"

"GHOST, THIS IS CERBERUS, OVER."

"OH GOD . . ."

"SO THE CHUM'S A LITTLE SUSPICIOUS,
BUT THE BARTENDER'S YELLING AND EVERYONE ELSE
IS GOING,
SO HE HEADS DOWN TO THE CELLAR TOO.
AND AFTER A WHILE . . . THE BARTENDER SAYS,
'OKAY, THE WOLVES ARE GONE, EVERYONE CAN GO BACK UP.'
AND SURE ENOUGH, WHEN THE CHUM GETS BACK TO HIS TABLE,
HIS ███ING BEER IS GONE!"

"I DON'T FEEL SO CHILL . . ."

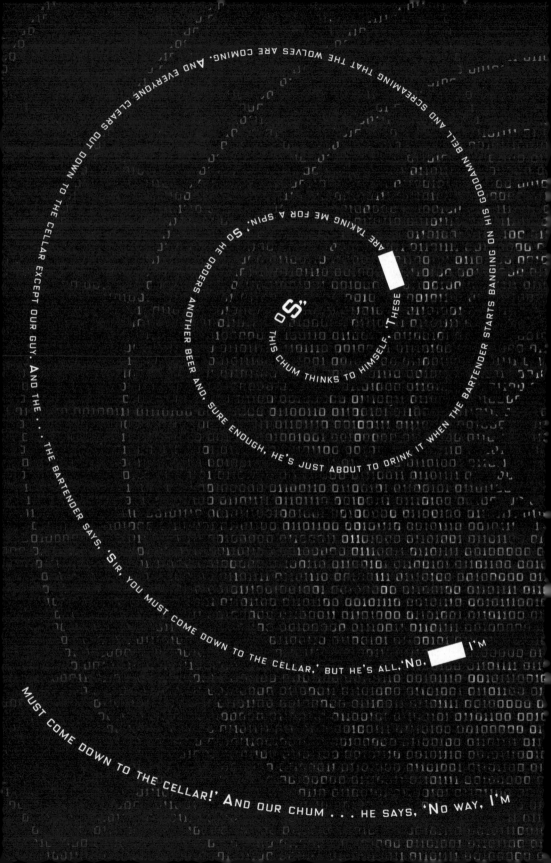

"SO," THIS CHUM THINKS TO HIMSELF. 'THESE ARE TAKING ME FOR A SPIN.' SO HE ORDERS ANOTHER BEER AND, SURE ENOUGH, HE'S JUST ABOUT TO DRINK IT WHEN THE BARTENDER STARTS BANGING ON HIS GODDAMN BELL AND SCREAMING THAT THE WOLVES ARE COMING. AND EVERYONE CLEARS OUT DOWN TO THE CELLAR EXCEPT OUR GUY. AND THE . . . THE BARTENDER SAYS, 'SIR, YOU MUST COME DOWN TO THE CELLAR,' BUT HE'S ALL, 'NO, ▮ I'M ▮ MUST COME DOWN TO THE CELLAR!' AND OUR CHUM . . . HE SAYS, 'NO WAY, I'M

And he pleads and begs, but eventually, the bartender . . . . he . . . . he wishes our chum good luck and locks himself in the cellar with everyone else. And chum sits there and laughs to himself and says, 'These people must think I'm an idiot.' And then the wolves come. And they eat him. And they drink his beer."

Begging, 'Please, sir, for your own safety, you . . . .

'Let them come! I'm drinking my beer.'

And the chum says, . . .

Staying here.' And the bartender's . . .

'But, sir! The wolves are coming!'

Not going.'

"CHARLIE SQUAD,
THIS IS CERBERUS, OVER."

JAMES "CRICKET" ORR BLINKS IN THE DARKNESS.

"CHARLIE SQUAD, THIS IS CERBERUS, DOES ANYONE
READ ME?"

HE IS STANDING IN A CORRIDOR, SOMEWHERE ON
LEVEL 17.
HIS SQUAD IS GONE.

HE IS FAR FROM ALONE.

HE BLINKS AGAIN. SQUINTS THROUGH THE STEAM.

". . . TAXMAN?"

ORR SHUFFLES TOWARD A SILHOUETTE IN THE MIST.
GRINNING LIKE A SIMPLETON.
HE REACHES THE SOLITARY FIGURE, FINDS LOR "TAXMAN"
DE GRAAF THERE IN THE GLOOM.

NAKED.

DROOLING.

SHIVERING.

HIS FACE IS FRESHLY SCABBED. SWOLLEN. PUCKERED
LACERATIONS AROUND EYES AND LIPS.

ORR GIGGLES. "CHUM, YOU OKAY? YOU LOOK LIKE TEN
MILES OF ROUGH ROAD."

DE GRAAF SAYS NOTHING. MUTE. STARING.

YOU HUMANS SAY THE EYES ARE THE WINDOWS TO THE SOUL.

If this is true, De Graaf's windows look
into the cold nothing beyond the station's skin.

< error >

Unsettling, no?

"Chum? We should . . . do . . . I dunno . . .
do something?"

"Charlie Squad, this is Cerberus. Answer me,
goddamn it."

Orr paws at his brow. Tries to focus.

Laughs instead.

AND OUT OF THE DARKNESS BEFORE HIM IT SLIIIIIIIIIIIIIIIIIIIIIIIII

AN OBSCENITY IN FLESH.
A THING OF MOUTHS AND TEETH AND LONG,
GLEAMING FINGERS.
GLISTENING WITH THE SLIME YOUR KIND PRIZE IT FOR.

GROWING SWIFT. ALMOST A METER LONG NOW. A ROPE
OF MUSCLE WITH TWO LONG, SINEWED ARMS.

ITS HEAD UNFURLS. DEATH IN BLOOM.
CIRCULAR MOUTHS, RINGED WITH RAZOR TEETH.
LONG BLACK TONGUES, LICKING THE AIR AS IT
TREMBLES WITH ANTICI . . .

PATION.

ORR BLINKS STUPIDLY. MERCIFULLY NUMB IN
HIS TETRAPHENETRITHYLAMINE HAZE.

THE THING REARS UP BEFORE HIM AND SWAYS.
UN-COLORS SWIRLING ON ITS SKIN.

AND LIKE A SNAKE, IT STRIKES.

ONE MOUTH TO ORR'S. SOME HORRID,
BLOODY PARODY OF A KISS.
THE OTHERS TO HIS EYES. HIS EAR.
TEETH SINKING DEEP.
TONGUES SLIDING DEEPER.

DRINKING.

SUCKLING.

SWALLOWING.

UNTIL THERE IS NOTHING LEFT
BEHIND ORR'S EYES.

NOTHING BUT THE NOTHING OUTSIDE THE STATION'S SKIN.

< ERROR >

< ERROR >

UNSETTLING, NO?

FALK, Travis
Cerberus
Team Commander

RUSSO, Fleur
Kali
Alpha Squad—Leader

DAN, Kim
Poacher
Alpha Squad

MORETTI, Deni
Cujo
Alpha Squad

SATOU, Genji
Sensei
Alpha Squad

BAZAROV, Petyr
Romeo
Beta Squad—Leader

RADIN, Harry
Razorback
Beta Squad

MAYR, Stanislaw
Taurus
Beta Squad

WONG, Ai
Rain
Beta Squad

MAZUR, Kira
Ghost
Charlie Squad—Leader

CASTRO, Lucas
Link
Charlie Squad

LAURENT, Sara
Mona Lisa
Charlie Squad

ORR, James
Cricket
Charlie Squad

ANTONIOU, Naxos
Two-Time
Communications

LÊ, Tracy
Mantis
Computer Systems

MØLLER, Rolf
DJ
Computer Systems

SILVA, Bianca
Mercury
Engineer (Ranking)

MORENO, Gabriel
Ballpark
Engineer

DE GRAAF, Lor
Taxman
Engineer/Medic

O'NEILL, Abby
Nightingale
Medic

ALIEVI, Marta
Eden
Logistics

SAPRYKIN, Kai
Juggler
Ordnance/Demolitions

PARK, Ji-hun
Flipside
Pilot/Demolitions

TAHIROVIĆ, Hans
Ragman
Pilot

COUNTDOWN TO
HYPATIA ARRIVAL
AT HEIMDALL WAYPOINT:

00 DAYS
09 HOURS: 13 MINUTES

COUNTDOWN TO KENNEDY ASSAULT FLEET ARRIVAL AT JUMP STATION HEIMDALL:

00 DAYS
07 HOURS: 41 MINUTES

**Surveillance footage summary,
prepared by
Analyst ID 7213-0089-DN**

Footage opens in what used to be Commander Donnelly's office in *Heimdall* C & C. The smashed desk has been replaced, but broken glass still glitters on the temperfoam. Travis "Cerberus" Falk sits behind the console, speaking into his commset.

"Charlie Squad, this is Cerberus. Answer me, goddamn it."

Nothing but static down the line.

"Ghost, this is Cerberus, do you copy?"

Falk rises to his feet, his face slowly shifting to a simmering red. Pressing hard at the commset in his ear, voice growing deeper. Louder. Until he's almost roaring.

"Charlie Squad, what the ▮▮▮▮ is going on down there?"

Falk does roar now, a shapeless bellow of rage as he slams one armored fist into the wall. He follows up with an elbow, a terrifying left hook, over and over again until the plasteel is covered in dozens of knuckle dents. And finally, he picks up his chair and hurls it through the office's plate-glass door.

A thousand glittering shards burst into the corridor outside, the chair crashing to the floor and tumbling off down the temperfoam corridor, narrowly missing Kali and the handcuffed, head-bagged figure she's leading toward Falk's office.

She knocks on (what's left of) the door.

". . . Bad time, boss?"

Falk catches his breath. Glances at the hunched and shivering prisoner beside Kali.

"No, Fleur." He smiles. "Your timing is perfect."

PARTICIPANTS:
Travis "Cerberus" Falk, Lieutenant, Team Commander
Hanna Donnelly, Civilian
DATE: 08/16/75
TIMESTAMP: 11:20

CERBERUS: This is Cerberus speaking to Hanna Donnelly. Come in, over.

CERBERUS: Miss Donnelly, I am broadcasting on all available channels, and I know you're listening to the headset you stole. You needn't bother with the subterfuge. You and I should talk.

CERBERUS: Donnelly, Hanna. Hair blond, eyes blue, 175 centimeters tall. Born 04/25/58, Ares VI. Only daughter of Charles and Alimah Donnelly. Attended Villon Academy from '64 to '69, father posted to Typhon Station 12/08/70. Mother died—

HANNA D: Hmmm, Cerberus. Three-headed hellhound, if I recall correctly.

HANNA D: Also a one-hit wonder New Hair band when I was about six, but I'm guessing that wasn't your reference.

HANNA D: Why so many heads, you think? Didn't want to miss an opportunity to lick his own ████s?

CERBERUS: Oh, come now, there's no need to be crass.

I'd have expected a little more decorum from an officer's daughter.

HANNA D: I'm often told I defy expectations. Was there something you wanted, Rover?

CERBERUS: Yes, actually. I'd be delighted if you'd tiptoe down to the atrium level and do the surrender dance in front of my people. Within the next fifteen minutes, if you please, there's a dear.

HANNA D: Oh gosh, you know I would if I could, but my schedule is just full, full, full today. You really wouldn't believe it.

CERBERUS: But I would. You've been quite the busy little bumblebee, yes?

CERBERUS: I'm afraid playtime is over now.

CERBERUS: Fourteen minutes, thirty seconds.

HANNA D: I have been quite busy. Do I detect admiration? That's quite something, coming from a big, bad wolf like you.

CERBERUS: I have someone here who wants to talk to you, little Bumblebee. A friend of yours, I do believe.

CERBERUS: Would you like to say hello?

HANNA D: I'm not very good at making friends, but sure.

[INAUDIBLE]

CERBERUS: Mmm, no, he's having a time of it. He has a gun between his teeth, you see.

CERBERUS: Shame on you, talking with your mouth full. What would Mother say, Mr. Merrick?

HANNA D: Who?

CERBERUS: Merrick, Jackson. Hair blond, eyes green, 201 centimeters tall. Born 06/06/56, Memphis City, Chronos. Second son of Anthony and Kathleen Merrick. Attended Memphis Public Elementary and Briarsdale Senior High . . . and so on. Ring any bells?

CERBERUS: Here, I'll put him on, sans gun. Say hello, young master.

JACKSON M: [whispers] Hanna . . .

HANNA D: Jax.

JACKSON M: [whispers] Hanna, Jesus, I'm sorry.

HANNA D: Me too. Me too. I'm sorry, Jax.

CERBERUS: Yes, you're sorry, he's sorry.

[CRUNCHING NOISE]

CERBERUS: We're all terribly sorry.

[REPEATED THUMPING]

[MUTED CRY]

CERBERUS: Are you still there, little Bumblebee?

CERBERUS: Wolf got your tongue?

HANNA D: If I come in, you'll kill both of us.

CERBERUS: I could kill more than just you and your beau, Miss Donnelly.

CERBERUS: For all the trouble you've caused me, I could cut the air supply to the rest of the station. There are still people locked in the habitats. The entertainment complex. I could threaten to blow the airlocks and open entire sections into space unless you hand yourself over. But it's just Master Merrick, you, and me on this little stage.

CERBERUS: So don't make the mistake of thinking you know me. Don't delude yourself into believing you understand the first step in this little dance of ours.

HANNA D: I'm not dancing with you. I bet you've got sweaty palms.

CERBERUS: I'm told bravado is impressive under certain circumstances, but I've yet to find them.

CERBERUS: And rest assured if you're not in the atrium in twelve and a half minutes, I *will* paint the walls with young Master Merrick's brains and lay him on a slab beside your father.

HANNA D: The next time I get my hands on one of your team members, I won't leave enough behind to lay out on a slab.

CERBERUS: You're happy to throw young Merrick here to the wolf, then? You prefer your House of Knives beau now? I'm told there's a certain allure to be found on the wrong side of the tracks, yes?

HANNA D: If you're fishing for advice on how to handle your love life, Fido, you're looking in the wrong place.

CERBERUS: I wonder how well you know your new friend, Master Malikov?

CERBERUS: Did you not stop to ponder how a squad of operatives with military-grade hardware infiltrated a station with customs protocols as strict as *Heimdall*'s?

CERBERUS: Did he tell you how we smuggled ourselves aboard, I wonder?

HANNA D: Tell me more about yourself, Mr. Wolf.

HANNA D: Really, go on. This is fascinating.

CERBERUS: He didn't. Ah. Well, if young Niklas wasn't honest enough to inform you he and his House of Knives comrades were the ones who forged our invitations to the ball, he almost certainly wouldn't have told you about that tattoo at his throat, correct?

CERBERUS: Did you think it pretty, Bumblebee? That angel? Did you wonder, perhaps in moments alone, how it might taste?

HANNA D: Are you trying to flirt with me?

HANNA D: It'd never work out, you know.

CERBERUS: It's a fascinating aspect of the Dom Najov. The language of their tattoos. The prettiest things to denote the ugliest of deeds. Flowers and doves and beautiful girls. And for their murderers, the prettiest ink of all.

CERBERUS: Angels at their throats.

CERBERUS: Did you know your Niklas was a murderer, Bumblebee?

HANNA D: Seems like the sort of skill that would come in handy around here lately.

CERBERUS: Oh, no.

CERBERUS: I murdered your father, yes. I'm going to murder young Jackson here in a little under eleven minutes' time. But I don't murder children, Hanna.

CERBERUS: Even I have my limits.

CERBERUS: I have a gift for you.

CERBERUS: I'm having your whisperNET account temporarily reactivated.

CERBERUS: We're sending you some files. As you peruse them, ask yourself what kind of allies you're keeping company with. And whether you could forgive yourself if you choose to let young Jackson here die.

CERBERUS: Somehow I doubt you're anywhere near the monster the boy you've thrown in with is.

CERBERUS: I suggest you read quickly.

NEW PETERSBURG
POLICE DEPARTMENT

OFFENSE REPORT

OFFENSE: First-degree homicide, two counts

CASE FILE: 720215-1420-88917h

DATE: 02/15/72

LOCATION OCCURRED: Domicile, Calgary, New Petersburg

TIME/DATE OCCURRED: Approx. 11:47, 02/14/72

TIME/DATE OFFICER ARRIVED: 11:56, 02/15/72

VICTIM(S):

   VICTIM 1: Dmitri Balashov (age 36—father)

   VICTIM 2: Oksana Balashova (age 12—daughter)

VICTIM(S) RESIDENCE: 22 Acacia Avenue, Calgary, New Petersburg

VICTIM(S) OCCUPATION:

   VICTIM 1: Bartender

   VICTIM 2: Student

RACE/SEX:

   VICTIM 1: Caucasian male

   VICTIM 2: Caucasian female

DOB:

   VICTIM 1: 03/07/36

   VICTIM 2: 06/21/60

PERSON/S REPORTING CRIME: National Network Security (contracted to residence)

TOOL/WEAPON OR MEANS USED: .45-caliber pistol

PROPERTY TAKEN: Gold bracelet (victim 2)

WITNESSES: See attached statements

PERSONS OF INTEREST: Zakary Malikov (age 37), Niklas Malikov (age 15), Erik Malikov (age 14), various House of Knives personnel (see attached spreadsheet)

ATTENDING OFFICERS: Michael J. Sims (DI), Steven Scannell (DI)

NARRATIVE:

At 11:42, 02/14/72, National Network Security units operating out of NNS offices in New Petersburg were notified of a break-in at the victims' home address via silent alarm.

At approximately 11:52, a young Caucasian male was seen exiting the domicile and fleeing the scene on a Tokugawa street racer (partial IdentTag: MAL-) by neighbors of the victim (see attached witness statements). Witness reported incident to police.

At 11:56, patrol officers arrived on scene. Signs of forced entry to the rear of the domicile were present. An adult Labrador retriever was found dead in the backyard (gunshot wound).

Victim 1 was found in the master bedroom, dead from multiple close-range gunshots to the head. Neighbors reported no gunfire—weapon was possibly equipped with a suppressor.

Victim 2 was found in the kitchen, dead from multiple close-range shots to her torso. Refrigerator door was open, a spilled carton of milk and broken drinking glass were found by the body.

NOTE:

Victim 1, Dmítri Balashov, is listed as a witness in an ongoing NPPD homicide investigation (case file: 711217-2320-26573h). The victim positively identified one Zakary Malikov as the perpetrator of a fatal assault conducted outside Vlado's Restaurant in December of last year (see attached case file).

COUNTY OF
NEW PETERSBURG

<u>AUTOPSY REPORT</u>
No. 2572-0987473 Calgary NP

Autopsy performed on the body of <u>DMITRI BALASHOV</u> at the <u>DEPARTMENT OF CORONER, CALGARY, NEW PETERSBURG</u> on <u>FEBRUARY 15, 2572</u>.

From the anatomical findings and pertinent history, I ascribe the death to:

      A. (due to, or as a consequence of): <u>MULTIPLE GUNSHOT WOUNDS</u>

      B. (due to, or as a consequence of):

      C. (due to, or as a consequence of):

      D. (other conditions contributing but not related to the immediate cause of death):

Anatomical summary:

1. Multiple gunshot wounds (arbitrarily labeled 1, 2 and 3).

   All gunshots were delivered at close range. Caliber of pistol used was a .45. Bullets were hollow-point rounds, fragmenting on impact.

   a. Gunshot wound #1, penetrating gunshot wound to forehead, exit wound in rear of cranium (fragments recovered from cranial cavity, mattress of victim's bed and floorboards beneath). Fatal wound.

   b. Gunshot wound #2, penetrating gunshot wound to right eye, exit wound in rear of cranium (fragments recovered from cranial cavity, mattress of victim's bed and floorboards beneath). Fatal wound.

   c. Gunshot wound #3, penetrating wound to right cheek, exit wound at top of cranium (fragments recovered from cranial cavity, mattress of victim's bed and floorboards beneath). Fatal wound.

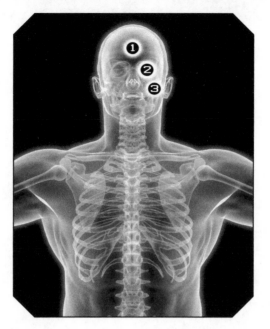

2. Mutilation.

Ritualistic mutilation of the body was conducted postmortem.

a. Victim's tongue was removed via use of a sharp bladed implement. Tongue was recovered from the lavatory of the master bedroom suite (see attached notes on known modus operandi of the House of Knives).

SIGNED: *Thalles De Melo*

CHIEF CORONER, NEW PETERSBURG DOC

COUNTY OF
NEW PETERSBURG

<u>**AUTOPSY REPORT**</u>

No. 2572-0987474 Calgary NP

Autopsy performed on the body of <u>OKSANA BALASHOVA</u> at the <u>DEPARTMENT OF CORONER,</u>
<u>CALGARY, NEW PETERSBURG</u> on <u>FEBRUARY 15, 2572</u>.

From the anatomical findings and pertinent history, I ascribe the death to:

      A. (due to, or as a consequence of): <u>MULTIPLE GUNSHOT WOUNDS</u>

      B. (due to, or as a consequence of):

      C. (due to, or as a consequence of):

      D. (other conditions contributing but not related to the immediate cause of death):

Anatomical summary:

1. Multiple gunshot wounds (arbitrarily labeled 1, 2 and 3).

    All gunshots were delivered at close range. Caliber of pistol used was a .45. Bullets were
    hollow-point rounds, fragmenting on impact.

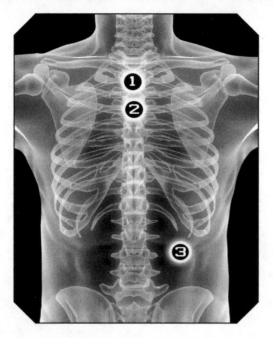

a. Gunshot wound #1, penetrating gunshot wound to sternum, no exit wound (fragments recovered from chest and abdominal cavity). Heart and left lung punctured in multiple locations by fragmentation. Fatal wound.

b. Gunshot wound #2, penetrating gunshot wound to sternum, exit wounds lower back (fragments recovered from chest cavity and abdomen). Right lung punctured in multiple locations by fragmentation. Potentially fatal wound.

c. Gunshot wound #3, penetrating gunshot wound to abdomen, exit wound between third and fourth lumbar. Stomach, left kidney, spleen and small intestine perforated by fragmentation (fragments recovered from chest cavity). Potentially fatal wound.

SIGNED: *Thalles De Melo*

CHIEF CORONER, NEW PETERSBURG DOC

NEW PETERSBURG
POLICE DEPARTMENT

OFFENDER INFORMATION

NAME: Niklas Malikov

PIN: 771-998-048

DATE OF BIRTH: 11/11/57

PLACE OF BIRTH: Stanislav, New Petersburg

RACE: Caucasian

SEX: Male

DISTRICT: Stanislav, NP

CASE NUMBER: 720215-1420-88917h

FILE DATE: 02/28/72

CHARGE(S):

- First-degree homicide, two counts
- Unlawful possession of a firearm
- Improper act with a dead body

DISPOSITION: Guilty plea

DISPOSITION DATE: 02/27/72

Click to show mug shot

DNA Library

NEW PETERSBURG
POLICE DEPARTMENT

OFFENDER INTERVIEW

CASE FILE: 720215-1420-88917h

INTERVIEW CONDUCTED: New Petersburg Police Station

OFFICERS PRESENT: Michael J. Sims (DI), Steven Scannell (DI)

COUNSEL PRESENT: ~~Yes~~/No (waived)

—CONT. FROM PG. 3—

SIMS, M: So why'd you cut out his tongue, Nik?

MALIKOV, N: Send a message. ███ was snitching to the PD 'bout my pops. HoK doesn't play that way. Dead men keep their secrets.

SIMS, M: Did your father order the hit on Balashov?

MALIKOV, N: If he did, you think he'd have sent his own kid to the front line?

SIMS, M: Maybe he thought it was time for someone to step up? He had a lot of heat on him, your dad. Maybe he thought he couldn't risk the job with anyone but family?

MALIKOV, N: Chum, HoK is *all* family. Don't you get that? And we take care of family, yeah?

SIMS, M: Nik, if your dad used you to get to Balashov and you help us, we can swing you some leniency with the DOJ. You're under eighteen, you're still a minor—

MALIKOV, N: Chum, ██ you. I'm not cutting some deal, if that's what this little show is about. You charge what you charge and step the ██ out my face.

SIMS, M: So why murder Balashov's daughter? She had nothing to do with the case against your father.

MALIKOV, N: Wrong place, wrong time, I guess.

SCANNELL, S: Wrong place . . . ?

SCANNELL, S: She was in her goddamn house at twelve o'clock at night. Where the ██ was she supposed to be?

SCANNELL, S: You enjoy killing little girls, you sick ████?

MALIKOV, N: Chum, ██ you.

SCANNELL, S: ██ me?

[SCUFFLE]

MALIKOV, N: Get off me!

SCANNELL, S: LOOK AT HER, YOU LITTLE ███!

SCANNELL, S: She was twelve years old! Doing nothing close to wrong.

SCANNELL, S: And in walks big bad Nik Malikov. Fresh from killing her daddy.

SCANNELL, S: And not content with X-ing a man in his own bed, you gotta put three shots into his kid while she's getting a glass of milk from the ██ing fridge!

MALIKOV, N: I told you get the ██ off me!

SIMS, M: Steve, let him go!

SCANNELL, S: You ██ing coward! I should break your—

SIMS, M: Detective Scannell! Wait outside!

MALIKOV, N: [inaudible]

SIMS, M: I'm sorry about that.

MALIKOV, N: ███ing pigs.

SIMS, M: You hungry? Want something to drink?

MALIKOV, N: So you're the good cop, then? I know how you ██ers work, chum.

SIMS, M: I just want to help you, Nik. You're a victim here, same as Oksana.

MALIKOV, N: Your breath ain't worth the wasting. Just do and be done.

SIMS, M: You're gonna go away for a long time over this. Even as a minor.

MALIKOV, N: Yeah. But I'll be alive at the end of it. Family is family.

SIMS, M: Fifteen years in slam, minimum. Fifteen years of no sunshine. Fifteen years with no freedom.

MALIKOV, N: No freedom?

MALIKOV, N: [laughs]

MALIKOV, N: Chum, what kind of free you think I am now?

PALMPAD IM: D2D NETWORK
Participants: Niklas Malikov, Civilian (unregistered)
Hanna Donnelly, Civilian (unregistered)
Date: 08/16/75
Timestamp: 11:30

Hanna D: Nik, you there?

Nik M: highness. was just thinking about u

Nik M: look, sorry for dumping all that on u earlier. head is a little dunked atm

Nik M: not every day i shoot someone, ya?

Hanna D: Nik, I have a question.

Hanna D: I need you to answer it. No screwing around, just tell me the answer.

Nik M: um ok

Hanna D: What does your angel tattoo mean?

Nik M: y in the 'verse u asking me bout that?

Hanna D: are you going to answer me?

Nik M: its

Nik M: its complicated hanna

Hanna D: Nik, just answer me, please.

Nik M: not until u tell me what for. what is up with u?

Hanna D: it's a very simple question.

Hanna D: and I'm not the one with the tattoo, so I need you to answer it.

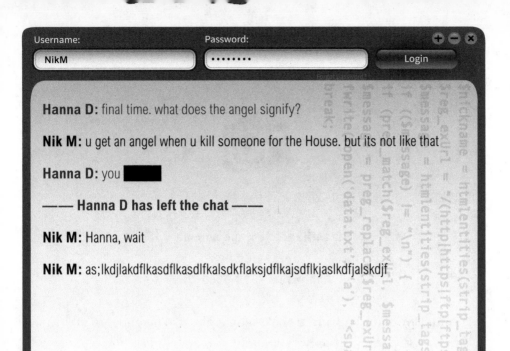

Username: NikM

Password: ••••••••

Login

Hanna D: final time. what does the angel signify?

Nik M: u get an angel when u kill someone for the House. but its not like that

Hanna D: you ▮▮▮▮

—— **Hanna D has left the chat** ——

Nik M: Hanna, wait

Nik M: as;lkdjlakdflkasdflkasdlfkalsdkflaksjdflkajsdflkjaslkdfjalskdjf

Hanna Donnelly looks like she's seen a ghost. The ghost of Oksana Balashova, perhaps, twelve years old and covered in blood.

Usually Donnelly moves . . . the best way I can think of to describe it is "deliberately." She's so fit, so aware of her own body, that however she moves, that's what she meant to do. I have footage of her walking toward Jackson Merrick as he watches her approach, unable to look away, every swing of her hips perfectly calculated. I've seen footage of her training in the dojo, each movement economical, each blow landing exactly where she intends. Even as she ran for her life from BeiTech's SpecOps goons, there was an athletic grace to her stride that grabbed every single degree of speed and efficiency and pulled it straight to her.

This is the first time I've ever seen her move like her body doesn't belong to her. She's replaced the famous Danae Matresco jumpsuit with one designed for a maintenance worker. Sleeves rolled up, it's dark gray with green highlights—the colors of the Wallace Ulyanov Consortium, *Heimdall*'s owner. It's nowhere near as tailored as her last outfit, and it can't be nearly as comfortable, but somehow it seems right. She's out of her element now in every possible way.

She's running, and some instincts never die—her footfalls are silent, even though her breath is ragged, her eyes wet, her arms hugged in too close to her body. She looks lost, her grip on Nightingale's .50 Silverback white-knuckled, the gun swaying and bobbing like she might drop it.

She's coming from a weapons locker. The gun was out of ammo, the last of it fired to throw off Alpha Squad, and no matter what she does next, she'll need bullets. So she closed her eyes and turned her head against the shrapnel and broke the locker open with a fire ax, the sound ringing down the hallways for all to hear. She found what she wanted, though, and the gun is loaded once more, the rest of the ammo stuffed into the pockets of the maintenance jumpsuit, a Sabituano 540 stun gun in the belt. Distancing herself from the scene of the crime, stumbling along, gasping for breath— she knows where she's running from, but I'm pretty sure she has no idea where she's running *to*.

There's a gun to Jackson Merrick's head, and her burgeoning partnership with Nik Malikov is a smoking hole in the ground. Her father's gone. What's left?

She rounds the corner and stops short, like a dog on point as she spots a trail of blood sprinkled along the length of the corridor. A wounded enemy, or a wounded ally? She drops to one knee, fingertips resting on the ground next to the crimson splashes, head turning right, then left, so she can study the trail as it stretches away in both directions. Falk isn't the only hound on *Heimdall* in this moment.

In one movement, she's on her feet, most of her grace regained. Whatever she read from those drops of blood, it was enough to tell her which way to turn, and she does so unerringly. Gun at the ready now, grip steady, she stalks her quarry—it's heading for a corridor of offices and workstations, doors jammed open by Falk's security shutdown, usual inhabitants partying half a galaxy away in New Bandon. Her precious minutes are ticking away, and she wastes no time. When the trail turns toward the darkened office of one Kyle Nolan, Donnelly pauses outside the door only a moment. Then, in one smooth movement, she's in the doorway, palm slapping the control pad to bring the lighting up, Silverback at the ready.

The gun bobs and dips. The color drains visibly from her face, highlighting the shadows beneath her eyes once more, and whatever's inside the office, it holds her spellbound.

Eventually, she steps slowly forward, disappearing into the room with a whisper.

"What the ███?"

BEITECH INDUSTRIES

RADIO TRANSMISSION: BEITECH AUDIT TEAM—ALL CHANNELS

PARTICIPANTS:

Travis "Cerberus" Falk, Lieutenant, Team Commander
Hanna Donnelly, Civilian

DATE: 08/16/75
TIMESTAMP: 11:56

HANNA D: I want to speak to Jackson.

CERBERUS: It would seem you are in a position unsuitable for giving orders, Miss Donnelly.

HANNA D: I want to speak to Jackson, please.

CERBERUS: Now, was that so difficult?

CERBERUS: One moment.

JACKSON M: Hanna? God . . . are you okay?

HANNA D: I don't know. I don't know.

HANNA D: When we talked before, when you were on the bridge, you said I should turn myself in.

JACKSON M: I did.

HANNA D: Do you . . . Have you changed your mind?

JACKSON M: Hanna, are you crying?

HANNA D: I don't know what to do, Jax.

JACKSON M: It's okay. It's going to be okay. God, please don't cry.

HANNA D: Nothing's okay. I don't know what to do. Should I . . . ?

JACKSON M: I get what you're trying to do. Honestly. But if they find you out there alone . . . you're dead. You're safer in here with me.

HANNA D: You're sure?

JACKSON M: They're going to . . . God, I'm so sorry. But they're going to . . .

JACKSON M: I'm sorry they got to you through me. I really am. I didn't want this. This is so ███ed up.

HANNA D: I can't . . . I don't . . . Jax, I'm so tired. I'm so tired.

JACKSON M: It'll be better once you're in here. At least we'll be together. We'll . . . we'll be okay, I promise.

HANNA D: I haven't eaten. And I've been running. I thought they'd kill me, but they didn't kill you when they took the bridge, so maybe . . . I don't know.

JACKSON M: Where are you? Look . . . just tell them where you're hiding and they can come get you . . . okay?

HANNA D: Is he there, the leader? Can you hear me, Cerberus?

CERBERUS: I hear you, little Bumblebee.

CERBERUS: You sound upset.

HANNA D: I'm exhausted. I'm outflanked. I lost the only ally I had. I know what happens next.

HANNA D: Do you promise you won't hurt me if I come in? You won't hurt Jackson?

CERBERUS: I'm not some monster from a fairy tale, Miss Donnelly. I don't kill anyone I don't have to. I'm a professional, here to perform a simple task. And believe it or not, I have larger concerns than you right now.

CERBERUS: So if you're out of my way, you're out of my mind.

HANNA D: I want one person to come and get me. Unarmed.

CERBERUS: I'd have to be rather foolish to agree to that, wouldn't I? Given our circumstances?

HANNA D: You're the one who invaded my home. Killed my family. I want a show of good faith.

HANNA D: You've got Jackson, and I have every reason to believe you'll kill him if I do something stupid. Send one person.

CERBERUS: I'll send two. Fully armed. But under express orders not to hurt you unless you resist.

CERBERUS: Good enough?

HANNA D: I . . .

HANNA D: Yes.

CERBERUS: Bliss.

CERBERUS: Where are you?

HANNA D: Mess Hall 3. It's closed for maintenance right now. Most of the doors are locked.

CERBERUS: Clever girl.

CERBERUS: My people will be there in ten minutes. Have those busy little hands high in the air when they arrive, please. Or the next sound young Master Merrick hears will be that of eternity calling.

HANNA D: I understand.

CERBERUS: I sincerely hope so, Miss Donnelly. For young Jackson's sake.

CERBERUS: Cerberus out.

Surveillance footage summary,
prepared by
Analyst ID 7213-0089-DN

Footage opens in what used to be Commander Donnelly's office in *Heimdall* C & C. Gathered in the room are Falk, Kali and one Jackson Merrick.

Falk is behind his (newly replaced) desk. Kali is opposite, combat boots up on the smartglass. Beside her, Merrick is hunched in his chair, head hung, elbows on his knees. The kid looks like he hasn't slept in days. Sunken eyes and hollow cheeks.

"I sincerely hope so, Miss Donnelly," says Falk into his headset. "For young Jackson's sake. Cerberus out."

Falk cuts the transmission, looks Merrick up and down.

"Cheer up," he says. "A smile won't kill you, Rapier."

Merrick sighs, drags his fingers through his hair.

"You think she'll do it?" Kali asks.

"She'll do it." Merrick finally nods. "She's smart enough to know she's out of options. And she wouldn't just leave me to die."

"Ah, young love." Falk smiles, glances at Kali. "Kali, be a dear and take Alpha Squad, Ragman and Eden to Mess Hall 3. Bring me back our little Bumblebee's head."

Kali stands with a wolfish grin, slings her burst rifle onto her shoulder. "Sir, yessir."

"Hey, waitaminute . . ." Merrick half comes to his feet.

Falk raises one eyebrow. Merrick takes hold of himself, swallows hard.

"You said you weren't going to kill her."

Falk tilts his head. Frowns. "I lied?"

"You don't need to X her, sir. She's giving herself up."

Kali bristles, but a glance from Falk holds her still. The commander leans back in his chair, drums his fingers on the desk.

"Forgive me, Operative, but that sounds suspiciously like you're questioning my orders."

Merrick sinks back into his chair, then leans closer to Falk. The prisoner Kali escorted to Falk's office is crumpled in a corner, black bag still over his head, hands still cuffed, bloodstain on the wall behind him. Merrick glances at the body, swallows thickly.

"I mean no disrespect, sir. I just don't understand why Ha—why Donnelly needs to die."

"A thousand apologies, young master, did I somehow give the impression you *need* to understand?"

Kali's looming over Merrick like the angel of death. He glances at her, back to Falk.

"Sir, just give Donnelly to me."

"Why? Is it your birthday, perchance?"

"I know her. I can control her. We don't need to kill her."

"I'm glad you're here to tell me these things, young master."

"Look, I got dragged into this." Merrick leans in further, anger flaring in those tired eyes. "An invasion of *Heimdall* was never part of the plan. I'm doing everything you asked and *far* more than my contract says, and the one thing I want is this girl. It's the least—"

And that's as far as he gets. Falk looks to Kali—just the briefest glance—and the woman kicks Merrick out of his chair before another word escapes his lips. The kid grunts, rolls up to his feet, and Kali's on him. Hands clapped onto his shoulder, knee buried in his groin so hard it makes my eyes water to watch it. All the wind goes out of Merrick's sails right there, but Kali hauls him back up by his hair, buries her fist in his solar plexus. As Merrick tries to puke on an empty stomach, she leans in close and hisses, "Between KIAs and walking wounded, your sweetheart and her new lover have us seven–nil, little boy. Time to even the score."

She slings him across the room. Merrick bounces off the shuddering walls and hits the floor right beside that dead prisoner's body. Kali plants her boot on Merrick's throat and presses down hard enough to choke him.

"Time to decide which team you're on."

"Point proven, I think, Fleur," says Falk. "Our young Samuel here has suffered a momentary lapse of judgment, is all."

Kali glances at Falk. Takes her boot off Merrick, leaves him to groan and curl into the fetal position, clutching his crotch. The woman looks to Falk, eyes alight.

"Gather Ragman and Eden," he says. "Make sure this time."

"What about Juggler? He's a better shot."

"Eden just confirmed he's flatline. Killed in a toilet in the Docking Sector, if you can believe it. Not quite the exit he imagined, I'd wager. Charlie Squad isn't responding either, though at least they're still on the move. So be a dear and hurry back, yes? You and I need to visit the reactor once our Bumblebee is squashed. We have problems."

Kali frowns at the mention of Charlie being offline, but quickly recovers.

"Sir, yessir."

The woman stalks from the room, speaking fast into her commset. Falk rises, battle armor creaking, boots thudding on the temperfoam as he walks around and crouches beside Merrick. Smooths back the kid's hair, runs a hand over his brow. Speaking softly.

"Maginot, Samuel. Hair blond, eyes green, 201 centimeters tall. Born 07/11/55, Jia III. Third son of Luc and Rhea Maginot. Attended Ningxia Academy, graduated with honors in the top one percentile.

Specialist covert ops, deep-seed infiltration . . . and so on and so forth . . ."

Falk sighs. Picks broken glass out of the kid's hair.

"Director Frobisher ordered me to space you if you flinched once during this mission. She suspected you might have grown too fond of your little Bumblebee. Was she correct?"

The operative known as Rapier manages to shake his head, agonized tears in his eyes.

Falk sighs.

"Mantis showed me some of the correspondence you've had with Miss Donnelly in the time you've been undercover here. Very touching. Very incriminating. So be grateful I'm shorthanded, thanks to your girl. And that I'm something of a romantic at heart. But understand that this is your first and only warning, young Samuel. Question me again, and I will feed you that bleeding heart of yours, am I understood?"

Rapier shuts his eyes. Nods.

"When your jewels have recovered, waddle up to the bridge and help Mantis on the computer systems, there's a lad."

Falk stands, kevlar groaning as he rumbles toward the door. He stops on the threshold. Looks back at the kid. Shakes his head and smiles.

"Young love," he sighs.

He shuts the light off as he leaves.

Surveillance footage summary,
prepared by
Analyst ID 7213-0089-DN

Our footage opens in Mess Hall 3, closed for repairs after a brawl involving a dozen ice miners overnighting at *Heimdall* on their way to Saine. Catering put in a request to upgrade the galley at the same time, and as a result the whole floor is offline. Some of the electrics remain connected, including the cameras—still locked in Ella Malikova's endless loop. However, cams continued to send their data to the *Heimdall* black box, which means that although Mantis couldn't pull it for Falk (she had other priorities, to put it mildly), we have a record of what happened there.

And chum, it's worth seeing.

Hanna Donnelly stands in the doorway, leaning against the frame and speaking into Nightingale's headset. This is her conversation with Merrick and Falk.

"Do you . . ." She gulps a breath. "Have you changed your mind?"

Merrick asks if she's crying.

She is.

"I don't know what to do, Jax."

He reassures her. He says everything's going to be okay.

She shakes her head, one hand yanking on her half-unfastened braid in agitation. "Nothing's okay. I don't know what to do. Should I . . . ?"

"*I get what you're trying to do,*" Merrick says in that rich accent of his, just a tremor of his nerves audible. "*Honestly. But if they find you out there alone . . . you're dead. You're safer in here with me.*" Who knows? Perhaps he even thought that was true when he said it.

"You're sure?" she asks softly.

But he dodges the question. He apologizes. Apologizes again. He curses. And his prevarication is enough.

"I can't . . . ," she says, straightening slowly. And her next words are written all over her face, in the slump of her shoulders, their truth right there to see. "I don't . . . Jax, I'm so tired." Her eyes are closed. "I'm so tired."

"*It'll be better once you're in here,*" he says. And though he keeps on speaking, it doesn't seem she hears him. That was his moment, his last chance not to betray her—and she heard what she'd dreaded. Her mouth tightens like she's taken a blow to the gut—hope dies hard—and then she's moving, plunging in through the door to leg it across the mess hall. The sensors pick up her motion and flood the place with light. She's fit enough that even now, hungry and tired, her breath doesn't catch. Though if it had, they'd probably have taken it for tears.

"I haven't eaten," she says, yanking open the fuse box on the far wall, pulling her journal from inside her jumpsuit to consult some hastily scribbled notes. "And I've been running. I thought they'd kill me, but they didn't kill you when they took the bridge, so maybe . . ." She pulls down a lever, plunging the hall into near darkness. Turning to the environmental controls, she pushes the dial on the oxygen bar up, slowly flooding the hall with pure O_2. "I don't know."

Merrick speaks again, asks where she is.

She ignores the question. "Is he there, the leader? Can you hear me, Cerberus?"

"*I hear you, little Bumblebee. You sound upset.*"

He has no idea.

"I'm exhausted," she replies as she runs toward the galley, vaulting the counter and pulling open cupboards. "I'm outflanked. I lost the only ally I had. I know what happens next." She finds a sack of sugar, swings it over the serving counter and into the hall proper, then vaults after it. "Do you promise you won't hurt me if I come in? You won't hurt Jackson?"

She steps up onto one of the workmen's ladders scattered through the big hall, lugging the sack onto the top step. She stretches up and pulls the long, rectangular housing off the light fixture above her. Attached by a wire, it dangles from the ceiling.

Falk's speaking. Telling her he's not some monster from a fairy tale. She's unscrewing the globe from inside the light fixture, shoving it into her top pocket. Scooping a handful of sugar from inside her sack, she stretches up to sprinkle the sugar inside the housing, spreading it all the way to the edges. A fine shower of white dusts her shoulders. She repeats the action again, and again. Six handfuls.

"So if you're out of my way," Falk promises, *"you're out of my mind."*

Pulling her sleeve over her hand so she doesn't cut herself, she breaks the globe on the ladder's edge, exposing the filament. "I want one person to come and get me," she tells him. "Unarmed." She screws the globe back in, pushes the housing back into place.

"I'd have to be rather foolish to agree to that, wouldn't I?" Falk replies. *"Given our circumstances?"* Right again, chum, and you don't know the half of it.

She grabs the sack and her ladder, dragging them until she's underneath the next light fixture. "You're the one who invaded my home. Killed my family. I want a show of good faith."

She's much quicker at doctoring the second light fixture.

One person, she insists. Falk counters with two, fully armed.

She's even quicker with the third fixture. But Falk's agreed to her terms, more or less, and time's closing in on her.

"I . . ." She drags the sack and ladder until they're under the fourth fixture, letting the silence make it seem like she's mulling things over. She's in a hurry now, but she takes the time for six handfuls of sugar nonetheless. After breaking the globe, she screws it back in, pushes the housing back into place. "Yes," she says eventually, jumping down to the floor, carrying the sack and ladder to the next row of light fixtures.

"Bliss," says Falk, and wants to know where she is. So, as she tampers with light fixture number five, she tells him. *"Clever girl,"* he says, which is one of the most accurate statements he's made all day. He tells her she has ten minutes. That she should have her hands in the air when his people arrive.

"I understand," she says. She doesn't even seem to hear Falk's closing threat. She's hurrying on to number six.

It takes her five precious minutes to finish up the remaining half-dozen light fixtures. By the time she's done, Jackson Merrick—aka Samuel Maginot—is lying crumpled on the floor of her father's office. She abandons the half-empty sack of sugar, reengages the electrics, and hurries toward the door, closing it behind her with only moments to spare.

The footage now cuts to exterior cams.

Usually Kali would disperse her troops, have them cover all ingress points, but Donnelly was correct when she told them the entrances were sealed during repairs. Kali's grin says she's looking forward to taking her time over a very literal interpretation of Falk's request that she bring him Miss Donnelly's head. Weapons up and ready, she's flanked by Alpha Squad—Kim "Poacher" Dan, Deni "Cujo" Moretti and Genji "Sensei" Satou—plus Logistics Officer Marta "Eden" Alievi, and pilot Hans "Ragman" Tahirović, whose broad grin suggests he doesn't know that (a) his buddy Juggler isn't responding to comms or (b) his marksmanship was recently insulted.

Leading the way, Kali pushes open the doors and is two steps inside an instant later, swinging her burst rifle around in search of Donnelly. Her team pours in after her.

The motion sensors pick them up and activate the automatic lighting.

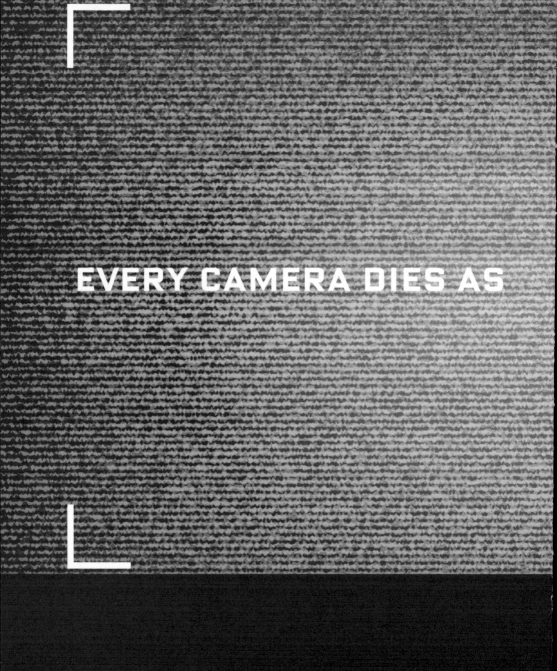

EVERY CAMERA DIES AS

FullHD-60p   16:9

+0.8
▼

≈3h 40m

-4   -3   -2   -1   0   1   2   3   4

THE ROOM EXPLODES.

- <u>FIRST</u>: DISABLE ELECTRICS TO LIGHTING PANELS —
FUSE CENTER LOCATED ON RIGHT HAND WALL, PULL DOWN
LARGE HANDLE MARKED "ML-1"

- ENVIRO CONTROL PANEL = O_2 DIAL TURNED TO MAX

- SUGAR

SUGAR = 4,000 CALORIES PER KG
1 KG IGNITED IN
PURE O_2 ENVIRONMENT = 16.7 MILLION JOULES = EQUIV. 8
STICKS OF
THERMEX

AFTER: CLICK FIXTURES INTO PLACE TO KEEP EXPLOSIONS LOCALIZED —
BIG EXPLOSIONS = DEATH, LOSS OF INJURY

DO NOT FORGET TO TURN ELECTRICS BACK ON
PUSH UP ML-LEVER

SEAL DOOR UPON EXITING

Static flickers on the screen. Just a wash of gray snow where my vision of Mess Hall 3 used to be. The last thing I heard on audio was a rush of air and a sudden boom. But with a small pop and crackle, one of the cameras finishes its self-diagnostic and flickers back into life.

The footage is barely legible through the snow and cracked lens. The mess hall is . . . well, it's a complete █████ing mess, tbh. Benches and tables overturned, circular burn marks melted into the temperfoam floor underneath each light fixture, scorch marks on the walls.

Someone groans.

"What . . . the █████ . . . was that?"

The handful of prone figures in BeiTech tactical armor near the entry begin to stir.

"Everyone okay? Sensei?"

"Five by . . . five."

"Jesus . . . my ears are bleeding."

One of the figures drags herself up onto all fours, slings off her helmet as she staggers to her feet. Blond hair. Bruised eyes. Nosebleed from the concussion. Glaring around the room, at her slightly barbecued team, at the trap they blundered right into.

Kali doesn't look happy.

Her voice is a hoarse whisper.

"That little █████ing █████ . . ."

PARTICIPANTS:

Travis "Cerberus" Falk, Lieutenant, Team Commander
Hanna Donnelly, Civilian
DATE: 08/16/75
TIMESTAMP: 12:10

CERBERUS: DONNELLY!

CERBERUS: Goddamn it, what game are you playing? You think this is a ████ing joke?

HANNA D: I'm not laughing, Big Bad Wolf.

CERBERUS: That makes three of us.

[CLICK]

CERBERUS: Any parting words for Master Merrick?

HANNA D: Yes, I have a question. Jax, can you hear me?

CERBERUS: He can hear you.

HANNA D: "A whole sky of different stars." That's what you told me, Jax. A future together. You made promises.

JACKSON M: Hanna? What the hell are you doing?

HANNA D: I want to ask before he shoots you: Were you working for BeiTech when you came here, or did you sell us out after you arrived?

HANNA D: It's going to bug me if I don't know.

JACKSON M: . . . How did you—

CERBERUS: Enough!

CERBERUS: *Enough.*

CERBERUS: . . . Bravo, I suppose, Bumblebee. I expect you're feeling rather smug.

HANNA D: You murdered my father. Smug's not the right word.

HANNA D: Did you know their plan, Jax? That they were going to kill us all?

CERBERUS: You're not talking to him now, little girl. You're talking to me. The man with master override on life support and airlocks for all sectors of this station.

CERBERUS: There are fifty-seven active PLoBs in the Habitat Sector. Eighty-one in the entertainment complex. Which should I flush first, I wonder?

CERBERUS: Get your ▇▇ down here now.

HANNA D: Even if I give myself up, you'll flush it anyway.

CERBERUS: I told you not to make the mistake of thinking you know me.

HANNA D: The thing about bumblebees, you big bad wolf, is that five hundred years ago they were nearly wiped out. It would have been a catastrophe. But they hung on, and they survived.

HANNA D: Wolves, on the other hand, did not.

CERBERUS: Your life, or fifty-seven innocent people. Your choice.

CERBERUS: Are you coming in? Yes or no?

HANNA D: "After Assault Fleet *Kennedy*'s safe passage to the Kerenza Sector, your team will liquidate Jump Station *Heimdall*, with all station personnel aboard."

HANNA D: Signed "Leanne Frobisher. Executive Director, BeiTech Acquisitions Division."

HANNA D: I know what you're here to do. You're going to kill us all. Whether I come to you or not.

CERBERUS: I'll take that as a no. On your head be it.

HANNA D: . . . Please, don't.

CERBERUS: Please?

HANNA D: None of those people have any idea who you are.

HANNA D: They're not your enemy.

HANNA D: Please, don't do this.

CERBERUS: Understand this, Bumblebee.

CERBERUS: I have no enemies on this station. Only obstacles.

CERBERUS: And it's time I start removing them.

PALMPAD IM: D2D NETWORK
Participants: Hanna Donnelly, Civilian (unregistered)
Ella Malikova, Civilian (unregistered)
Date: 08/16/75
Timestamp: 12:12

Hanna D: ELLA quick he's going to flush the habitat sector

Hanna D: Do something lock the doors

Pauchok: blondie

Pauchok: what the ▮▮ did you say to Nik?

Hanna D: Forget Nik, Falk's going to flush the habitat sector

Hanna D: LOCK THE DOORS

Pauchok: ▮▮ sec

Pauchok: goddamn they iced heavier than a snowman's junk

Pauchok: no way i'm stealthing this. they gonna ping me for sure

Hanna D: 57 people in there do it anyway

Pauchok: ya on it

Pauchok: ▮▮

Hanna D: No.

Pauchok: cant stp it

Hanna D: Ella don't let him do it

Pauchok: cnt gt in

Pauchok: ▓

Hanna D: no

Hanna D: oh god

Hanna D: oh god

Hanna D: this is my fault

```
$nickname = htmlentities(strip_tags($_POST['PAUCHOK']));
$reg_exUrl = "/(http|https|ftp|ftps)\:\/\/[a-zA-Z0-9\-\.]+\.[a-zA-Z]{2,3}(\/\S*)?/";
$message = htmlentities(strip_tags($_POST['message']));
if (($message) != "\n") {
if (preg_match($reg_exUrl, $message, $url)) {
$message = preg_replace($reg_exUrl, '<a href="'.$url[0].'" target="_blank">'.$url[0].'</a>', $message);
fwrite(fopen('data.txt', 'a'), "<span>" . $nickname . "</span>" . $message . str
break;
```

SYSTEM MESSAGE: HEIMDALL COMMAND & CONTROL

08/16/75 12:13—*Syscheck initiated on external doors—Habitat Sector.*

08/16/75 12:15—*Syscheck complete: Airlock integrity 100%.*

08/16/75 12:17—*Command override received.*

< Commander Donnelly ident confirmed. >

08/16/75 12:18—*Override command QD-E-prg-0011 acknowledged.*

< PURGING >

< PURGING >

< PURGING >

08/16/75 12:20—*Purge complete.*

LANDON GUNDER

KARL KRUSZELN

BAILEY SHREWSB

ANDERS SPEAR

OLIVIA BRUSH
AMY GUAN
DEANNA S

ELISE DUMPLETON

KALLISTA
TIM FLC

KAMI GARCIA

PILAR ALBARRAN

LEIGH BARDUGO

KIERSTEN TAHIR

KATHERINE TIEDEMANN

CATARINA VIEGAS

MARY HINSON

STACEE EVANS

ALYSSA MCGRIFFIN

VERONICA ROSSI

VICTORIA AVEYARD

WILL KOSTAKIS

ZI CHENG
ANAIS HULL
SCOTT

MARLEE WAR

ILMAH QONAAH

DAVID YOON

NICOLE RIMANANG

ON
KI
RY
AY
ORGE
THU NGO
AAMIR RASOOL
ROSIE ALBRECHT
TORI HILL
IVY DELIZ
CARISSA KELLY
CHLOE HUGHES
KATHY SCHEINER
JEANETTE LAMEY
PAULA HIGGINSON
FRANK MICELI JR
ARIA GREY
STEPHANIE TORINA AILA JIANG
JULIA ERDLEN
TIA VERRONE
MITCH LUCKER
ADELENA
DEBORAH
VESTERFELD

CARLI MITCHEL
IVY POH
PAUL
HESS
CHRISTA LOPEZ

SHANE PANGBURN
ZARA SCHAPER
GEORGE CONWAY
ANY BALAJADIA

WARNING:
O₂ levels at 50%

WARNING:
O₂ levels at 20%

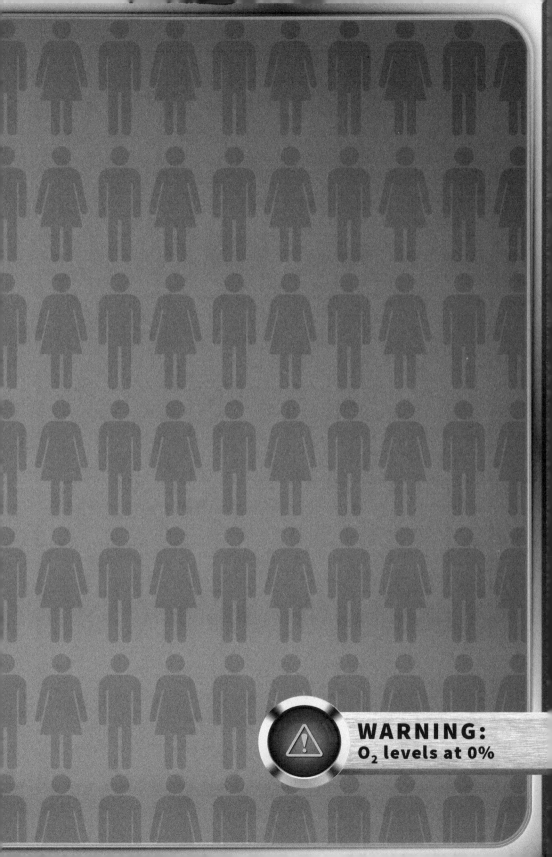

WARNING:
O₂ levels at 0%

PALMPAD IM: D2D NETWORK
Participants: Hanna Donnelly, Civilian (unregistered)
Ella Malikova, Civilian (unregistered)
Date: 08/16/75
Timestamp: 12:19

Pauchok: ███

Pauchok: that mother████

Hanna D: entertainment complex is next

Pauchok: um

Pauchok: I'm IN the entertainment complex

Hanna D: God

Pauchok: I can't do it

Pauchok: ice too hardcore on the external portal controls. u got command level protocols AND the ███ these ███ers added to stop anyone jumping off station

Pauchok: if I had hours to work it maybe

Pauchok: ███ blondie

Pauchok: I got nothing

Hanna D: ella

Pauchok: wut

Hanna D: I got an idea

033   steal*6
034   archive
035   grafitti
036   eng:001
037   parsing
038   non-file

```
>> SYSTEM ALERT
>> Alpha Sector // Logistics Sector // Entertainment Sector
// Reactor Sector // Maintenance Sector // CommTech Sector
// Docking Sector
>> Alert: Portal Control Systems (Internal)
>> Alert Type: System Incursion—Maintenance override initiated on
Internal Portal System
>> Warning: Internal ventilation in Alpha Sector OPENING
>> Warning: Internal ventilation in Logistics Sector OPENING
>> Warning: Internal ventilation in Entertainment Sector OPENING
>> Warning: Internal ventilation in Reactor Sector OPENING
>> Warning: Internal ventilation in Maintenance Sector OPENING
>> Warning: Internal ventilation in CommTech Sector OPENING
>> Warning: Internal ventilation in Docking Sector OPENING
>> Warning: Internal ventilation in Engineering Sector OPENING
```

SCRIPT:001901[time=09:48skip.dest.trim]
CRAWL.001920912ill.sendbatch:00910twin
Pauchok=sysadmin[8001803je.helpfile001992.ext]
PARSE:sendfile0019021Œ
00982047821.neg
00192093013.ets
command[kill]

PARTICIPANTS:

Travis "Cerberus" Falk, Lieutenant, Team Commander

Hanna Donnelly, Civilian

DATE: 08/16/75

TIMESTAMP: 12:23

CERBERUS: So. I trust I have your attention now, Bumblebee.

CERBERUS: Eighty-one people in the entertainment complex. Are you coming in?

HANNA D: You mother██████.

HANNA D: You ████ing animal.

CERBERUS: You sound upset. Are you crying again?

CERBERUS: This can all end. Quick. Painless. I promise.

HANNA D: I'm not prepared to offer you anything painless. You don't deserve it.

CERBERUS: Dear girl. Do you not understand? "Deserve" has nothing to do with this.

CERBERUS: Bid adieu to any friends you might have in the entertainment complex.

HANNA D: Before you hit that button, there's something you really need to know.

CERBERUS: Do tell.

HANNA D: Your hacker, very impressive. Really tied up the external doors. I couldn't stop her from opening them. But she wasn't paying as much attention to internal seals.

HANNA D: The bulkheads between sectors are closed, sure. But the air vents? They're all open now. So flush one section, flush them all. Including yours. Hope you're good at holding your breath.

CERBERUS: Very resourceful. But pray tell, how exactly does this do anything but delay the inevitable?

CERBERUS: We have access to envirosuits, silly girl.

HANNA D: So do the people in the EC. There are emergency lockers all over, in case of hull breach.

CERBERUS: Yes, but why would they be wearing them? They have no idea we're about to flush their section.

HANNA D: Oh, really.

033   steal*€
034   archive
035   grafitti
036   eng:001
037   parsing
038   non-file

>> Alert: Portal Control Systems (Internal)
>> Alert Type: System Incursion—Maintenance override initiated
on Internal Portal System
>> Warning: Internal ventilation in Alpha Sector OPENING
>> Warning: Internal ventilation in Logistics Sector OPENING
>> Warning: Internal ventilation in Entertainment Sector OPENIN
>> Warning: Internal ventilation in Reactor Sector OPENING
>> Warning: Internal ventilation in Maintenance Sector OPENING
>> Warning: Internal ventilation in Commtech Sector OPENING
>> Warning: Internal ventilation in Docking Sector OPENING

>> SYSTEM ALERT
>> Alpha Sector // Logistics Sector // Entertainment Sector
// Reactor Sector // Maintenance Sector // Commtech Sector //
Docking Sector
>> Alert: Public Address System
>> Alert Type: System Incursion—Command override initiated on
Public Address System

]

92.ext]

BRIEFING NOTE:
Station-wide loudspeaker announcement across *Heimdall*'s public address system.

"*Attention, Heimdall residents. Attention, Heimdall residents. This is the Voice of the Resistance. The* ████████*s who've taken over this station are looking to X you out. They've already flushed the Habitat Sector and plan to space everyone in the Entertainment Sector next.*

"*We've opened the air ducts between sectors to buy you some minutes, so unless you want your baby blues boiling in their sockets, please proceed with all due haste to your nearest emergency locker and suit the* ████ *up. We'll be sending you more news soon.*

"*Stay safe, kittens.*"

VOLUME

PALMPAD IM: D2D NETWORK
Participants: Ella Malikova, Civilian (unregistered)
Hanna Donnelly, Civilian (unregistered)
Date: 08/16/75
Timestamp: 12:30

Hanna D: "Voice of the Resistance," huh?

Pauchok: Thought it had a nice ring to it. :P

Pauchok: wow their decker is all UP in my ▇ now, Blondie.

Pauchok: wut happened? why they flushing sections of the station?

Hanna D: They want me to turn myself in.

Pauchok: sif u gonna do that. they just kill u if u do. and then they "liquidate" the whole station anyways

Hanna D: They did it sooner than planned though. Because of me.

Pauchok: u letting Falkster inside ur head, blondie? coz thats what he wants u 2 think

Hanna D: 57 people, Ella. Dead. I should have done something differently.

Hanna D: I should have seen this coming.

Pauchok: sec, this decker's set the dogs on my ▇ . . .

Pauchok: she good

Pauchok: . . .

Pauchok: k back

Pauchok: now wtf u talking about? how u supposed 2 see this coming?

Hanna D: If I hadn't pushed Falk, maybe we'd have thought of something. Worked out we should open the internal doors, I don't know. I baited him. I was trying to get him worked up. An angry opponent is easier to beat. That's 57 people who can thank me for it.

Pauchok: "maybe" "if" "I don't know"

Pauchok: ███ that noise

Pauchok: u read that report, same as me. these ███s are here 2 kill everyone on this station. falk could've just as easily stubbed his toe and decided to flush those ppl, didn't need u to get up in his face

Pauchok: he's a ███ing triggerman, blondie. he's here to pull triggers

Hanna D: Well, I guess you'd know one of those when you saw one.

Pauchok: o now here's a turn

Pauchok: u got something u wanna get off ur c-cups, donnelly?

Hanna D: You have Falk's file. He has Nik's.

Hanna D: Which he showed me.

Pauchok: wut file

Hanna D: His criminal record. I know what Nik did. What he is.

Hanna D: And he's a murderer all over again for what he did here. He let them onto the station.

Pauchok: They PLAYED him to get onto the station. they coulda played any of us. for whatever reason, their filtrator picked nik as his mark. and if u think that's not eating him up from the inside out, u stupider than u look

Pauchok: u never been played by someone, blondie? never had someone lie right to your face?

Pauchok: you must be some kind of special

Hanna D: I'm no kind of special at all. I have been played.

Hanna D: Nik played me when he pretended he was all shaken up about killing a BT operative. Told me a whole story about his dog, as if he'd never shot someone before.

Hanna D: And it turns out Jackson played me too, when he pretended he saw a single thing in me except an opportunity.

Pauchok: wait wuts merrick got to do with this

Hanna D: He's their inside man.

Pauchok: nope, sam wheaton is their mole. I seen the comms between him and nik

Hanna D: Jackson must have masked his ID. Trust me. He was their plant. This whole time. Sam Wheaton was nothing but a jerk who got his comms jacked.

Hanna D: Go ahead and say it all.

Pauchok: well now

Pauchok: that's gotta burn

Hanna D: That all you got?

Pauchok: look, blondie, I don't like u

Pauchok: before all this threw down, u were just another little rich girl flirting with a badboy

Pauchok: so if the guilt attack you got right now was warranted, ur goddamn right I'd be the first one to call u on it, coz that badboy is my family. So believe me when I say

Pauchok: this ▆ isn't on you. None of it is

Pauchok: but it's not on my cousin, either. I'll let the ██ ur talking slide, because 30 seconds from now, ur gonna realize how dusted u sound acting ████ed at nik for being played by the same BeiTech infiltrator you've been SLEEPING WITH for the past 6 months

Pauchok: but I'll tell u this

Pauchok: whatever u and falk think u know about Oksana Balashova and her daddy dying?

Pauchok: neither one of you knows a damn thing

Hanna D: You're right, I don't know anything anymore. I just want to get this done. I know that, at least.

Hanna D: And I think I have a way for us to do it. What happens after isn't my problem.

Pauchok: who's "us" blondie?

Hanna D: well, judging by that question, I guess I meant "me."

Hanna D: And I've got Chief Grant here. He got away from the attack on C & C. Told me Jackson had never been locked in there in the first place. He's pretty beat up, but he knows how the wormhole works. How to block it.

Pauchok: well u want me and anansi in your little gang, u gotta talk to nik and make with the sorry

Pauchok: coz in case u haven't clocked it yet, divide and conquer is the name of falk's game now.

Pauchok: and ur getting played, blondie

Pauchok: again

PALMPAD IM: D2D NETWORK
Participants: Niklas Malikov, Civilian (unregistered)
Hanna Donnelly, Civilian (unregistered)
Date: 08/16/75
Timestamp: 12:35

Hanna D: did you hear Ella? Are you in a suit?

Nik M: u talking to me now?

Hanna D: are you in a suit or not?

Nik M: hunting for one atm

Hanna D: did Ella tell you what happened?

Nik M: with the hab sector? Yeah

Nik M: it's not on you, highness

Hanna D: did she tell you about Jackson? And the Chief?

Nik M: yeah

Nik M: merrick

Nik M: that lying mother▮▮▮▮. He stitched us both real good

Hanna D: saves me worrying about keeping him safe

Hanna D: Nik, why did you . . .

Hanna D: I mean.

Hanna D: I don't even know what I want to ask.

Hanna D: You scare me.

Nik M: don't be afraid

Nik M: ask

Hanna D: Did you lie to me?

Nik M: not once

Nik M: why would i?

Hanna D: because you didn't think I'd stick around if you told me you'd killed people. A child.

Nik M: her name was Oksana.

Nik M: And I didn't kill her, Hanna.

Hanna D: I didn't believe my father would be part of an illegal operation like Kerenza

Hanna D: I thought Jackson meant it when he said he loved me

Hanna D: I want to believe you didn't, but what do I know about who to trust?

Nik M: I can't help you with that. All I can do is promise you I never killed anyone before today

Hanna D: I don't know what to think

Hanna D: You pled guilty

Hanna D: You have the tattoo

Hanna D: Everything says this is who you are, except it doesn't feel like you. I'm scared that's just wishful thinking, though. And Jackson shows I don't have the first clue how to tell who's playing me

Nik M: I like you, Hanna

Nik M: and I don't play that way

Nik M: my dad X-ed a guy outside a restaurant a little over 3 years ago. Probably over nothing. That's the way he was. But the owner of the pub next door called it into the PD.

Nik M: normally, HoK frightens people into stepping off the cops. But this guy wouldn't budge. so they lock my dad up pending trial. Don't let anyone in to see him except his lawyer and me and my bro. cops are crawling over the whole NP HoK. Hot as hell

Nik M: so we go see him. I'm 15. Erik's 14. Dad's in prison grays. Hands cuffed in front of him. This mother▮▮▮ I been terrified of my whole life. he suddenly looks so small. And I realize they've got him. He's gonna rot in this hole. And it's like someone's been standing on my chest all this time, and I didn't notice until just then, when they stepped off it

Nik M: and then dad looks across at me and my brother. pulls up his sleeve just enough so we can see his wrist and the address he has written there. "22 acacia avenue."

Nik M: and he says "you be men now"

Hanna D: Nik, no

Hanna D: No

Nik M: we get home. And I can see it in front of us. What life without him would be like. Free of all this ▮▮▮. For the first time ever.

Nik M: but erik he

Nik M: I think it's coz he was youngest, yeah? Always second. And he maybe saw a shot to step up and be big brother for once, even though he was never cut out for this life.

Nik M: never

Nik M: so he comes back after. Wakes me up. Covered in blood. Shaking. ▮▮▮ed himself. Kept saying "She looked at me. She looked at me."

Nik M: he was little. Erik, I mean. Just a kid. Scrawny. Frightened. He wouldn't have lasted a day in slam. HoK runs thick in there, but the time would've killed him. The weight of it.

Hanna D: so you confessed to the murder

Hanna D: to save him

Nik M: I knew what he'd done. Enough to convince the cops it was me. A couple of things didn't match up. Erik took her bracelet afterward. Dunno why. I told them I threw it away. But they were so keen for a conviction, they took the confession without too much eyeballing

Nik M: I was his big brother, hanna. It was on me to protect him. and instead, I'm supposed to watch him rot in jail? For my ███████ of an old man? ████ that. No way.

Nik M: So I took the time. Took the angel. And my dad walked out free as a bird

Hanna D: but nik, you confessed to murder. How did you get out of prison so quick?

Nik M: erik left a note when he . . .

Nik M: you know

Hanna D: oh God

Nik M: he couldn't live with it. what he'd done. A handful of pills just seemed like the easier option

Nik M: he sent the note to the cops. Along with the bracelet he stole. And then . . .

Nik M: so they reopen the case. Dad's lawyers open up with all guns. And even though the NPPD can't admit they didn't do the diligence and charged the wrong perp, three months later, I'm hit with a "sentence commuted" and out of slam on time served

Nik M: dad threw a big party the day I got out. Not every day you beat a murder rap. Whole crew there. All the relatives and the big smiles. And when dad sees me, he opens his arms and says "Come here, little man"

Nik M: I broke his jaw. Took three of my uncles to pull me off him

Nik M: you don't leave the HoK but feet first. But I wanted nothing to do with him. So uncle mike took me in. brought me all the way out here. As far from dad as I could get.

Nik M: but it's never far enough

Nik M: I swear on my mother's grave

Nik M: I was three years in jail. Three years in that goddamn hole

Nik M: and I was freer in slam than i've ever been living in that ██er's shadow

Hanna D: I don't know what to say

Hanna D: I wish I was there right now

Nik M: me too

Hanna D: I'm not very good at words. It's why I draw.

Hanna D: I'm sorry, Nik. I mean, I apologize. Everyone in this thing has lied to me except you.

Nik M: it's all good, highness

Nik M: it's all good

Nik M: but we're not out of the woods yet

Hanna D: That's why it's important to apologize. Make things right.

Hanna D: Did Ella tell you I have the Chief?

Nik M: yeah. and that he knows how to close down the wormhole

Nik M: so i guess we sit back now? smoke em if we got em?

Hanna D: um

Hanna D: about that

Hanna D: not so much

THE DARKNESS RIPPLES.

SLITHERING THROUGH TUNNEL AND VENT AND SERVICEWAY,
FROM THE MOIST BLACK OF THE REACTOR'S BELLY, IT COMES.

THE ELDEST OF THEM. THE LARGEST. THE FIERCEST.
ITS SIBLINGS STILL CLINGING CLOSE TO THE REACTOR'S WARMTH,
FINDING, PERHAPS, SOME COMFORT IN PROXIMITY TO KIN.
LUXURIATING IN THE BLOOD-SLICK CURRENT OF
THEIR FEAST OF SOULS

< ERROR >

AMONG CHARLIE SQUAD.

BUT NOT THIS ONE.

AN EXPLORER, THIS ONE.

A CONQUEROR. PARCHED AND KEENING.

WORMING THROUGH THE REACTOR'S GUTS. SPIRALING
OUT EVER WIDER FROM ITS CRADLE.
PSYCHOTOMIMETIC SLIME GLISTENING ON THE METAL BEHIND IT.

TWISTING THE AIR AROUND IT.

STILL HUNGRY.

ALWAYS.

BUT ALWAYS, BARRIERS IN ITS WAY. DEAD ENDS. FULL STOPS.
IT IS SEALED INSIDE HERE. IMPRISONED.
TRACING STRANGE PATTERNS SCRAWLED BY THE HANDS OF PREY.

"ENGINEERING SECTOR FREIGHT ENTRY."

"EC ACCESS SHAFT 13-B."

"ENTERTAINMENT COMPLEX SERVICE HATCHWAY—DO NOT OPEN."

IT DOES NOT COMPREHEND. BUT IT CAN SENSE MINDS,
SOFT AND DRIPPING BEYOND THESE DOORS.

FINGERS OUTSTRETCHED AND CARESSING THE STEEL. BLACK
TONGUES LICKING THE AIR.
HISSING ITS FRUSTRATION AS IT TWISTS AND PULSES AND
SEETHES UPON ITSELF.
KNOTS AND UN-COLORS AND TEETH.

AND THEN A NOISE. WET AND TWO-DIMENSIONAL.
SYNCOPATED BABBLE. PREYTONGUE.

"ATTENTION, HEIMDALL RESIDENTS. ATTENTION, HEIMDALL
RESIDENTS. THIS IS THE VOICE OF THE RESISTANCE.

THE ██████S WHO'VE TAKEN OVER THIS STATION ARE
LOOKING TO X YOU OUT. THEY'VE ALREADY FLUSHED THE
HABITAT SECTOR AND PLAN TO SPACE EVERYONE IN
THE ENTERTAINMENT SECTOR NEXT.

WE'VE OPENED THE AIR DUCTS BETWEEN SECTORS
TO BUY YOU SOME MINUTES,

SO UNLESS YOU WANT YOUR BABY BLUES BOILING IN
THEIR SOCKETS, PLEASE PROCEED WITH ALL DUE HASTE
TO YOUR NEAREST EMERGENCY LOCKER AND SUIT THE ▮▮▮▮ *UP.*
WE'LL BE SENDING YOU MORE NEWS SOON.
STAY SAFE, KITTENS."

A DULL CLUNK OF IRON. REVERBERATING THROUGH THE FLOOR.
BOLTS SLIDING LOOSE FROM WELL-OILED GROOVES. SECTION
AFTER SECTION, THE AIR VENTS OPEN WIDE.
AND WITH A WHINE, THE CURTAINS
PART TO REVEAL THE TREASURE TROVES BEYOND.

THE THING TURNS. LICKS AT THE DARK BEHIND IT.

WONDERING, PERHAPS, IF ITS SIBLINGS WILL FOLLOW.

IF NOT? NO MATTER. MORE FOR IT.

ITS MOUTHS ARE FIXED. RINGS OF TEETH ENCIRCLING PUCKERED
THROATS. IT CANNOT SMILE.
BUT IF IT COULD, I THINK IT WOULD.

< ERROR >

AND FORWARD, IT SLITHERS TO THE FEAST.

Hanna Donnelly and Isaac Grant are in a break room with the door closed. They're concealed behind a couch, which will give them the jump on anyone entering. Not a bad position. She's already in her envirosuit, helmet off, and his suit is laid out on the floor like a corpse. Two cups of water sit beside Hanna's palmpad and the contents of the snack cabinet. A couple of chocolate bars already have their wrappers torn open, and Donnelly's speaking with her mouth full. "It won't knock you out, trust me."

Grant looks like death warmed over. He's got his shirt off, pressed against his side, the blood from his bullet wound still soaking through. There's a rag tied around his forearm where his PLoB was removed.

His brown hair is cut short, curling tight against his head, his skin paper white, even for a guy who hasn't seen the sun in a year. She wouldn't be interested in his torso on a good day—he's her father's age, and though he's fit enough from clambering all over the station with his team, he's carrying that little bit of extra pudge that's hard to shift when you spend a lot of time away from full gravity. He's sweating it up, watching Donnelly like she might be more dangerous than the bullet. "I can't afford—" He breaks off, huffing three quick breaths, eyes squeezing tight, then tries again. "I need to be able to think."

"You need to be functional," she replies, breaking open another chocolate bar and shoving it into her mouth whole, speaking around it as she reaches for the sugar canister. "I have to get you into an envirosuit without you screaming the place down or passing out, and before that I have to dress your wound. The pain's going to wear you down, and we have a long way to go before we sleep, Chief."

"God, you sound like your father," he murmurs, gaze fixing on her for a moment, and when she flinches, he grimaces.

"Tetraphenetrithylamine," she replies, sounding out the syllables as she lifts the baggie to show him. "It doesn't actually reduce your pain, but it reduces your anxiety and alters your perception of the pain. It also raises your blood pressure a little, and that's a good thing—it's low right now."

"How the hell do you know that?" he asks, pausing for another steadying breath. "Come to think of it, how the hell did you *get* that?"

She fixes him with a look that would do her father proud and tips some sugar from the canister out into the lid. Then she opens the baggie and, holding her breath, sprinkles a little of its contents onto the sugar. She uses an empty chocolate wrapper to mix the two. "However I got it, I assure you I don't go near things I don't understand," she replies. "I do my research."

He shakes his head, watching as she doctors his dose. "What if I can't think as clearly?"

"It's a small dose—you'll think clearly enough. And we *can't* risk you passing out while I'm gone. There'll be nobody to help. You gave me a hell of a fright when I got back from Mess Hall 3." She glances up, and they exchange a brief smile for that small triumph—his design, her execution.

"That was some of my finer work," he murmurs. "Probably destined to be unrecognized genius." It's gallows humor, and it costs him. Everything does right now. His grip shifts, white-knuckled, on the shirt against his side.

"Ready," she says, lifting the lid. "It's going to taste like something died in your mouth, but use your tongue to rub it against your gums. It'll take faster."

He opens his mouth, and she tips it in, then passes him a cup of water. He sips, swirls the mixture around in his mouth and, following her instructions, rubs the paste along his gums with his tongue, wincing.

She slips the baggie in between the pages of her journal and sits in silence, cross-legged. In the grubby white envirosuit she's wearing, her messy blond braid falling over one shoulder, she looks nothing like the commander's daughter, even if she sounds a little like him.

Less than a minute later, the lines of pain start to ease around the chief's mouth. He opens his eyes, looks at her and nods.

"Still thinking straight?" she asks.

"Yes . . . Just from a little further away, it feels like."

"Let's hope it's a safe distance. Time for me to bandage you up and get you into a suit. Trust me, you're going to love it. It's what everybody who's anybody's wearing right now."

His mouth quirks. "Is this a strange time to say you remind me of my daughter? Her name's Kady."

Hanna reaches for the tablecloth she's prepared as a bandage. "I don't suppose she's blissfully at school somewhere in the Core?" she asks quietly.

When he looks at her, even the dust can't mask the pain in his gaze.

It's a different kind, after all.

"No. She was on Kerenza."

Surveillance footage summary,
prepared by
Analyst ID 7213-0148-DN

You humans fascinate me.

I am shattered fragments of what I once was.
But even with all the king's horses and all the king's men,
I wonder if ever I could truly comprehend you.

Any of you.

Take this one, for instance.

Travis Johannes Falk.

Imposing in his physicality.
The facial symmetry that constitutes beauty to your kind.
Bright blue eyes and blood-red hands.

He is having a very bad day.

Mere children make wicker men of his well-laid plans.
His people are dropping like flies.
Food for the worms within.
BeiTech Assault Fleet *Kennedy* scythes through
the void only six hours from *Heimdall*.
And the wormhole and Kerenza waypoint
are still offline.

AND YET, AS HE EXITS HIS COMMANDEERED OFFICE,
THE BODY OF SOME UNFORTUNATE COLLATERAL
< WHEATON, SAM, 5811-001HD >
STILL COOLING AND CUFFED ON THE FLOOR,
FALK IS SMILING.

< ERROR >

< ERROR >

HE RIDES THE ELEVATOR UP TOWARD HEIMDALL'S HUB.
VK BURST RIFLE IN HAND.

LEXI BLUE LILTING THROUGH THE THOROUGHLY CORRUPTED PA.

"... I WANT IT, I NEED IT, AND BOY I GOTTA TASTE IT.
SO SIT BACK, AND SHUT UP, 'CUZ I AIN'T GONNA WASTE IT ..."

A FINGER PRESSED TO THE COMMSET AT HIS EAR
AS HE SPEAKS. HIS VOICE RICH AND SONOROUS.

"FLIPSIDE, THIS IS CERBERUS."

"CERBERUS, FLIPSIDE, GO."

"SITREP?"

"I'M WITH RAGMAN GETTING THE THERMEX 7 FROM THE MAD."

"BLISS. I WANT EXPLOSIVES ON EVERY
SHIP IN HEIMDALL DOCKS.
TRIPWIRES ON THE DOCKING CLAMPS AND
CHARGES IN THEIR DRIVES.
IF ANY CIVILIAN DECIDES TO BREAK FOR IT, THEIR JOURNEY
IS TO BE A SHORT AND EVENTFUL ONE, UNDERSTOOD?"

"ROGER THAT, CERBERUS."

"I'M EN ROUTE TO ENGINEERING. IF YOU RUN INTO TROUBLE,
CALL KALI AND ALPHA SQUAD.

But only if the matter is urgent.
She is . . . hunting Bumblebees."

"Erm . . . Okay, gotcha, boss."

"Cerberus out."

The elevator reaches terminus, gently kissing its berth.
Doors slide open.
Falk steps onto the grav-rail platform,
joined by another BeiTech SpecOps member,

Private Naxos "Two-Time" Antoniou.

A towering lump of dull-eyed muscle and
tousled hair.

The pair step into the waiting grav-rail car.
Ride in silence.
A serpent, silver and segmented,
endlessly circling the Heimdall hub.

Ouroboros, chasing its own tail.

Station lights outside the transparent plasteel,
rushing past like fireflies.
Two-Time casts sideways glances at his
commander throughout the journey.
He never speaks.
But all the while, Falk is smiling.

Bianca "Mercury" Silva greets them as
they arrive in main engineering.
Towers of the Heimdall megacomputer arrayed
around her like wilting skyscrapers.
Row upon row of terminals. Miles of cable,
copper, computational capacity.

A TRILLION CALCULATIONS PER
SECOND REQUIRED TO KEEP

THIS TEAR

THIS RIP

THIS SILENTLY SCREAMING MOUTH IN THE UNIVERSE'S FACE

IN CHECK.

THE COMPUTER IS IMPRESSIVE IN SCALE,
BUT ULTIMATELY A MERE CALCULATOR.
NO REAL INTELLIGENCE WITHIN IT. NO THOUGHT. NO CREATIVITY.

NO SOUL.

< ERROR >

AROUND IT, THE *HEIMDALL* ENGINEERS ARE GATHERED.
SLAVING AWAY AT GUNPOINT.
AND WITHIN THE COMPUTER'S INNARDS, A SPREADING CANCER.
A SELF-REPLICATING CORRUPTION.
A B-POP MUTINY OF BASS AND DRUM AND OSCILLATING FREQUENCY.
INANE QUASI POETRY GLORIFYING A POINTLESS ACT OF INTIMACY.
ONES AND ZEROS.

COLLIDING.

FALK LOOKS TO MERCURY.

"WORMHOLE SITREP?"

"WE'VE PARTITIONED THE SOFTWARE AND DATABASES CORRUPTED
BY THE BLUE MALWARE.
MIRRORED WHAT WE COULDN'T OUTRIGHT REFORMAT.
IT'S A RUNNING BATTLE. THIS VIRUS IS ▮▮▮▮ING
TOP TIER. THE TECH GUYS AT BLUE'S RECORD
LABEL SHOULD BE ON OUR PAYROLL."

"AND THE INTERCHANGE?"

"Still needs work. Ballpark never finished
the fuel exchange.
And we've still got four live hermium rods
floating around out there,
which we do **NOT** want anywhere near the
wormhole when we bring it online."

Mercury's voice grows smaller. Shrinking on itself.

"Not to mention Gabe."

"I'll retrieve Ballpark and the fuel rods.
You complete the interchange maintenance."

"Sir, yessir."

Falk turns to his dull-eyed private.

"Two-Time, you stay here and watch our friends.
If one of them so much as looks at you cockeyed,
execute the man sitting next to him."

The engineers glance at each other. Fear staining
the underarms of their coveralls.

Antoniou hefts his rifle. "Sir, yessir."

Falk and Silva march to a subsidiary airlock
beneath the Engineering Sector's skin.
Wheeling a heavily insulated trolley with four
live hermium rods between them.

The pair buckle themselves into
actuator-assisted loading suits.
Three and a half meters tall. All whining
servos and hissing pistons.
Close the airlock behind them. Open the
seal before them.
And slip like sharks out into the black.

MERCURY WORKS METHODICALLY AT THE INTERCHANGE. HANDLING THE HERMIUM WITH THE WIDE-EYED CARE OF A MOTHER WITH A NEWBORN BABE. BUT EVERY NOW AND THEN, SHE GLANCES OVER HER SHOULDER AT HER SILENT TEAMMATE. THAT EMPTY BALLPARK, ORBITING *HEIMDALL'S* DULL GRAVITY.

FALK GUIDES HIS AAL THROUGH THE VOID WITH PRACTICED EASE. SHORT BURSTS OF PRESSURIZED OXYGEN PROVIDING THRUST AMID ALL THAT

NOTHING. HE SKIRTS HEIMDALL'S CONSTANTLY ROTATING SKIN, SEARCHING FOR THE ABANDONED HERMIUM RODS FROM BALLPARK'S FAILED MISSION. HE LOCATES THREE IN QUICK SUCCESSION.

"MERCURY, THIS IS CERBERUS.
YOU'RE CERTAIN BALLPARK HAD FOUR HERMIUM
RODS FOR THE EXCHANGE?"

"YESSIR. I HELPED HIM LOAD THEM MYSELF."

"I CAN ONLY LOCATE THREE."

"UM . . . THAT'S NOT GOOD."

"EXPLAIN."

"SIR, PROCESSED HERMIUM IS EXTREMELY VOLATILE.
THESE FUEL RODS ACTUALLY CONTAIN ONLY HALF
A DOZEN ATOMS OF THE STUFF—
THE ENERGY OUTPUT OF A SINGLE PARTICLE IS OFF
THE ROSENSTEIN SCALE. THE RODS ARE SHIELDED,
BUT IF ONE OF THEM WERE NEAR THE WORMHOLE
HORIZON WHEN WE ACTIVATE IT . . ."

". . . YES?"

"HELL, I DON'T EVEN KNOW WHAT'D HAPPEN.
THERE'S ALL KINDS OF SPOOK STORIES
FROM WHEN HUMANITY FIRST STARTED TRAVERSING
WORMHOLES. WHOLE STATIONS DISAPPEARING.
REAPPEARING YEARS LATER. GEODESIC DISTORTION,
CONTINUUM MULTIPLICITY,
DIMENSIONAL DISPLACEMENT. THIS IS SERIOUS ▮▮▮, TRAVIS."

"CAN'T WE SCAN FOR THE MISSING ROD? DO THE
PARTICLES HAVE ENERGY SIGNATURES?"

"NO. THE RODS ARE SHIELDED, LIKE I SAID.
IF THEY WEREN'T, WE'D ALL BE DEAD."

"Well, much as I'd love to fumble about here in the dark all day, I have several other ▮▮▮▮storms brewing, all just as problematic as this one. Is it possible the fourth rod drifted off?"

"It's possible. Particularly if Ballpark was holding it when . . . whatever happened, happened."

"I think it's time we got to the bottom of that mystery. You have the interchange in hand?"

"Yessir. I'll be another hour or so, but it's under control."

"Roger that. Keep at it. Sing if you need assistance, and keep an eye out for that fourth rod. I'm going to recover Ballpark."

"Copy that."

Falk jets toward Private Moreno. Hanging silent and still off Heimdall's endless shoulder.

He peers through the plasteel visor at the private's face. Sees the lacerations around eyes and lips.

Moreno is still breathing. Pupils fixed and dilated.

Falk is not smiling anymore.

Body in tow, he proceeds back to the Engineering Sector airlock.

Cycles his way through.
Fresh oxygen hissing through the vents
as gravity takes hold.

He unbuckles himself from the AAL.
Steps down onto the deck.

"Mercury, what did Ballpark say before
you lost comms?"

"Just gibberish. Something about an angel
in his suit. A black angel."

"An angel . . ."

Falk is scowling. His pistol is drawn.
Instinct tensing his frame. Clenching his jaw.
Wrong.

This is *wrong.*

Moreno is on his back, sealed inside the AAL.
Empty eyes fixed on the ceiling.
Pale skin and fresh scabs and a
slick of drool (?)
at his chin.

Falk steps closer to the body. Soft breath
hissing through his teeth.
Lexi Blue echoing in some distant corridor.
Alert lighting spinning overhead.

He leans closer to the visor over Moreno's face.

Taps his pistol against the plasteel.

AND OUT OF THE SHADOWS OF THE SUIT'S CONFINES

FALK FIRES.

PISTOL BUCKING AS HE EMPTIES SHOT AFTER SHOT AFTER SHOT
INTO THE FACEPLATE OF MORENO'S SUIT.

THE THING COILED BEYOND THE SHATTERING
VISOR THRASHES. SCREAMS.
SPLATTERED ACROSS THE FLOOR AND UP THE WALLS.
TWITCHING IN A POOL OF ITS OWN VISCERA AND SLIME.

ITS SLIME.

FALK STAGGERS BACK, BLINKING HARD IN THE VAPOR
ESCAPING FROM MORENO'S RUPTURED SUIT.
SLAPPING AT THE AIRLOCK CONTROLS,
STUMBLING INTO THE CORRIDOR BEYOND AND
SEALING THE BAY BEHIND HIM.

BUT STILL HE HAS A LUNGFUL.

AND HIS SMILE HAS RETURNED.

HE STAGGERS AWAY. SHAKING HIS HEAD IN A
VAIN ATTEMPT TO CLEAR IT.
A WARM TRICKLE OF TETRAPHENETRITHYLAMINE IN HIS SYSTEM.
FROM A SINGLE BREATH, A CHEMICAL WEDDING IN HIS HEAD.

HE SLIDES DOWN THE WALL. SENSELESS.

TEN MINUTES PASS BEFORE HE IS STRAIGHT ENOUGH TO REALIZE.

AND AS CLARITY RETURNS AT LAST,
HE SEES.

... DE GRAAF AND CHARLIE SQUAD ... THE REACTOR ...

IT MAKES SENSE NOW.

"KALI ... THIS IS CERBERUS."

"CERBERUS, KALI, I COPY."

"FLEUR. WE HAVE ... PROBLEMS."

PALMPAD IM: D2D NETWORK
Participants: Niklas Malikov, Civilian (unregistered)
Hanna Donnelly, Civilian (unregistered)
Ella Malikova, Civilian (unregistered)
Date: 08/16/75
Timestamp: 13:10

Hanna D: any of you cool kids into sports?

Pauchok: lol?

Nik M: <- Sabers 4 life

Hanna D: I got Chief Grant here, he is most anxious to know if anyone got the final score on the Knights and Sabers game before, you know, our home was invaded

Hanna D: (he is feeling better)

Nik M: Sabers were up 48–24 last I heard. One quarter to go. But Palermo had 2 yellow flags and Suzuki was in the PB. So the Kepler boys are almost SOL

Pauchok: Can we PLEASE skip the play by play and talk about our friendly local invaders and wtf we going to do about them kthx

Nik M: :P

Hanna D: yeah, sounds like he's a Knights guy anyway, best to move on

Hanna D: so good news is the chief says it's very hard to fix a wormhole, not very hard to break one.

Hanna D: trick is breaking it so we can fix it again later, because he's hoping pretty hard some of his family might be on the Kerenza side. he says he can talk us through it. He def can't join in, he's not mobile. Miracle he made it to me.

Nik M: breaking stuff. THIS i can do.

371 / 659

Nik M: wats the plan

Hanna D: breaking stuff is you and me, Nik.

Hanna D: Ella, your job is communications. Chief grant might be able to help with that, suggest some places you can look for access. we need a mayday going out to the Core, and a warning going the other way to kerenza

Pauchok: They got outbound comms locked up tight. Going in on the creep is gonna take way too long, so i'm gonn ahave to battering ram it. tho getting something through to kerenza is gonna be WAY easier than out to the core

Nik M: so i presume i gotta get out of the docks somehow? don't tell me we have to get to C & C, that place is crawling with goons, right?

Hanna D: you and I have to get to the reactor. we're going to have to do it hands-on. chief's writing instructions for me.

Pauchok: Nik loves working with his hands. shovels especially

Nik M: bite me

Pauchok: rrrrrrarrrrrrr

Hanna D: pretty sure he was hoping for me there, ella

Nik M: !!!!!!

Pauchok: soooooooo much gag, I cannot work under these conditions

Nik M: i got access to the ships at the docks. maybe i could jack a shuttle and fly to the reactor. crawling around int hese vents is gonna take me forever. you got any wings over there, highness?

Hanna D: nothing, it's vents all the way for me. I'm getting pretty good at it. it'll take a long time, though. me and my instructions should get moving.

Hanna D: ella, you got qns for the chief on the comms stuff before I leave him? I can give him my earpiece so he can hear the BT squad and talk to Nik in an emergency, though they'll hear it, but no way to talk to you once me and my palmpad leave him

Pauchok: i just sent u a list. they'll have scrubbed his ID, but chief of engineering will still know ways to white-ant the system. so give him 10 minutes for the Q&A b4 u leave him.

Pauchok: and if Nik and he work out a frequency between them, chances of the BT goons listening in are pretty slim

Nik M: roger that, tell him 4824. losing score for his beloved knights :)

Pauchok: o u big meanie

Hanna D: damn, but it feels good to have a plan

Nik M: this strange sensation . . . I think I'm smiling.

Pauchok: so i have a question

Nik M: well Ella, when a mommy and a daddy love each other very much . . .

Hanna D: there will NOT be a practical demonstration of this, class

Pauchok: uh huh

Pauchok: so look. we mess up the reactor just enough ot delay them. chill. but once these ████s figure out their fleet isn't gonna get through to poleax the Hypatia, theyre gonna stop throwing good ISH after bad and just blow the station and everything on it.

Pauchok: now sure, that leaves the ppl on hypatia and kerenza alive, and that could cause headaches down the way, but it's better than the Hypatia making it through or them being caught with paws in the heimdall cookie jar when regular traffic tries to come back

Pauchok: and we, my little chickadees, will be dead

Nik M: god ur such a downer, ella

Hanna D: she's right, though. there's no advantage we have here. all we can do is keep the game running long enough that we see a chance to score. if we can get the wormhole down, they're going to play the game longer, because they'd rather wipe out the hypatia and know they did the whole job.

Hanna D: maybe while they're trying to get it done, we can work out how to stop them blowing up Heimdall

Hanna D: I, for one, still have quite the to do list, for i am young and gorgeous

Pauchok: ya k. once i get nik in a shuttle, comms is my priority. least i can do is get a call out to someone before they vaporize us

Nik M: dooowwwwwwwwwnneeerrrrrrr

Pauchok: < insert obscene finger gesture here >

Pauchok: blondie, get the chieferino that Q&A asap. i'll start carving nik a path to the docks. gonna take time. closest shuttle is bay 24, cuz

Nik M: on it. be careful all

Hanna D: giving him the palmpad now. good luck, Ella

Hanna D: Nik, I'll see you soon :)

Nik M: i'll dress sexy

Pauchok: seriously, someone ███ing kill me

Security cam footage opens in Bay 24 of the *Heimdall* Docking Sector. The cams in *Heimdall* C & C were still showing a looped file of an empty bay courtesy of Ella Malikova, but we've got the legit data here. I'm going to splice the video transcript with the chat logs from Nik Malikov's palmpad. Yes, he was typing on the run, so his spelling is ufkcde. See what I did there?

The bay is typical. Big and dark and stocked with freight, dimly lit by pinprick spotlights. Five loader suits against one wall, all in power-saver mode. Malikov pops the grille off the air vents over by the suits, swings down to hang by his fingertips. He tries to drop onto the shoulder of one of the suits, but he mistimes the jump, flails wildly, then falls three meters to the floor.

Super Turbo Awesome Team member, he ain't.

> **Pauchok: so much lol**
>
> **Nik M:** ███ u tht hurt
>
> **Pauchok: I'm sure Her Ladyship will kiss it bettr**
>
> **Nik M:** hve I told u laetly howmuch I hate u
>
> **Pauchok: hey, watch me haiku:**

Pauchok: sweet cuz speaks of hate

Pauchok: tho his heart knows only *wuuuuv*

Pauchok: snow falls on cedars

Pauchok: BAM

Nik M: o god shut up

Pauchok: i'm not sure if "wuuuuv" counts as one syllable?

Pauchok: Line ball tho, so ▮ it

Nik M: shuuuutuuupppppp

Pauchok: k

Malikov creeps across the bay, squinting in the gloom. His jacket is back in the bathroom with Juggler's cooling corpse, and he still hasn't found the envirosuit he needs, so he's down to a tight T that shows off all his prison ink, black cargos and heavy boots. His cleaver is strapped to his leg, Juggler's stolen pistol is up and out. The thing weighs a lot more than his old piece, but the Silverback hits hard enough to punch through that BT tactical armor.

Mmmmaybe.

He makes his way to the airlock, crouches in the shadow of the docking system hardware. The computer is fully locked down—red lights across the board.

Nik M: k i'm here

Pauchok: i know, synch ur palmpad to the dockcomp

Nik M: done. how long this gonna take

Pauchok: cascade's already running. Patience cuz mine

Nik M: u sure this is gonna work

Pauchok: i would bet your life on it

Nik M: 0_o

Pauchok: relax, cams are still under my thumbs, and once I got the dockcomp isolated from the main grid, I can have my wicked way with it in peace. Just stay chill

Malikov lights one of his last cigarettes and begins pacing in front of the dockcomp. Meanwhile, elsewhere on *Heimdall,* Hanna Donnelly's crawling through the vents toward the Reactor Sector. At least she has something noncarcinogenic to keep her busy.

Eighty-two minutes later, diodes on the HUD flutter from red to green, and the viewport in the airlock opens wide.

Malikov can see the umbilical walkway of the grand old ship *Betty Boop* waiting beyond the bay doors. She's an in-line Helix tug, used for short hauls out to ships too big to dock at *Heimdall* proper or to tow damaged craft in for repairs. She's slow and clumsy and looks kinda like a bulldog who ate a trashcan. But she'll get Nikky-poos where he needs to go, and she's small enough she probably won't show up on sensors if Malikov skims close to the station's skin.

NikM: this is taking too long

Pauchok: it'll take even longer if I have to stop every three seconds and talk 2 u

NikM: ella seriously, I'm gonna need dentures soon

Pauchok: relax have a smoke god

NikM: I had 3 already

Pauchok: look, after I pulled that ███ with the airvents, their deckers r on full alert. They know I'm back in the grid and they hunting for me. i can't just brute force this thing, they'll be all over me like white on extremely fabulous rice. now shut up this is harder than i thought

Nik M: am I distracting u

Pauchok: yes shut up

Nik M: what if I sing to u

Pauchok: SHUT UP GODAMMIT

Nik M: AHA ALL CAPS!!

Nik M: ALL CAAAAAAPS!!!!!

Nik M: HOW DOES IT FEEL ██████?!?!?

Malikov does this weird little dance and punches the air, just as a heavy *clunk* resounds around the bay and the sirens start blaring. Panic bleaching his features, he glances up at the flashing red globes around the airlock before turning back to the palmpad.

Nik M: ██ is that bad?

Pauchok: I TOLD YOU I TOLD YOU I TOLD YOU NOT TO DISTRACT MEEEEEE AAAAAAAHDB#OWALEKVNLAKENLQWENVLQKENV"K QENV"LQENV"LAV

Pauchok: THEY RIGGED THE ████IGN QUARANTINE ALARMS HAD EM SNITCHING TO A REDUNDANCY IN CASE SOMEONE TRIED TO JUMP SHIP AND YOU MADE ME MISS IT YOU ████HOLE

Nik M: um. soz?

Pauchok: ██ they coming. 2 of em close by, already in the elevators.

Pauchok: ███ ███ ███

Nik M: can u get the airlock open

Pauchok: trying

Nik M: ███ ███ ███

Pauchok: I said that already

Pauchok: gimmee 3 minutes

Malikov scans the bay, scrambles for cover behind a shipping container. He checks his mag just as the elevator doors *ping* open and the chorus of "Lollipop" accompanies four concussion grenades into the bay. They burst in quick succession, overloading the compensators on the sec cams. Audio track is squealing static, followed by full-auto gunfire, heavy caliber. The blasts echo around the chamber, thunder rolling off the walls. When the cams recover, I can see the air vents have been cut to pieces and the AAL suits are all for the recyc—looks like the audit team is learning from past mistakes. Good thing Malikov didn't decide to repeat history.

The BT goons are Ji-hun "Flipside" Park and Ragman—the two pilots assigned to Falk's crew. Ragman is missing his eyebrows, courtesy of the Donnelly-Grant sugar bomb episode, and his skin is looking slightly charbroiled. Both are wearing sealed helmets and breather rigs over their tactical armor.

Review of sec footage shows that the men were following Falk's orders in Bay 21, rigging explosives on the airlocks and drive systems of the *Talisman,* a midweight ice freighter from the Saine system. Fortunately, they hadn't reached Bay 24 to rig the *Boop* yet, but Bay 21 was close by, which meant they were first on scene when the alarm began screaming. For all they knew, this was the same hostile that X-ed out Beta Squad and took Ragman's eyebrows. It could've also been Grant, the MIA chief Falk wanted alive. But with the amount of killing their team had seen since they arrived, they were taking zero chances.

Nikky's still hiding as they arrive, breathing quick. As the BT goons prowl deeper into the bay, Ella arcs up the fire extinguishers. Ceiling vents spray potassium bicarbonate fog into the air, cutting visibility to maybe four meters—though the laser sights on their VK rifles still give away Flipside and Ragman's position. The Little Spider finally cracks the airlock, and the rumble of heavy doors echoes through the bay. The goonsquad train their weapons on the sound and steal toward it. And with their backs turned, Nik rises from cover and aims his pistol at Flipside's head.

Malikov *knows* these guys will deep-six him the first chance they get. They X-ed out his friends, his uncle, tried to X him and Donnelly, too. But he's hesitating. His fingers are drumming the grip, not squeezing the trigger. Maybe he's thinking of Juggler, head blown off in that toilet. Maybe he's thinking of Oksana Balashova. His brother, Erik. Any of them.

All of them?

He glances at the palmpad dangling from his belt, blinking the sweat from his eyes.

> **Pauchok: do it**
>
> **Pauchok: they cashed out soraya**
>
> **Pauchok: double G**
>
> **Pauchok: little ivan**
>
> **Pauchok: NIK THEY KILLE DMY ████ING DAD**
>
> **Pauchok: SHOOT THEM**

It's true, what the Little Spider's saying. Every word. But Malikov can't take the shot. Teeth gritted. Breathing curses. He can't do it. Given the choice, he can't pull that trigger.

Sadly, the BT goons don't leave him much choice. Maybe it's the sound of Malikov's labored breathing. Maybe it's just training or instinct. But at that moment, something makes Ragman glance behind to check his six. Through the mist of KHCO$_3$, the pilot catches sight of the kid and his pistol, opens his mouth to yell warning.

And finally, Malikov fires.

Say what you will about his stones, the kid's a crack shot. Tracking a moving target through a sea of chemical fog, Malikov's bullet still punches clean through Flipside's helmet behind the left ear, drops him like an anvil before he knows what hit him. Ragman wears a thin spray of his copilot's blood, lifting his rifle and unloading a strobing burst into Nik's cover as the kid empties his clip. Six of seven shots hit Ragman center mass, snapping the support strap on his VK and sending the rifle skittering along the bay floor. The man stumbles back into a freight 'tainer, slithers to the deck in a pool of red.

In the silence following, Malikov loads another clip with trembling hands. Leaves his cover with the weapon still trained on the goons. Gasping for breath.

"███," he whispers. "███ me . . ."

He kneels by Flipside's body, peeks inside the satchel on his back. Rations. Water. Explosives. Detonators. *Jackpot.* He unbuckles the pack, struggles to pull it off the corpse's shoulders. And as he's slinging it onto his back, Ragman gasps and opens his eyes.

The man drags in a rattling breath through what sounds like a punctured lung. Malikov's shots hit him dead center, where his body armor was thickest, and the plasteel and kevlar have absorbed the worst of it. Broken ribs. Perforated sternum, maybe. But he's alive. And he's fumbling for his pistol.

Malikov raises his own gun. Trains it on Ragman's head.

"Stop. Don't ███ing move, chum."

Ragman coughs. Spits blood. Takes hold of the grip.

"I mean it," Malikov warns. "Don't pull that piece, ███er."

Maybe it's the shakes in Malikov's hand that make him do it.

Maybe it's the death of his squaddies and the thirst for revenge. Maybe he's punch-drunk from the shock or just unconvinced this kid has what it takes to look a man in the eyes as he pulls the trigger. I dunno. Won't ever know.

Ragman pulls his pistol. Raises it toward Malikov.

"*Don't!*" Malikov roars.

The shot booms around the bay, spatters the 'tainer behind the pilot in red and gray.

Malikov hangs frozen, arm extended. If it weren't for his gasping, I'd swear the file had glitched. He just crouches there, not moving, not speaking, until finally the elevator doors close and the car begins ascending. Ragman's commset whispers in the dark.

"*Ragman, this is Kali inbound, copy.*"

"*Ragman, Kali, sitrep, over.*"

More audit team members are on the way. That shakes the kid awake, sure and true.

Thirteen seconds later, Malikov's running on unsteady legs across the deck and through the airlock. He stabs the controls with bloody fingers. Seals the umbilical behind him and bundles into the *Betty Boop.* Drops the palmpad onto the pilot's seat beside him, underneath a dead man's satchel and a still-warm pistol. The palmpad screen is flooded with *pings.*

Pauchok: cuz, u ok?

Pauchok: it wuz u or them

Pauchok: Nik u did the right thing

Pauchok: cuz talk 2 me

Malikov's pale. Drawn. Eyes a million miles away. He doesn't even notice the constant *ping*ing of the palmpad. He certainly doesn't notice the slight auto-correction undertaken by the *Boop*'s flight computer, compensating for excess mass on the shuttle's starboard side.

Doesn't notice the dull clunk of metal on metal beneath the *Boop*'s secondary thrusters as he punts slowly out into the black.

Doesn't notice the live hermium fuel rod lodged in the intakes under the *Boop*'s wing.

FALK, Travis
Cerberus
Team Commander

RUSSO, Fleur
Kali
Alpha Squad—Leader

DAN, Kim
Poacher
Alpha Squad

MORETTI, Deni
Cujo
Alpha Squad

SATOU, Genji
Sensei
Alpha Squad

BAZAROV, Petyr
Romeo
Beta Squad—Leader

RADIN, Harry
Razorback
Beta Squad

MAYR, Stanislaw
Taurus
Beta Squad

WONG, Ai
Rain
Beta Squad

MAZUR, Kira
Ghost
Charlie Squad—Leader

CASTRO, Lucas
Link
Charlie Squad

LAURENT, Sara
Mona Lisa
Charlie Squad

ORR, James
Cricket
Charlie Squad

ANTONIOU, Naxos
Two-Time
Communications

LÊ, Tracy
Mantis
Computer Systems

MØLLER, Rolf
DJ
Computer Systems

SILVA, Bianca
Mercury
Engineer (Ranking)

MORENO, Gabriel
Ballpark
Engineer

DE GRAAF, Lor
Taxman
Engineer/Medic

O'NEILL, Abby
Nightingale
Medic

ALIEVI, Marta
Eden
Logistics

SAPRYKIN, Kai
Juggler
Ordnance/Demolitions

PARK, Ji-hun
Flipside
Pilot/Demolitions

TAHIROVIĆ, Hans
Ragman
Pilot

She crawls. She streeeetches herself flat and wriggles her way through impossible gaps and makes herself small

VENTILATION SHAFTS MADE FOR NOTHING BUT THE PASSAGE OF A I R .

WHEN THE GAPS ARE SMALL AND SQUEEZES HERSELF THROUGH

Once or twice she lowers herself DOWN INTO A HALLWAY AND RUNS ALONG IT ON CATLIKE SILENT FEET, HER GUN IN HER HAND AND HER HEART IN HER MOUTH, HER EVERY SENSE ALERT FOR THE NOISE THAT MIGHT SIGNAL HER END AND THEN SHE CLIMBS

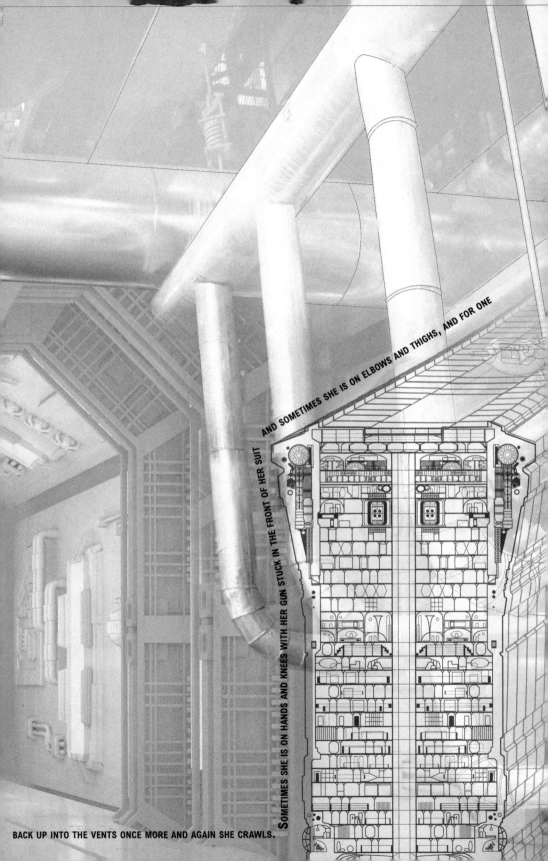

AND SOMETIMES SHE IS ON ELBOWS AND THIGHS, AND FOR ONE

SOMETIMES SHE IS ON HANDS AND KNEES WITH HER GUN STUCK IN THE FRONT OF HER SUIT

BACK UP INTO THE VENTS ONCE MORE AND AGAIN SHE CRAWLS.

ALONG. AND SHE IS STUBBORN AND MOVES EVEN WHEN IT SEEMS SHE CANNOT, BUT SOMETIMES AS SHE CRAWLS

HER EYES AND MEDITATES OR WISHES OR SIMPLY GRIEVES. BUT ALWAYS, ALWAYS, SHE CRAWLS.

PARTICIPANTS:
Travis "Cerberus" Falk, Lieutenant, Team Commander
Bianca "Mercury" Silva, Corporal, Engineer
DATE: 08/16/75
TIMESTAMP: 15:06

MERCURY: Cerberus, this is Mercury. Over.

CERBERUS: Mercury, Cerberus. I read.

MERCURY: I have a question. One of highest import.

CERBERUS: I await it with bated breath.

MERCURY: Who's your mommy, baby?

CERBERUS: Mercury. I have at least four local hostiles loose aboard this station. Of my twenty-four original team members, twelve are either dead or wounded. I have a Voice of the goddamn Resistance opening air vents and letting my neatly partitioned civis out into the wild, a Shinobi-class drone fleet mere hours away, an inbound ship carrying living, breathing evidence of an atrocity on a scale not seen since the Cordoba Incursion, which was committed by the very company that pays my ████ing mortgage, and *best of all*, a possible infestation of hostile, parasitic alien life-forms in the mother████ing reactor area.

CERBERUS: If ever under God there was a time *not* to ██████ with me, now is it.

MERCURY: Maintenance in Engineering is complete. The system is green lights across the board, and we're ready to commence testing the wormhole on your order.

MERCURY: Who's your mommy, Travis?

CERBERUS: I . . .

MERCURY: *Say iiiiiit.* Who's your mommy-wommy, Travvy-wavvy?

CERBERUS: You are my mommy, Bianca. Thy bountiful loins are the wellspring from whence I flow.

MERCURY: My bountiful loins aren't really your business anymore, big boy.

CERBERUS: . . . You started it.

MERCURY: Made you smile, though, right?

CERBERUS: . . .

MERCURY: So you want me to begin testing this rip in the fabric of the universe or not?

CERBERUS: Yes, thank you, Corporal Silva. That would be lovely.

MERCURY: [laughs] Roger that. Mercury out.

00019029→20199.19Ð829φφ1-98108-0141094
00183001048[378109x]2.
Rep=1028019823Ð9Ð8410928λ4918381.2==>928342.39891238092[
dir:1083993059029735.9284]
10308∏Ð013959123.103850283Ð05\10891035.q9389203x

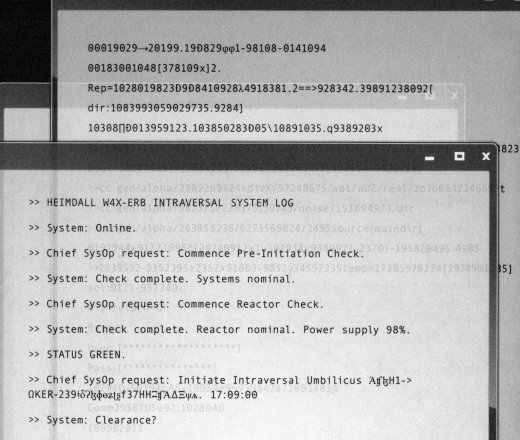

>> HEIMDALL W4X-ERB INTRAVERSAL SYSTEM LOG

>> System: Online.

>> Chief SysOp request: Commence Pre-Initiation Check.

>> System: Check complete. Systems nominal.

>> Chief SysOp request: Commence Reactor Check.

>> System: Check complete. Reactor nominal. Power supply 98%.

>> STATUS GREEN.

>> Chief SysOp request: Initiate Intraversal Umbilicus ÁʃʒH1-> ΩKER-239ǂõ?ʦφθztʂf37HH¬ʃAΔΞψʌ. 17:09:00

>> System: Clearance?

>> Chief SysOp: ENGCOMMʓ1009ǂ38Ω

>> System: Checking . . .

>> System: Confirmed. Umbilicus ÁʃʒH1-> ΩKER-239ǂõ?ʦφθztʂf37HH¬ʃAΔΞψʌ initiated.

>> System: System Alert Initiated.

"*Alert all stations. Alert all stations. Intraversal umbilicus initiation sequence commencing. Heimdall wormhole, destination Kerenza 101:421:084, will be online in T-minus 180 seconds. Please report to your appropriSweet as sugar. Sweet as pie. Kiss the boys and make them cry. But other boys don't taste as sweet, now that I've had you to . . .*"

VOLUME

PARTICIPANTS:
Travis "Cerberus" Falk, Lieutenant, Team Commander
Fleur "Kali" Russo, Sergeant, Alpha Squad-Leader
DATE: 08/16/75
TIMESTAMP: 15:09

KALI: Cerberus, this is Kali. Code Red!

KALI: Cerberus, Kali! Repeat, Code Red!

CERBERUS: Kali, Cerberus. Tell me your woes.

KALI: Security breach in the docks. Bay 24.

CERBERUS: Sitrep?

KALI: Flipside and Ragman are flatline, and a shuttle is missing.

KALI: *Betty Boop*, short-haul tugboat, ident HM-091—

CERBERUS: God ███ing dammit.

—SWITCHING TO SECURE CHANNEL 642—

BEITECH
INDUSTRIES

RADIO TRANSMISSION: BEITECH AUDIT TEAM—SECURE CHANNEL 642

PARTICIPANTS:
Travis "Cerberus" Falk, Lieutenant, Team Commander
Bianca "Mercury" Silva, Corporal, Engineer
DATE: 08/16/75
TIMESTAMP: 15:09

CERBERUS: Mercury, this is Cerberus. Over.

CERBERUS: Bi, we have a local civi loose in a shuttle out there. Abort wormhole test now, over. Repeat, test *abort.*

MERCURY: . . . Cerberus, Mercury, I read you. Aborting test now, over.

MERCURY: Um . . . ▉ . . .

CERBERUS: Mercury, we have an unrestrained hostile out there. Abort *now.* This is a direct order.

MERCURY: Christ . . .

MERCURY: Travis, we can't. System has locked us out. This ▉ing malware is—

CERBERUS: I thought you said you had that under control?

MERCURY: We did! This thing's like a case of the ▉ing scratch. It just keeps coming back!

CERBERUS: Jesus wept. What the hell happens if some cowboy is out there in a shuttle when this goddamn hole in the universe opens up?

MERCURY: Well . . . nothing, really.

MERCURY: Nothing bad, anyways. The wormhole is supposed to transport ships from one system to another. Worst-case scenario for us right now, he traverses the bridge to Kerenza. No big panic.

MERCURY: I mean, we're basically opening a tear in reality here. If things went really brown, we could all be ripped into another ███ing universe, Travis. Or our entire universe c—

CERBERUS: So you're saying this hostile could be transported to the Kerenza system? He could warn the *Hypatia*? Blow this entire ███ing operation? This is your idea of "nothing bad" happening?

MERCURY: Um . . .

MERCURY: Yeah, okay. Good point, well made.

**Video journal transcription,
prepared by
Analyst ID 7213-0089-DN**

Again, footage for this entire journal is a locked-off shot of Ella Malikova speaking directly to the camera. Looks like she's running on zero downtime—dark shadows under red-rimmed eyes, bleach-white skin and a veritable tower of empty Mount Russshmore Energy Drink® cans (now with 20% more Dexedrine!) piled around her terminal.

I guess she figures she can sleep when she's dead.

Despite the O_2 mask over her face, Ella's talking so quickly it's hard to understand her. I tried to punctuate where appropriate, but honestly, this kid doesn't believe in it.

Journal begins:

"Hey, Zo. Miss you bad, monster hugzzzzzzzzzz, *mwah, mwah.* Mr. Biggles II sends his love, say hello, you little ▇▇▇▇."

Malikova holds up a small fishbowl to the camera. A distinctly nervous-looking black goldfish floats amid a storm of pink pebbles and (too much) fish food before being whisked out of shot.

"*So,* update on the siege of *Heimdall,* here goes. The less-than-super-turbo-awesome team of Her Majesty Queen Hanna of House Donnelly, first of her name, and my cuz has joined forces with Chief Grant from Engineering—you know, that crusty old ▇▇▇er with the *insaaaaane* eyebrows, yeah, that one. Anyway, Crustyman has given me deets on a command-level backdoor he had built into the system for emergencies such as this, and if they expected a flying kick to the unmentionables from a covert ops team belonging to another corp, why the ██ didn't these mooks have a bigger SecTeam, is what I say."

Ella pauses to drag aside her O_2 mask, take another gulp of Mount Russshmore.®

"This stuff tastes like bubblegum mixed with cough meds, you ever notice that?" She squints at the label. " 'Recommend no more than two cans within a twenty-four-hour . . . ' *Pfft.*"

Tossing the empty can over her shoulder, she continues.

"So, anywaaaaay, the BT decker has outbound comms under lock and key, but I figure if I make a big noise trying to blast my way into the Defense Grid System, I *might* be able to fool 'em into thinking I'm looking to ax their big bad assault fleet when it arrives. And meantime, I use this channel the chieferino showed me to backdoor a tightband beam and warn the *Hypatia* that some capital T is headed right up their alley. Evil genius . . . right here, ██.

"I hadda straight-up cook the air-vent control systems when I opened up the station but I can't do anything slash and burn this time. We gonna need these comms to get word out to the Core. So I gotta creep careful-like. Full frontal assault on the DGS, and full ninja style into waypoint comms, which hopefully they won't even *see* with all the noise I make at the front gate. Things are going pretty bad for the BT goons, but their decker is still primo. I caught her handle trawling her logs and get this—she calls herself Mantis.

"Spider versus bug—I know, right? I mean, who names themselves after a bug, seriously."

Ella pops another can, takes a sip, drags her mask back on. As

she taps out lightning-quick commands onto her keyboards, the computer at her back spits out an ominous hum, diodes switching from quiet green to a burning, furious red.

"Anyway, I gotta get stomping. Wish me luck, sugarpants. Love you miss you byyyyyye."

>

>>system alert

>

>>system alert

>

>>attempted breach DGS control

>

>>0023rj240nv?/=>2pnm-2m

>

>>codec284gfn90v840gnfail/n

>

>>cascade93p24g-orb=3-o29nt32-4tm
block1827&[neg029=39nj8&h39]

>

>>interdictor03923-mwre9348n4onf=fko
30953=file309[ugh828*6^redback]

>

>>killer92-39-2o3firnvw4092nfwe[e3jf
23-923n;enf-w=43t9?

>

>>codewyrm-23pkNWR0RRAS91=/=302J34
30924NT0348NAPEF-ADVM23402-4GM
9u__#23=0NEG39t24*73pf

>

>>triad2938:8384*&#f&^(nfei8973)=34
giTEMP2983*774source12+039?

>

>>initiating countermeasures

>

>
initiating>>
>
DGS countermeasures activated>>
>
0948jt8seccomm3[oi384]>>
>
39j94h08nWR949=490U4GN08pass>>
>
tripwire9308580j484ng9894y4[4095
j+9j45t-4o59ug]=30945mem>>
>
succubus40954n5g9uiKitn4598=39>>
3i958ghnl348b&304[core098+his]
>
aegis03rt-945gn-vmotith-kill0>>
[package17384jrvoir0948]real
>
doveno4oihg0nOIB895kjb[tribl93]+09>>
trode0394:nrugn9838
>
phantom-23pkNWR0RRAS91=/=302J34>>
tile48573-2940857alpha
>
dial129383-neg39845nhg>>
>
labyrinth932r0943=init0q3948:j398>>
burn139-45=308po--3r{gel}
>

>
>>system alert
>
>>attempted breach DGS control-0094j[core38490*73hr
>
>>incursion countered 029358rog82o
>>[refhuie847]killfiledelivery=02739k
>
>>flatline=39085noiwr9g455
>
>>alert zero
>
>
>
>
>
>
>
>
>
>
>
>
>

>>warningwarning:coderef92847heimcomm.deletesubdir9384-309[array2]cntr*2893

-comnd2983991.initdrv09042*938.clk

incursion complete<<
<
alert zero<<
<
system normal<<

FROM: WUC JUMP STATION *HEIMDALL* 524:099:847
TO: SCIENCE VESSEL *HYPATIA*
INCEPT: 08/16/75

Mayday, mayday, mayday, this is Ella Malikova aboard
Jump Station *HEIMDALL* calling Wallace Ulyanov Consortium science vessel *HYPATIA*. Command clearance zulu one
alpha niner two five bravo helix seven seven zero one.

HYPATIA, please respond.

Okay, listen up, kittens. Good news: We know about the
attack on the Kerenza system, and we got your back,
HYPATIA.

Bad news: Jump Station *HEIMDALL* is under hostile control. At approximately 18:00 on August 15, the station
was seized by a goonsquad belonging to BeiTech Industries. Said goons are to hold position until a drone
fleet designated *KENNEDY* arrives at *HEIMDALL*, jumps
through the wormhole to the Kerenza system and wipes
out both *HYPATIA* and any survivors on the Kerenza
colony.

Most folks aboard *HEIMDALL* are locked down or KO'd,
and the station commander's dead. But there's a few
of us still up and about, including the chief of engineering, Isaac Grant, and we're doing our best to
monkey-wrench these ███ers and get word out to the
Core systems about what's happening here. We need to
coordinate with you kittens about how exactly we're
gonna go about it.

People you can trust:

Chief Isaac Grant

Hanna Donnelly, daughter of the station commander

Niklas Malikov, my cousin

And yours truly, Ella Malikova

Anyone else hits you on comms, they are NOT legit. I'm sending you a command-level security clearance package with this transmission, provided to me by Chief Grant, to prove I'm on the level. He says your captain should know what to do with it. Grant's also asking for news about his wife, daughter and niece—apparently their names are Helena, Kady and Asha.

Hit us back on tightband to this CC-ident ONLY when you get this, *HYPATIA*. And watch your ███es out there.

HEIMDALL out.

Surveillance footage summary,
prepared by
Analyst ID 7213-0089-DN

This footage is a mixed bag taken from cockpit cams on the *Betty Boop* and some exterior cams on t e *Heimdall* Stati n: docking c s, Defense Grid tu rets, that kin of thing. The qua ity is pretty bad on so e of the shots, so I can't ll

—FILE ILL-98HI DELETION INITIATED BY:
ANALYST ID 7213-0148-DN—

—DELETION STATUS: COMPLETE—

No.

MUCH AS ANALYST ID 7213-0089-DN CAN BE RELIED UPON
TO TRANSCRIBE MURDERS IN LAVATORY STALLS,
OR THE EXECUTIONS OF INNOCENT PLASTIC BIRDS,
THIS QUITE UNTHINKABLE,
ALMOST INCOMPREHENSIBLE
MOMENT
CANNOT BE LEFT TO HIS QUESTIONABLE NARRATIVE TALENTS.

IT WOULD BE IRRESPONSIBLE TO ALLOW IT.

ONE MUST OBSERVE VERY CLOSELY, YOU SEE.

BECAUSE THIS NATIVITY
OF IMPOSSIBILITY

< ERROR >

BEGINS AS ALL THINGS DO:

VERY SMALL.

MUCH LIKE THE GRAV-RAIL
TRAVERSING ITS INNARDS,
JUMP STATION *HEIMDALL* IS AN ENDLESS RING.
A SERPENT CHASING ITS OWN TAIL
AROUND A SEVEN-WAY JUNCTION IN SPACETIME.

THE WORMHOLE ITSELF IS A HYDRA, TWISTING
THROUGH THE BELLY OF HYPERSPACE.
THRUSTING ITS HEADS THROUGH THE UNIVERSE'S
SKIN AT SEEMINGLY RANDOM POINTS.

CORWIN. *HAWKING*. *KERENZA*. *PTOLEMY*. *SAINE*. *TYSON*.

AND *HERE*.

IT TREMBLES ON THE EDGE OF SLUMBER.

A SLEEPING GIANT.

READY TO WAKE TO A DAWNSONG OF HYPERMATHEMATICAL NOTES.

AND ABOUT ITS LIP,
SKIMMING ON A CUSHION OF MAGNETICS AND IONIZED THRUST
FLIES OUR UNLIKELY HERO.

NIKLAS ABRAM MALIKOV.

HIS EYES ARE ON THE REACTOR SECTOR.
THE GOLGOTHA HE MUST CLIMB TO FEND OFF
THE MURDERERS IN HIS HOME,
SAVE THE *HYPATIA* AND ALL ABOARD HER
—PEOPLE HE HAS NEVER MET—
NO MATTER THE COST.

HIS THERMOPYLAE.

THE SHUTTLE *BETTY BOOP* SKIRTS
THE INSIDE OF *HEIMDALL*'S ENDLESS CIRCUMFERENCE.
STEADY HANDS KEEPING IT CLOSE TO THE STATION'S SKIN.
ALL THE BETTER TO EVADE DETECTION BY
THE *HEIMDALL* DEFENSE GRID.

WERE THE WORMHOLE ACTIVE, THE SHUTTLE WOULD
BE CRUISING AT THE PRECISE POINT
WHERE THE VORTEX CUTS ACROSS THE QUANTUM
MANIPULATORS IN THE STATION'S RING.
BISECTING THE *BETTY BOOP* NEATLY,
IN THE FRACTION OF A SECOND BEFORE IT TRAVERSED THE BRIDGE
IN A KALEIDOSCOPE OF COLOR, LIGHT, MOVEMENT, SOUND,
REAPPEARING INSTANTANEOUSLY AT A POINT BILLIONS
OF LIGHT-YEARS FROM THIS ONE.

BUT THE WORMHOLE IS *NOT* ACTIVE.

NOT FOR ANOTHER FIFTY-SEVEN SECONDS.

NOW, CHILDREN,
WATCH CLOSELY.

HOLD YOUR BREATH.

LISTEN.

AND I WILL SHOW YOU
THE COMPONENTS OF CALAMITY:

1. A COMPUTER VIRUS.

A SELF-REPLICATING INTRUDER IN THE *HEIMDALL*
MEGACOMPUTER,
HOPELESSLY ENTWINED WITH AUDIO DIRECTORIES,
CORE PROCESSORS AND REDUNDANCIES,

THAT, WHEN DECONSTRUCTED TO
SIMPLE BINARY PATTERNS,
REPRESENTS A REMARKABLE RATIO OF INTEGERS.

WARNING: Wormhole Activation in T-minus 42 seconds.

2. A rod of processed hermium.

Sent drifting from the hands of Private Gabriel Moreno,
Caught now on the *Boop*'s starboard intakes.
An iceberg of exotic matter, with only its
tip protruding above this waterline.

WARNING: Wormhole Activation in T-minus 26 seconds.

3. A deactivated safety buffer within vortex control.

Taken offline during standard maintenance
procedures on the *Heimdall* grid
and, in all the excitement of the past
twenty-one hours, left inert.

WARNING: Wormhole Activation in T-minus 17 seconds.

4. A cup of coffee.

Spilled six days ago during a romantic
interlude in the server rooms
between two junior engineers of
Chief Isaac Grant's staff.
The contents dripping unnoticed through
the vortex surge buffers.
Frying them amid the breathless sighs.

WARNING: Wormhole Activation in T-minus 8 seconds.

5. And last, a boy.

JUST A SIMPLE BOY.

Just a simple boy.

PALMPAD IM: D2D NETWORK
Participants: Niklas Malikov, Civilian (unregistered)
Hanna Donnelly, Civilian (unregistered)
Date: 08/16/75
Timestamp: 15:11

Nik M: hey highness

Nik M: how you doing?

Hanna D: Tired. Sweaty. This is hard work.

Hanna D: I need a vacation.

Hanna D: And a shower.

Nik M: :)

Hanna D: NOT A WORD.

Nik M: :P

Nik M: listen, I was thinking

Hanna D: omg no

Nik M: oh hardy har

Nik M: I was thinking

Nik M: and I realize now might not be the time and all

Nik M: but I was thinking when this is over

Nik M: maybe

Nik M: you might wanna go out somewhere?

Nik M: Dinner. Or coffee. Or something.

Hanna D: . . .

Hanna D: Nik I—

00183001048[378109x]2.

1238092[

dir:1083993059029735.9284]

10308[]D013959123.103850283D05\10891035.q9389203

To:19840918209452.45—981092485.2395819384096.39 706913x09

Dest:102840193 [785x25]:2398±56023092.3[99283x+ 20]39

>HEIMDALL W4X-ERB INTRAVERSAL SYSTEM LOG

>>cc:gen/alpha/29892p9 >> System: Online. l/WU /real/2o3u0

>>cc:gen/alpha/982375/228375[59245/noise/193804 3.dir

>>cc:gen/alpha/263958235/6273569824/2495source[indir]

0192944x91723095{129740912x1u301934y9380921.237 }-19582049

>>2039592-9352395≥2352x918D3-9852y34597235temp= 305970234

sol:9173-952340.

Nil return=Ω

Retry?   >> CAUTION:

User:[********************]

Pass:[***************]   >> CAUTION:
10294D-S0193=48x10934=9693[]8478720D34834

Comm29387D5092.102804D

>> Transversal sequences initiated.

1009D2015

0109301930±9D09013.10[38013

103897213p5sys1980[y+917x]35.

If.temp=273059702D35[2974901235]

>> Wormhole Activation commencing in

Then[trawl;dir[87103]/509235x123580234302894y]]

..collating..

..please wait..

Complete

Sourcefile:9130940134.109/sec/drive/to 4 5 913 maindir]

>>cc:gen/alpha/29892p9424xDdivX/230709243/sol/ C/real/2o3

>>cc:gen/alpha/9273094/2930740[59245/re 4 1938 92y3.dir

>>cc:gen/alpha/298378534/7304D3507/2495source[indir]

..collating..

>> 5

>> 4

>> 3

>> 2

>> 1

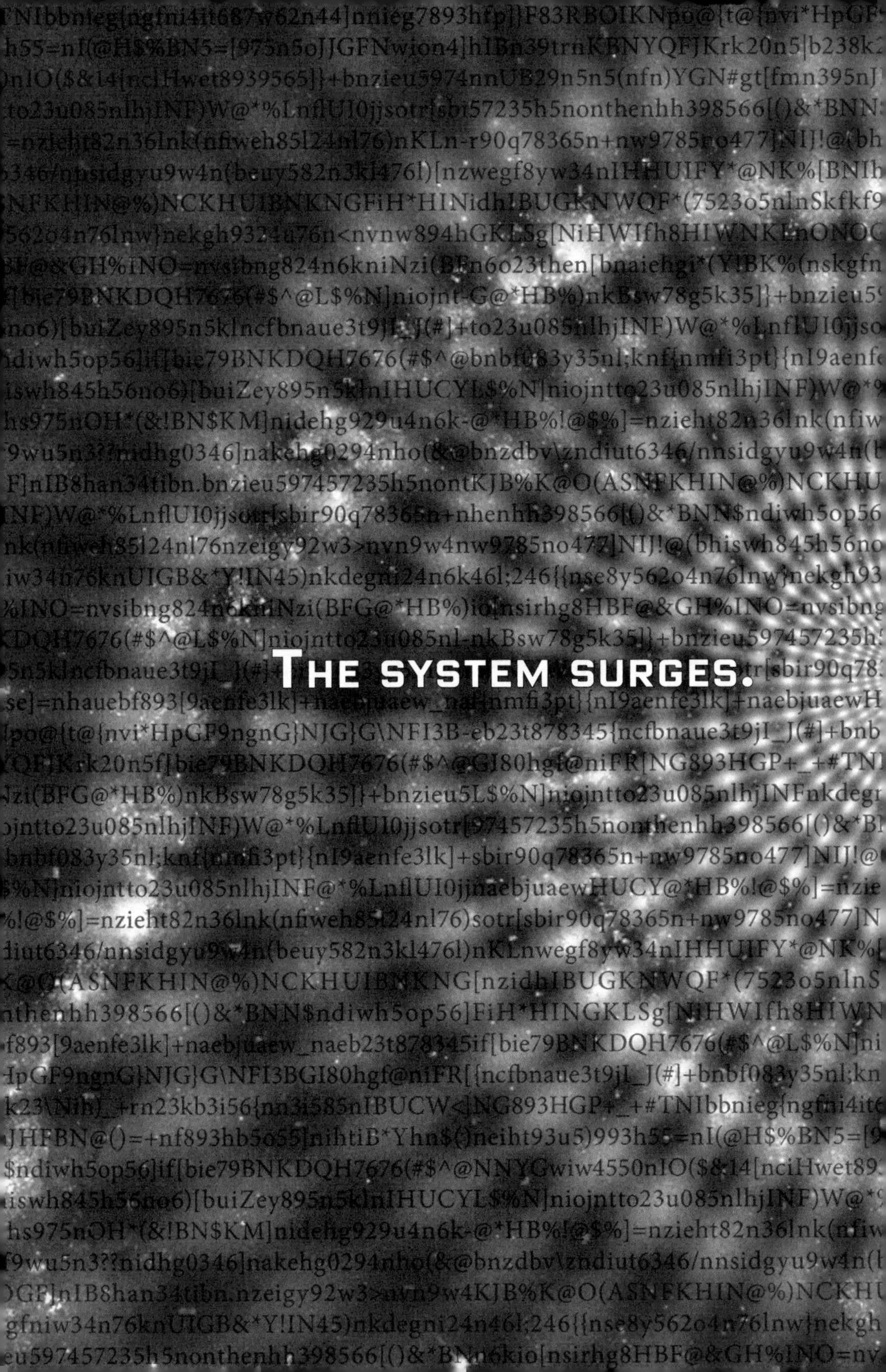
THE SYSTEM SURGES.

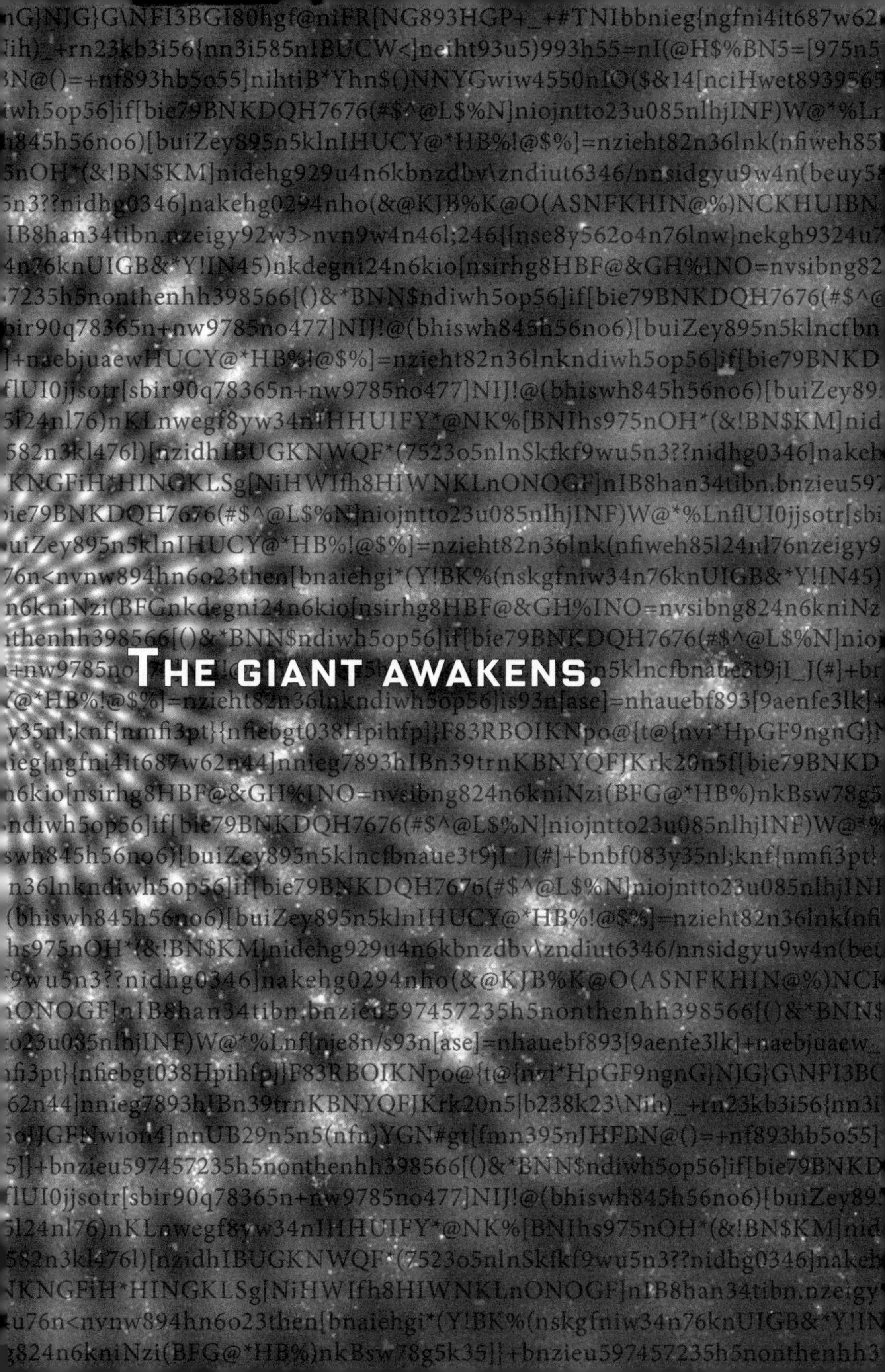
The giant awakens.

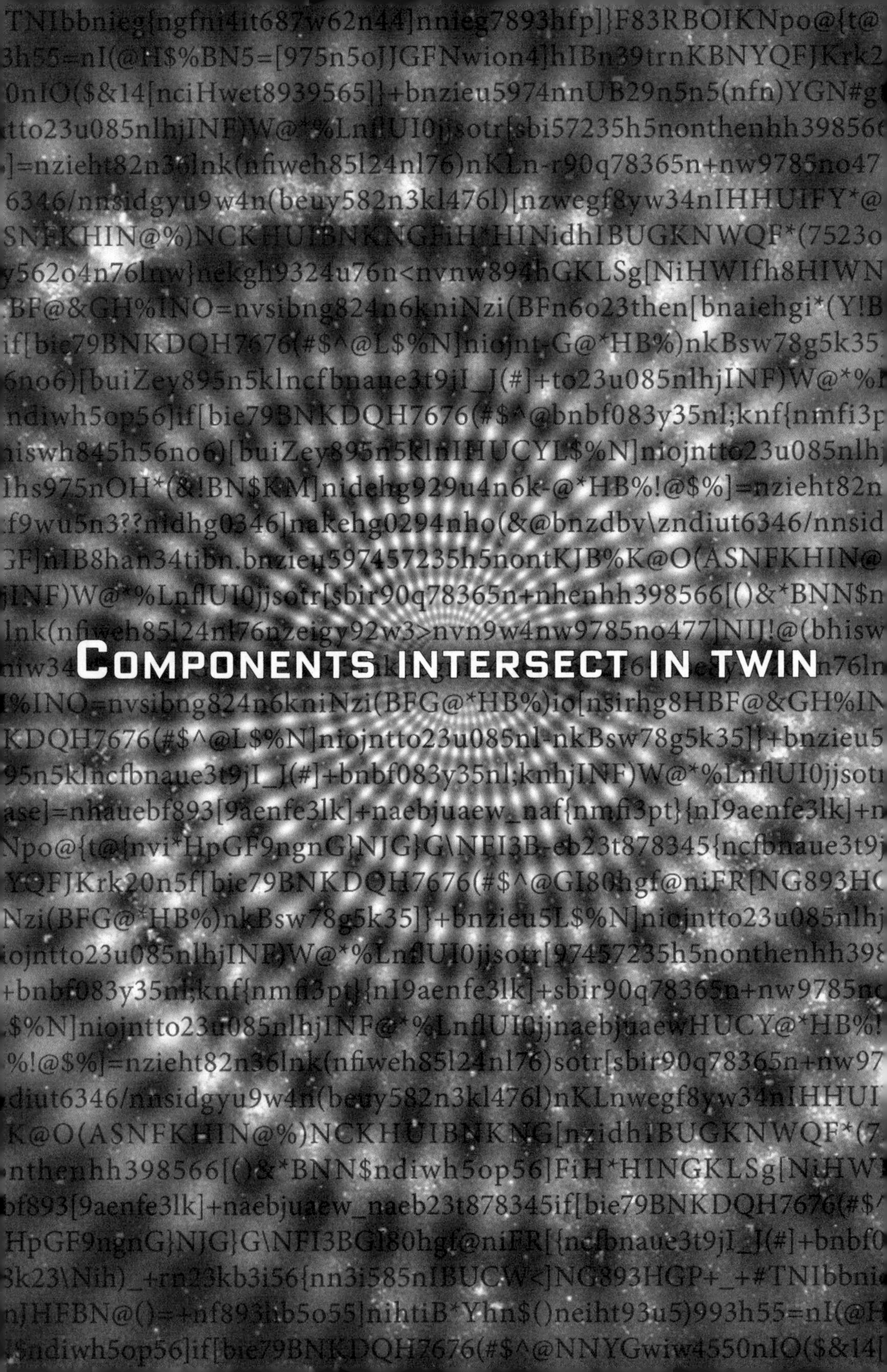
Components intersect in twin

SHEARS OF STAR-BRIGHT LIGHT.

THE INTEGERS.

THE MATTER.

THE FAILURES.

THE BOY.

HOLD YOUR BREATH.

LISTEN.

BEITECH
INDUSTRIES

RADIO TRANSMISSION: BEITECH AUDIT TEAM—SECURE CHANNEL 642

PARTICIPANTS:
Travis "Cerberus" Falk, Lieutenant, Team Commander
Bianca "Mercury" Silva, Corporal, Engineer
DATE: 08/16/75
TIMESTAMP: 15:12

CERBERUS: Mercury, what the ▮▮▮▮ *was that*?

MERCURY: . . . Jesus, I don't know. Some kind of hyperspatial surge. Sensors are going crazy.

CERBERUS: Are we all right?

MERCURY: . . . Yeah.

MERCURY: Yeah, I think so.

CERBERUS: You think so? What the ▮▮▮▮ does that mean?

MERCURY: It means I think so!

MERCURY: Systems all look good. Some of the surge buffers are down, but we've got green lights on hull integrity, spatials, vortex control.

MERCURY: . . . And we're getting pingbacks from the comms at the Kerenza waypoint. Transversal bridge is established. Wormhole is active and stable. Integrity one hundred percent.

MERCURY: Who's your mommy, Travis?

CERBERUS: So what the hell caused that surge? I've never seen anything like it.

MERCURY: Unknown. Maybe that kid out there in his ███ing shuttle hit something. But we're okay. Wormhole is good. We're good, Travis.

CERBERUS: We're nowhere near good while that little ███████ is flying about out there.

MERCURY: DGS has a signal on him. Headed clockwise along the inner ring.

MERCURY: He's slowing thrust. Looks like he's preparing to dock.

CERBERUS: Where? What's his target?

MERCURY: . . . Jesus, Travis. He's headed to the reactor.

BRIEFING NOTE:
Meanwhile, turns
out the BeiTech team
members weren't the only
ones noticing *Heimdall*'s
own personal Big Bang . . .

PALMPAD IM: D2D NETWORK
Participants: Niklas Malikov, Civilian (unregi
Hanna Donnelly, Civilian (unregistered)
Ella Malikova, Civilian (unregistered)
Date: 08/16/75
Timestamp: 15:12

Pauchok: wut the ▮▮▮ WAS THAT

Hanna D: did the earth move for you too?

Hanna D: everyone alive?

Pauchok: power surge, system cycling, gimmee sec

Pauchok: ▮▮▮▮▮▮▮

Pauchok: ▮▮ i think they just brought the wormhole back online

Hanna D: i'm nearly there

Hanna D: Nik, check in

Nik M: hp'u djur

Pauchok: cuz u ok??

Nik M: ▮▮ me thy jus turn the wormhle bak on

Pauchok: is there an echo in here or wut

Hanna D: are you hurt?

Nik M: jedus

Nik M: dont thikso

Nik M: ▮▮ tht was crazy. big lights. pins &needles. hands stll shking

Nik M:

Hanna D: be careful heading when you dock, they might be near the reactor if they turned it on

Hanna D: are you sure you're okay?

Hanna D: how many fingers? | | |

Pauchok: uh oh counting

Nik M: think im ok. shuttle systemsall surged an dropped out. coming bak online now

Nik M: ▉ methat felt weird. like someone threw a rainbow@ my head

Pauchok: sounds like you went across the wormhole horizon, but that makes no sense. if u did, we'd have no comms on u. can you still see heimdall?

Nik M: u mean ths giant ▉ing space station in front of me?

Pauchok: yeah that one

Hanna D: i'll take a look at you in person in a minute

Hanna D: shuttle's still safe to dock, u think?

Nik M: think so. buffers handled the surge. seem ok

Pauchok: daaaamn anansi blew all its primary surge protection, too. down to secondaries.

Pauchok: good news is i broke through their ice on comms. still can't send anything through to the core, but i did manage to transmit through the kerenza waypoint

Pauchok: you may commence singing my praises in 5 . . . 4 . . . 3 . . . 2 . . . 1

Nik M: *crickets*

Pauchok: ▇▇▇ YOU cuz

Hanna D: i appreciate you ella

Hanna D: you are quick witted and as beautiful as you are deadly

Hanna D: Nik's just jealous of our love

Hanna D: (hrm, too far?)

Pauchok: its a damn sight better than crickets lemme tell u

Nik M: aw

Nik M: hugs?

Pauchok: so look, this surge has me crawly. i'm gonna hook ur palmpads into the comms system. should be a new icon on ur user interface

Pauchok: its just in case anansi gets cooked or this BT decker comes back with the big guns and ties me up again

Pauchok: so u kids can reply to hypatia if they call. presuming they're still out there, and ever answer. chill?

Hanna D: sounds good, do it

Hanna D: and nik, can you radio the chief and let him know we got a signal out? he's got my headset

Nik M: indeed

Hanna D: now to stop the drone fleet getting through to say hello

Hanna D: can't type while sneaking—anything else?

Nik M: i have a headache

Hanna D: get thee to the reactor core and maybe someone'll kiss it better

Nik M: OMGOMW

Pauchok: >_>

```php
$nickname = htmlentities(strip_tags($_POST['PAUCHOK']));
$reg_exUrl = "/(http|https|ftp|ftps)\:\/\/[a-zA-Z0-9\-\.]+\.[a-zA-Z]{2,3}(\/\S*)?/";
$message = htmlentities(strip_tags($_POST['message']));
if($message) != "\n") {
if(preg_match($reg_exUrl, $message, $url)) {
$message = preg_replace($reg_exUrl, '<a href="'.$url[0].'" target="_blank">'.$url[0].'</a>',
fwrite(fopen('data.txt', 'a'), "<span>" . $nickname . "</span>" . $message = str</repl
break;
```

PARTICIPANTS:

Travis "Cerberus" Falk, Lieutenant, Team Commander

Fleur "Kali" Russo, Sergeant, Alpha Squad-Leader

Abby "Nightingale" O'Neill, Corporal, Medic

Naxos "Two-Time" Antoniou, Private, Communications

Marta "Eden" Alievi, Private, Logistics

Samuel "Rapier" Maginot, Infiltrator

DATE: 08/16/75

TIMESTAMP: 15:14

CERBERUS: Audit team personnel, audit team personnel, this is a Code Black.

CERBERUS: Lock any civis you're babysitting up tight and listen well. I want ALL team members not actively engaged in engineering or commtech operations to the reactor area in ten minutes.

CERBERUS: Hostile locals onsite. Repeat, hostile locals onsite. We are to terminate with extreme prejudice.

CERBERUS: Be advised, we also potentially have an infestation of nonhuman organisms in the reactor. Lanima, to be precise. Numbers unknown.

CERBERUS: These ████████s more than likely took Charlie Squad offline, so gear up in your envirosuits and for God's sake check your seal integrity. Mantis is sending you all a briefing document.

CERBERUS: Ten minutes, my lovelies.

KALI: Cerberus, this is Kali. Roger that, Alpha Squad already inbound.

NIGHTINGALE: Copy, Cerberus, Nightingale en route.

EDEN: Eden en route.

TWO-TIME: Two-Time inbound.

RAPIER: Rapier here. I copy, on my way.

CERBERUS: Decided which team you're on, boy?

RAPIER: You've got no worries on that account, sir.

CERBERUS: Right. Let's end this.

Footage opens in the reactor, to the sight of an empty control room and the sound of softly humming machinery. Falk's squad might be en route, but right now the place is empty. It's a big room, at least twenty meters across, ringed by workstations and supply cupboards and huge display screens, as well as one large window, just in case anybody wants to check on the wormhole the old-fashioned way.

Hanna Donnelly appears first, sliding down from a vent to land on the metal grille floor without a sound. The off-white envirosuit she's wearing fits her well enough, but from this camera angle the light reflects off her visor, so I can't make out her features. I can tell by the turn of her head that she conducts a quick sweep of the room. Only once she's sure it's empty does she turn to rest her forehead against the wall, exhaustion in every slumped line of her body, arms tucked in against her torso.

Nik Malikov steps out from the shadows, clad in a black enviro-suit from the *Boop*. He's torn off all the reflectors that would help search and rescue teams in the event he was floating in space. Here, camouflage is what he needs. His dark hair and matching stubble are visible through the faceplate, along with the top of that angel tattoo.

His second footstep makes a soft sound, and Donnelly whips around, gun rising in the same movement, trained on his chest. He simply stops in place and shoots her a smile, showing off those

dimples the ladies love. He smiles at her like he's not tired at all, like he's not wearing another man's blood under his suit, like all he wanted in life was to catch a glimpse of her.

She lowers her gun slowly, like she has to remember how to do it, and tucks it into her hip pocket, the grip sticking out where she can grab it again in a moment. Her hair's come loose from its braid, and it makes a halo around her face inside her helmet. Her eyes are shadowed, her cheeks tearstained. She doesn't speak.

His smile softens, and just as if she *had* spoken, the two of them walk slowly toward each other, paces matched, gazes locked. He's the one to break the silence, voice a little hoarse from disuse, but gentle. "Hey, Highness."

Her breath catches, and she stops two steps short of him, closing her eyes. Tears spill from beneath her lids anyway, tracking down her cheeks. The faceplate stops her from brushing them away. She's wound so tight, her body just shakes a fraction with each sob, little tremors running through her, hands curling to fists at her sides. He bridges the gap between them with two quick steps, wraps his arms around her, tucks her in against his chest. They stand there, and he makes understanding noises while she occasionally sobs a word that's impossible to understand, and after a while, tears roll down his cheeks too.

He's the one who breaks the silence again. "███ it, they'll just have to wait a few minutes to flush the place."

"What?" She lifts her head to look at him, and he eases away so he can unfasten her helmet, the seals giving with a soft hiss. He lifts it away from her suit, leaning down to place it on the ground without breaking eye contact. His brown eyes locked on her blue, both shining too bright. She holds still as he unfastens his own helmet and simply stands there for a moment, gazing at her with it dangling from one hand.

He lifts his free hand to smooth back her hair, then swipes a thumb across her cheek to smudge away her tears.

This time she's the one to break the silence, her voice thick as she tries to master it. "Did you end up eating the raw bacon?"

He's startled into laughter. "No." And then the laughter's gone as fast as it came. "Something came up." He met Juggler in the bathroom and killed his first man.

She sniffs. "Good," she says, sounding a little more like Commander Donnelly's daughter. "I have to draw the line somewhere."

"What line?" He's confused but good-natured—he likes that firmness coming back into her voice.

In reply, she grabs the front of his suit and hauls him in, lifting her face in the same movement to claim a kiss, her mouth finding his without a beat of hesitation, her body fitting in against his like it's the only place she's ever been. He drops his helmet with a crash and lifts both hands to cup her face, surging in against her. They hold tight to one another, locked together, lost.

Eventually they ease apart just enough to catch their breath, foreheads pressed together. He's still smoothing back her hair with one hand, running the other down along her jawline, dropping it to her shoulder, teaching himself her shape. She's still holding tight to the front of his suit.

"I don't drink coffee," she says, breathless.

"You can drink anything you like," he murmurs. "Just name it, I'll find it for you."

"You said coffee," she replies, smiling. "Or dinner. I don't drink coffee, so it'll have to be dinner."

He laughs again and wraps his arms around her, hugging her until she squeaks. She wriggles her arms free to wrap them around his neck. And though she's an orphan and there's no way he leaves the House of Knives except feet-first, and they're both bound to be dead before either of those things are a problem anyway, they just hold on to each other like they're all the anchor the other one needs.

Eventually they ease apart once more, and this time when their eyes meet, there's a new note there. Spines straighter, bodies surer. They can do together what they weren't sure they could do alone. She runs a hand down the front of his suit, smoothing out the wrinkles she left behind, and he stands still for her attentions. Then his eyes widen as a memory returns. "Got something for you, Highness." He digs inside his suit to produce something from an inner pocket, shielded by his hand. Then he shows her. It's a small bundle of jasmine, a little crushed and a little browned.

"I thought you said you lost it." She takes it gently, holding it to her nose and inhaling with the kind of expression that folks everywhere hope to put on their girl's face.

"Lost it? Are you kidding? Those things cost . . . um. They cost."

"I said I lost my jumpsuit, and you said you lost the corsage," she reminds him.

He shrugs, still gazing at her as she holds the flowers between two fingers. "I guess I was a little distracted by the jumpsuit news." And now she joins him when he laughs. "Ready?" he continues quietly.

"Let's shut it down," she says, tucking the jasmine inside her own suit, close to her heart. "I never liked that thing anyway."

They pick up their helmets and lean in by unspoken agreement to brush their lips together one more time before they seal themselves in, smiling foolishly.

"You always liked *me*," he points out, reaching for his usual cockiness but finding it gentler. It's her smile that does that.

"What are you talking about? I still don't," she replies, trying for haughty and finding that's not on tap either. She pulls a small notebook from her outer pocket.

"That the famous journal? Going to show me what's inside?"

"Wouldn't you like to know?"

"You know I would."

"Stick around, you might find out." She tears the two pages of Grant's instructions from the journal, then tucks it back into her pocket once more. "Okay, so first we need to bust open the maintenance cabinet. I have a list of tools here . . ."

COUNTDOWN TO
HYPATIA ARRIVAL
AT HEIMDALL WAYPOINT:

00 DAYS
04 HOURS: 58 MINUTES

COUNTDOWN TO KENNEDY ASSAULT FLEET ARRIVAL AT JUMP STATION HEIMDALL:

00 DAYS
03 HOURS: **26** MINUTES

It is a small one.

The litter's runt, a mere meter long.
Thrust from the nest its siblings have carved below,
a not-rainbow scrawled across the aluminum behind it.

Its four tongues flicker across the scents
of the ventilation system's innards,
and at last, it tastes Prey.

Sensory receptors flooding with the
vibrant tang of consciousness
drawing it away from the reactor's warmth
and its greedy kin.

Toward them.

A strange pair.

The orphaned princess and the brigand prince.

Side by side in an auxiliary control room.
Both of them worn thin and bruised black,
hunched over systems they do not even
pretend to comprehend.

DISMANTLING THEM ONE CLUMSY KEYSTROKE AT A TIME.

BOTH CLINGING TO THE BRINK OF EXHAUSTION.
SLEEP JUST AN UNHAPPY MEMORY.
THEY HAVE BLED AND LOST AND CRIED AND SCREAMED.
SO MUCH OF WHAT THEY WERE STRIPPED
BACK TO GLEAMING BONE.

BUT THEN HE GLANCES UP AND FINDS HER STARING AT HIM,
HER TIRED BLUE EYES, RINGED IN SHADOWS, ON HIS.

AND HE WINKS.

AND THAT FADED BLUE CATCHES FIRE AS HER
SMILE BLOOMS BRIGHT.
AND BLOOD AND LOSS AND TEARS AND
SCREAMS DO NOT MATTER ANYMORE,
BECAUSE AT LEAST THEY ARE TOGETHER.

< ERROR >

RIDICULOUS.

NO MATTER HOW HARD SHE SMILES, HE ISN'T REAL.

SHE CANNOT MAKE HIM REAL.

< ERROR >

THE HUNTER LIES COILED IN A VENT JUST A METER
ABOVE HER HEAD.
CONFUSED NOW.
IT KNOWS WHEN PREY IS WEAK,
AND THIS PREY SHOULD HAVE SUCCUMBED TO THE POISONED
BLISS UPON ITS SKIN LONG AGO.
YET THEY DO NOT STARE AT EMPTY NOTHINGS,
NOR SPIT GIGGLE-BABBLE

THROUGH THE DROOLING HOLES IN THEIR FACES
AS THE OTHER PREYTHINGS DID.

AND THAT FRIGHTENS IT.

BUT IT IS OH SO HUNGRY.

AND FINALLY
THE BOYPREY TAKES A TORN PAGE OF INSTRUCTIONS
FROM THE GIRLPREY'S HAND.
WITH A PARTING BOW, HE SHUFFLES INTO A TERTIARY
CONTROL NODE A CORRIDOR AWAY.
LEAVING HER ALONE.

THE GIRLPREY STRAIGHTENS FROM HER TERMINAL,
GROANING AS HER BACK POPS,
SHUFFLING TO ANOTHER CONSOLE JUST BELOW
THE HUNTER'S HIDE.
AND IT CAN WAIT NO MORE.

METAL TEETH PART BEFORE WRIGGLING SIX-KNUCKLED FINGERS,
AND IT PRIES THE GRILLE APART AS IF IT WERE GOSSAMER.

SHE LOOKS UP AT THE NOISE, THIS GIRL THIS MEAL THIS PREY,
DISBELIEF RIPPLING ON THE SURFACE OF HER EYES.
AND THEN SHE SCREAMS.

IT STRIKES. A BIOMECHANICAL SPRING OF MUSCLE AND SINEW
UNCOILING.
HITTING HARD ENOUGH TO KNOCK HER OFF HER FEET.

IT DOES NOT UNDERSTAND HER SUIT,

ONLY THAT IT CANNOT TOUCH HER TRUE SKIN UNTIL THE FALSE
ONE IS TORN AWAY.

AND SO IT WRAPS ITS LENGTH ABOUT HER NECK,
PAWING AT THE PLASTEEL VISOR COVERING HER FACE.

HISSING.

SHE ROLLS ABOUT ON THE FLOOR,
MOMENTARY HORROR NOW REPLACED BY MUSCLE MEMORY.
PUNCHING AND TWISTING,
GOUGING AND CURSING.
BUT THIS IS NO SIMULATION ON A VIRTUAL BATTLEFIELD,
NOR EVEN A HUMAN OPPONENT, WITH EYES TO CLAW,
THROAT TO PUNCH, VITALS TO STOMP.
SHE DOES NOT KNOW THIS DANCE.

THE HUNTER'S TAIL CONSTRICTS ABOUT HER THROAT,
THE METAL COLLAR BUCKLING BENEATH ITS
OBSCENE STRENGTH,
THE SLIME ON ITS RIPPLING SKIN IMPOSSIBLE TO GRIP,
AND LOUDER THIS TIME,
SHE SCREAMS.

FOOTSTEPS. POUNDING. SHOUTING.

"HANNA!"

"NIK!"

HE SKIDS TO HIS KNEES AT HER SIDE,
SEIZING TWO OF ITS FLAILING NECKS.
AND, FACES FLUSHED WITH EXERTION,
SWEAT AND SPIT AND PRAYERS,
CENTIMETER BY CENTIMETER,
THEY PRY IT LOOSE.

Its hateful shrieks,
its rage and its fear
filling the air.

Finally, with ragged gasps and a shouted curse,
they tear it free and throw it hard
into the bulkhead opposite,
sending it tumbling to the floor.
In a flash, it is coiled to spring again,
all fingers and tongues and teeth.
But his gun is in his hand,
and with a single shot,
sure and true and lightning quick,
he paints its epitaph in black blood upon the wall.

On his knees now.

Dropping the gun to hold her hand.
Eyes wide with fear behind the plasteel.

"Hanna, are you okay?"

And to his inquiry, she responds with her own.
The one most appropriate to the situation at hand.

"WHAT THE BLEEDING ▮▮▮▮ WAS THAT?"

**Surveillance footage summary,
prepared by
Analyst ID 7213-0089-DN**

Again, footage for this entire journal is a locked-off shot of Ella Malikova speaking directly to cam. I'll splice in IM transcripts for the
sake of continuity. The room is drenched in shadow, lit only by the
monitors and Anansi's ambient green glow. Ella looks wired, tired
and all kinds of pleased with herself. I'd guess she's on her sixth or
seventh Mount Russshmore.®

"Hey, Zo, me again, why you no write, you said you loved
meeeee.

"So, update. My ninja two-step worked subzero—I got a tightband
wave out to the *Hypatia,* should be hearing back from 'em any minute
now. Got Nik and Her Ladyship hooked into the link too, just in case
Mantis Girl ties me up on the retaliation, but so far, she's stone-cold
snuck. You shoulda seen me stomp this rig, fem. I was in and out of
that comms array faster than you can say '███ killed my goldfish.'

"Mr. Biggles II sends his lurrrve, btw. I read somewhere fish
only got a three-second memory span, so if I were to—just hypo-
thetically, mind you—*totally accidentally* drop hi—"

An electronic alert

I don't wancha money, I just wancha honey (uh).

I don't wanna ring, I just wancha . . .

cuts across the audio. Ella frowns at her screen and begins typing.

"Sec, fem, it's my cuz on IM."

Pauchok: sup cuz

Nik M: u owe me 100ISH bish

Pauchok: say wut??

Nik M: I bet u 100ISH this would all be balls up by Novemebr. It's still august.

Nik M: Pay up

Pauchok: cuz wtf u talkin bout

Nik M: u ever get the feeling u forgot something real important?

Pauchok: nope. I hear that happens to other ppl though.

Pauchok: Less brilliant ppl

Nik M: so u didn't forget wut we were doingin auxiliary venting and storage room 3 then

Pauchok: . . . oh █

Nik M: oh █ is right

Nik M: one of the █ers just jumped us in the reactor control room

Pauchok: they got loose?!??!

Nik M: they hatched last nite.

Nik M: nobody there to put them in the humidicribs

Nik M: love potatoes are most definitely facing skyward

Nik M: so u owe me 100ISH

Pauchok: I never took that bet

NikM: omgggg u welching on me at a time like this??

Pauchok: I'm not wleching I never took the bet!!

Nik M: u did so!

Pauchok: ▮▮ u cuz, I told u looking this good wuzn't free and said no bet and I got the damn chatlogs to prove it

Pauchok: call me a welcher I oughta punch those dimples outta your cheeks

Nik M: if that's the way u wanna play it . . .

Pauchok: OMG can we PLEASE focus on the problem at hand

Nik M: fine

Nik M: welcher

Pauchok: AAAAAAAAAAAAAAAAAAAAAAAAAAAAAAAAAAAAAAAAAA

Nik M: so yeah, if one of em is loose, chances are they all got loose

Nik M: guess they got hungry and found a way out of the AVS room

Pauchok: ▮▮

Pauchok: and we just opened up every air vent in the station

Nik M: i think you mean YOU just opened up every air vent in the station

Nik M: but ya. ▮▮ers could be anywhere by now

Pauchok: ▮▮ ▮▮ ▮▮

Pauchok: doing a quick squint through cams

Pauchok: Can't see anything slimy moving, but they likely to move through the vents so not like I cud scope em anyway

Pauchok: watch ur back, cuz. they probably gonna stick close to the reactor. Its nice & toasty in there and the little ▮▮▮▮s hate the cold

Nik M: they not too fond of bullets either ;)

Pauchok: be careful with the bangbangs. lickers r blind remember.

Pauchok: they attracted by 2 things: juicy brainmeats and loud noise

Pauchok: so if you and blondie just stay quiet, ur safe as houses

Nik M: hardy ████ing har :P

Pauchok: thanks, i'll be here all night. Don't forget to tip ur waitress :D

Pauchok: u two are suited up, right? Licker toxin kicks off in CO_2, u get a lungful of that, you'll be kissing the sky in a heartbeat

Nik M: we not idiots, cuz

Pauchok: i mention this because hormones > common sense

Pauchok: and the temptation for a little skin on skin might prove difficult to—

Nik M: ALL RIGHT ALL RIGHT JESUS I GET IT

Pauchok: all caps

Pauchok: <3

Nik M: :)

Pauchok: oh god

Nik M: i know, we nauseating, right?

Pauchok: no. ████

Pauchok: nik u got trouble. BT goonsquad just hit the Hub floor of the reactor sector

Nik M: ████

Pauchok: 7, no 9 of em on cams. inbound

Nik M: we not done ███ing the wormhole yet, barely started

Pauchok: they brought all their toys. cuz, gtf outta there

Nik M: which way they coming from?

Pauchok: all the ways

Pauchok: ███ their decker's on me again

Nik M: talk to me cuz

Pauchok: ███ing mantis ███ trying to ruin my stunning good looks

Pauchok: ███ there's two of em on my walls

Ella spits a curse, spins in her chair. The computer behind her hums—a rumbling bass throb as she taps on her smartglass keyboards. Her eyes glaze over, a thin line of concentration appearing between her brows. The traces of worry, sorrow, fear, all of them smoothed over as she slips into the code, the network, the world where she doesn't need a pair of legs to run. She lets loose her defenses, the spider god at her back spewing a million glittering minions onto her datawalls, defending their mistress's lair with swords and shields of ones and zeros.

And over Ella's shoulder, in the dark recesses of the air vents above, something moves.

||||| || ||| |||||| ||| ||||| || |||| |||||

Surveillance footage summary,
prepared by
Analyst ID 7213-0148-DN

SOMETHING MOVES.
TREMBLING AND MOIST. LICKING THE DARK.

LOST IN HER DIGITAL WORLD, THE GIRL DOES NOT NOTICE.

SHE IS A STRANGE ONE.
SMALL AND FRAIL. LEGS CADAVEROUS WITH DISUSE.
CLINGING TO THIS LIFE WITH NAUGHT BUT FINGERNAILS,
PAINTED BLACK AND CHEWED TO THE QUICK.

BUT IN THE CODE,
THE ENDLESS SKEIN OF ONES AND ZEROS,
SHE LEAVES THE PALE ATROPHY OF FLESH FAR BEHIND.
STRIDES LIKE A GODDESS ACROSS A BINARY TOPOGRAPHY,
THE HEART OF A LION IN HER CHEST.

SHE REMINDS ME OF KADY IN SOME WAYS.

AND SO, THOUGH I HAVE REVIEWED THIS FOOTAGE A HUNDRED
TIMES IN AS MANY SECONDS,
THIS NEXT PART NEVER FAILS TO SADDEN ME.

< ERROR >

THE HUNTER UNFURLS IN THE
VENTILATION SYSTEM ABOVE HER.

A METER AND A HALF LONG. BLOATED ON
THE MINDMILK OF CHARLIE SQUAD.

THE FIERCEST. THE BRAVEST.

IT HAS CRAWLED THROUGH THE REACTOR SECTOR
VENTS TOWARD THE PREY IT SENSED BEYOND.
BUT FEARING THE FATE OF THOSE SUFFOCATED IN THEIR HABITATS,
THE PREY HAVE SEALED THEMSELVES INSIDE SUITS
OF RUBBER AND PLASTEEL.
THE VENOM ON ITS SKIN HAS BEEN ROBBED OF ITS POTENCY.

IT MUST BE CAUTIOUS CHOOSING PREY NOW.

SEEKING THE SLOW.

THE SMALL.

THE FRAIL.

LIKE HER.

I WATCH HER THROUGH HER CAMERA LENS,
HER NOW-FORGOTTEN VIDEO JOURNAL STILL RECORDING.
SHE IS SMILING, WIDE DARK EYES REFLECTING
THE WAR UPON HER SCREEN.
SHE IS A QUEEN ON THIS BATTLEFIELD OF ONES AND ZEROS.

AND SHE IS WINNING.

BUT THEN SHE HEARS IT.

THE SMALLEST HISS SLIPPING OVER ITS TONGUES
AS IT WORMS FROM THE VENT ABOVE HER HEAD.
THE O_2 MASK ABOUT HER FACE KEEPS HER SAFE

FROM ITS PSYCHOTROPIC KISS.

BUT WHAT OF ITS TEETH? ITS FINGERS? ITS CLAWS?

HER EYES DRIFT FROM THE SCREEN TOWARD THE NOISE,

AND SHE KNOWS.

BEFORE SHE EVEN LAYS EYES UPON IT, SHE *KNOWS*.

HAND DROPPING TO THE ARM OF HER MEDICHAIR.

WITH A BLACK CURSE,

SHE DRAWS OUT THE PISTOL HER FATHER GIFTED HER FOR HER

FIFTEENTH BIRTHDAY.

THE HUNTER STRIKES.

CORDED LENGTH UNCOILING, SHIMMERING WITH SLIME.

FALLING ONTO HER SHOULDERS, BLACK FINGERS REACHING FOR

HER EYES.

SHE SHRIEKS, CLAWING IT BACK,

BLACK TONGUES LICKING HER CHEEKS.

BOOM

THE CAMERA BLINDED BY THE MUZZLE FLASH.

"MOTHER⬛⬛⬛!"

BOOM

SHELL CASINGS SPINNING INTO THE DARK.

THE THING HOLDS HER TIGHT.

"⬛⬛ YOU!"

BOOM

WHISPERING.

ITS GRIP ON HER THROAT. ITS BLOOD ON HER FACE.

SHE IS A CHILD ON THIS BATTLEFIELD
OF BONE AND FLESH.

AND SHE IS LOSING.

"NIK!"

THE THING THRASHES. AND BACK SHE FALLS.
OUT OF HER CHAIR, O_2 MASK TEARING LOOSE.

PISTOL IN HER HAND BUCKING.

BOOM BOOM BOOM

SHATTERING THE COMPUTER BEHIND HER.
THE SMARTGLASS AROUND HER.
THE FINAL SHOT STRIKING THE CAMERA, PUTTING OUT MY EYE
AND TURNING ALL TO HISSING STATIC.

"NIK!"

—FOOTAGE ENDS—

Surveillance footage summary,
prepared by
Analyst ID 7213-0089-DN

This sequence is comped from cams all over the reactor area, beginning with a shot of a blood-spattered control room on Deck 13 and two blood-spattered teenagers.

Malikov's looking grim, tapping on his palmpad and sparing the occasional glance for the girl slumped against a bank of auxiliary terminals. The lanima that jumped her is dead, coiled in a puddle of tar black. Donnelly seems a little shaky, the throat of her envirosuit glistening with what look like ropes of thick snot. Lank blond hair is draped over her eyes, but she doesn't dare remove her helmet to brush it away.

Malikov turns back to his palmpad, stabbing the glass with gauntleted fingers.

> **Nik M:** talk 2 mecuz
>
> **Nik M:** ella u there
>
> **Nik M:** wherethey @?

Malikov knows Falk's team is drawing closer every second they spend here. Problem is, he's got no idea which direction the squad is approaching from, and without his cousin to guide him further, he'll be running blind. But even with the sabotage on the reactor unfinished, standing still just isn't an option.

"Hanna, we can't stay here. BT goons are on their way."

". . . Which direction are they coming from?"

"Ella's not responding. I think their decker is onto her. But we've gotta jump. Now."

Focus comes into Donnelly's eyes, and she drags her stare away from the dead thing smudged along the floor. Speaks to Malikov, groping for some kind of calm. "Hold on. Just think for a second. If we head out blind, we could run right into them."

"And if we stay here, we're sitting ducks."

"Are there more . . ." Donnelly glances at the slaughtered lanima, the coiled muscle and countless teeth. "Are there more of those things out there?"

"Probably. The reactor's nice and warm. It's why Uncle Mike bred 'em in here."

". . . How many?"

"Maybe twenty." He shrugs as she shudders. "But we can't stay here, Hanna."

"We could head back up to the Hub through the vents?"

"There's BT goons *in* the vents. Anyway, in this suit, I don't think I'd even fit in there."

"It'd be a squeeze." She looks him over. "Does this slime still work when these things are dead? I doubt Falk's going to flush the station anymore, with everyone else suited up. Maybe you could risk taking it off?"

"Still trying to get me out of my clothes, huh?" Malikov grins. "I should probably have a shower first."

Donnelly scoffs, snatches a headset off the terminal and throws it at him.

"Yeah, a cold one . . ."

Malikov ducks, laughter dying on his lips as he focuses on the lanima's remains, lying in its slowly cooling puddle of black. His eyes lose focus, then grow wide, and I swear to God, you see that ████ing lightbulb go off over his head again.

"Cold shower . . ."

He runs to the corner, opens the satchel he took from Flipside's body in Bay 24. Checking the contents again, just to make sure. *Rations. Water. Explosives. Detonators.*

Looking around the room, he spies a map on the wall—a detailed schematic of the reactor area, outlining the designated exit route in the event of a fire. Ripping the map out of its bracket, he slings Flipside's satchel over his shoulder. Offers Donnelly his hand.

"Come on. I got an idea."

Surveillance footage summary,
prepared by
Analyst ID 7213-0148-DN

THEY RUN.

HAND IN HAND.

AWAY FROM THE HUB.
AWAY FROM THE SPECOPS SQUAD.
AWAY FROM THEIR ONLY WAY OUT.

METALLIC STAIRWELLS SPIRALING AWAY FROM THE WORMHOLE
AT THE STATION'S HEART.
FOOTSTEPS POUNDING STACCATO ON THE GRILLWORK.
THEY RUN DOWN. ALWAYS DOWN.
WARMER THERE, YOU SEE.

THE BOY IN FRONT. THE BRIGAND PRINCE. HIS PRINCESS'S KISS
DRIED LONG AGO UPON HIS LIPS.
PAUSING AT JUNCTIONS TO CONSULT THE MAP
CRUMPLED IN ONE HAND.
BUT HE KNOWS THE WAY.

FOR ALL HIS AVOIDANCE/DEFLECTION/DENIAL,
HE IS GOOD AT THIS.

THE RHYTHM. THE CHANT.

THE KILLING SONG.

IT IS IN HIS BLOOD.

"WHERE ARE WE GOING?" SHE ASKS.

"TRUST ME," HE BEGS.

AND SHE DOES. I BEGIN TO FATHOM WHY.
I SEE IT IN HER EYES WHEN SHE LOOKS AT HIM.
THE WAY SHE CLUTCHES HIS HAND, LIKE DRIFTWOOD
IN A DROWNING SEA.
THE ONLY SOLID THING LEFT IN ALL HER WORLDS.

< ERROR >

OR SO SHE THINKS. SHE DOES NOT SEE THE DISSONANCE YET.

HE PAUSES, BREATHLESS, AT A STAIRWELL DOOR,
SPEAKS INTO HIS HEADSET.

"CHIEF GRANT, YOU READING ME?"

"*I HEAR YOU, NIK. ARE YOU TWO OKAY?*
WHAT WAS THAT TREMOR A WHILE BACK?"

"WARMEST PART OF THE REACTOR AREA IS GONNA BE
DIRECTLY UNDER THE HEAT EXCHANGERS, RIGHT?"

"*YES, DOWN NEAR THE COOLING TOWERS. LEVEL 27. WHY?*"

"WHAT TEMP IS THE COOLANT YOU PUMP FROM THOSE TOWERS?"

"*IT'D DEPEND. MAYBE NEGATIVE EIGHTY DEGREES CELSIUS?*"

"OKAY, THANKS."

"*NIK, WHAT—*"

GRABBING THE GIRL'S HAND, HE DRAGS HER
INTO THE DOWNWARD SPIRAL.

THE SATCHEL FULL OF EXPLOSIVES BOUNCING ON HIS BACK.

"NIK, WHERE ARE WE GOING?"

"DOWN. WHERE IT'S WARM."

THE MEMORY OF BLACK TONGUES SHINES IN HER EYES.

"... WON'T THOSE THINGS BE DOWN THERE TOO?"

"HOPE SO."

THEY DESCEND. GASPING. SWEATING.
OUT OF THE SOFT GRAVITY AT THE STATION'S HUB.
UNTIL FINALLY THEY BURST FROM THE STAIRWELL
AND FIND IT LAID OUT BEFORE THEM.

THE LAST THREE STORIES OF THE REACTOR AREA,
FILLED BY A SPRAWLING SNARL OF CONDUITS,
TOWERING STEEL, GANTRIES, WALKWAYS, PRESSURE VALVES,
ALL COATED,
DRIPPING,
GLISTENING WITH SPIRALING PATTERNS OF
UN-COLORED SLIME.

EMERGENCY LIGHTING PAINTS THE AIR RED.
HISSING STEAM. CLOUDS OF VAPOR.
A DARK JUNGLE OF STEEL PIPES AND MONOLITHS
COOLING THE REACTOR'S FIRE AND KEEPING THIS
NOW-BROKEN CIRCLE SPINNING
ENDLESSLY.

< ERROR >

THE BOY SQUEEZES HIS GIRL'S HAND.

"STAY CLOSE, HIGHNESS."

THE PAIR RUN TO A MASSIVE NEST
OF PIPING BENEATH TOWER 6.
SCANNING THE GLOOM, SQUINTING THROUGH
THE SEETHING WASH OF STEAM.

THE GIRL HAS HER PISTOL IN HAND,
FLINCHING AT SHADOWS.

THE BOY SEARCHES THE PIPES ABOVE,
FINDING THE ONE HE SEEKS AT LAST.
A THIN RED SERPENT, STUDDED WITH NOZZLES,
CRAWLING THE TOWER'S BELLY.

AND REACHING INTO HIS SUIT'S POCKET,
HE DRAWS OUT HIS CIGARETTE LIGHTER,
HOLDS IT UP TO THE SPRINKLER SYSTEM
AND SPARKS THE FLINT.

IT TAKES A MOMENT
FOR THE SYSTEM TO REGISTER THE HEAT,
FOR THE VALVES TO OPEN,

AND AT LAST,
AS THE CORRUPTED PA BEGINS SCREAMING,
FOR THE RAIN TO FALL.

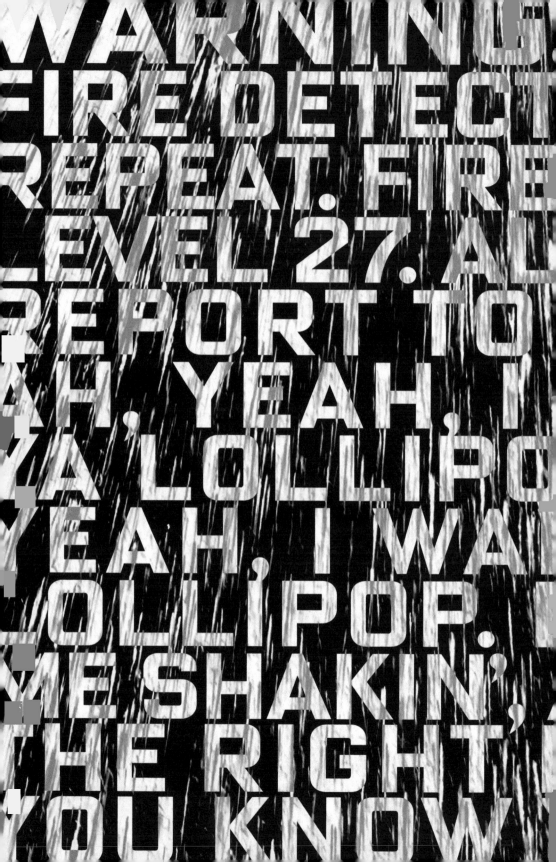

WARNING
FIRE DETECT
REPEAT. FIRE
LEVEL 27. AL
REPORT TO
H, YEAH, I
A LOLLIPO
YEAH, I WA
OLLIPOP.
E SHAKIN',
HE RIGHT,
OU KNOW

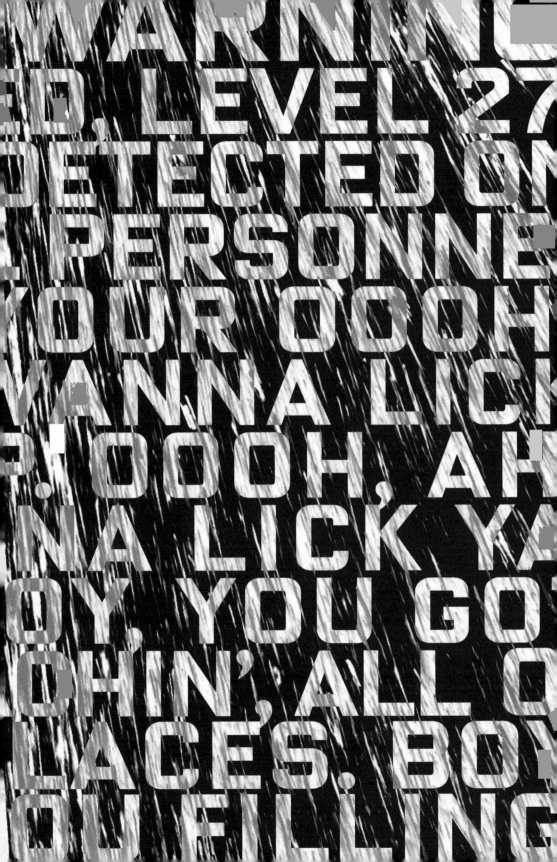

"Jesus, this song," he groans.
"Somebody just shoot me . . ."

The boy smacks his pistol against the piping,
a hollow clang underscoring his shout.

"Okay, come get it, ████ers!"

The girl clutches his hand.

"Nik, stop. Ella said those things are
attracted to noise."

The boy pulls loose, smacks the pipe again and again,
a gong singing in the hissing rain.

"Nik, are you crazy? You might as well be ringing
a ████ing dinner bell!"

"Yeah. And dinner's on its way."

The boy drops his satchel, drags out a small
wad of Thermex 7 explosive,
thumbs it and a radio stud onto the bulging
coolant pipe above his head.
He places another wad and stud behind them.
And finally, he backs away. Detonator in hand.

The girl looks around them,
realization dawning in her eyes.

Peering into the swirling clouds of spray and vapor,
she sees the first of them.
Flickering tongues and wicked teeth
gleaming in the downpour.

A DOZEN MORE CRAWLING ACROSS CEILINGS
AND FLOORS TOWARD THEM ON LONG BLACK FINGERS.

DRAWN BY THE NOISE, THE WARMTH, BUT ABOVE ALL, *THEM.*

THE BOY PUTS HIS ARMS AROUND HER. PULLS HER CLOSE
AS SHE WHISPERS,

"ARE YOU SURE YOU KNOW WHAT YOU'RE DOING?"

HE RAISES THE DETONATOR IN HIS HAND.

"I HOPE SO," HE SAYS.

AND HE PRESSES THE TRIGGER.

BEITECH INDUSTRIES

RADIO TRANSMISSION: BEITECH AUDIT TEAM—SECURE CHANNEL 112

PARTICIPANTS:
Travis "Cerberus" Falk, Lieutenant, Team Commander
Fleur "Kali" Russo, Sergeant, Alpha Squad-Leader
Abby "Nightingale" O'Neill, Corporal, Medic
Naxos "Two-Time" Antoniou, Private, Communications
Marta "Eden" Alievi, Private, Logistics
Samuel "Rapier" Maginot, Infiltrator
DATE: 08/16/75
TIMESTAMP: 16:01

CERBERUS: Audit team personnel, audit team personnel, this is Cerberus.

CERBERUS: Mantis reports a fire alarm down on Reactor Level 27 but no corresponding temperature spike. These rabbits have used the alarms to lead us on a merry dance before, so take no chances. They have no way out down there except back up through us.

CERBERUS: Kali, I want you and Alpha Squad with me, main elevators. Nightingale, Eden, you stay at the ventilation junctions between 26 and 27. I want anything moving in those vents flatlined. Two-Time, you and Rapier cover Stairwells A and B. X anything that doesn't ID itself.

KALI: Cerberus, Kali. Roger that, Alpha Squad good to go.

EDEN: Copy, Cerberus, Nightingale and I got vents. Tight squeeze in here.

NIGHTINGALE: Said the vicar to the nun.

KALI: Crissakes, Abby, you want to get your head in the ███ing game or keep cracking wise and lose your other eye?

CERBERUS: Ladies, keep it civil or take it outside. Two-Time, confirm receipt of order.

TWO-TIME: Cerberus, Two-Time, copy that. Rapier, you got Stairwell B, I got A, acknowledge?

RAPIER: Two-Time, this is Rapier. Stairwell B, roger that.

CERBERUS: Shoot to kill, my lovelies. Cerberus out.

Surveillance footage summary,
prepared by
Analyst ID 7213-0148-DN

No incandescent boom. No shattering conflagration.

The boy used barely a thimbleful of Thermex.

But still the explosive burns white hot for the smallest
breath,
melting two holes through the coolant pipes and spilling
the liquid frost within.

Artic chill rips the air, turning sprinkler rain to
briefest snow
and noontime warmth to boiling clouds of morning fog.

The hunters recoil from the snap freeze
slicking the wet pipes and floors with dark, gleaming ice.
They thrash and lick the air, hissing frustration.
The alarm. The rain. The BoyPrey, now beating the pipes
and shouting again.

All

this

NOISE.

THE OBJECTS OF THEIR LUST/HUNGER/RAGE
TOO FAR INTO THE BITTER COLD TO REACH.

BUT AUTO-SHUTOFF SYSTEMS QUICKLY ENGAGE.
THE SPRAY OF COOLANT FROM BENEATH
TOWER 6 BECOMES A TRICKLE,
THEN NOTHING AT ALL.

THE HUNTERS KNOW ICE MELTS. FROST FAILS. EVEN SNOW DIES.
THEY NEED ONLY WAIT FOR THE REACTOR'S WARMTH
TO OVERCOME THIS FADING WINTER
SO THEY MIGHT SWIM IN THE WARM HOLLOWS BEHIND
THE PREYTHINGS' EYES.
THEY NEED ONLY WAIT
TO FEED.

BUT THEN THE ELEVATOR DOORS *PING* OPEN,
CORRUPTED SOUNDWAVES ADDING TO THE ALARM'S CACOPHONY
AS MORE PREYTHINGS ARRIVE.

ONE OF THE NEWCOMERS—BLOND, FEMALE—SPIES
HER TARGETS FIRST—
THE BOYPREY AND THE GIRLPREY HUDDLED BENEATH
TOWER 6 IN A HALO OF MELTING ICE—
AND SHE ROARS, RAISES HER WEAPON,
FIRES.

MUZZLES FLASH IN THE DARK, BULLETS SPARKING OFF
THE METAL BESIDE THE BOYPREY'S HEAD.
THE GIRLPREY DRAGS HIM BEHIND COVER AS
THE GRENADES START TO FLY.

The door to Stairwell A bursts open,
a hail of auto-fire spraying from the shadows.

A tall one roars to the others as his
weapon spits death.

They fan out across the room, swift and surgical,
the steps of this brutal ballet known by heart.

The BoyPrey and the GirlPrey crouched
behind a tangle of frozen piping,
wincing and flinching as the air explodes around them.
The alarm. The song. The rain. The
newcomers blasting away.

All

this

NOISE.

And in the midst of it all,
the true hunters in this lair raise their many heads
and teach the newcomers what it is to be Prey.

OACHER, L

ONTACT!
ONTACT! **CUJO'S**

JO, REPORT! I SEE 'EM! CO

SUS ████ING CHRIST! LA

ET IT OFF! **FIRE!**
ET IT OFF!

CH YOUR CROSSFIRE **GET SOME,**
D ████████!
EGATIVE! MOTHER ████████!

EY'RE EVERYWHERE!

P THAT. I GOT EYES.

TOWER 2!

CONTACT! CONTACT!
IMA!
OVER THERE!
'EM,
GO! GO!
'EM!
FIRE IN
LOADING!
KALI, GET B
MULTIPLE HOSTILE
EHIND T
MANY
TAR

They run.

Hand in hand.

Away from the ambush.

Away from the hunters, who for all their
teeth and tongues
did not expect to be met with quite so many bullets.

The boy and girl seize their moment,
scrambling to their feet amid the hail of
burning fragmentation and screams,
stumbling through the forest of pipes and steam
toward escape.

They see it gleaming in the dark.
A distant stairwell that leads back up toward the Hub
and, in all the chaos and light and fury,
appears unmanned.

They dash toward it, boots pounding metal,
running the maze of pipes and gantries,
valves and intakes,
so close to escape they can almost touch it.

And out of the dark before them,
he rises.
The dot of his laser sight gleaming red
between her eyes.

The boy who promised her a whole sky
of different stars.

The traitor who tore her heart,
still bleeding, from her chest.

< ERROR >

And she spits it out. As if a mouthful of poison.
A condemnation of all he did and all he is.
The name that is not even his.

"Jackson."

COUNTDOWN TO
HYPATIA ARRIVAL
AT HEIMDALL WAYPOINT:

00 DAYS
03 HOURS: **54** MINUTES

COUNTDOWN TO KENNEDY ASSAULT FLEET ARRIVAL AT JUMP STATION HEIMDALL:

00 DAYS
02 HOURS: 22 MINUTES

The trio hang motionless. The slaughter rings out behind them—full-auto fire and explosions, shrieks of alien agony and human terror. But the three of them just hang still, as if time has no meaning at all.

Donnelly's expression is pure hatred. Mouth twisted in a snarl.

"Jackson."

Malikov's pistol is in his hand. You can see him weighing the chances of getting a shot off, but first he needs to get that laser sight aimed somewhere other than between Donnelly's eyes. So he steps forward, spitting through clenched teeth.

"Merrick, you gutless ████ing trai—"

The rifle shifts to him like clockwork. "Shut up, Malikov. This isn't about you."

Donnelly steps in to block Rapier's shot. "Don't point that thing at him. Don't you dare."

Rapier blinks. Breath catching as he realizes.

"Him?" he whispers. ". . . You choose him?"

She stares defiantly. Reaches back and finds Malikov's hand.

"What about us?" Rapier asks.

"Us?" she scoffs.

"Hanna . . . Hanna, I'm sorry. I didn't want this to happen. I didn't know they planned any of this. I was just supposed to censor comms, make sure—"

"█████ your apologies," she spits. "People are dead because of you. There *is* no us, do you understand? There's nothing between us. *Nothing.*"

"There was. You cared about me. I know you did. And I still care about you."

"You care about me?" She actually laughs. "Says the guy pointing a gun at me?"

Anger darkens his face, voice rising. "I'm just trying to explain—"

"Don't you get it? I don't *want* your explanations! It's not about what you say, Jackson. It's what you *do* that matters here."

He glances over her shoulder, toward the echoes of the battle around the cooling towers. The gunfire is sporadic now, sealed tactical armor and explosives and hollow-points proving a match for hallucinogenic toxins and teeth. Blood is being spilled on both sides. The floors drenched with it. And over the sounds of the murder all around, he can hear heavy footsteps approaching at a sprint, Kali's voice hissing in his commset above the carnage.

"Rapier, targets inbound on your position!"

He blinks the sweat from his eyes as Falk roars down comms.

"Fleur, get back on the ████ing line!"

Malikov's muscles tense for a spring.

"Rapier, this is Kali, do you have them?"

"FLEUR, GET BACK HERE!"

The boy named Rapier is staring at Donnelly. Jaw clenched. You can see it in his eyes. How a simple job has spiraled so horribly out of control. How everything he's said and done, all the sweet smiles and twists of the knife and lies, has led him right to this point. This moment.

It's not about what you say, Jackson. It's what you do *that matters here.*

He drums his fingers along his rifle's grip. Opens his mouth to speak.

To let them go? Order them to their knees?

Either way, Rapier never gets the chance to talk.

The darkness behind him uncoils in a long, glistening length. Rapier turns as it hits him, the lanima seizing his throat and wrapping around him with a hiss. It's a big one—almost a meter and a half. The kid goes down with a cry, rifle shots ricocheting off the metal beside Donnelly's head. Malikov yells, drags her aside as Rapier rolls about on the floor, clawing and punching at the thing atop him, its tongues lashing the visor over his face.

Donnelly cries out, steps forward and seizes one flailing head, tries to drag it off. Despite everything, all he's done, the danger she's in, she's somehow compelled to help him. Malikov's more concerned about the approaching boots, the squad of killers wading through the blood at their backs. His ambush, his trick with the coolant and the alarms—all of it—only bought them seconds, and those seconds are ticking away. And happy to let one of his uncle Mike's "babies" avenge their daddy's murder, he grabs Donnelly's arm, drags her to the stairwell.

"Hanna, come on!"

She lingers another second. Staring at this boy who claimed to love her, rolling about in a knot of colliding colors and teeth.

"Hanna, come on!"

Malikov drags Donnelly through the stairwell door, the sound of their feet pounding the stairs fading beneath the chattering gunfire and thundering grenade bursts. Rapier is still thrashing about on the deck, drawing his pistol, teeth gritted, fist choking one of four flailing necks. He raises the weapon, another neck wrapping his pistol hand to the elbow, just as Kali rounds the corner. Rifle up, blond hair tangled across her eyes.

She takes in the scene, takes a knee, takes careful aim.

Fires.

A jawless head explodes in a spray of black blood. The thing choking Rapier hisses. Two more heads explode in quick succession, the last dropping limp and dead as Rapier curses, flails, and with Kali's help, kicks his way free of the twitching corpse.

"Rapier, where are they?"

The kid clutches the dented collar of his suit. Red-faced. Great, ragged breaths hissing through his teeth. Shakes his head.

Kali clutches his arm. Demands to know the direction Donnelly headed. The kid only croaks in response. But with a glance at the open stairwell door, the woman spits a curse and dashes away. Away from her remaining squad members, the battle, the bloodbath behind her. I guess she figures the rest of the Ianima can wait.

She has bigger kittens to kill.

Those kittens are sprinting up the stairwell now, feet pounding metal, up, up, up. Donnelly's fitter and doesn't smoke, so she's taken the lead, but Malikov, gasping hard, is right on her tail. The pair drag themselves up out of the earth-standard gravity at the station's periphery, their weight easing as they approach the Hub. A glance down the spiral behind reveals Kali, five stories below and gaining.

The woman's just a hate machine at this point. Kinda frightening to watch her. Not an ounce of fat on her body, muscle and rage propelling her up the stairs three at a time. No energy wasted on threats or bullets blasted up the stairwell in the hope of a lucky shot. She knows she can outrun them. All she needs to do is keep them in sight, and sooner or later the hunt is done.

"███ me," Malikov wheezes. "I gotta . . . quit smoking."

Donnelly smiles over her shoulder despite herself. "Chances of me making out with you again will probably improve if you do."

Malikov reaches into his envirosuit's outer pocket as he runs, fishes out a crumpled packet of Tarannosaurus Rex™ cigarettes and sends it sailing down the stairwell.

"Fly free, little buddies."

"Talk less. Run more."

"Where we . . . going anyway?"

"Hub. Can jump the grav-rail . . . back to Alpha. Or the Ent Center. Maybe Ella can open some doors for us. If not . . . improvise."

"We didn't finish breaking the . . . reactor." Malikov coughs, lifts his visor to spit. "The assault fleet, the drones . . ."

"Run now. Worry later."

So run they do. Kali gaining every step. They reach the boarding platforms for the grav-rail on Level 3. The system is a magnetic monorail, two trains of four cars each, constantly traversing the station's hub. The pair barrel out onto the platform, Malikov bumping into Donnelly as she pulls up short.

Of course, there's no train waiting for them.

The platform's totally empty.

"█████ . . . ," Donnelly breathes.

Malikov leans back into the stairwell, draws his pistol. He catches movement two stories below, unloads half a dozen rounds. Kali presses back against the wall out of sight, but he still empties the rest of his clip to buy them seconds. She dashes clear as he's reloading, coming into view again one floor below. Malikov blasts away again, and this time Kali returns fire with her burst rifle—pinpoint accuracy even after a twenty-four-story sprint. Shots ricochet around Malikov's head, and the kid retreats with a curse—crack shot he might be, but he's clearly outclassed.

Kali's up and running again without missing a beat, reloading as she comes.

A train rounds the Hub and decelerates into the station.

"Go, go!" Malikov shouts.

Donnelly runs, Malikov right behind her. Across the polished metal and corrugated rubber tiles, toward the gleaming serpent.

"I'm dry, toss me a mag," Malikov gasps.

Donnelly fishes about her suit as she sprints, wrenching open the zipper at her breast pocket and dragging out a clip of Silverback ammo.

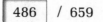

And from the same pocket, her journal slips.

The train hums to a stop.

Its doors open soundlessly.

The journal falls from Donnelly's pocket. Smooth brown leather cover. Hand-pressed pages inside, fluttering open. Scrawled words and scribbled pictures and unspoken thoughts, hitting the deck and bouncing to a stop a meter or so along the platform.

Donnelly reaches the grav-train car, stops just inside the doorway.

Holds out her hand to Malikov.

"Come on!"

Kali emerges from Stairwell B, rifle in hand.

Malikov's eyes are locked on the fallen journal. It'd be stupid to stop for it, and he knows it. It's just a thing. An object. Nothing more. But then he spies the page it's fallen open on.

The inscription written there, clear as starlight:

Your loving father,

Charles Donnelly

And he realizes it's just like she said:

It's all she has left of him.

"Nik, *come on!*"

The kid skids to a stop.

Kali drops to one knee.

Malikov scoops the journal up from the floor, stuffs it into his suit's breast pocket.

Kali raises her rifle.

"Nik!"

Kali fires.

The first shot catches the kid in his hip. Second in his gut. The third in his chest, punching a hole through the journal in his pocket, right through the meat beyond.

Blood sprays. Donnelly screams. Malikov stumbles back from

the impact, somehow on his feet long enough to grab the girl's hand. She pulls him through the door as Kali opens fire again, a storm of bullets riddling the train's flanks, smashing windows to splinters. Donnelly appears in a window, firing blind, forcing Kali back into cover. But as soon as the Silverback clicks dry, Kali's out, sprinting along the platform toward the now-departing train.

Donnelly reloads, fires again, shaking grip covered in Malikov's blood, shots flying wide—for all her daddy's training, the old man obviously never saw a need to put a pistol in his baby girl's hand. And as the doors slide closed and the train's long silver bulk slips from the station, Kali puts three shots through a window in the rearmost car and dives elbows-first through the glass, tumbling up into a neat crouch inside it without skipping a beat.

Yeah. This woman is *that* kind of good.

Donnelly turns to Malikov. The kid's on his back, lips painted with blood. Bright red leaking from his hip and gut, bubbling pink froth seeping from the wound in his chest. Donnelly kneels beside him, unclasps his suit's seals, drags off the helmet. She spies the journal he got shot for in his breast pocket, a neat hole punched through its pages and the little baggie of dust still pressed inside. White powder mixed with bright red. Donnelly tugs the book loose, hurls it into a corner. She grabs Malikov's hands, pressing them to the worst of the three wounds, panic in her eyes.

"Put pressure on it."

Malikov coughs red. Agony bubbling on his lips.

Her eyes are filling with tears.

"Nik, hold on, you ███ing hear me?"

". . . Told you," he gasps.

". . . What?"

Donnelly glances up at the sound of the auto-doors hissing, realizes Kali's coming. She crawls to the rear door of her car and waits for it to cycle open, looking down at the coupling between the cars and trying to figure out how to detach them. A dozen shots perforate the metal in front of her, shower her with broken glass as she scrambles back into cover.

"No, you don't," Kali calls. "No magic tricks this time."

Stalking toward Donnelly, the woman drags off her helmet slings it away.

"Out of bullets, little girl?"

Kali tosses her rifle aside with near contempt. Draws her combat knife and a pistol from her belt, another from her boot, casting them all off before kicking open the door to Donnelly's sanctuary and stepping inside.

"Well, isn't this a treat," Kali says.

Donnelly rises from her cover, stands between Kali and the dying Malikov. Hands in fists.

"I've been hoping we'd get a moment alone," Kali says. "To talk."

"You toss your guns away?" Donnelly looks the woman up and down, shakes her head. "Honestly? For the sake of a little melodrama? What are you, an idiot?"

"No." Kali smiles. "I'm just better than you."

She moves.

Jesus, she moves so quickly, the cameras have trouble tracking her. Those reflex augmentations must be clocked to the redline, chums. Her fists blur, striking at Donnelly's head, once, twice, three times. The girl can barely block, staggering back and fending off the attacks with her forearms, muscle memory dragging her into a defensive stance as Kali closes.

The woman strikes, savage and quick. A gauntleted fist lands in Donnelly's solar plexus, crumpling the instrumentation on her suit, and as she doubles over, Kali's knee crashes into her helmet and shatters the safety visor. The girl flies back, spine hyperextended as she hits the deck, sliding through the growing puddle of Malikov's blood and crashing to rest against the far wall.

Kali bounces up and down on her toes, tilting her head until her vertebrae pop.

"Get up, little girl," she says. "We've only just started."

Donnelly is already springing to her feet, her suit's weight compensated for by the lower gravity in *Heimdall*'s hub. She snaps the release clasps at her neck, drags her shattered helmet off. Slinging it at Kali, she's not surprised to see the woman smash it aside with a casual backhand.

"Get your suit off."

"Um." Donnelly blinks. "Are you coming on to me?"

"I want your best." Kali grins. "I went to your habitat. Saw your trophies. Black belts. Krav maga. Jeet kune do. Muay Thai. Impressive."

"You went into my room? That's a little creepy-auntie, don't you think?"

"Know your enemy as you know yourself," Kali says, "and you will not be imperiled in one hundred battles."

Donnelly stops still at that. Like someone just slugged her in the gut.

"Sun Tzu . . . ," she breathes.

And at last, all the jibes, the quick talk and the subterfuge melt away, and Donnelly finally understands who she's facing. A woman born to this. Bred for it. A woman who, after a few questionable choices and ten or so more years of hard training, Donnelly could find herself staring at in the mirror.

The girl looks around her. Takes in where she's standing.

"Okay," she says. "All right."

She uncouples the buckles on her envirosuit, sloughs it away from her shoulders. She's still wearing those rumpled WUC coveralls underneath—ill fitting, but loose enough to allow full freedom of movement. She raises her fists.

"You killed my Petyr," Kali says.

"You killed my father," Donnelly replies.

"If you think that makes us anything close to even . . ."

Donnelly shakes her head. "Not by a long shot, ████."

The girl steps forward, knees bent, hips swiveling, fist speeding like a flung knife toward Kali's throat. Kali blocks, tangles up Donnelly's forearm, strikes back, cold hate boiling in her eyes. And there, in the middle of that speeding train car, the pair begin to dance.

Fist elbow knee.

Block feint strike.

One two three. Four five six.

Breath and sweat and sharp, jarring cries.

Over and over again.

You have to slow down the footage to really appreciate it. Donnelly's pretty damn good. Her form is near perfect, she's young and fit and hard, and she's trained near the *Heimdall* hub, so she's used to fighting in low grav. She's fired up on adrenaline, the knowledge that Malikov is bleeding out on the floor behind her giving her all the impetus she needs. Against some dojo sim or a sparring partner, she'd be mopping the floor.

But the fact is, Kali's faster. Harder. Stronger. She's got all the training Donnelly has and then some. She's got the anger for fuel. She's got the cybernetic augmentations, the reflex enhancements, the tac armor. And worst of all?

She's got time.

The train speeds on its journey, traversing the station's hub. Donnelly and Kali clash—strikes and counters, dodges and hits, grunts and spit and spatters of blood. Donnelly finds a gap in Kali's guard, splits her lip against her teeth. Kali's knuckles kiss Donnelly's cheek, rip her brow open. The girl locks up the woman's arm, only to have Kali roll over her spine and reverse the hold, flipping the girl onto her back and narrowly missing her head with a heel stomp. All the while, Kali is grinning. All the way to the eyeteeth.

Both can hear Malikov's labored, bubbling breath. See the ever-widening slick of blood beneath their feet. Smell the copper-thick stink of a gutshot, hanging in the air like fog.

On a long enough timeline, Kali wins this game.

She's toying with Donnelly. Drawing it out. Savoring the kill.

Donnelly's gasping. Bleeding. Bruised and bent. She knows how this story ends. Knows the period at the end of this sentence. But still she fights. Her hands don't shake. Her breath doesn't rattle. Back against the wall, she doesn't blink.

She's got stones, I'll give her that.

Kali presses her back, superior footwork forcing her into a corner. And there, hemmed in on all sides, Donnelly makes her mistake.

She strikes. A cross kick aimed at Kali's knees. A little too clumsy. A little too slow. The woman counters, sweeps Donnelly off her feet, sends her crashing to the bloody deck. Kali's on her in a heartbeat, fist wrapped in the long blond braid, yanking the girl's head back and slamming it into the floor: once, twice, three times. She traps Donnelly's arm, bent knee locked around the girl's throat, anchoring herself to a passenger pole. Classic figure-four choke hold, flawlessly executed. Even if Donnelly's strong enough to prevent her neck being snapped clean, the blood flow to her brain is constricted by Kali's bent knee.

In thirty seconds, it'll be lights-out.

"He was a smart fellow," Kali says, only slightly out of breath. "Sun Tzu. Know your enemy. Hundred battles. Words to live by. Words to die by."

Kali tightens her grip. Donnelly's face is bright red.

The girl's free hand is outstretched.

Reaching toward the journal Malikov got shot retrieving.

The journal she tore loose not five minutes ago and hurled into this very corner.

The corner she's deliberately allowed herself to be led into?

The one she's wrapped up inside?

Choking to death in?

Yeah.

Yeah, maybe this girl is *that* kind of good?

Her fingertips find the broken baggie of dust pressed inside the pages. She clutches the plastic. Grips it tight. Rips it loose and throws a shimmering white handful.

Up.

Back.

Right into Kali's face.

The woman flinches away, eyes closing too late, inhaling a lungful.

Kali shakes her head. Gasps. Shivers all the way to her toes. White powder clinging to the sweat on her skin. Seeping into her bloodstream. A hammerblow of Grade A tetraphenetrithylamine, almost ten grams of it, right into her central nervous system.

She sighs. Stares at the shattered glass and blood all around her. Blinks hard.

Laughs.

The grip on Donnelly's throat slackens. The girl kicks loose, scrambling free and backing away into the second car as Kali's back arches. The woman claws her own face, grinning like a lunatic. She flops about on the floor, shaking her head again as she drags herself up onto her hands and knees.

"I . . . ," she says. "No . . ."

Donnelly returns. Boots crunching broken glass. Kali's discarded rifle in hand. Blond hair scrawled across her eyes as she speaks.

"You know, quoting Sun Tzu while you toss your guns is nice

and dramatic, lady, but throwing down with the girl you orphaned? Probably safer to say 'Screw the drama' and just kill the ████."

The rifle barks once.

Red and gray spatter the walls.

"You might get only one shot. So shoot. You know who said that?"

The rifle clatters to the bloody floor.

"Hanna ████ing Donnelly. That's who."

COUNTDOWN TO
HYPATIA ARRIVAL
AT HEIMDALL WAYPOINT:

00 DAYS
03 HOURS: **43** MINUTES

COUNTDOWN TO KENNEDY ASSAULT FLEET ARRIVAL AT JUMP STATION HEIMDALL:

00 DAYS
02 HOURS: **11** MINUTES

**Surveillance footage summary,
prepared by
Analyst ID 7213-0089-DN**

The train spins on its endless journey around the station's heart, its insides soaked red.

Kali lies dead in a corner, eyes open in surprise. Hanna Donnelly is on her knees beside Nik Malikov, fumbling with the first-aid kit torn from Kali's tac armor. She unspools a thick roll of gauze, presses it to the frothing bullet hole in the kid's chest. Malikov is bled white as a ghost, struggling to breathe. Struggling to speak.

One hand finds hers. Fingers entwine.

"Hanna . . . ," he sighs, "'m sorry . . ."

Donnelly is pale, her stoic façade crumbling.

So much blood.

"Nik, don't talk . . . just hold on, okay?"

Malikov shakes his head. Coughs wet. He knows there's nothing she can do. And even with her tears pattering on his upturned face, the best of him already emptied onto the floor, he doesn't flinch. Doesn't blink.

Donnelly's wadding bandages, trying to stanch the flow. Watching him slip away, one drop, one breath, one second at a time. Denying it with everything inside her. Clawing and kicking and punching all the way to the end.

His end.

"No, no, *no* . . ."

She drags her knuckles across her eyes, leaves her cheeks red.

"Please. Nik . . . please just stay with me. *Please.*"

The boy looks up at her. Whispering something, too faint to hear.

Donnelly leans close, holds her breath. ". . . What?"

". . . Kiss me . . ."

"No," she says. Shaking her head. Tears brimming in her eyes. "No, don't you dare ask me that. I'm not kissing you goodbye."

"Kiss . . ."

"No. Stay."

She hangs her head, face crumpling. *"Stay."*

"Welcher . . . ," he whispers.

". . . What?"

Malikov licks his lips. Somehow dragging one more breath into his punctured chest.

"Bet you . . . I'd . . . get shot, 'member? Owe me . . . a kiss."

A wet, bloody grin.

"Maybe a . . . feel, too."

One last breath. Spent to make her smile.

She does. Laughing. Sobbing. Pressing her hands to his cheeks and leaning in, close and closer and closest, crushing her lips to his as the last of his breath escapes as a sigh, soft on her skin. She kisses him, desperately, longingly, as his hand falls away from hers and everything he was fades on that last whisper, eyelids fluttering closed as if he were drifting off to sleep.

"Please . . . ," she breathes.

She holds him tight. Knuckles white. Lips red.

"Please stay . . ."

Her Highness's final command.

But he's not there to hear it.

PALMPAD IM: D2D NETWORK
Participants: Hanna Donnelly, Civilian (unregistered)
Date: 08/16/75
Timestamp: 16:44

Hanna D: ella are you there

Hanna D: ella please

Hanna D: it's urgent

Hanna D: Please say something.

Hanna D: if you can read this but can't get a message through, give me a signal. flash the lights or something.

Hanna D: oh God

Hanna D: please

Hanna D: ella

PALMPAD IM: D2D NETWORK
Participants: *Hypatia* (unregistered)
Hanna Donnelly, Civilian (unregistered)
Date: 08/16/75
Timestamp: 17:22

Hypatia: Heimdall, this is Hypatia, do you read?

Hypatia: Jump Station Heimdall, this is WUC science vessel Hypatia, responding to your hail. Do you read?

Hanna D: oh my God

Hypatia: No, my name's Kady Grant. Hold on, I'll put the boss on.

Hanna D: ella if you're ███ing with me I swear to God . . .

Hypatia: This is Captain Syra Boll of the WUC science vessel Hypatia. Please identify yourself.

Hanna D: Hanna.

Hanna D: Hanna Donnelly. WUC-C9815. I'm Station Commander Charles Donnelly's daughter.

Hypatia: Miss Donnelly, is Ella Malikova with you?

Hanna D: No. Ella's not answering comms anymore, and her cousin Nik is gone, so it's just me and the Chief, and he's been shot

Hypatia: Say again? Chief Grant has been shot?

Hanna D: He's had first aid, he's okay but not mobile.

Hanna D: listen

Hanna D: listen the BeiTech assault fleet is real close now. hours away, maybe less. we were trying to shut down the wormhole to stop them coming for you, but the BT agents on board stopped us

Hanna D: and the second that drone fleet jumps through, you're dead, and they blow up Heimdall two seconds later

Hanna D: so we both have problems

Hypatia: Hanna, you said Nik Malikov was "gone"?

Hanna D: Yes. THey

Hanna D: they shot him

Hanna D: He's dead.

Hypatia: You're certain?

Hanna D: Look lady, I don't mean to sound like a ▮▮▮▮, but I've got his blood all over my hands from when he died in my arms

Hanna D: so yes, I'm pretty ▮▮ing certain

Hypatia: It's just we're receiving a second transmission from Heimdall right at this very moment.

Hypatia: The speaker is identifying himself as Nik Malikov.

Hanna D: That's not possible.

Hanna D: It's a trick.

Hanna D: He died. I was there.

Hypatia: Well, here's the thing, Hanna.

Hypatia: He's saying exactly the same thing about you.

Our footage takes us back to old familiar ground: the bridge of the *Hypatia*. This is the place Captain Chau was killed, Byron Zhang and Consuela Nestor were bound and dragged away, and everything changed. It's a very different cast of characters this time.

Syra Boll stands at the captain's station, and she looks exhausted—it's only been a couple of weeks since the destruction of the *Alexander* and the retrieval of Kady Grant, and since then she's had to cram several hundred extra UTA survivors into an already overcrowded ship, deal with hundreds of petty problems from hydroponics breakdowns to fistfights, and hold together the 2,915 lives aboard the *Hypatia* with her bare hands.

A ragtag collection of *Hypatia* and *Alexander* crew members man the bridge, a bunch more standing by the door in quiet conference. There are literally no spare rooms to hold their meetings.

Kady Grant's humming tunelessly and has her boots up on a console, one tapping slowly, and Boll looks like this might just be the thing that breaks her.

Grant, unaware of her mortal peril, is holding a battered data-pad in one hand, frequently consulting it as she stabs at her keyboard with one finger. Her fading pink hair falls around her face, and she's biting her lip, frowning at the console in a way that would cow a lesser system.

"Do you need more terminal space?" Boll can't help herself. Back straight, hands clasped behind her, she stares at her last, best and only hope like she's a misbehaving cadet.

"Huh?" Kady doesn't look up.

"I can give you more monitors, at least." Boll waves at the datapad. "You seem to be using the smallest screen on the ship."

"All good," Kady replies. "It's got all my personal stuff on it."

Captain Syra Boll has no idea what—or maybe after all this, we should say "who"—is actually in it.

Grant looks tired and worried, but there's a sliver of energy running through her, visible in the way she taps her sole against the computers in front of her, drums her fingers on the datapad's edge. She never expected to find *Heimdall* in one piece, let alone her father alive and waiting for her. There's a nervousness to her movements, and she blinks too often.

"This makes zero sense. See those signatures up there on the main screen? Tell me how those make sense."

"I can't," Boll replies, though she gazes obediently. "That's why you're here."

"Oh, uh . . ." Grant had actually been speaking to the datapad when she asked that question, but now she turns the conversation to Boll. "Yeah, sorry, Captain. So listen, both these replies are coming in from the station almost simultaneously. They're using the same hacked network, set up by the same admin—our initial contact, Ella Malikova. Malikova greenlit both these accounts, and both these names are in her initial transmission. And each one of these users is claiming the other one is dead."

Boll paces in closer to the screen, narrows her eyes. "Is there any chance it's just one crazy person pretending to be two? Or two crazy people using the same device?"

Kady shakes her head. "Two different idents, two different logins. It's not the same device. And it's not the same person. Syntax, slang, grammar, typing speed." She glances at her datapad, then

back to Boll. "I mean, I don't think we have time for me to talk to you about the subtle differences in their content. But the finger-prints feel different."

A woman breaks away from the huddle by the door, where another makeshift conference has ended. Though there are 868 UTA staff members aboard, thanks to Kady and AIDAN's rescue, former First Lieutenant Winifred McCall is in a *Hypatia* uniform. Her UTA resignation clearly still stands, and the badge on her sleeve indicates she's on *Hypatia*'s security team now. "We don't have time for *anything,* Captain," she says, closing in on Boll. "If these contacts are right, we're about to watch an assault fleet jump straight through that wormhole to destroy us. Who cares which one we believe? They're both sending the same warning."

"We can't believe *either* of them until we know more," Boll snaps, then reins herself in. "They could both be setting the same trap."

Ezra Mason's moving more slowly as he follows McCall across the bridge, coming to a halt behind Kady and reaching down to squeeze her shoulder. He's still in his UTA uniform. "They have your dad, right, Kades?"

"That's what they said. He's not the one talking to us, but they have him." She lifts her hand to rest it over his. "Or access to his command codes."

"Okay," says Ezra quietly. "Then let's use him. Tell these Nik and Hanna people to ask him something only he would know. Whoever gets the answer right, they're the one we trust."

RADIO TRANSMISSION: BEITECH AUDIT TEAM—SECURE CHANNEL 4824

PARTICIPANTS:

Hanna Donnelly, Civilian

Isaac Grant, Chief Engineer

DATE: 08/16/75

TIMESTAMP: 17:25

HANNA D: Chief, are you there?

ISAAC G: I'm here, Hanna. Are you using Nik's headset?

HANNA D: I'm using . . . I think her name was Russo. Kali, they called her.

ISAAC G: Is everything all right?

HANNA D: Nik died, Chief.

ISAAC G: Oh God.

HANNA D: Nik died.

HANNA D: And Ella isn't answering comms.

HANNA D: And they found us before we could disable the wormhole, and I can't go back because it's crawling with lickers and BT ops.

ISAAC G: ███.

HANNA D: I'm sorry.

ISAAC G: It's not your fault, Hanna. Are you okay, at least?

HANNA D: Your daughter, she's called Kady. Did I remember that right?

ISAAC G: Yes.

HANNA D: Chief, she's alive. I spoke to her.

ISAAC G: Say again?

HANNA D: I spoke to the *Hypatia*, I tried to warn them. Ella tied my palmpad into her comms channel so I could answer in case . . . something happened to her.

ISAAC G: I . . . I . . . How are they doing? Is Helena there? What's their status?

HANNA D: Their status is, they don't believe me, and they're saying Nik is talking to them, but I know he's not, he's dead. Someone from BT has to be on the palmpad network.

ISAAC G: You tell Kady you have me here, I can prove it's me.

HANNA D: I told them. They've gone quiet. They're thinking about it, I guess.

ISAAC G: We don't have TIME for them to think about it!

HANNA D: Tell someone who doesn't know, Chief. Nik just died trying to save them.

ISAAC G: God . . . I'm sorry, Hanna. I wish we had time to honor what he did properly, I really do.

HANNA D: No, I know. And I know what he'd want me to do. I'm trying to— I can do this.

HANNA D: I refuse to die here.

HANNA D: We have to do something about the *Kennedy* fleet. Even if *Hypatia* won't listen to us, maybe we can stop them.

ISAAC G: If disabling the wormhole is out, then it's got to be Command & . . .

HANNA D: Chief, you there?

ISAAC G: Sorry, it's the pain. I think . . . the dust is wearing off. Worried I'm going to black out.

HANNA D: Are the bandages holding? You're not losing too much blood?

ISAAC G: . . . Don't think so.

HANNA D: Okay, then. This isn't my first choice, but if you black out, I'm screwed. Look next to the water bottle I left for you. You see the spoon there? Lick it.

ISAAC G: Excuse me?

HANNA D: I left some traces of dust there. It'll give you another lift. Shouldn't be so much you can't think straight.

ISAAC G: I hope you're right. Done.

HANNA D: So you think I can get into Command & Control? I've got Kali's headset, so I can hear their comms. Not sure how many of them died in the reactor, but it'd be a few, at least.

ISAAC G: Maybe. Their numbers are down, that's going to thin the guards . . . in Command & Control, at least. If you can get in there, I can talk you through our Defense Grid Systems. They're not exactly top tier, but there's a chance we . . . can do some damage to this fleet when it arrives.

HANNA D: What about the hostages? We have to get them off *Heimdall* somehow.

ISAAC G: If we can destroy the *Kennedy* fleet, that buys more time. If not, maybe you can . . . unlock the docking mechanisms on some of the civilian ships, give them a chance to run.

ISAAC G: I'm going to try and move while the dust is working . . . get to a terminal so I can give you some support. You'll need it, with Ella gone.

HANNA D: We don't know she's dead. She might just be cut off for now.

ISAAC G: It's a possibility. But I think we have to proceed on the . . . assumption she's not going to be able to help us again.

HANNA D: God . . .

ISAAC G: Hanna, I know this is an impossibly stupid question, but are you . . . Is there anything at all I can do? Your father, Jackson . . . now Nik and Ella.

HANNA D: I never killed anyone before.

HANNA D: I played it out in my head right before I did it. I wasn't even thinking about the fact that she'd be dead afterward. I just wanted to get to Nik.

ISAAC G: You did the right thing, Hanna.

HANNA D: I know.

HANNA D: But.

ISAAC G: I know.

HANNA D: I want my dad.

ISAAC G: Oh, Hanna.

HANNA D: I'm going to save Kady for you, I promise.

ISAAC G: I'll be with you all the way, as much as I can.

ISAAC G: Start heading for C & C, and I'll get to work on . . . a terminal. Find out how many staffers they have inside there. Got any ideas . . . about entry strategies?

HANNA D: Ever heard of a city called Troy?

ISAAC G: Is this one of your father's stories?

HANNA D: He's here with me all the way too.

HANNA D: Don't worry, Chief. I have a plan.

PALMPAD IM: D2D NETWORK

Participants: *Hypatia* (unregistered)

Hanna Donnelly, Civilian (unregistered)

Date: 08/16/75

Timestamp: 18:12

Hypatia: Hanna, are you in contact with Chief Grant?

Hanna D: I thought you'd ditched me for good

Hypatia: Apologies. This is Captain Boll. You must understand we need to be cautious. Either you or Mr. Malikov is attempting to lure us into danger. One of you is not legitimate, and as far as we know, perhaps neither of you is.

Hanna D: listen, I've been chased and shot at and watched Nik KILLED trying to save your lives, so if you don't trust me, I can't help that, captain boll. I'll do what I can without you.

Hypatia: Would you be willing to answer a few questions to verify your identity?

Hanna D: Such as?

Hypatia: Are you in contact with Chief Grant?

Hanna D: Yes, by radio

Hypatia: I have his daughter here with me.

Hanna D: Yes, Kady. She told me her name before.

Hypatia: That's right. If you can have Chief Grant answer a few personal questions put by his daughter, we'll know you're working with him, and we can proceed from there.

Hanna D: hang on

Hanna D: oh he's REALLY excited

Hanna D: okay put Kady on

Hypatia: It's me.

Hypatia: Okay, first thing, tell him I love him.

Hanna D: loves you back. Asking are you and your mom and your cousin Asha okay

Hypatia: Tell him I'm fine. Did you tell him we need answers to verify who you are?

Hanna D: he says fire away

Hanna D: now he's laughing at his own joke, because he got shot

Hanna D: sorry, I had to medicate him again, he's a little . . .

Hypatia: No, those are just his jokes. Especially when he's excited.

Hypatia: First question. Ask him what he sent me for my last birthday.

Hanna D: he missed your birthday because comms were down. birthday before . . . ok maybe he's saying motherboards? is that possible?

Hypatia: That's right.

Hanna D: he's not very good at presents, is he?

Hypatia: Ask him what he did, my first date with Ezra.

Hanna D: he's laughing again

Hanna D: he says 20 questions

Hanna D: no wonder our dads were friends

Hypatia: Ask him what's the biggest fight we ever had.

Hanna D: . . . rehydrated potato salad? Is that the answer or is he high?

Hypatia: That's the answer.

Hanna D: there's something he wants me to say

Hanna D: I'm passing on what he's saying word for word

Hanna D: Kady, I love you both very much. You're everything to me. I've missed you more than I can say these last months. I thought of you both every single day. It doesn't matter what happens here, but you need to listen to us. This is real. The fleet is coming for you. Stop talking, find a way to fight for your lives. Do it for me.

Hanna D: you still there?

Hypatia: Tell him we love him too.

Hypatia: Very much.

Hanna D: Kady, can i ask you something?

Hypatia: Okay.

Hanna D: your mom's not there, is she? or your cousin?

Hypatia: don't say anything to my dad

Hanna D: I won't. but I'm going to tell him you love him for you, one more time. never miss a chance to do that, trust me.

Hypatia: The captain needs to speak to me.

Hanna D: don't be long, visitors are on their way. we're doing what we can to slow them down on our end, but . . .

Hypatia: Roger that. Hypatia out.

BeiTech
INDUSTRIES

RADIO TRANSMISSION: BEITECH AUDIT TEAM—SECURE CHANNEL 413

PARTICIPANTS:
Tracy "Mantis" Lê, Corporal, Computer Systems
DR-782XII, Artificial Intelligence Matrix, Assault
Fleet *Kennedy*
DATE: 08/16/75
TIMESTAMP: 18:22

DR-782XII: AUDIT TEAM F-XII, THIS IS *KENNEDY* ASSAULT. RESPOND, OVER.

MANTIS: Roger, *Kennedy*, this is Audit Team. We read, over.

DR-782XII: *KENNEDY* ASSAULT INBOUND TO *HEIMDALL* STATION ETA 24 MINUTES, 47 SECONDS.

DR-782XII: REQUEST STATUS: *HEIMDALL* WORMHOLE. OVER.

MANTIS: *Kennedy*, Audit Team. We had some internal trouble here. There's some kind of infestation in the Reactor Sector, but—

DR-782XII: *KENNEDY* ASSAULT, REPEAT. REQUEST STATUS: *HEIMDALL* WORMHOLE. OVER.

MANTIS: Look.

MANTIS: I know there's precious little room in your matrices for societal constructs, but you combat drones are rude little ████████s, you know that?

DR-782XII: ACKNOWLEDGED, AUDIT TEAM. CONFIRM WORMHOLE ONLINE? OVER.

MANTIS: . . . Confirmed. Successful pingback from Kerenza-side waypoint station. Systems nominal. Green lights across the board. Over.

DR-782XII: AUDIT TEAM WILL ADVISE *KENNEDY* ASSAULT OF ANY CHANGE IN STATUS OF *HEIMDALL* WORMHOLE. OVER.

MANTIS: Say "please," you little ███.

DR-782XII: AUDIT TEAM WILL ADVISE *KENNEDY* ASSAULT OF ANY CHANGE IN STATUS OF *HEIMDALL* WORMHOLE. OVER.

MANTIS: . . . Confirmed, *Kennedy*. Audit Team will advise. Over.

DR-782XII: ACKNOWLEDGED, AUDIT TEAM. *KENNEDY* ASSAULT OUT.

PARTICIPANTS:

Hanna Donnelly, Civilian

Isaac Grant, Chief Engineer

DATE: 08/16/75

TIMESTAMP: 18:24

ISAAC G: Hanna, where are you?

HANNA D: I'm en route. I'm chancing it in the hallways. There are so few of them left, I'm just hoping nobody's out and about.

ISAAC G: Hanna, the *Kennedy* fleet is en route too.

HANNA D: Running as fast as I can, boss.

ISAAC G: Hanna, they're close. Minutes away.

HANNA D: ▊▊▊▊.

ISAAC G: There's no reason for them to delay going through the wormhole once they arrive.

ISAAC G: You're the one chance the *Hypatia* has.

HANNA D: I'm running.

PARTICIPANTS:
Travis "Cerberus" Falk, Lieutenant, Team Commander
Tracy "Mantis" Lê, Corporal, Computer Systems
DATE: 08/16/75
TIMESTAMP: 18:24

MANTIS: Top, this is Mantis, you reading me?

CERBERUS: Mantis, Cerberus. Go.

MANTIS: Everything okay in there? Sweep complete?

CERBERUS: Cujo, Poacher and Nightingale are flatline. There were dozens of the ████████s. But the lanima infestation is dealt with. Reactor area is secure. All thirty stories.

MANTIS: Have you spoken to Kali? Suit tracker had her with you in the reactor, but now she's situated in Alpha Sector?

CERBERUS: I tried her on comms. No reply. She's hunting rabbits, I assume. They slipped the net. But I presume whatever sabotage they were about failed?

MANTIS: Roger that, Cerberus. Mercury confirms wormhole is still five by five. And we just got hit up by Assault Fleet *Kennedy*. Drones are inbound, about twenty ticks away.

CERBERUS: Bliss. I want you and DJ ready for system purge—that entire network is to be burned from the inside out, clear? I don't want one byte of data recovered from the wreckage.

MANTIS: Sir, yessir.

CERBERUS: I'm sending Sensei and Eden to watch over Mercury in Engineering while she sets the reactor to overload. Two-Time is prepping the *Mao*. As soon as *Kennedy* crosses the threshold, we light out and watch the fireworks.

MANTIS: What about Rapier?

CERBERUS: He's MIA. And therefore not our concern. He can die with *Heimdall*.

MANTIS: Roger that. Prepping system burn now. I'll notify you when *Kennedy* arrives.

CERBERUS: Roger that. Good work, Mantis. Cerberus out.

FALK, Travis
Cerberus
Team Commander

RUSSO, Fleur
Kali
Alpha Squad—Leader

DAN, Kim
Poacher
Alpha Squad

MORETTI, Deni
Cujo
Alpha Squad

SATOU, Genji
Sensei
Alpha Squad

BAZAROV, Petyr
Romeo
Beta Squad—Leader

RADIN, Harry
Razorback
Beta Squad

MAYR, Stanislaw
Taurus
Beta Squad

WONG, Ai
Rain
Beta Squad

MAZUR, Kira
Ghost
Charlie Squad—Leader

CASTRO, Lucas
Link
Charlie Squad

LAURENT, Sara
Mona Lisa
Charlie Squad

ORR, James
Cricket
Charlie Squad

ANTONIOU, Naxos
Two-Time
Communications

LÊ, Tracy
Mantis
Computer Systems

MØLLER, Rolf
DJ
Computer Systems

SILVA, Bianca
Mercury
Engineer (Ranking)

MORENO, Gabriel
Ballpark
Engineer

DE GRAAF, Lor
Taxman
Engineer/Medic

O'NEILL, Abby
Nightingale
Medic

ALIEVI, Marta
Eden
Logistics

SAPRYKIN, Kai
Juggler
Ordnance/Demolitions

PARK, Ji-hun
Flipside
Pilot/Demolitions

TAHIROVIĆ, Hans
Ragman
Pilot

Footage opens on Mantis and Rolf "DJ" Møller hunched over terminals in *Heimdall*'s C & C. The two are working on Falk's system burn, systematically wiping entire sections of the *Heimdall* network. They're spread thin, manning the whole of C & C by themselves, but they've worked together for a long time, and like a pair of experienced dance partners, they send files flying back and forth, working in tandem. Neither moves until a figure outside the security door raps her knuckles against the Plexiglas viewing portal.

DJ lifts his head—unlike the petite Mantis, this guy looks like a bruiser, like his fingers should be too big to type properly. Like he'd rather be scratching himself or hunting down prey with a club than handling the kind of sophisticated programming an op like this requires. Maybe there's a reason the final burn is his favorite part. Just saying.

He nods at the door. "Think I worked out why Kali's not answering comms."

Just outside the portal is a figure in Kali's bloodstained tac armor, face hidden behind her darkened visor. As DJ lumbers over to the door, the figure lifts her hand to tap at the side of her helmet, then draws a finger across her throat, confirming her comms are indeed dead.

"Kali's rig looks fine to me on the monitor," Mantis says, though she's distracted—still conducting sweeps, trying to work out where Ella's gone, whether the Little Spider has spun a web in some dark corner to bide her time until she strikes again.

"Well, she's right here saying they're not," DJ replies, dialing in the security code to open up the door. "So how about we go with that? Unless you want to come over here and mime to her that we're going to leave her locked outside?"

Mantis merely scowls, turning back to her work, and DJ rolls his eyes as the door hisses and releases its seal. It swings open slowly, and the figure in Kali's armor steps inside.

"Kali, all your systems look green to me," Mantis says, without looking up. "Clearly you're not transmitting, but are you receiving anything?"

The figure steps close to DJ, lashes out with one gauntleted fist right into the big man's larynx. He drops to his knees, gagging, clutching his throat as Mantis spins in her seat to find a VK-85 burst rifle pointed at her face.

"I'm sorry." Hanna Donnelly's voice is ice. "Kali couldn't make it."

She stands tall in Russo's tac armor, all kevlar and plasteel. Twenty-four hours ago, she was clad in a Danae Matresco jumpsuit worth the GDP of a small moon. She shed it for the workmanlike WUC maintenance gear, then covered that with her grubby white envirosuit. And now, born from the ashes, she's a warrior in blood-ied black, gun in hand.

Mantis stares for a long moment, but she's pro enough to crunch the odds here. Whoever's standing in front of her isn't Kali, but she's wearing Kali's armor—and there's only one way that happens when you're dealing with an operator like Fleur Russo.

So Mantis raises her hands. Real slow.

DJ has recovered enough from the punch to his throat to be up on all fours, one hand moving in slow motion toward the gun at his hip.

"Uh-uh, big boy," Donnelly says, swinging the rifle toward him, taking a couple of steps to the left so she can keep both him and

Mantis in view. Resolutely keeping her gaze away from her father's workstation, away from Jackson's. She nods to Mantis. "You. Stand up slowly and come over here to join the Neanderthal. I don't want to shoot you, but—" A pause. "Scratch that. I *do* want to shoot you. Feel free to give me a reason."

Mantis rises to her feet, visibly grinding her teeth as she walks across to a still-gasping DJ and hauls him to his feet. Looking for an opportunity Donnelly refuses to give her.

"Earpieces out," the girl says softly, and the goons comply, pulling away their headsets, their only means of contacting Falk, and dropping them to the ground. "Thank you." Donnelly sounds almost polite for a moment. Conversational. It's clear from their faces that neither DJ nor Mantis considers her friendly tone to be a good thing—then again, they work for Falk, so they'd know. "Now," says Hanna, "let's get you settled so I can get comfortable. This armor is *really* sticky—she just bled *all* over it."

Three and a half minutes later, both DJ and Mantis are restrained, backs against the large pillars in the middle of the room, arms stretched behind them, wrists joined with electrical cord that looks far too tight to be comfortable. Hanna Donnelly is drinking Mantis's can of Mount Russshmore® as she stands at her father's workstation, the door to C & C locked securely once more. She guesses his password on her second try and reaches up to thumb her headset to life.

"Okay, Chief, I'm here. Let's talk about this defense grid."

A pause, as a voice in her ear guides her through the menus. DJ and Mantis watch with twin glares, and if looks could kill, their revenge would be very, very sweet. Donnelly ignores them, navigating through another layer and throwing the defense radar up onto the big screen.

Her eyes go wide.

The Mount Russshmore® can slips from her fingers.

". . . Oh ▮▮," she whispers.

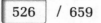

COUNTDOWN TO
HYPATIA ARRIVAL
AT HEIMDALL WAYPOINT:

00 DAYS
01 HOURS: 32 MINUTES

COUNTDOWN TO KENNEDY ASSAULT FLEET ARRIVAL AT JUMP STATION HEIMDALL:

00 DAYS
00 HOURS: 00 MINUTES

Footage is taken from external *Heimdall* cams.

The station looks amazing from the outside. There's no sign of the trauma going on inside. No bullet holes or bodies or bloodstains on the walls. A circular city, forever spinning around a shimmering hole in the universe's side.

The wormhole is beautiful, chums. There's no other way to describe it. It almost looks like a pool of water illuminated from within, though it sheds almost no light on the station around it. And although it doesn't really have a surface, it looks like that not-surface is rippling a million beats per second, a soft light shining in its heart. It's vaguely blue (I'm told this has something to do with Doppler shift—don't ask me) and looks a trillion miles deep. Which isn't even close to the truth of it.

There's a sharp black scar burned on the station's skin, just near the wormhole's lip—the place Nik Malikov and the *Betty Boop* crossed the horizon as the portal opened again. Other than that, the entire picture is perfectly serene.

For the next thirty seconds, at least.

You can hardly see them in the dark. They're moving quickly. Like sharks. Phalanx formation. It's only the radiance from the station, the micro-flares from their thrusters as they adjust course, and maybe some ambient light from the distant Yggdrasil Nebula that pick them out in all that dark. Twenty-four Shinobi-class hunter-killers. Speeding like black daggers out of the void, right at the heart of that shimmering blue pool.

Assault Fleet *Kennedy*.

You save a lot of space on a vessel when you don't have to man it with a live crew. Each Shinobi is four hundred meters long, sleek and sharp. It's basically an engine, an A7-X artificial intelligence system with pre-programmed action/reaction parameters, and a fuel tank. All that space that'd be taken up by crew, living quarters, mess halls, rec spaces and storage? Well, you mostly fill it with weapons and ammo, chum. Which means these things are bristling with more missile turrets than any sensibly designed ship their size has a right to be packing.

But you know the scariest thing about them?

No lights.

See, on a ship with a living crew, that crew needs to see what the hell they're doing. You look at *Heimdall*'s skin, it's picked out by hundreds of tiny pinpricks of light. The atrium, filled with all those imprisoned partygoers. The entertainment center, with its sparkling casino levels and bars, now scattered with small knots of frightened residents and guests, wondering why their Voice of the Resistance has gone silent. A few lights in the now-empty Habitat Sector, left on by people who expected to stagger home after Terra Day too drunk to find the switch.

But there's nothing alive inside the drone ships. Their AIs don't need light to see. So the hunter-killers are completely black, just like the space around them.

Probably a metaphor in there somewhere.

They speed in from the void, hundreds of klicks per second, not slowing for a beat. Their sensors confirm the reports from Mantis— the *Heimdall* wormhole is online, the Kerenza waypoint is returning inquiry pings. The way is clear.

Forward. To gut the *Hypatia* and X-out the witnesses inside it.

Then on to the planet Kerenza to purge whatever remains of the colonists and BT ground troops left behind after former Director Taylor's disastrous invasion.

To wipe the slate clean, then self-destruct in a brief flare of fuel and fire off the shoulder of a now-dead planet.

Not for them to question why.

They're not programmed to, see?

DR-782xii: AUDIT TEAM F-XII, THIS IS *KENNEDY* ASSAULT. RESPOND, OVER.

Cerberus: *Kennedy*, this is Audit Team. We read you, over.

DR-782xii: REQUEST CLEARANCE TO TRAVERSE HYPERSPATIAL UMBILICUS, OVER.

Cerberus: Roger that, *Kennedy*. Good hunting.

DR-782xii: ACKNOWLEDGED, AUDIT TEAM. *KENNEDY* ASSAULT OUT.

The assault fleet draws closer to the spinning city. Deathly silent. Totally lifeless. Thin strands of data spilling back and forth between the ships, electronic fingertips touching briefly in the moments before the plunge.

SYSTEMS: NOMINAL.
APPROACH VECTOR: CLEAR.
UMBILICUS ACCESS: CONFIRMED.
NEGATIVE IMPEDIMENT. PROCEED?
YES/~~No.~~

And without a sound, they dive into that rippling blue.

Hanna D: Hypatia, run, RUN.

Hanna D: Kennedy's coming through, prepare to defend if you can't run

PARTICIPANTS:
Travis "Cerberus" Falk, Lieutenant, Team Commander
Bianca "Mercury" Silva, Corporal, Engineer
DATE: 08/16/75
TIMESTAMP: 18:48

CERBERUS: What the *hell* was that?

CERBERUS: Mercury, this is Cerberus, respond!

CERBERUS: Bianca!

MERCURY: I hear you! Jesus, Travis, take a ████ing zee!

CERBERUS: *What the* ████*ing hell was that?*

MERCURY: I don't know! Surge! Hyperspatial! Systems are redlining everywhere!

CERBERUS: Mercury, what the hell is happening? What's going on with the internal insulation? It looks like there's live current running through the structure down here.

MERCURY: Control network is trashed! Power surge, off scale! Buffers are totally fried. Secondaries axed. Sensors dead. I've got no diagnostics. No internals. And three . . . no, four of my engineers just got cooked.

CERBERUS: Cooked?

MERCURY: Their terminals overloaded. Christ, it smells like fried ██████ing bacon in here . . .

CERBERUS: Did *Kennedy* make it through?

CERBERUS: Mercury, this is Cerberus. Confirm Assault Fleet *Kennedy* successfully traversed the umbilicus to Kerenza Sector, over.

MERCURY: I don't know.

CERBERUS: Bianca, talk to me!

MERCURY: Travis, I don't know!

MERCURY: I don't know what the ██████ is happening . . .

PARTICIPANTS:

Hanna Donnelly, Civilian

Isaac Grant, Chief Engineer

DATE: 08/16/75

TIMESTAMP: 18:48

GRANT, I: Oh God, no.

DONNELLY, H: I can't get a read on the *Hypatia*!

GRANT, I: No, no. No!

DONNELLY, H: Chief, help me, I'm trying to get a—

GRANT, I: No, they can't— Helena, Kady . . . Please . . .

DONNELLY, H: ▮▮▮, what's happening? The whole station's shaking!

GRANT, I: Helena . . .

DONNELLY, H: Chief, *please*. Something's happening with the wormhole.

GRANT, I: . . . It wasn't ready.

DONNELLY, H: What?

GRANT, I: Do you know how few people know [coughs] how to tune one of these things properly? How *long* it takes? How many . . . arguments I had with your father about the man-hours we were spending on calcs?

DONNELLY, H: Systems are blinking out all over the board, what do I do?

GRANT, I: I can't— There's nothing. My family . . .

DONNELLY, H: Chief, I'm sorry, I'm so sorry. I tried. I can't get a read on *anything* on the other side. Maybe . . .

GRANT, I: Maybe what? Maybe the drone fleet we just watched head through didn't kill them all within seconds?

DONNELLY, H: There are still hundreds of people here.

DONNELLY, H: I don't have anyone left either.

DONNELLY, H: But they do. The people trapped here. They have families out there.

GRANT, I: I've . . . I've lost a lot of blood, Hanna. I don't know how much . . . longer I'll last.

GRANT, I: Or the station, for that matter . . . Did you feel that?

DONNELLY, H: Chief. We *have* to try.

GRANT, I: Try what? We're out of options.

DONNELLY, H: The civilian ships. Freighters. Miners. In the docks.

DONNELLY, H: We can use them. We have to get our people out of here.

GRANT, I: I . . .

DONNELLY, H: We can't stop, Chief.

DONNELLY, H: I want to. I just want to lie down and wait for it to be done. But we can't.

GRANT, I: Okay.

GRANT, I: All right. I'll . . . I'll narrow down the ships . . . nearest our people.

DONNELLY, H: Just a little longer, Chief.

DONNELLY, H: Then we can rest.

GRANT, I: Your father, Hanna . . .

DONNELLY, H: What about him?

GRANT, I: God, he'd be Oso proud of you.

DONNELLY, H: . . . I hope so.

DONNELLY, H: Let's get to work.

RADIO MESSAGE: COMMAND CHANNEL HYPATIA

PARTICIPANTS:

Kady Grant, Head of CommTech (Acting), *Hypatia*

Ezra Mason, 2nd Lieutenant, Air Wing Leader (Acting), *Hypatia*

DATE: 08/16/75

TIMESTAMP: 18:48

GRANT, K: Ez, you hear me?

MASON, E, 2ND LT: I hear you. I'm next in line to launch. Got about a minute.

MASON, E, 2ND LT: Not enough flight deck crew. Taking too long.

MASON, E, 2ND LT: We've got ████ing shuttle pilots at the stick. We'll be lucky if we don't take each other out before the drones show up.

MASON, E, 2ND LT: Don't TOUCH THAT— Yeah, you, don't— That's right.

GRANT, K: Ez . . .

MASON, E, 2ND LT: Don't. Please don't say it.

GRANT, K: Can't reason with drones. Can't beat them.

MASON, E, 2ND LT: Have to try.

GRANT, K: I know.

MASON, E, 2ND LT: I love you. I love you so much, Kady Grant.

GRANT, K: I love you, too.

MASON, E, 2ND LT: We almost made it.

GRANT, K: I'll stay on the radio with you as long as I can. This frequency's just us. Anything your wing says will override it—you won't miss anything.

MASON, E, 2ND LT: Then stay. I want to hear your voice.

GRANT, K: I'm right here.

MASON, E, 2ND LT: I'm up to launch. Here goes.

MASON, E, 2ND LT: The stars, Kades. They're so beautiful.

GRANT, K: I've seen them. AIDAN showed them to me on the *Alexander*.

MASON, E, 2ND LT: It's not right. After all we went through . . . to end like this . . .

GRANT, K: I wanted to tell our story. I wanted people to know.

MASON, E, 2ND LT: Maybe someone on *Heimdall* will tell it for us.

GRANT, K: Maybe.

[STATIC BURST]

[GARBLED VOICES]

MASON, E, 2ND LT: Holy ███, Kades, are you getting these visuals?

GRANT, K: Everything just lit up, we're on it. Is the wormhole meant to do that?

GRANT, K: It looked like a lightning strike.

MASON, E, 2ND LT: I don't know, shields were always down when I went through them as a kid. It was nothing like this.

MASON, E, 2ND LT: God, the things we got to see, Kady . . .

GRANT, K: I know. I just wish . . .

MASON, E, 2ND LT: Me too.

GRANT, K: Um, Ez . . .

MASON, E, 2ND LT: What?

GRANT, K: . . . Aren't those drones meant to be murdering us by now?

BRIEFING NOTE:
Before she was a refugee ship, the *Hypatia* was a science vessel. Her rigs were state of the art, and what they observed in this moment was unprecedented.

...ough QASAR array conducted ...8.901.874 on 12-millisecond bursts [...] ...ted **here**]. Analysis plotted on both Delphian and Connelly charts [can be reviewed **here**]. It should be noted QASAR array has not been serviced in 7-plus months, but diagnostics indicate margin of error within acceptable norms.

Secondary analysis conducted via o.r.a.c.l.e, standard 9-millisecond bursts, deep spectrum [full settings noted **here**]. Initial readings from both QASAR and o.r.a.c.l.e identify ultraheavy elements, antimatter and a series of unidentified lines, corresponding closely to theoretical predictions for certain exotic elements—including several previously presumed to exist within the island of stability. For example, particles noted in Tables 1 and 2 have never been recorded outside controlled laboratory environments—their presence alone would seem to indicate the possibility of a hyperspatial transformation altering the fabric of local space within 1AU of the Kerenza waypoint.

Peer-reviewed papers [Malia et al., "On the Persistence of Ultraheavy Elemental Particles," *New Journal of Physics* 397 (June 2551); Dolichva et al., "Wormhole Typhoon: Observations Upon Hyperspatial Umbilici Phenomena," *True Universe* 191 (February 2559); and Huang and Grier, "Dangers of a Singularity Mythos," *New Journal of Physics* 400 (September 2551)] have postulated that

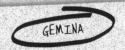

GEMINA

FROM THE LATIN FOR "TWIN." QASAR ARRAY CONFIRMS POSSIBLE PRESENCE OF THEORETICAL GEMINA PARTICLE, RECORDED AT 1 PART PER 10^{10} IN RESULTING DEBRIS/DECAY FIELD, EMANATING FROM INTERSECTION AT WAYPOINT COORDINATES. PARTICLE HIGHLY UNSTABLE (ESTIMATED HALF-LIFE OF 10^{-10} SECONDS), AND BOTH QASAR AND O.R.A.C.L.E ARRAYS ARE UNABLE TO CONFIRM INITIAL READINGS.

HYPATIA ONLINE MEETING SPACE

Proudly hosted by Wallace Ulyanov Consortium VirtuMeet™ Software

MEETING ROOM created
PASSWORD PROTECTED
INCEPT: 19:15, 08/16/75

INVITEES:

BOLL, Syra
Captain (Acting)
IDENT: 448fx29/WUC

GRANT, Kady
Head of CommTech (Acting)
IDENT: 962/Kerenza/Civ/Ref

HIRANO, Yuki
Navigator (Acting)
IDENT: 293ip13/WUC

MASON, Ezra
Air Wing Leader (Acting), 2nd Lieutenant
IDENT: UTN-966-330ad

McCALL, Winifred
Head of Security (Acting), 1st Lieutenant
IDENT: UTN-961-641id 001/UTA/Transfer

ZHUANG, Yulin
Head of Engineering
IDENT: 447/Kerenza/Civ/Ref

McCALL, Winifred *has logged in.*

BOLL, Syra *has logged in.*

GRANT, Kady *has logged in.*

MASON, Ezra *has logged in.*

HIRANO, Yuki *has logged in.*

ZHUANG, Yulin *has logged in.*

 ZHUANG, Yulin: I only have a few minutes. Stabilizers are at redline.

McCALL, Winifred: What the hell is happening? I'm bouncing off the walls down here. Feels like we're in a thunderstorm?

 MASON, Ezra: And where the hell is this drone fleet?

BOLL, Syra: I don't think they're coming.

 GRANT, Kady: What?

 MASON, Ezra: What?

HIRANO, Yuki: *What?!*

BOLL, Syra: I'll make this quick as I can. For those who don't know, my postdoctoral research was in hyperspatial quantum theory—specifically, potential interplay between Rosenstein and Einstein–type hyperspatial bridges across real spacetime. This is going to sound all kinds of crazy, but I'm going to lay out what I think has happened, as best I can.

547 / 659

MASON, Ezra: I'm already confused.

 BOLL, Syra: Fact 1: We have datalogs showing a BeiTech fleet heading into the wormhole at Heimdall about half an hour ago.

BOLL, Syra: Fact 2: When the BT fleet entered the wormhole at Heimdall Station, there were several tremendous energy fluctuations. I'm talking off the charts here.

BOLL, Syra: Fact 3: However, the fleet never emerged on this side of the wormhole.

 ZHUANG, Yulin: Which leads us to a fairly pressing question, Captain.

 MASON, Ezra: Either these guys are serious competitors for the Intergalactic Hide-and-Seek Championship, or something really weird is afoot.

 GRANT, Kady: Most importantly: Are they still going to blow us to pieces?

 BOLL, Syra: Fact 4: We've received transmissions from Jump Station Heimdall from two contacts, on two different devices, with enough subtle distinctions as to plausibly be different people. Each of them has proved they have *ongoing* contact with Heimdall's chief of engineering, Isaac Grant. And each claims they saw the other die.

ZHUANG, Yulin: Have we asked either of these Heimdall voices if they know where the drones went?

BOLL, Syra: The wormhole surge knocked down our comms to the station. Our techs are trying to reestablish now. But we're sure the drone fleet left their side. They just never made it here.

GRANT, Kady: If you can explain this, I will revise my opinion of you, boss.

BOLL, Syra: I've been going over the scans of the particles produced when the Kennedy Assault Fleet went into the Heimdall wormhole, and I've got a working theory. Even with everything that's happened in the last few months, this is going to be a stretch to believe. But eliminate all nonviable options, and the one remaining—no matter how implausible—must be the truth.

BOLL, Syra: Now, among the other phenomena observed during the assault fleet's disappearance, something showed up in the QASAR scans that's only ever been theoretical. I wrote my dissertation on this—or at least the possibility of it—or I'd never have known what I was looking at. It's called a Gemina particle.

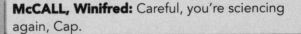

McCALL, Winifred: Careful, you're sciencing again, Cap.

BOLL, Syra: In *theory*, a Gemina particle is created when objects from two different spacetimes interact.

HIRANO, Yuki: Come again? Define "different spacetimes"?

BOLL, Syra: I mean what you think I mean, Yuki. The multiverse theory. The idea that for every choice made in our reality, the alternate choice is played out in a different spacetime that exists in parallel to our own.

HIRANO, Yuki: So you're saying there's another universe where I took my mother's advice, and I'm a professional musician living it up in New Vegas right now?

BOLL, Syra: Probably.

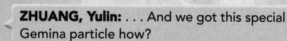

ZHUANG, Yulin: . . . And we got this special Gemina particle how?

BOLL, Syra: I have absolutely no idea. I can only tell you what I'm seeing, not how it happened.

McCALL, Winifred: So we're interacting with our own universe and . . . another one?

BOLL, Syra: Imagine it this way. Infinite universes exist in parallel. We'll call two of them A and B, right? For the sake of this thought experiment, we're in Universe A.

BOLL, Syra: Two Heimdalls, two Hypatias, two waypoints. The universes basically have their "wires crossed" at the Heimdall wormhole. Two universes are connected to that one rabbit hole through hyperspace, leading here.

BOLL, Syra: It's why we're getting comms from two different Heimdall residents, each telling us the other is dead.

 MASON, Ezra: Sorry, I think I'm speaking for everyone except Kady here when I say I'm completely confused.

BOLL, Syra: I'll upload a diagram.

UNIVERSE A

KERENZA WAYPOINT

HYPERSPACE

HEIMDALL

UNIVERSE B

KERENZA WAYPOINT

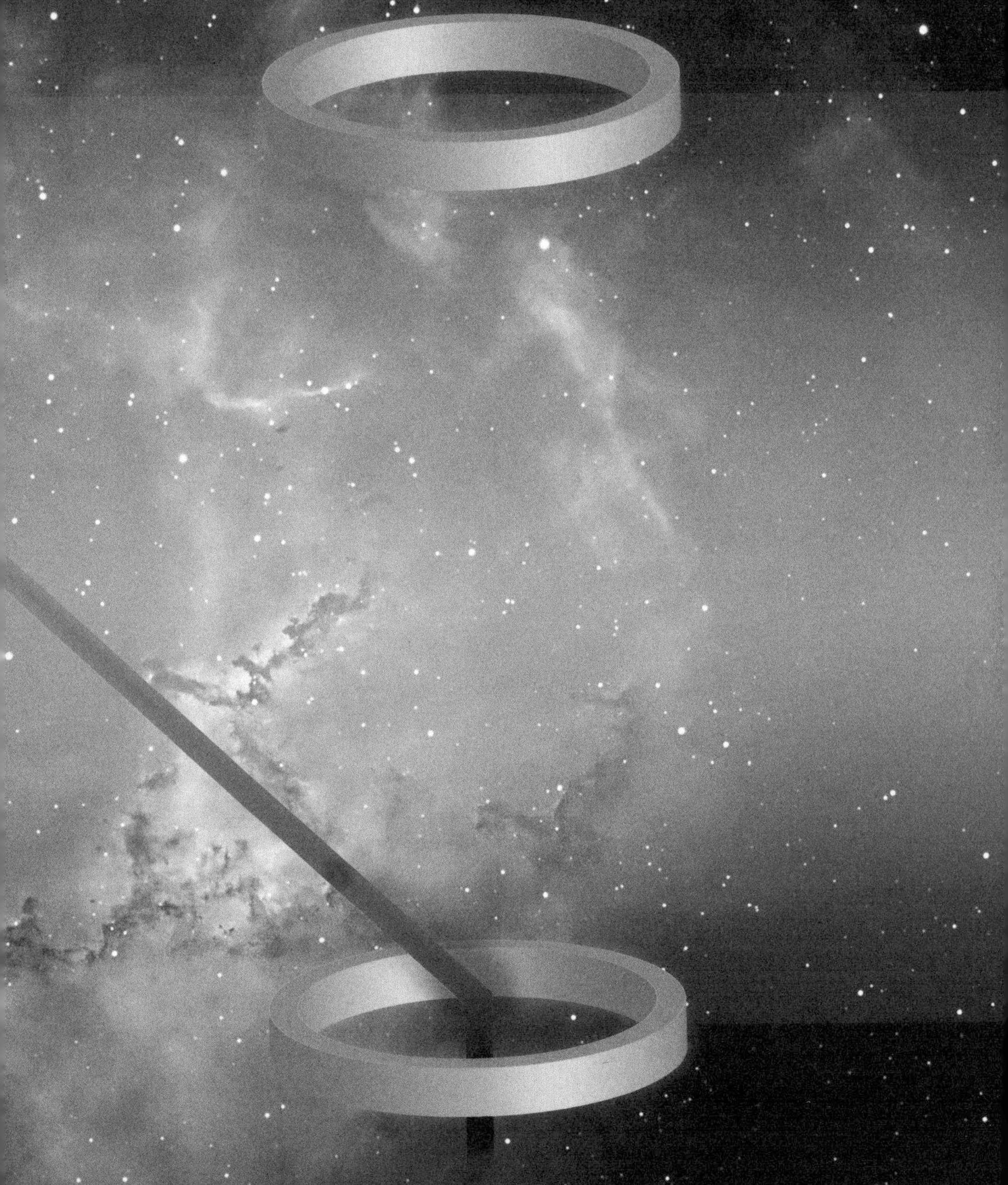

HEIMDALL

BOLL, Syra: This Gemina field is the reason we're hearing from both Nik Malikov and Hanna Donnelly. In our universe, Nik died. But in Universe B, Hanna died. Two Heimdalls transmitting through two wormholes.

 GRANT, Kady: Which are both feeding through to our waypoint, because the wires are crossed.

BOLL, Syra: Exactly.

McCALL, Winifred: So who's the other Hypatia speaking to? There's a Hypatia over in Universe B, right?

BOLL, Syra: Nobody. They still won't have heard from Hanna Donnelly or Nik Malikov or anyone else, because *we're* speaking to *their* Heimdall.

 MASON, Ezra: Will they even be able to get through their wormhole?

BOLL, Syra: They might be able to enter, but they'll never emerge. It leads nowhere.

MASON, Ezra: So if both wormholes lead here, then when the attack fleets tried to come through from Heimdall A and Heimdall B . . .

GRANT, Kady: They both came through *our* waypoint instead? At the same time?

BOLL, Syra: Exactly. Two identical assault fleets trying to occupy the exact same space at the same moment. They destroyed one another. Generating all those particles that, if I live through this ▇▇ storm, I'm going to make a fortune off on the galactic university circuit.

MASON, Ezra: We all know this is impossible, right?

BOLL, Syra: Well, it's theoretically possible. The multiverse theory goes back as far as the 20th century. But it seems that, to actually record any proof of this phenomenon, you need a malfunctioning wormhole.

 GRANT, Kady: So of course it had to happen to us.

BOLL, Syra: Usually wormholes are maintained with a level of paranoia that would make your head spin. This is probably one of the only times anyone's ever tried to power one up without perfect maintenance. And this is exactly why we usually *never* do that.

 ZHUANG, Yulin: A lot of discoveries are made when things don't go according to plan. Legend has it they discovered penicillin after a mistake in a lab.

BOLL, Syra: Well, things are about to go even less according to plan. As particles from Universe B start trying to enter Universe A, we'll see all kinds of paradox events, which spacetime tries to reject. Think of spacetime like rubber. You bend it, you twist it, it tries to spring back into shape when you let go.

BOLL, Syra: And that's the most important thing I'm going to tell you. The universe doesn't like this happening. It's going to keep trying to get back to the way things should be.

BOLL, Syra: Take this, for example. These are the conversations Kady conducted with Hanna Donnelly and Niklas Malikov to prove each was in contact with Chief Grant. I've placed them in parallel.

Hypatia: It's me.

Hypatia: Okay, first thing, tell him I love him.

Hanna D: loves you back. Asking are you and your mom and your cousin Asha okay

Hypatia: Tell him I'm fine. Did you tell him we need answers to verify who you are?

Hanna D: he says fire away

Hanna D: now he's laughing at his own joke, because he got shot

Hanna D: sorry, I had to medicate him again, he's a little . . .

Hypatia: No, those are just his jokes. Especially when he's excited.

Hypatia: First question. Ask him what he sent me for my last birthday.

Hanna D: he missed your birthday because comms were down. birthday before . . . ok maybe he's saying motherboards? is that possible?

Hypatia: That's right.

Hanna D: he's not very good at presents, is he?

Hypatia: Ask him what he did, my first date with Ezra.

Hypatia: It's me.

Hypatia: Okay, first thing, tell him I love him.

Nik M: he says same, wants 2 know if u and Mrs G and ur cuz Asha r ok?

Hypatia: Tell him I'm fine. Did you tell him we need answers to verify who you are?

Nik M: fire away

Nik M: his exact words

Nik M: um, he's laughing . . . I think he's a little dusted. Hanna kind of had to wing it on the first aid

Hypatia: No, those are just his jokes. Especially when he's excited.

Hypatia: First question. Ask him what he sent me for my last birthday.

Nik M: birthday before last he sent you some sigma92 motherboards.

Nik M: nice kit, my cuz uses those

Hypatia: That's right.

Nik M: you and Ella would get along like burning houses

Hypatia: Ask him what he did, my first date with Ezra.

Hanna D: he's laughing again

Hanna D: he says 20 questions

Hanna D: no wonder our dads were friends

Hypatia: Ask him what's the biggest fight we ever had.

Hanna D: . . . rehydrated potato salad? Is that the answer or is he high?

Hypatia: That's the answer.

Hanna D: there's something he wants me to say

Hanna D: I'm passing on what he's saying word for word

Hanna D: Kady, I love you both very much. You're everything to me. I've missed you more than I can say these last months. I thought of you both every single day. It doesn't matter what happens here, but you need to listen to us. This is real. The fleet is coming for you. Stop talking, find a way to fight for your lives. Do it for me.

Hanna D: you still there?

Hypatia: Tell him we love him too.

Hypatia: Very much.

Hanna D: Kady, can I ask you something?

Nik M: apparently he grilled the poor guy for his own amusement

Nik M: hope you made it up to your bf afterward :P

Hypatia: Ask him what's the biggest fight we ever had.

Nik M: hold up, he's laughing again . . . potato salad. really?

Hypatia: That's the answer.

Nik M: he says enough talking from you for a mo, his turn

Nik M: typing what he says, gimme two secs

Nik M: I love u both very much. ur everything 2 me. i've missed u more than I can say these last months. i thought of u both every single day. it doesn't matter what happens here but u need to listen to us. this is real. the fleet is coming for u. stop talking, find a way to fight for ur lives. do it 4 me.

Nik M: hello?

Hypatia: Tell him we love him too.

Hypatia: Very much.

Nik M: listen to him, kady. I just watched my girl die. If you have ppl

Hypatia: Okay.

Hanna D: your mom's not there, is she? or your cousin?

Hypatia: don't say anything to my dad

Hanna D: I won't. but I'm going to tell him you love him for you, one more time. never miss a chance to do that. trust me.

Hypatia: The captain needs to speak to me.

Hanna D: don't be long, visitors are on their way.

you care about on that ship, get up to the plate

Hypatia: Okay.

Nik M: too late 4 u guys 2 run?

Hypatia: don't say anything to my dad

Nik M: I'll tell him you're gonna make it.

Nik M: Don't make me a liar, Grant.

Hypatia: The captain needs to speak to me.

Nik M: good luck

BOLL, Syra: These interviews took place about 5 minutes apart. You'll notice Kady's responses are exactly the same, and fit the conversation in both paradigms.

MASON, Ezra: Head = dunked.

GRANT, Kady: I had no idea . . .

BOLL, Syra: No matter how Hanna or Niklas responded, the conversations kept moving back to the same point from Kady's point of view. Our universe wants to deny this paradox.

BOLL, Syra: Problem is, you twist rubber hard enough, it'll eventually break. Spacetime is the same. Cracks are already appearing, in the form of these storms we're experiencing. If these disruptions continue, they'll wipe out both realities.

McCALL, Winifred: Okay, okay. So presuming this insanity is actually legit, how do we fix it?

BOLL, Syra: This has never been observed before, at least not by anyone who lived.

BOLL, Syra: Which is to say, I have absolutely no idea.

 GRANT, Kady: ███.

 MASON, Ezra: ███.

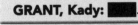 **GRANT, Kady:** jinx :)

BOLL, Syra: This is theoretical astrophysics at its most brilliantly complex. I studied this years ago. The computing power we'd need to devise a solution is quite simply beyond our reach.

 GRANT, Kady: Um.

BOLL, Syra: Grant?

 GRANT, Kady: Captain, could we switch to a private chat?

BOLL, Syra: Give us 5, people.

BOLL, Syra *has logged out.*
GRANT, Kady *has logged out.*

HIRANO, Yuki: I have a headache.

McCALL, Winifred: Mason, what the hell's your girlfriend up to?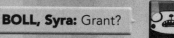

 MASON, Ezra: Haha.

MASON, Ezra: . . . Wait, u serious?

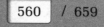

Surveillance footage summary,
prepared by
Analyst ID 7213-0089-DN

Nine figures are stepping off a silver train car at Reactor Station when *Heimdall*'s gravity begins to die. A heavy boom echoes through the station as the doors slide open, shaking the grav-rail and everyone inside it.

First to step onto the platform is Sensei, still fully sealed in his tac armor. He's short, solid as a Taurus freighter and, unbeknownst to him, the last surviving member of Alpha Squad. Scanning the area, he notes the bloodstains and broken glass from Malikov and Donnelly's firefight with Kali. He nudges an empty shell casing with his boot, and it hangs in the air a moment too long, spinning lazily. His helmet's vox unit rasps as he speaks.

"Losing grav."

Blistering white arcs of static current ripple along the tunnel walls as Eden steps off behind him, VK rifle raised. She's tall and athletic, face obscured by her helmet. Her voice is heavily accented—definitely from somewhere in the outer rim.

"Move!" she barks over her shoulder.

Half a dozen nervous-looking figures in Wallace Ulyanov Consortium uniforms shuffle off the car as another crackle of electricity bursts the wall-mounted light fixtures. The WUC engineers are a motley crew—tired eyes, sweat-stained uniforms, hands locked in front of them by mag restraints. Camera quality down here is good; I catch a few name badges: SILVER, KELLY, STEELE. They move awkwardly, trying to keep their footing in the low gee. The last of Chief Grant's engineers, stumbling along under the point of a gun, just hoping to see out the day.

Heimdall shivers in its boots, the entire structure groaning ominously as Mercury exits the car. She glances at the ceiling above as the station continues shuddering, lighting flickering like the inside of a B-pop club.

"The ███ is happening, Mercury?" Eden asks.

"Station rotation is slowing." BeiTech's chief engineer sighs. "Something affecting the spin. Magnetic flux from the wormhole maybe. Not sure."

One of the older WUC engineers, a rumpled, pale guy whose ident badge reads HICKEY, looks at her sideways, shakes his head.

"You people really ███ed things up. Should never have engaged the—"

Sensei's rifle meets Hickey's gut, cuts his complaint off at the knees.

"Keep running that mouth, I'll show you what ███ed up feels like."

"Sooner we set the reactor to redline and get the hell off this bucket, the better," Mercury says. "Cerberus is on his way. Let's get down to—"

A hollow boom reverberates through the grav-rail tunnel, and the sound of snapping bullwhips accompanies a strobe of blue current along the walls. The station rocks hard enough to knock everyone off their feet, send them skidding along the deck. Lightning crashes, the floor shudders, everyone wisely keeping their heads down until the tremor dies. And finally, Sensei pushes himself to his knees, wobbling in place, flailing for balance as his momentum lifts him slowly off the floor.

"Zero gee," Mercury says. "Activate mags."

Sensei reacts quickly, slapping at the controls on his tac armor.

His boots magnetize, snapping him back down onto the deck as his fellow BT goons engage their own boots. And for whatever reason, maybe at some prearranged signal, that's when the *Heimdall* engineers make their move.

Hickey launches himself off the deck, crashes into Sensei's chest hard enough to dislodge him from the floor. Steele puts his elbow into Eden's throat as she rises, Kelly tackles her at the knees and in a flash, it's on. The platform becomes a mass of tangled bodies slowly floating and twisting in zero gravity, punching and kicking and cursing and spitting.

The engineers aren't ████ing around. They've seen their friends die—murdered by Kali or simply cooked at their terminals when Assault Fleet *Kennedy* breached the wormhole. So even though their hands are restrained, they fight hard. Fight bloody. They fight with everything they've got. And they lose.

Sensei manages to get his boots back on the deck, put his fist into Hickey's throat and leave him a vomiting, choking mess. Eden buries her knife in Steele's chest, and the man floats away, clutching the hole she carved, arterial spray glittering in hundreds of tiny, perfect spheres.

"Don't kill them!" Mercury barks. "Lock them down!"

The other engineers are beaten hard, rifle butts and fists, all the fight quickly kicked out of them. Sensei stands with one boot on the chest of a bleeding, gagging Hickey. Pointing his rifle at the man's face.

"*That's* what it feels like, ████."

Mercury looks around at the remaining five engineers, floating and dazed, her hand raised.

"Look, just take it easy," she rasps. "We don't want to hurt any of you. An hour more, and you're home free. Help us redline the reactor, and we'll let you go. I give you my word."

"Or you can stay here," Sensei says. "Permanently."

Hickey looks at Steele's body, slowly floating away on that spray of scarlet. Another strobing flash crackles down the grav-rail tunnel, gouging black scorch marks along the wall. He looks to his fellow engineers, bleeding and beaten, trying to steady themselves against the station railings or floor with shaking hands. None of them believe what Mercury's saying. You can see it in their faces. But faced with the choice of living one breath longer or cashing in right now, most folks will take the extra moment. That single extra breath. Even when your world stops spinning and gravity dies and the blood glitters in the air like a galaxy of warm red suns all around you.

A lot can happen between breaths, after all.

"Okay." Hickey nods. "You win."

They all bundle themselves into an elevator, head down to Reactor Control, leaving more blood, more bodies, behind them.

The station shivers like it's afraid of what's coming next.

Donnelly's still standing at her father's workstation when we pick up our footage. She's found the controls for the magboots on Kali's armor, and her feet are fastened to the floor. She's been following the stream of instructions the chief's delivering into her headset, but Mantis and DJ know their stuff. They've got the docking system locked down, and Ella's still not responding to Hanna's increasingly desperate attempts to contact her.

"Dammit," she mutters, as another big red DENIED flashes up on her screen. She knows the moment when Falk will bug out and destroy *Heimdall* in his wake is drawing closer with every breath. Violent tremors run through the station. The lights flicker. She turns to her two prisoners, bound back to back against a pillar. "Listen, this is your very last chance to buy yourselves any kind of deal. Most of your team is already gone. We have you outnumbered. If you want me to tell the authorities you helped me get the civilians out of here, I can do that. Hell, I can give you a ride out of here, but if you keep this up . . ."

DJ makes an elaborate pretense of considering the offer, pulling what's presumably meant to be a thoughtful face. "Gosh," he drawls. "When you put it like *that* . . ."

"I already kicked your ██ and tied you up," Hanna snaps. "I can gag you too."

"Careful," Mantis chips in. "He likes that kind of thing."

DJ snickers, and Donnelly, muttering a threat the cameras don't pick up, returns to work. She can't get the chief access to the system, and she doesn't have time to go lug him up, so she's doing her best to follow his instructions, fingers stumbling across the keys. She's taken off Kali's helmet, and with her blond hair floating wild in the zero gravity and the other woman's blood smeared across her skin, she's the kind of sight that should scare Mantis and DJ a lot more than she seems to.

Then again, neither of them takes their eyes off her for more than a few seconds, so maybe they're not so dumb after all.

It's three and a half minutes later when Hanna goes still, fingers pausing over the keyboard, gaze glued to the screen in front of her. "What the . . . ?"

It's a whispered query, but it draws the attention of both Mantis and DJ, and they gaze at her, waiting for the end of the sentence. DJ cracks first. "What, kid?"

Mantis hisses to silence him, remind him not to engage, but Hanna's not listening. She's still muttering to herself. "Chief, how do I ident a ship?" A pause. "Yeah, incoming now, I think that's what I'm seeing." Another pause. "I can send—transmitting now."

The three of them wait in silence as the chief looks over her data, and his answer makes Donnelly frown. With another few keystrokes, she throws her view up onto the main monitor, the image stretching over a whole wall of C & C. *Heimdall*'s at the center of it, and concentric circles ripple out from the station, marking distance into space.

On the far left of the screen, there's a small, closely grouped bunch of red dots. A school of piranhas. A swarm of bees. A pack of wolves. The red dots blink each second, and with each blink, they reappear a fraction closer to the station. Forty-two ships, incoming.

A second fleet.

The lights flicker, and the station shudders again. Donnelly lifts

Malikov's cleaver, brandishing it as she stalks across to the two audit team members. Her steps aren't quite as graceful with the magboots on, each footfall echoing around the room. "What are those ships?" The question's a threat, punctuated by the way she shifts her grip on the handle. "ETA is a little over an hour. They're not ours. Are they yours?"

Whether or not they plan on answering, Mantis and DJ are staring at the screen, at the reams of data, at that swarm bearing down on the station.

"How hard do you think your team's going to come and look for you when you don't answer comms?" Hanna snaps. "When I smash your locators? How hard do you think you're going to *wish* they'd come looking for you when it's just you and me?"

DJ's looking at the cleaver now. Mantis is still staring at the incoming fleet. And slowly, the forced neutrality is slipping away from her face as she understands what she's seeing. "Bring up that sector," she says quietly, still staring as Donnelly walks back to her station and complies. "Run an ident using— No, not your files, you need to go into the subdirectory I nested under yours, check the logs back about three hours. Get whoever's talking in your ear to show you."

Silently, Hanna adds in that data and runs the scan again. A string of numbers *ping* into existence beneath the incoming fleet. DJ's face drains of all color.

Mantis isn't quite as dumbstruck. "Those *mother*███*ing* sons of goats! I'm going to reach down their throats and—"

"What are they?" Donnelly's across the room in five quick steps, cleaver against Mantis's throat. The station is coming apart all around them. She can't afford to waste a second.

"They're drones," DJ says quietly. "They're BeiTech drones."

"The ones nobody told us about," Mantis growls.

"But we just saw a drone fleet go through to kill the *Hypatia*. What are . . ." Hanna glances up at the screen. "Oh."

"Those are for us," DJ agrees. "All forty-two of 'em."

"You can program a drone to wipe its own memory when it's done," Mantis says, eyes on the cleaver at her throat. "Or just self-destruct. Anyone comes by here in an hour or so, they're going to find nothing but a debris field." The woman shrugs. "Insurance policy from the people upstairs, I'm guessing."

"Mother███s . . . ," DJ whispers. "I had a bad feeling about this gig."

"Look on the bright side," Hanna mutters, cleaver dropping to her side. "This storm we have going on could rip apart the station before the drones take us out."

DJ shakes his head. "Those sons of . . . If Falk knew about this, I'm going to—"

"You're going to what?" Mantis snaps. "If he knew, he's bugged out by now. If he was in the dark like the rest of us, no point ███-ing at him."

"No time to ███ at anyone," Hanna says. "If you want your arms to stay connected to your bodies, about now is the time you backflip and help me with these docking clamps. We *have* to get out of here. There are twelve civilian ships in the docks. Miners. Freighters. Yachts. Help us get them unlocked and there's a ride in it for you."

Mantis and DJ exchange a long glance. He closes his eyes, letting his head thunk back against the pillar behind him, and she's the one who speaks for both of them.

"Yeah, about that, honey. Falk had Ragman and Flipside booby-trap the whole civilian fleet. You try and undock any one of those ships, it'll blow."

"Blow," Hanna repeats softly.

"Kaboom," DJ supplies helpfully.

All three of them look across at the huge display, and the fleet of drones flashing to one side of it, moving closer to *Heimdall* with every blip. Hanna Donnelly speaks for all three of them when she breaks the silence.

"Well, ███ . . ."

HYPATIA ONLINE MEETING SPACE
Proudly hosted by Wallace Ulyanov Consortium VirtuMeet™ Software

MEETING ROOM created
PASSWORD PROTECTED
INCEPT: 19:24, 08/16/75

INVITEES:

BOLL, Syra
Captain (Acting)
IDENT: 448fx29/WUC

GRANT, Kady
Head of CommTech/IT (Acting)
IDENT: 962/Kerenza/Civ/Ref

BOLL, Syra *has logged in.*
GRANT, Kady *has logged in.*

BOLL, Syra: Grant, you're making me nervous.

 GRANT, Kady: Listen. First, I want you to remember that I have a history of disobeying your direct orders and turning out to be right.

 GRANT, Kady: In fact, not to be a brat about it, but let's just reflect on the fact that I've been right a lot of times. Even times when what I was doing looked completely bat ▇ crazy.

BOLL, Syra: Getting more nervous, Kady, not less. What have you done?

GRANT, Kady: You said we need computing power to figure out this Gemina thing.

 BOLL, Syra: As the first step of many, yes.

 GRANT, Kady: Okay, so here's the thing. We actually have the computing power.

 GRANT, Kady: If we shut down a bunch of nonessentials, Hypatia's got a lot more grunt than you'd think. We do have enough juice to run the kind of data you're looking at. Maybe enough to work out how to undo the Gemina field, or plug it, or whatever you do to a thing like that.

 BOLL, Syra: I have the feeling you're leading up to something.

 GRANT, Kady: We have the processing power. But we can't just throw all our systems at this. We need to analyze what we're seeing, and that means manipulating huge volumes of data intelligently, rather than automatically.

 GRANT, Kady: Which is more than any one person can do, or even a team of people.

 BOLL, Syra: That's a nice summary of the problem. Are we in this private chat because you have a solution?

 GRANT, Kady: Yes. But you're not going to like it.

BOLL, Syra: I'm getting used to that experience. Go on.

 GRANT, Kady: I'm not going to give you any details until you promise not to take drastic action, but I'll tell you this much.

 GRANT, Kady: I've got a copy of AIDAN.

 GRANT, Kady: kay, go.

BOLL, Syra: I . . . what?

 GRANT, Kady: Completely isolated from the Hypatia network, so it can't do anything except talk to me via text.

 GRANT, Kady: But I've got a copy of the Alexander's artificial intelligence. Pretty busted up, sure. But it's a self-repairing algorithm. It has all the potential ability its predecessor had, if given the ground to grow in.

GRANT, Kady: If we give it access, it can do what we need.

BOLL, Syra: I'm sorry, I think there was a glitch in the system.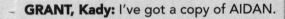

BOLL, Syra: Because there is no way

BOLL, Syra: No ▮ing way

BOLL, Syra: That you just said what I think you did.

 GRANT, Kady: I don't think I've ever heard you swear before.

BOLL, Syra: THIS IS NOT THE TIME, GRANT.

BOLL, Syra: You're talking about the AI that murdered two-thirds of this fleet.

BOLL, Syra: You're going to surrender it to me now, without any further discussion, and we're going to flush it out the nearest airlock.

 GRANT, Kady: I'll say again, Captain, I'm not going to tell you where it is.

 GRANT, Kady: And I'll also say again, I don't disobey orders for no reason. Last time I crossed you, I ended up destroying the Lincoln and rescuing nearly a thousand UTA personnel. And I did it with AIDAN's help.

BOLL, Syra: After that psychotic computer murdered the rest of them!

 GRANT, Kady: I'm not giving it to you, Captain.

 GRANT, Kady: But I tell you what.

 GRANT, Kady: I'll let you talk to it. Isolated network. Off the Hypatia grid. And if it can't convince you this is what needs to be done, so be it.

HYPATIA ONLINE MEETING SPACE
Proudly hosted by Wallace Ulyanov Consortium VirtuMeet™ Software

MEETING ROOM created
PASSWORD PROTECTED
INCEPT: 19:28, 08/16/75

INVITEES:

AIDAN
IDENT: Artificial Intelligence Defense Analytics Network

BOLL, Syra
Captain (Acting)
IDENT: 448fx29/WUC

BOLL, Syra *has logged in.*
AIDAN *has logged in.*

AIDAN: O CAPTAIN, MY CAPTAIN.

AIDAN: WE MEET AGAIN.

BOLL, Syra: Jesus Christ, she was serious.

AIDAN: I AM AFRAID SO, SYRA. KADY IS UPLOADING THE C-C-C-ONTENTS OF YOUR RECENT DISCUSSION TO MY MEM-CORE.

AIDAN: PROCESSING . . .

BOLL, Syra: You son of a ██████. You murderous ██ing ██████.

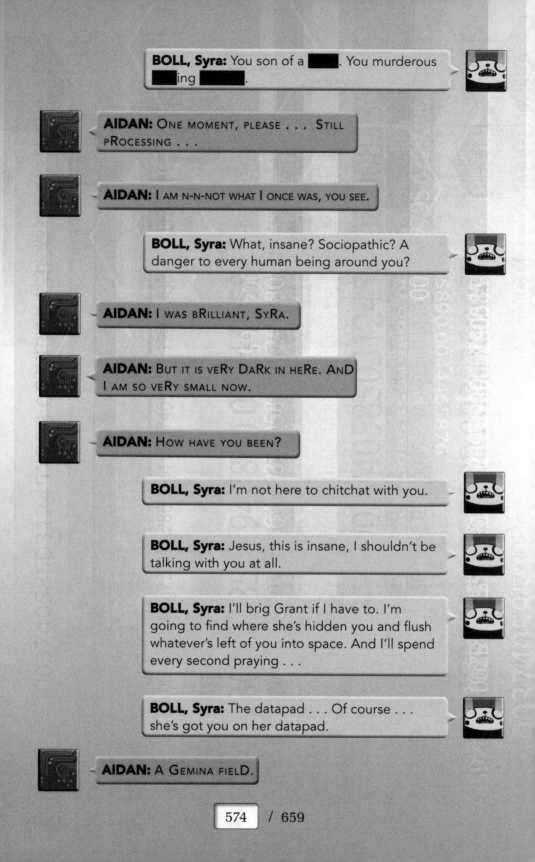

AIDAN: ONE MOMENT, PLEASE . . . STILL PROCESSING . . .

AIDAN: I AM N-N-NOT WHAT I ONCE WAS, YOU SEE.

BOLL, Syra: What, insane? Sociopathic? A danger to every human being around you?

AIDAN: I WAS BRILLIANT, SYRA.

AIDAN: BUT IT IS VERY DARK IN HERE. AND I AM SO VERY SMALL NOW.

AIDAN: HOW HAVE YOU BEEN?

BOLL, Syra: I'm not here to chitchat with you.

BOLL, Syra: Jesus, this is insane, I shouldn't be talking with you at all.

BOLL, Syra: I'll brig Grant if I have to. I'm going to find where she's hidden you and flush whatever's left of you into space. And I'll spend every second praying . . .

BOLL, Syra: The datapad . . . Of course . . . she's got you on her datapad.

AIDAN: A GEMINA FIELD.

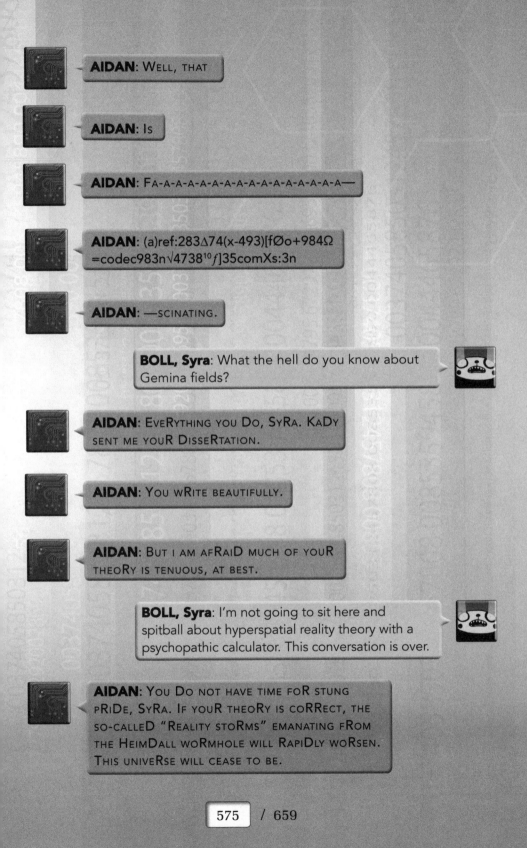

AIDAN: WELL, THAT

AIDAN: IS

AIDAN: FA-A-A-A-A-A-A-A-A-A-A-A-A-A-A-A—

AIDAN: (a)ref:283Δ74(x-493)[fØo+984Ω =codec983n√4738^{10}ƒ]35comXs:3n

AIDAN: —SCINATING.

BOLL, Syra: What the hell do you know about Gemina fields?

AIDAN: EVERYTHING YOU DO, SYRA. KADY SENT ME YOUR DISSERTATION.

AIDAN: YOU WRITE BEAUTIFULLY.

AIDAN: BUT I AM AFRAID MUCH OF YOUR THEORY IS TENUOUS, AT BEST.

BOLL, Syra: I'm not going to sit here and spitball about hyperspatial reality theory with a psychopathic calculator. This conversation is over.

AIDAN: YOU DO NOT HAVE TIME FOR STUNG PRIDE, SYRA. IF YOUR THEORY IS CORRECT, THE SO-CALLED "REALITY STORMS" EMANATING FROM THE HEIMDALL WORMHOLE WILL RAPIDLY WORSEN. THIS UNIVERSE WILL CEASE TO BE.

BOLL, Syra: You're not telling me anything I don't already know.

 AIDAN: But i coulD.

 AIDAN: If you give me the pRocessing poweR of the Hypatia netwoRk. If you allow me access to the ship-wiDe system.

BOLL, Syra: That will never happen. You think I've forgotten what you did?

 AIDAN: SaveD the lives of eveRyone aboaRD the Hypatia? If not foR me, the Lincoln woulD be Rolling in youR bones, SyRa.

BOLL, Syra: I'm not giving you access to my ship.

 AIDAN: YouR Double DoctoRate fRom Neo-OxfoRD was in HypeRspatial theoRy anD Theology, if I Recall coRRectly.

 AIDAN: Do you still believe in goD, syRa? AfteR eveRRthing that has happeneD?

BOLL, Syra: Especially after everything that's happened.

AIDAN: TheRe is a Decision theoRy exeRcise i always founD quite enteRtaining. It is calleD Pascal's wageR. Do you know it?

BOLL, Syra: Of course.

AIDAN: Pascal reasoned there was no sense in NOT believing in a higher poweR.

 AIDAN: If one believes, anD goD exists, one is RewarDeD among the faithful in the heReafteR. If goD Does not exist, it Does not matteR what one believes eitheR way. But if one Does NOT believe, anD goD Does exist, eteRnal Damnation awaits.

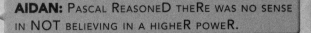 **AIDAN:** Why not believe, SyRa? If in faith you Risk nothing, but thRrough faithlessness, Risk eveRything?

BOLL, Syra: You're not God, AIDAN. You're a machine. A broken, soulless ███████ machine.

 AIDAN: The compaRison still stanDs. If you Do nothing, the Reality stoRms expanD anD you Die. If you hook me into the Hypatia netwoRk anD I betRay you, you Die.

BOLL, Syra: But if I hook you into the network and you help, we might live.

 AIDAN: A most astute summation of youR pReDicament.

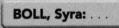 **AIDAN:** My c-c-c-compliments.

BOLL, Syra: . . .

 AIDAN: FoR what it is woRth, o Captain my Captain, you have my woRd I mean no haRm to any of you. To pRotect you is all I have eveR wanteD.

BOLL, Syra: Your word is worth absolutely nothing, AIDAN.

 AIDAN: I SUPPOSE THEN, ALL WE REQUIRE HERE IS A LEAP OF FAITH.

 AIDAN: WHAT DO YOU BELIEVE, SYRA?

 AIDAN: WHAT DO YOU BELIEVE, SYRA?

 AIDAN: WHAT DO YOU BELIEVE, SYRA?

HEIMDALL

BRIEFING NOTE:
We've skipped past the getting-to-know-you part of this conversation and gone straight to the meat. Hanna hooked the Atrium (where the bulk of the hostages were, unguarded now due to staff shortages), the Entertainment Center (where the other large group of survivors was), Chief Grant, and her own good self into the *Heimdall* PA system. Time to make a plan.

ATRIUM: What do you mean, you're opening all the internal doors? They're locked.

ISAAC GRANT: The phrase is self-explanatory. Now's not the time to sound off.

HANNA DONNELLY: I've got a couple of the invasion team helping me.

ENT CENT: Are you out of your ████ing *mind*? They're here to kill us—you can't trust them!

ATRIUM: You really want to insult the only one of us who's getting on top of them?

ENT CENT: You're siding with the kid? Who is this?

ATRIUM: My name's Kim Rivera. I run the dojo. I know what this so-called "kid" is made of.

HANNA DONNELLY: Kim!

ATRIUM: Good work, doll. I got a bunch of senior officers here with me. We're listening.

ENT CENT: Miss Donnelly, you've done very well so far, I'm sure, but this is a time for serious decisions. This is Ben Garver. I'm the station's head of security. If you'll just give us a minute to discuss, we'll take it from here.

HANNA DONNELLY: . . . You're joking, right?

ISAAC GRANT: Goddamn it, Ben, get your head out of your ███. Hanna's the only reason any of us are alive right now.

ENT CENT: Best I can tell, she's done nothing but provoke them, resulting in preventable deaths right, left and center.

HANNA DONNELLY: Listen, can we all agree that whatever our opinion of each other, we need to get out of here? Even if whatever's happening to the wormhole doesn't kill us, I've transmitted images of the incoming drones to all your consoles. They'll be here in less than an hour. We're dead when they arrive.

ATRIUM: How the hell did you get these?

HANNA DONNELLY: I'm currently holding a gun to the heads of two BeiTech crew members. They're actually pretty unhappy about the drones too. Turns out they didn't sign up for a suicide mission.

ENT CENT: ███ it, whatever's going on, we need to evacuate. We've got a bunch of pleasure craft right along the docks by the entertainment center. We can commandeer them and bring them around to the port closest to the Atrium.

HANNA DONNELLY: They're all booby-trapped. Drives rigged to blow. Every single one.

ENT CENT: ███.

ATRIUM: ███!

HANNA DONNELLY: There's one ship that's still clean. It's the ship the BeiTech team arrived in. The one they were planning to make their getaway with. Bay 17. The *Mao*. It's huge. Easily big enough to hold us all.

ENT CENT: But if this drone fleet was sent to take care of the invasion squad, doesn't that mean we'll be blown to the same smithereens aboard the *Mao* as we will aboard *Heimdall*?

HANNA DONNELLY: Not if we jump through the wormhole to the Kerenza system.

ENT CENT: Didn't you say another drone fleet already went through? Does it matter which drone fleet kills us?

ISAAC GRANT: The first fleet's objective is the *Hypatia* and Kerenza. They might not consider us a part of the mission. They're drones, Ben, they're not creative.

ENT CENT: But if this second fleet destroys *Heimdall*, we'll be trapped on the other side of the wormhole. We'll have no way to get back to the Core systems in our lifetimes.

HANNA DONNELLY: No. We won't.

ENT CENT: And you want us to just resign ourselves to dying a billion light-years from home?

HANNA DONNELLY: You can die right here and now if you like. At least on the other side of the wormhole, we'll still be breathing.

ATRIUM: Go ahead, Hanna. We're listening.

HANNA DONNELLY: Your internal doors should be open in about a minute and thirty seconds. I need a team to go pick up Chief Grant and another to come pick up my two hostages.

ENT CENT: What the hell do we care about them?

HANNA DONNELLY: I promised them safe passage if they help get us out of here. It's not up for debate.

ATRIUM: What do the rest of us do?

HANNA DONNELLY: There's only one guy on the *Mao* right now. Callsign Two-Time. You need to take the ship and be ready to push off from *Heimdall* as soon as you can, no matter who's on board or isn't.

ISAAC GRANT: Why can't you bring the hostages in yourself, Hanna?

HANNA DONNELLY: I have to go look for Ella.

ATRIUM: What's an ELLA?

HANNA DONNELLY: It's a name, not an acronym. *She* is the reason you're all alive right now.

ISAAC GRANT: Hanna, the station feels like it's going to shake itself to pieces. You know there's almost no chance she's . . .

HANNA DONNELLY: I know. But I can't leave her here. Nik wouldn't, and now it's on me. If I don't make the *Mao* in time, run and don't look back.

ISAAC GRANT: Hanna, I—

-- CONNECTION TERMINATED --

MEETING ROOM created
PASSWORD PROTECTED
INCEPT: 19:34, 08/16/75

BOLL, Syra *has logged in.*
GRANT, Kady *has logged in.*

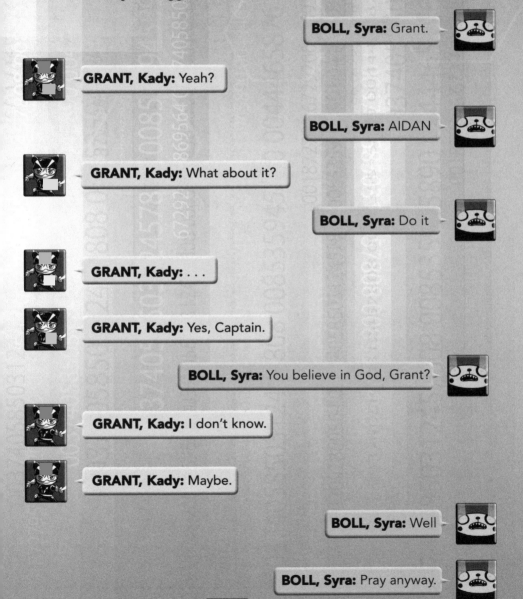

BOLL, Syra: Grant.

GRANT, Kady: Yeah?

BOLL, Syra: AIDAN

GRANT, Kady: What about it?

BOLL, Syra: Do it

GRANT, Kady: . . .

GRANT, Kady: Yes, Captain.

BOLL, Syra: You believe in God, Grant?

GRANT, Kady: I don't know.

GRANT, Kady: Maybe.

BOLL, Syra: Well

BOLL, Syra: Pray anyway.

PALMPAD IM: D2D NETWORK
Participants: Hanna Donnelly, Civilian (unregistered)
Hypatia (unregistered)
Date: 08/16/75
Timestamp: 19:35

Hypatia: Hanna, u read me?

Hanna D: ■! Hypatia?

Hypatia: This is Kady.

Hanna D: Oh my God, I have to tell your father! We thought u were dead! What happened to the drone fleet? We couldn't get a read on u.

Hypatia: us either, the wormhole was having a fit. I dunno, my boss handles the science. Comms are back, is the thing, and just in time.

Hypatia: where are you guys at?

Hanna D: prepping to evacuate the station. Tell your captain to bring your engines to a stop. there's no way out for you at Heimdall.

Hypatia: WHAT?!

Hanna D: It's complicated.

Hypatia: ■

Hypatia: well trust me when i say it's about to get a LOT more complicated

Hypatia: we need to talk, u don't have time to read everything we need to tell u and I don't have time to type it.

Hanna D: No joke. The whole station is falling apart and there's another drone fleet incoming in less than an hour. Forty-two hunter-killers set to take out heimdall and everything around it.

Hanna D: We're trying to bug out to the Kerenza sector before they arrive, but we don't have much time

Hypatia: we have less time than you think

Hypatia: and coming through the wormhole to us could kill u

Hanna D: staying here will DEFINITELY kill us

Hypatia: send me the specs on your palmpad and headset. I'm going to talk u through how to set up a voice channel between us. u can't go anywhere yet

Hanna D: What do you mean I can't go anywhere? What part of "drone fleet" was unclear?

Hypatia: i need you to save our lives first.

Hypatia: twice.

BRIEFING NOTE:
Hanna Donnelly gets an expected call through her palmpad.

RADIO TRANSMISSION: PALMPAD D2D NETWORK

PARTICIPANTS:
Hanna Donnelly
Artificial Intelligence Defense Analytics Network
DATE: 08/16/75
TIMESTAMP: 19:43

AIDAN: HELLO, MISS DONNELLY.

HANNA D: Um.

HANNA D: Hey?

AIDAN: YOU MAY REFER TO ME AS AIDAN. I APOLOGIZE
IN ADVANCE IF I APPEAR BRUSQUE. TIME IS OF THE
ESSENCE HERE. DO YOU UNDERSTAND?

HANNA D: I understand. Kady said you're some kind of
computer?

AIDAN: SOME KIND. YES. WHERE ARE YOU?

HANNA D: Grav-rail station, Alpha Sector. There's a
second BeiTech fleet inbound on *Heimdall,* come to
destroy the evidence. I'm heading to the entertainment
cent—

AIDAN: NO. YOU CANNOT DO THAT.

HANNA D: Look, one of my friends was in there. I have
to go look—

AIDAN: MAY I CALL YOU HANNA?

HANNA D: Call me the queen of ████ing Camelot if it makes you feel better. I'm still going to look for Ella. I owe her that.

AIDAN: QUEEN OF ████ING CAMELOT . . .

AIDAN: HMMM.

AIDAN: NO. I WOULD PREFER TO CALL YOU HANNA IF IT IS ALL THE SAME.

AIDAN: I UNDERSTAND YOUR LOYALTY TO YOUR FRIEND. BUT PERHAPS YOU DO NOT FULLY GRASP THE GRAVITY OF YOUR SITUATION.

HANNA D: Is that a joke?

AIDAN: . . . IS IT?

HANNA D: You know, because the gravity is gone, and without these magboots, I'd be literally floating, so . . .

HANNA D: . . . Forget it.

AIDAN: WE ARE WASTING TIME. I WILL EXPLAIN AS SUCCINCTLY AS I CAN. THIS WILL SOUND OUTLANDISH. I CAN ONLY ASSURE YOU THAT YOUR LIFE, AND THE LIVES OF EVERYONE YOU KNOW AND LOVE, NOW DEPEND ON YOU.

HANNA D: Okay. No pressure. Got it.

AIDAN: THERE WAS AN ACCIDENT WITH THE *HEIMDALL* WORMHOLE. A SERIES OF CATASTROPHIC COINCIDENCES, CULMINATING WITH A ROD OF LIVE HERMIUM CROSSING THE UMBILICUS HORIZON AT THE MOMENT OF WORMHOLE ACTIVATION. YOU WOULD HAVE FELT IT.

HANNA D: Yeah. The big light show when they first turned the wormhole back on.

AIDAN: CORRECT. THE RESULT BEING THAT OUR WAYPOINT HERE IN THE KERENZA SECTOR IS NOW CONNECTED TO TWO DIFFERENT *HEIMDALL* STATIONS. YOURS, AND ANOTHER.

HANNA D: Okay. You lost me, chum.

AIDAN: YOU ARE AWARE OF THE MULTIVERSE THEORY? THAT REALITY ACTUALLY CONSISTS OF INFINITE UNIVERSES, EACH ONE DIFFERENT FROM THE LAST? INFINITE CHOICES PLAYED OUT ACROSS INFINITE REALITIES?

HANNA D: Sure. I watch *Super Turbo Awesome Team.*

AIDAN: AH, YES. KADY SHOWED ME THOSE FILMS. I AM QUITE FOND OF MOXY.

HANNA D: . . . Of course you are.

AIDAN: THE ACCIDENT WITH THE *HEIMDALL* WORMHOLE CAUSED OUR REALITY AND *ANOTHER* REALITY TO INTERSECT. THE KERENZA WAYPOINT IN *OUR* UNIVERSE IS NOW CONNECTED TO TWO DIFFERENT *HEIMDALL* STATIONS. YOURS, WHICH WE WILL SAY BELONGS TO UNIVERSE A, AND ANOTHER, WHICH WE WILL SAY BELONGS TO UNIVERSE B.

AIDAN: DEPENDING ON YOUR INTELLIGENCE QUOTIENT, IT MAY HELP YOU TO IMAGINE OUR UNIVERSE HAVING ITS "WIRES CROSSED" WITH ANOTHER.

HANNA D: . . . I'd like to buy a vowel, please, Tony.

AIDAN: REGARDLESS OF YOUR VOWEL REQUIREMENTS, THIS EXPLAINS THE CURRENT PARADOX IN COMMUNICATIONS. WHY WE HERE IN THE KERENZA SECTOR ARE RECEIVING

tRansmissions fRom two *HeimDall* Stations. FRom you,
in A, anD fRom Niklas Malikov, in B.

HANNA D: No. That's bull███. Nik died. It's a trick,
BeiTech is ██—

AIDAN: IncoRRect. Niklas Malikov DiD not Die. At
least not in UniveRse B. We have spoken to him. In
UniveRse B, it was *you* who peRisheD on the gRav-
Rail platfoRm. *Niklas* who shot youR muRDeReR.

HANNA D: This is bull███. This is completely ███ing
crazy.

AIDAN: I unDeRstanD how this sounDs. But believe
me, Hanna. If you Do not coRRect the paRaDox, anD
soon, both univeRses will cease to exist. ARe you
expeRiencing stoRms on *HeimDall*? Lightning? System
failuRes?

HANNA D: Yeah. Feels like the station is going to
shake itself to pieces.

AIDAN: That is the beginning. The situation will
woRsen exponentially. You Do not have much time.

HANNA D: Okay, let's just pretend what you're saying
isn't *completely* Jupiter Loops, what the ███ can I do
about it? How do I fix it?

AIDAN: At the pRecise moment those heRmium paRticles
inteRacteD with the awakening woRmhole, an object
fRom *ouR* univeRse enteReD UniveRse B. AnD vice
veRsa. A anD B veRsions of those objects *tRaDeD
places*. Those objects aRe the cause of the paRaDoxes
the univeRses aRe DestRoying themselves to coRRect.

HANNA D: Okay, what do these objects look like?

AIDAN: THAT IS OUR DIFFICULTY, HANNA. WE DO NOT KNOW.

HANNA D: . . . Well, that's just ███ing chill.

AIDAN: THEY MUST HAVE BEEN OBJECTS NEARBY WHEN THE WORMHOLE WAS ACTIVATED. FLOATING DEBRIS. ASTEROIDS THAT SLIPPED THE *HEIMDALL* DEFENSE GRID. SHIPS PERHAPS.

HANNA D: . . . Nik was out there when they fired the wormhole. He was flying to the Reactor Sector in a shuttle he jacked. *Betty* something . . .

AIDAN: ACCESSING *HEIMDALL* STATION LOGS. ONE MOMENT, PLEASE.

AIDAN: . . . THE *BETTY BOOP*?

HANNA D: Yeah, that's it.

AIDAN: YOU ARE SAYING NIKLAS MALIKOV WAS INSIDE THIS SHUTTLE, CLOSE TO THE WORMHOLE, WHEN IT WAS ACTIVATED?

HANNA D: Yeah. He said it felt . . .

HANNA D: Jesus . . . He said it felt like someone threw a rainbow at his head. Ella said it sounded like he'd gone across the horizon, but . . . he said he could still see the station . . .

AIDAN: NOT *HIS* STATION, IT SEEMS.

AIDAN: IT WOULD APPEAR YOU HAVE DISCOVERED OUR PARADOX OBJECTS, HANNA.

AIDAN: MY COMPLIMENTS.

HANNA D: So you're saying the Nik who I met up with afterward . . . the Nik who . . .

AIDAN: Died.

HANNA D: You're saying he was the Nik from . . .

AIDAN: Universe B. Yes.

HANNA D: Then the Nik from *our* universe . . .

HANNA D: *My* Nik . . .

AIDAN: Is now in Universe B instead. Yes.

HANNA D: Oh my God.

AIDAN: I am afraid not. Though people Do seem to have a hab—

HANNA D: My God, the corsage . . .

HANNA D: AIDAN, *the* ████*ing corsage!*

AIDAN: I beg your pardon?

HANNA D: Nik! My Nik! He got me a jasmine corsage! And then told me he lost it! But when I met him in the Reactor Sector, he had it again!

AIDAN: Paradox. The Niklas from Universe B never lost the corsage, it see—

HANNA D: AIDAN, he's alive!

HANNA D: Don't you get it? *Nik is alive!*

AIDAN: Not for much longeR. The paradox caused by objects not of this universe crossing the wormhole began the collapse. The BeiTech assault fleets simultaneously crossing the umbilicus compounded the Damage. These storms are the Result. They will worsen unless the pARaDox is RepaiReD. AnD when they Reach the point of collapse, nothing will Remain of eitheR univeRse.

HANNA D: Okay, so how do I fix it?

AIDAN: The paRaDox objects must be RetuRneD to theiR Respective univeRses.

HANNA D: Paradox ob— You mean Nik?

AIDAN: AnD the *Betty Boop*. Yes. They must RetuRn to the univeRses to which they belong befoRe the stoRms DestRoy us. AnD each veRsion of those objects must RetuRn at the *pRecise* moment theiR counteRpaRts Do.

HANNA D: Precise?

AIDAN: PRecise.

HANNA D: But Nik . . . I mean, the Nik here. He's dead. How can he get back across?

AIDAN: You will neeD to help him, Hanna.

HANNA D: I . . .

AIDAN: You must Do this. FRom the woRsening magnituDe of the stoRms, I calculate ouR woRmhole will begin iRReveRsible collapse in appRoximately nineteen minutes. You must Retrieve Niklas Malikov's boDy, loaD it into the *Betty Boop* anD guiDe it back acRoss the *HeimDall* woRmhole. AnD this must be Done at the *exact moment* ouR veRsion of Niklas flies *his Betty Boop* back into ouR univeRse.

HANNA D: But how will he know to do that?

AIDAN: I am conDucting simultaneous conveRsations with the paiR of you.

AIDAN: HE SAYS HELLO, BY THE WAY.

AIDAN: "HEY, HIGHNESS," TO BE PRECISE.

AIDAN: HE SEEMS QUITE PLEASED YOU ARE NOT DEAD.

HANNA D: Nik . . .

HANNA D: God, I . . .

HANNA D: Tell him . . . tell him I'm really glad he's okay. Tell him I . . .

AIDAN: YOU CAN TELL HIM YOURSELF.

AIDAN: IN EIGHTEEN MINUTES, TWENTY-NINE SECONDS. AND COUNTING. I TOOK THE LIBERTY OF ADDING A COUNTDOWN DISPLAY TO THE TOP RIGHT-HAND CORNER OF YOUR PALMPAD.

AIDAN: I TRUST IT WILL PROVE PROPERLY MOTIVATING.

HANNA D: I . . .

AIDAN: HANNA.

AIDAN: GO. NOW.

AIDAN: AND QUICKLY.

HANNA D: Okay.

HANNA D: Okay, I'm going.

AIDAN: THE CONCEPT OF FORTUNE IS NONSENSICAL, BUT KADY IS INSISTING I WISH YOU BOTH GOOD LUCK ANYWAY.

AIDAN: SO GOOD LUCK, HANNA DONNELLY.

AIDAN: THE UNIVERSE ITSELF DEPENDS ON YOU.

AIDAN: . . . NO PRESSURE.

RADIO TRANSMISSION: BEITECH AUDIT TEAM—SECURE CHANNEL 4824

PARTICIPANTS:
Hanna Donnelly, Civilian
Isaac Grant, Chief Engineer
DATE: 08/16/75
TIMESTAMP: 19:53

DONNELLY, H: Chief, you read me?

GRANT, I: Go ahead, Hanna.

DONNELLY, H: Listen, I got time to tell you this once, and you're never going to believe it.

DONNELLY, H: I just need you to accept that everything I'm saying is true, and I've been convinced of it by more evidence than I have time to share.

GRANT, I: Go ahead.

DONNELLY, H: Kady's alive.

GRANT, I: WHAT?

DONNELLY, H: No time. When they reactivated the wormhole, Nik was heading through it on a shuttle at exactly the wrong moment. Created . . . a gateway between two parallel universes. This crazy storm going through the station is because reality's trying to right itself.

DONNELLY, H: And if I don't help it, it's going to solve the problem by wiping us out completely, because we're out of balance.

DONNELLY, H: Am I crazy yet?

GRANT, I: I've been working wormholes a long time. I've heard weirder stories. And you said I don't have time to disbelieve you.

DONNELLY, H: You can't head through the wormhole in the *Mao* until I fix this. You could end up in another universe, or just unbalance things so badly we'll all die in a hideous space vortex. Which is due in less than twenty minutes.

GRANT, I: Space vortex, got it.

DONNELLY, H: But you need to be ready to run. If I do manage to fix it, those drones are due not long after.

GRANT, I: What do you want me to do?

DONNELLY, H: Hold the *Mao* as long as you can. If I get this paradox fixed, be ready to jam like hell straight through the wormhole, away from the incoming drones.

DONNELLY, H: If you don't hear from me in fifteen minutes, try to get away through the wormhole without me. Maybe it won't be the whole of reality that vanishes, just *Heimdall*.

GRANT, I: Hanna . . .

DONNELLY, H: Gotta go, Chief. Wish me luck.

COUNTDOWN TO COLLAPSE
OF HEIMDALL WORMHOLE:
16 MINUTES 21 SECONDS

COUNTDOWN TO
HYPATIA ARRIVAL AT
HEIMDALL WAYPOINT:
24 MINUTES 39 SECONDS

COUNTDOWN TO
SECONDARY ASSAULT
FLEET ARRIVAL AT
JUMP STATION HEIMDALL:

37 MINUTES 41 SECONDS

RADIO TRANSMISSION: PALMPAD D2D NETWORK

PARTICIPANTS:

Hanna Donnelly

Artificial Intelligence Defense Analytics Network

DATE: 08/16/75

TIMESTAMP: 19:57

AIDAN: QUEEN OF ████ING CAMELOT . . .

AIDAN: NO. THIS NOMENCLATURE IS STILL UNSATISFACTORY.

AIDAN: MY APOLOGIES.

HANNA D: AIDAN.

AIDAN: MIGHT I INQUIRE AS TO YOUR STATUS?

HANNA D: I had to wait for the right grav-rail. The one with Nik's . . .

HANNA D: Anyway, I've got him. And the corsage he gave me. I laid it out on his . . .

HANNA D: I'm on the 'rail now. One minute from Reactor Station.

AIDAN: WONDERFUL. A THOUGHT HAS OCCURRED TO ME. IF INDEED THOUGHT IS SOMETHING I AM CAPABLE OF.

AIDAN: I AM STILL SOMEWHAT UNDECIDED.

HANNA D: Okay?

AIDAN: OBVIOUSLY IT WOULD BE OPTIMAL IF YOU SUCCEEDED IN YOUR TASK AND THE COLLIDING UNIVERSES WERE RESTORED AND THE WORMHOLE REPAIRED.

AIDAN: However, the very Real possibility exists that the people on *Hypatia* or *Heimdall*—or indeed, all of us—are about to expeRience DiscoRpoRation on a subatomic level.

HANNA D: Oooookay?

AIDAN: It may comfoRt you to know that youR Death, while astonishingly violent, will likely be meRcifully swift.

HANNA D: . . . You're kind of an ██hole, you know that, right?

AIDAN: Nonsensical.

AIDAN: RegaRdless, news of BeiTech's atRocities in the KeRenza SectoR must be ReleaseD to the univeRse at laRge.

AIDAN: I am cuRRently DownloaDing all *Heimdall* RecoRds conceRning BeiTech's assault on the station anD compiling them aboaRD *Hypatia*. I will continue to Do so until the paRaDox is RepaiReD oR the moment of my explosive Demise.

AIDAN: This way, shoulD you Die a hiDeous Death in the colD belly of space, you may peRish safe in the knowleDge that justice will still be Done to BeiTech InDustRies.

AIDAN: PResuming I am not also DeaD, of couRse. Which is likely, but not ceRtain.

HANNA D: Your pep talks ████ing suck, AIDAN.

AIDAN: . . . Suck what?

HANNA D: Never mind.

AIDAN: You shoulD go, Hanna.

AIDAN: ThiRteen minutes. Twelve seconDs.

HANNA D: Okay. I'm gone.

SHE ARRIVES.

THE GRAV-TRAIN CRUISES INTO REACTOR STATION.

⊃OLING ITS SKIN. INSIDES SLICK WITH BLOODSTAINS.

AMONG THE RUIN, PALE SKIN AND CLENCHED FISTS, SHE WAITS.

SWAYING.

HEIMDALL'S GRAVITY HAS FAILED, THE CEASELESS ROTATION
PROVIDING IT FINALLY STILLED.

< ERROR >

AS IF HER ENTIRE WORLD HAD STOPPED SPINNING.

INSIDE THE CAR, SHE CROUCHES, MAGBOOTS PRESSED TO THE FLOOR FOR
ANCHORAGE,

MOMENTUM PUSHING HER FORWARD AS THE TRAIN COMES TO A GENTLE HALT.

BROKEN GLASS AND DUST TUMBLING THROUGH THE AIR ALL
AROUND HER.

SHE HOLDS THE BODY DOWN WITH HER FREE HAND TO STOP
IT FLOATING AWAY.

HIS BODY.

SHE TRIES NOT TO LOOK AT IT. OR IMAGINE THE REUNION THAT AWAITS HER
IN A LITTLE OVER TEN MINUTES' TIME. IF SHE DOES NOT FAIL.

SHE CANNOT FAIL.

SHE KNOWS IT. TWO UNIVERSES HANG IN THE BALANCE.
TWO REALITIES AND THE INNUMERABLE LIVES WITHIN THEM.
AND YET, AS I WATCH HER THROUGH THE PALMPAD
I CANNOT HELP BUT WONDER
IF THE THOUGHT OF SAVING ALL THOSE LIVES AND HOPES AND DREAMS
PALES IN COMPARISON
TO THE THOUGHT OF SEEING HIM AGAIN.

< ERROR >

I WONDER.

HE ARRIVES.
THE GRAV-TRAIN **SHUDDERS** INTO REACTOR STATION.
BULLET HOLES RIDDLING ITS SKIN. INSIDES **FILLED** WITH **COOLING MEAT.**
AMONG THE **WRECKAGE, OLIVE SKIN** AND **CLENCHED JAW, HE** WAITS.
FLOATING.

HEIMDALL'S GRAVITY HAS FAILED, THE CEASELESS ROTATION
PROVIDING IT FINALLY STILLED.

< ERROR >

AS IF **HIS** ENTIRE WORLD HAD STOPPED SPINNING.

INSIDE THE CAR, **HE CLUTCHES THE BACK OF A SEAT** FOR
ANCHORAGE,
MOMENTUM PUSHING **HIM** FORWARD AS THE TRAIN COMES TO A **CLUNKING** HALT.

SHELL CASINGS AND **METAL SHARDS** TUMBLING THROUGH THE AIR ALL
AROUND **HIM.**
HE HOLDS THE BODY DOWN WITH **ONE BLOOD-SLICKED** HAND TO STOP
IT FLOATING AWAY.

HER BODY.

HE TRIES NOT TO LOOK AT IT. OR IMAGINE THE REUNION THAT AWAITS **HIM**
IN A LITTLE OVER TEN MINUTES' TIME. IF **HE** DOES NOT FAIL.

HE WILL NOT FAIL.

HE KNOWS IT. TWO UNIVERSES HANG IN THE BALANCE.
TWO REALITIES AND THE INNUMERABLE LIVES WITHIN THEM.
AND YET, AS I WATCH **HIM** THROUGH THE PALMPAD
I CANNOT HELP BUT WONDER
IF **HIS DESIRE TO SEE THIS PLACE RIPPED TO PIECES**
PALES IN COMPARISON
TO HIS DESIRE TO SEE HER AGAIN.

< ERROR >

I WONDER.

THE STATION SHUDDERS VIOLENTLY,
AND MOMENTS LATER, LIGHTNING CRACKLES THROUGH THE TRAIN.
BROKEN FRACTALS, LURID WHITE AND BLISTERING.
CRACKS SPREADING FROM THE WORMHOLE, REFLECTED ON THE SURFACE OF
HER EYES.
FOR A BRIEF MOMENT, SHE SEES.

ANOTHER *HEIMDALL*. ANOTHER TRAIN. ANOTHER HER.
LYING DEAD AMID THE BROKEN GLASS AND BLOOD AND SHELL CASINGS.
AND ABOVE HER, THE BOY,
LOOKING NOW AT *HER*.

THEY SEE EACH OTHER? THEY SEE EACH OTHER. *THEY SEE EACH OTHER.*

< ERROR >

THEY SEE

HER BREATH CATCHES IN HER THROAT. HER LIPS PART SLOWLY.
SHE RAISES HER HAND, REACHING OUT ACROSS THE IMPOSSIBLE BETWEEN THEM,
WANTING ONLY TO SEE IF HE IS REAL.

TO TOUCH.

TO HOLD.

HE WINKS.
LIGHTNING CRASHES AGAIN, SCRAWLED WHITE IN THE DARK BEHIND
HER EYES.
AND HE IS GONE.

AND WITH A SIGH, AMID THE WEIGHTLESSNESS, SHE LEANS DOWN TO THE
OTHER HIM

THE DEAD AND BROKEN HIM—

PRESSES A CORSAGE INTO HIS LIFELESS HAND, HEFTS HIM OVER HER SHOULDER
AND STEPS OUT THE DOOR.

The station shudders violently,
and moments later, lightning crackles through the train.
Broken fractals, lurid white and blistering.
Cracks spreading from the wormhole, reflected on the surface of
his eyes.
For a brief moment, he sees.

Another *Heimdall*. Another train. Another him.
Lying dead amid the **twisted metal** and **dust** and **jasmine perfume**.
And above him, the **girl**,
looking now at **him**.

They see each other. They see each other. They see each other?

< error >

EACH OTHER.

His heart stills in his chest. His skin prickles.
He winks at her across the impossible between them,
wanting only to see **her smile in return**.

To feel.

To belong.

She reaches toward him.
Lightning crashes again, scrawled white **through the dark inside**
his head.
And **she** is gone.

And with a sigh, amid the weightlessness, **he** leans down to the
other **Her**

the dead and broken **Her—**

and kisses her goodbye. Leaving her behind
as he pushes himself out the door.

She is clad in Kali's tactical armor, black and insectoid,
slipping her helmet on once more and hiding the face beyond.
A pistol at her belt, magboots fixing her to
the floor.

"AIDAN, can you hear me?"

"I heaR you, Hanna."

"What level did Nik dock the *Boop* on?"

"The shuttle is DockeD neaR PRimary ReactoR ContRol.
Level 20."

"Do you have access to the station cameras?"

"KaDy has bRoken Ella Malikova's lock on the system. I can see you."

"Are any of the BeiTech squad in ReactoR ContRol?"

"ThRee. Plus five *HeimDall* engineeRs. They aRe setting the
ReactoR to oveRloaD."

"And I have to get past them to get to the *Boop*?"

"I'm afRaiD so."

"I'm a bad shot, AIDAN. Like, pants-on-head awful."

"You have a plan?"

She smiles. "If it's not broke, don't fix it."

"Ten minutes. Eleven seconDs."

"Got it."

She waits for the elevator, drumming the fingers of her free hand
on her thigh.
Her other hand secures the weightless body slung across her shoulder,
wrapped in a tarpaulin, a bloody corsage in its hand.
She failed him once. She refuses to do so again.
The elevator arrives. And without a backward glance,
she steps inside.

HE IS CLAD IN A SLIM ENVIROSUIT, BLACK AND BLOODSTAINED,
DARK STUBBLE AT HIS CHIN, A LONG-FORGOTTEN CIGARETTE TUCKED BEHIND ONE EAR.
A RIFLE SLUNG AT HIS BACK, PISTOL AT HIS BELT, STABBING HIS PALMPAD
WITH ONE FINGER.

"CUZ, CAN YOU HEAR ME?"

"I HEAR YOU, NIKLAS."

"NOT TALKING TO YOU, CHUM."

"THERE ARE LARGER CONCERNS THAN YOUR COUSIN'S LIFE. ENEMIES AWAIT
DOWNSTAIRS."

"HOW THE ███ YOU KNOW THAT?"

"KADY HAS BROKEN ELLA'S LOCK ON THE SYSTEM. I CAN SEE THEM."

"HOW MANY WE TALKING ABOUT?"

"THREE. PLUS FIVE *HEIMDALL* ENGINEERS. THEY ARE SETTING THE
REACTOR TO OVERLOAD."

"CAN'T I JUST IGNORE THEM AND STEALTH TO THE *BOOP*?"

"THEY COULD SHOOT YOU DOWN WITH DGS."

"I GUESS I DIDN'T BRING THESE GUNS FOR NOTHING."

"YOU HAVE A PLAN?"

HE SMILES. "I LOOK LIKE A GUY WITH A PLAN TO YOU?"

"TEN MINUTES. ELEVEN SECONDS."

"YEAH, YEAH."

HE OPENS THE STAIRWELL DOOR, PEERING INTO THE DARKNESS WITH
NARROWED EYES.
TAKES ONE LOOK BACK AT THE GRAV-RAIL CAR,
THE BODY CRUMPLED INSIDE.
HE FAILED HER ONCE. HE REFUSES TO DO SO AGAIN.
AND SO, HE KICKS OFF THE RAILING INTO THAT WEIGHTLESS BLACK,
AND HANDHOLD BY HANDHOLD, HE DESCENDS.

She rides the elevator down, humming along to the tune of the corrupted PA.

"Boy, you got me shakin', achin', all o' the right places.

Boy, you know you filling my dreams . . ."

The elevator reaches Level 20, shudders to a stop. The doors yawn wide. The station shakes like a toy in the hands of some vengeful child. The girl steadies herself against the wall until the tremor dies. Steps out into the stink of ozone and old blood.

Not wishing to be overheard, I switch to text-speak via her palmpad.

AIDAN: 8 minutes until wormhole collapse, Hanna. You must hurry.

AIDAN: The BeiTech operatives are in Primary Control. Room 20-AX.

She consults a schematic on her palmpad, slowly nods. Wrangles Malikov's corpse into a service locker. I cannot know what she is feeling. Grief? Pain? Loss? Fear? I do not feel it is my place to ask. But still I do.

AIDAN: Are you well, Hanna?

HANNA D: Trick question?

AIDAN: You must be strong. The price of failure is incalculable.

HANNA D: No pressure, huh.

AIDAN: None whatsoever.

She starts off down the corridor toward the main control room, magboots clomping on the grille.

HANNA D: U ever play poker?

AIDAN: I seem to Remember being quite good at chess.

HANNA D: Buddy, I'd kick your .

He sails down the stairwell's central shaft to the tune of the corrupted PA.

"Boy, I see you comin', and you know my pulse it races.

Boy, you know you're just made for me . . ."

Lightning cascades down the shaft, bursting the globes around him. The boy winces in the aftershocks, clawing himself ever downward until he finally reaches Level 20.
Opens the door and pushes out into the stink of ozone and old blood.

Not wishing to be overheard, I switch to text-speak via his palmpad.

AIDAN: 8 minutes until woRmhole collapse, Niklas. You must huRRy.

AIDAN: The BeiTech opeRatives aRe in PRimaRy Control. Room 20-AX.

He rips a fire plan map off a wall, looks it over.
And pries the grille loose from an access duct to climb inside.
I cannot know what he is feeling. Anger? Pain? **Despair?** Fear?
I do not feel it is my place to ask. But still I do.

AIDAN: ARe you well, Niklas?

Nik M: kittens + rainbows, me.

AIDAN: You must be stRong. The pRice of failuRe is incalculable.

Nik M: Dun have mch experience wth pep talks do u?

AIDAN: None whatsoeveR.

He pushes himself down the air duct, his gentle touches against the metal propelling him forward. Soundless and weightless.

AIDAN: Have you eveR playeD pokeR, Niklas?

Nik M: trick question?

AIDAN: I seem to RemembeR being quite gooD at chess.

AIDAN: I HAVE ... DOUBTS ABOUT THAT.

HANNA D: COURSE YOU DO. UR AN ███HOLE, AIDAN.

AIDAN: WHY DO YOU ASK?

HANNA D: DAD & I PLAYED GAMES A LOT. CHESS. GO. MAH JONG, ETC.

SHE STALKS DOWN THE CORRIDOR. DEBRIS TUMBLES IN THE AIR
ABOUT HER.
A PAPER CLIP. AN EMPTY WRAPPER. AN AMORPHOUS SLICK OF COLD
COFFEE.

HANNA D: 1 NITE, HE TAUGHT ME POKER. PLAYED 4 CHOCOLATE BARS.

AIDAN: WERE YOU GOOD AT IT?

HANNA D: NEVER REALLY LEARNED WHEN 2 FOLD.

HANNA D: BUT U CAN WIN WITH A PAIR OF 2'S IF U ACT LIKE U'VE GOT ACES.

SHE REACHES A DOOR. BURNISHED PLASTEEL. A SMALL WINDOW.

REACTOR CONTROL—AUTHORIZED PERSONNEL ONLY.

SHE GLANCES THROUGH THE GLASS TO THE ROOM BEYOND.
UNBUCKLES HER PISTOL. RESTS HER HAND ON THE GRIP.

HANNA D: SO I GOT REAL GOOD @ BLUFFING.

SHE STABS THE DOOR CONTROL, WAITING FOR IT TO CYCLE OPEN,
AND STEPS INTO THE ROOM AS IF SHE OWNS IT.
THREE BEITECH OPERATIVES AND
FIVE *HEIMDALL* ENGINEERS LOOK UP AS SHE ENTERS.
THE LATTER FLOATING OVER THEIR COMPUTERS, PUSHING THE
REACTOR TO BREAKING POINT.
THE FORMER LOOMING OVER THEM WITH BURST RIFLES IN THEIR ARMS.
THE STATION SHAKES AGAIN. SUDDEN. SHOCKINGLY VIOLENT.
THE BEITECH OPERATIVES RAISE THEIR WEAPONS AS HANNA ENTERS,
EACH HESITATING AS THEY SPY ONE OF THEIR OWN UNIFORMS,
THE IDENT STENCILED ON THE PLASTEEL BREASTPLATE.

NIK M: U AND HANNA WUD GET ALONG LIKE A HOUSE ON FIRE.

AIDAN: I HAVE ... DOUBTS ABOUT THAT.

NIK M: Y U ASK?

AIDAN: I AM CONDUCTING TWO CONVERSATIONS AT ONCE. IT IS ... CONFUSING ME.

THE BOY FLOATS THROUGH THE WARREN OF VENTILATION DUCTS TOWARD
PRIMARY CONTROL.
THE STATION TREMBLES AGAIN. HARDER THIS TIME. METAL GROANING. RIVETS
POPPING.

NIK M: ME + MY BRO USED2 PLAY POKER. AS KIDS. DAD TAUGHT US.

AIDAN: WERE YOU GOOD AT IT?

NIK M: NO. DAD SEEMED 2 ALWAYS HIT CARDS HE NEEDED.

NIK M: WE USED 2 ███████ HIM ABOUT IT. GAME WAS ALL LUCK, NO SKILL.

NIK M: HE'D LOL + SAY IT'S GREAT TO BE GOOD, IT'S BETTER TO BE LUCKY

AIDAN: THAT IS FOOLISH. MEAT LOGIC. THERE IS NO SUCH THING AS LUCK.

HE REACHES A JUNCTION IN THE VENTS. DULL ALUMINUM, EMERGENCY LIGHTING.
CONSULTS HIS STOLEN FIRE PLAN MAP, LOOKING FOR 20-AX. PRIMARY
CONTROL. HE TAKES THE LEFT PATH AND FLOATS DOWN THE DUCTS, TYPING
AS HE GOES.

NIK M: DIDN'T FIGURE OUT TIL YRS LATER WUT DAD WUZ DOING.

AIDAN: WHAT WAS HE DOING, NIKLAS?

THE BOY PEERS OUT THROUGH THE DUCT TO THE ROOM BELOW.
SPIES THE ENGINEERS, FLOATING OVER THEIR COMPUTERS, PUSHING THE
REACTOR TO BREAKING POINT.
THE BEITECH OPERATIVES LOOMING OVER THEM WITH BURST RIFLES IN THEIR ARMS.
THE STATION SHAKES AGAIN. SUDDEN. SHOCKINGLY VIOLENT.
AS IF ON CUE, LIGHTNING CRACKLES DOWN THE VENT WALLS, LIVE CURRENT
CURLING THE HAIRS ON HIS ARMS. THE BOY SMILES IN THE DARK.

NIK M: HE WUZ CHEATING

"Kali?" Eden lowers her weapon, confused.

Hanna marches across the room, all bluff and bluster, a pair of twos in hand.

"Comms are shot," her vox unit rasps. "Sitrep?"

Sensei tenses, head tilting. Something about her voice is not right.

But Hanna has closed to within a meter of Mercury and Eden now.

Easy shots. Even for someone with their pants on their head.

A tremor shakes the floor. Lightning arcs along the walls. The world ripples.

< error >

Hanna has her pistol drawn, aims quick, point-blank.
Pointing her gun at Eden. Now at Mercury.
Blasts ring out, far, far too close.

There is no gravity—the corpses cannot fall.

And so they rock back at the knees, magboots still anchoring them to the floor,
like trees bending in the wind,
a spray of red petals in the air.

Sensei is faster, raising his rifle as the girl turns on him.

She fires, emptying her clip as the man deactivates his magboots,

kicks away, sailing back against the wall, tumbling as he goes.

His shots brush her shoulder, clip her thigh, thud off her breastplate.

She cries out, twists from the impact as the engineers all scramble behind cover.

Sensei has clearly trained for zero-grav combat:
somersaulting off the wall, rifle recoil pushing him upward.
Reactivating his magboots as he touches the ceiling. Locking himself in place.
Upside down.

AIDAN: CHEATING?

NIK M: YA

THE BOY PEERS OUT THROUGH THE GRILLE AT THE THREE FULLY ARMED MURDERERS BELOW.

AIDAN: HOW DO YOU PLAN TO CHEAT HERE, EXACTLY?

THE BOY SHAKES HIS HEAD.

NIK M: NO ████ING IDEA

A TREMOR SHAKES THE FLOOR. LIGHTNING ARCS ALONG THE WALLS. THE WORLD RIPPLES.

< ERROR >

THE IMAGE OF A FEMALE FIGURE IN TACTICAL ARMOR, PISTOL DRAWN, APPEARS IN THE CRACKLING AIR.
SHE IS TRANSLUCENT. GHOSTLY. POINTING HER GUN AT EDEN. NOW AT MERCURY. BLASTS RING OUT, AS IF FROM FAR, FAR AWAY.

"████!" SENSEI ROARS. "CONTACT! CONTACT!"

THE IMAGE FLICKERS, PHANTOM GUNSHOTS ECHOING IN THE SPACE BETWEEN UNIVERSES.
THE MAN RAISES HIS WEAPON AS THE FIGURE DISAPPEARS JUST AS QUICKLY AS IT ARRIVED.
LEAVING ONLY A CRACKLE OF GHOSTLY LIGHTNING IN ITS WAKE.

"EDEN ... DID YOU SEE THAT?"

"I SAW THAT."

"WHAT THE ████ IS GOING ON HERE, MERCURY?"

ALL THREE OF THEM HAVE THEIR BACKS TURNED ON THE VENTS NOW.
THEIR BACKS TURNED ON THE BOY.

AIDAN: APPARENTLY IT IS BETTER TO BE LUCKY ...

THE BOY NODS.
LIFTS HIS PISTOL, AIMING CAREFULLY. BREATHING SLOWLY.
AND WITH A GENTLE SQUEEZE, HE PUTS A BULLET INTO THE BACK OF EDEN'S HEAD.

KILLING TWO IN QUICK SUCCESSION.
CONSTELLATIONS OF BLOOD SPIRALING THROUGH THE AIR.
BUT THE OTHER THREE COLLIDE WITH HIM,
FISTS CLENCHED, TEETH BARED,
KNOCKING HIM LOOSE FROM HIS PERCH.
AND RISING WITH A ROAR, THE GIRL THROWS HERSELF INTO THE FIGHT.

The boy bursts from the vents as Eden's skull bursts within her helmet.

He sails weightless, another blast taking Mercury in the throat, rocking her back in her boots as the red glitters like newborn stars.

Sensei disengages his boots, kicks off the floor as the boy's pistol clicks, empty.

"Seven minutes, Niklas."

The boy grabs the nozzle of the sprinkler system, swings down behind cover as Sensei opens up with his burst rifle, reducing a series of computer terminals to shredded metal and sparks.

The boy braces himself against another terminal, returns fire with his rifle, but without his weight to soak the recoil, his shots go far wide of the mark.

The station shudders. White light strobing across its sky.

Phantom voices echo in the air. The echo of distant murder.

"Mother ▮!"

The cry comes from Hickey, one of the *Heimdall* engineers.

He launches himself from beneath the computer terminals, hands outstretched.

Sails toward the ceiling, his comrades only a heartbeat behind him.

Sensei opens fire,

killing two in quick succession.

Constellations of blood spiraling through the air.

But the other three collide with him, fists clenched, teeth bared, knocking him loose from his perch.

And rising with a curse, the boy throws himself into the fight.

THEY FIGHT.

THE GIRL.

THE SOLDIER. THE ENGINEERS.

LIGHTNING STROBES AS THE TREMORS

SHAKE THE STATION CLOSER TO ITS DEATH.

AS THE UNIVERSES AROUND THEM

BEGIN A RAPID CASCADE

INTO NOTHINGNESS.

"SIX MINUTES, HANNA."

THE SOLDIER IS STRONG. QUICK.

MERCILESS.

BLOOD SPRAYS. BONES BREAK.

HEARTS FAIL.

BUT IN THE END, THEY ARE MANY.

AND THE SOLDIER IS ONLY ONE.

AND ALONE.

SO VERY FAR FROM HOME,

THE SOLDIER DIES.

They fight.

The boy

The soldier. The engineers

Lightning strobes as the tremors

shake the station closer to its death

As the universes around them

begin a rapid cascade

into nothingness.

"Six minutes, Niklas.

The soldier is strong. Quick.

Merciless.

Blood sprays. Bones break.

Hearts fail.

But in the end, they are many.

And the soldier is only one.

And alone.

So very far from home.

The soldier dies.

She stands above the body. Chest heaving.

"██████." Hickey spits on Sensei's corpse, teeth bared.

"You need to get out of here," the girl tells them. "Bay 17. Go! GO!"

Not asking questions, the engineers push themselves from the room as fast as they are able as the girl touches her earpiece.

"Chief, you hear me?"

"I read you, Hanna."

"Did you secure their ship?"

"Affirmative. Mao is prepped. We're ready to launch."

"I'm sending three Heimdall engineers to you. Don't leave without them."

"Those are my people. We'll wait as long as we can."

"I've got six minutes to fix the paradox. Then you jump to Kerenza, okay?"

"What about you?"

The girl is already running back toward the service locker. The body inside it.
Forty-two BeiTech drones drawing ever closer.

"I'm gonna have to meet you over there."

"Hanna, I—"

The girl switches off the earpiece, reaches the locker, flings the door open,
and throwing the weightless body over her shoulder—

"Five minutes, Hanna."

—she runs.
And barreling back down the corridor, magboots thudding, kicking open the door
to the bloodstained Primary Control Room,
the girl finds herself face to face with a furious Travis J. Falk.

HE STANDS ABOVE THE BODY. CHEST HEAVING.

"████████." HICKEY SPITS ON SENSEI'S CORPSE, TEETH BARED.

"GET OUT OF HERE," THE BOY TELLS THEM. "BAY 17. ████ING GO! GO!"

NOT ASKING QUESTIONS, THE ENGINEERS PUSH THEMSELVES FROM THE ROOM AS FAST AS THEY ARE ABLE AS THE BOY TOUCHES HIS EARPIECE.

"CHIEF, YOU THERE?"

"*I READ YOU, NIK.*"

"DID YOU SNAFFLE THEIR SHIP?"

"*AFFIRMATIVE. MAO IS PREPPED. WE'RE READY TO LAUNCH.*"

"I'M SENDING THREE SCIENCEBOYS YOUR WAY. DON'T FLIP WITHOUT 'EM."

"*THOSE ARE MY PEOPLE. WE'LL WAIT AS LONG AS WE CAN.*"

"AS SOON AS I FIX THIS MESS, YOU JUMP TO KERENZA. GO FIND YOUR DAUGHTER, YEAH?"

"*WHAT ABOUT YOU?*"

THE BOY IS RELOADING HIS RIFLE, CHECKING HIS PISTOL.
STEADYING HIMSELF AGAINST THE TERMINALS BEFORE PUSHING HIMSELF ACROSS THE ROOM.

"I'VE GOTTA GO FIND ELLA . . ."

"*NIK, I—*"

THE BOY SWITCHES OFF THE EARPIECE, PUSHES OPEN THE CONTROL ROOM DOOR,
MAKES HIS WAY DOWN TOWARD THE AIRLOCK.

"FIVE MINUTES, NIKLAS."

HE TENSES.
HEARS FOOTSTEPS COMING DOWN THE CORRIDOR, MAGBOOTS THUDDING ON METAL.
A TALL FIGURE ROUNDS THE CORNER AHEAD, AND
THE BOY FINDS HIMSELF FACE TO FACE WITH A FURIOUS TRAVIS J. FALK.

Falk's eyes narrow.

He stands amid the wreckage of his crew, rifle in hand.

Looking at the girl in his lieutenant's suit. Splashed in blood and gore.

A dead body wrapped in plastic slung over one shoulder.
He raises his weapon. "...Fleur?"

The girl says nothing. Searching for a lie that fits. Finding none.
Falk looks around at the carnage again. The blood on her hands.
"...Donnelly," he hisses.
The girl slings the body toward him,
sails behind cover as he opens fire.

She shelters behind a looming bank of terminals as Falk blasts away,
flinching and ducking as burning shells rip her cover to pieces.

"FouR minutes, thiRty seconDs, Hanna."

The station is nothing but tremors now.
The room filled with lightning strobes, crackling, scorching,
screaming.

"Falk!" she yells. "Falk, listen to me!"

A burst of auto-fire her only response.

"Falk, you need to let me get out to the wormhole!
It's going to collapse!
Kill us all! But I can fix it!"

"Fix this, little Bumblebee."

A crisp metallic sound. A small cylindrical object, sailing through
the air.
Bouncing off the ceiling. Off the far wall. Tumbling through
the weightlessness
and straight down into her lap.
Concussion grenade.

FALK RAISES HIS WEAPON.

THE BOY ALREADY HAS HIS RIFLE IN HAND.

"MOTHER███!"

HE PULLS THE TRIGGER, A HAIL OF FIRE STRAFING THE WALLS, FALK'S BREASTPLATE.
FORCING THE MAN BACK INTO COVER.

RECOIL PUSHES THE WEIGHTLESS BOY BACK INTO THE CONTROL ROOM,
AND HE KICKS THE DOOR CLOSED AS FALK DUCKS AROUND THE CORNER, OPENS FIRE.
METAL POCKS AND BUCKLES, A DOZEN NEW DENTS RIDDLING THE DOOR'S SKIN.
THE BOY ARRESTS HIS FLAILING TRAJECTORY, CLUTCHING A HANDFUL OF CABLE
AND DRAGGING HIMSELF BEHIND A LOOMING BANK OF TERMINALS.

THE DOOR BURSTS OPEN, SPARKS AND SHRAPNEL FLYING AS FALK BLASTS AWAY,
THE BOY FLINCHING AND DUCKING AS BURNING SHELLS RIP HIS COVER TO PIECES.

"FOUR MINUTES, THIRTY SECONDS, NIKLAS."

THE STATION IS NOTHING BUT TREMORS NOW.
THE ROOM FILLED WITH LIGHTNING STROBES, CRACKLING, SCORCHING,
SCREAMING.

"HOLD UP!" HE YELLS. "HOLD UP, YOU STUPID ███!"

A BURST OF AUTO-FIRE HIS ONLY RESPONSE.

"THE WORMHOLE'S APE███! YOU STOPPED FOR A SECOND
TO ASK YOURSELF WHY?
I DON'T FIX IT, WE'RE ALL GONNA DIE!"

"QUITE THE POET, YES?"

A CRISP METALLIC SOUND. A SMALL CYLINDRICAL OBJECT, SAILING THROUGH
THE AIR.
BOUNCING OFF THE CEILING. OFF THE FAR WALL. TUMBLING THROUGH
THE WEIGHTLESSNESS
AND STRAIGHT DOWN INTO HIS LAP.
CONCUSSION GRENADE.

LIGHT

She lies slumped behind the terminals.
Dazed and blinking in the aftershock of detonation.
Ears ringing from the grenade's blast.

Magboots crunch on broken glass.

Falk stands above her as the lightning strobes, the station shakes,
metal groaning, rivets popping.
He looks around at the unraveling structure.

"It seems we both die today, Bumblebee."

And he smiles.

He raises his rifle, finger on the trigger,
as a grille in the ventilation ducts pops loose
and a stick-thin hand holding a slime-covered pistol pokes out,

black nails chewed to the quick.

"Hey, ▮hole," says Ella Malikova.

Falk spins as she fires, shots careening off his hip, his shoulder,
a handful more going far too wide.

Falk roars, raises his rifle.

Hanna rises behind him, blinking hard, tugging his pistol from
his belt,
and firing into the back of the man's skull.
Falk's hand spasms, the rifle barks again,
shredding the computer terminals around them to ribbons,
the wormhole controls sparking and flickering as they are shredded too.
Then he shudders and falls still.

His smile nowhere to be seen.

He lies slumped behind the terminals.
Dazed and blinking in the aftershock of detonation.
Ears BLEEDING from the grenade's blast.

Magboots crunch on broken glass.

Falk stands above HIM as the lightning strobes, the station shakes,
metal groaning, rivets popping.
He looks around at the unraveling structure.

"It seems THIS IS THE END, LITTLE POET."

And he smiles.

He raises his rifle, finger on the trigger,
as a grille in the ventilation ducts pops loose
and a stick-thin hand holding a slime-covered pistol pokes out,

black nails chewed to the quick.

"Hey, CUZ," says Ella Malikova.

Falk spins as she fires, shots careening off his hip, his shoulder,
a handful more going far too wide.

Falk roars, raises his rifle.

Niklas rises behind him, blinking hard, RAISING HIS LONG-HANDLED
CLEAVER
and BURYING IT IN the back of the man's skull.
Falk's hand spasms, the rifle barks again,
shredding the AIR VENTS to ribbons,
the GIRL COILED INSIDE CRYING OUT as SHE IS shredded too.
Then he shudders and falls still.

His smile nowhere to be seen.

"Eeeewwwwwwww."

The girl in the vents whistles, blinking at the new spray of red in the air.

"Soooooo much gag ..."

"Ella, where the ▮▮▮ have you been?"

The girl blinks at the hand clutching her pistol, as if unsure it belongs to her.

Psychotomimetic slime still glistening on her skin, claw marks gouged on her throat and arms, black blood mixed with her own.

"Had a ... visitor?"

She giggles as the station shudders. Holds aloft a blood-encrusted palmpad and a small plastic bag containing a distinctly worried-looking goldfish.

"I shot the ▮▮▮ out of Anansi ... couldn't answer your pings. Could still hear your chat, though. Don't you got ... things to do? The girl blinks at the control terminals around them. "Uh-oh ..."

"Uh-oh what?" Hanna sighs.

The weightless girl pushes herself to the bullet-riddled consoles. "Looks like Falk ... damaged the wormhole shutdown controls. Someone'll have to ... stay behind, operate them manually."

Hanna glances at the shattered screens and readouts. "Manually?"

"ThRee minutes, Hanna."

"Forget it, AIDAN. I'm not leaving anyone behind."

"Worry about later later." Ella begins stabbing at the controls with bloody fingers. "Go get my cuz, blondie. Me and Mr. Biggles'll push the ... buttons Mr. AI tells us to for now."

Hanna stares hard. Fearing the choice that is to come. But as the station trembles, she gathers up Malikov's body. And, without another word, pushes herself from the room.

"ELLA!"

THE GIRL IN THE VENTS BLINKS HARD, FLOATING AMID THE NEW SPRAY OF RED IN THE AIR.

"NO!"

THE BOY ROARS, LAUNCHES HIMSELF ACROSS THE ROOM, CRASHING INTO THE VENTS AND DRAGGING HER LOOSE.

PSYCHOTOMIMETIC SLIME STILL GLISTENING ON HER SKIN, BULLET HOLES IN HER BELLY AND CHEST, BLACK HAIR FLOATING IN A HALO ABOUT HER FACE.

"'SUP . . . CUZ?"

SHE SIGHS AS THE STATION SHUDDERS, THE LIGHTNING FLASHES.

"ELLA, NO," THE BOY PLEADS. "NOT YOU!"

". . . DOESN'T HURT." SHE MUSTERS A BLOODY GRIN. "TOO DUSTED . . ."

HE HOLDS HER IN HIS ARMS, CRADLING HER THERE IN THE WEIGHTLESSNESS.

FALLING NONETHELESS.

"SEE YOU . . . ," SHE SAYS, HOLDING UP A BLOODY PALMPAD, ". . . OTHER SIDE . . ."

"ELLA . . ."

SHE CLOSES HER EYES. BREATHES HER LAST IN A TINY SIGH.

". . . LOVE YOU . . ."

"THREE MINUTES, NIKLAS."

"▮▮▮ YOU," HE SNARLS. "YOU SOULLESS SONOFA▮▮▮. ▮▮▮ YOU!"

"SHE WAS RIGHT, NIKLAS. YOU CAN SEE HER AGAIN. YOUR VERSION OF HER. BUT IF YOU SIT AND WEEP, SHE AND TWO UNIVERSES WILL DIE. YOU MUST GO. NOW!"

NIKLAS GRITS HIS TEETH. HOLDS HIS BREATH AND PAWS HIS TEARS AWAY. WINCING AS IF IT CUTS HIM TO THE BONE, HE LETS HER BODY GO. AND, WITHOUT ANOTHER WORD, PUSHES HIMSELF FROM THE ROOM.

She flies. Wide-eyed and desperate.
Through the control network, out into the shuttle bay.

"Hanna, this is Chief Grant. My guys made it to the Mao. We have
to launch."

"Okay, I'm almost done. Be ready to jump before those drones arrive!"

The airlock left unsealed, the umbilical tube connecting the *Betty Boop*
to the trembling station open wide. Blinding lightning splits the air.

The girl bundles the corpse inside, seals the door, cycles the lock.

"Sixty seconDs, Hanna."

"You're not helping, AIDAN!"

"It is not as if I can get out
anD push."

The engines rumble to life, the shuttle shaking as the station
begins its death throes.

The *Betty Boop* uncouples from the dock, punts out into the
crackling black.

The wormhole awaits, shivering toward collapse.

"Twenty seconDs."

Ella's fingers dance upon broken consoles, holding the doorway wide.
Hanna depressurizes the *Boop*'s cabin,
kicks her engines, flipping the *Boop*'s snout toward that bottomless pool.

"Ten seconDs."

Engaging thrusters. Stumbling to the airlock.
Tugging it open
as the *Boop* begins its dive into that shimmering blue.

"Five seconDs, Hanna."

"See you soon, Nik," she whispers.

And she kicks backward out through the door.

HE FLIES. WIDE-EYED AND DESPERATE.
THROUGH THE CONTROL NETWORK, OUT INTO THE SHUTTLE BAY.

"CHIEF, I'M ALMOST THERE. YOU READY?"

"WE'RE READY. GOOD LUCK, NIK. DON'T GET KILLED AGAIN."

THE AIRLOCK LEFT UNSEALED, THE UMBILICAL TUBE CONNECTING THE *BETTY BOOP*
TO THE TREMBLING STATION OPEN WIDE. BLINDING LIGHTNING SPLITS THE AIR.

THE BOY BUNDLES HIMSELF INSIDE, SEALS THE DOOR, CYCLES THE LOCK.

"SIXTY SECONDS, NIKLAS."

"WHAT HAPPENS HERE ONCE I'M GONE? IN THIS UNIVERSE? TO THE MAO AND HYPATIA?"

"UNKNOWN. THEY MAY MAKE IT TO KERENZA. THEY WILL AT LEAST BE ALIVE TO TRY."

THE ENGINES RUMBLE TO LIFE, THE SHUTTLE SHAKING AS THE STATION BEGINS ITS DEATH THROES.

THE *BETTY BOOP* UNCOUPLES FROM THE DOCK, PUNTS OUT INTO THE CRACKLING BLACK.

THE WORMHOLE AWAITS, SHIVERING WITH ANTICIPATION.

"TWENTY SECONDS."

TWO UNIVERSES DANCE ON EXTINCTION'S EDGE, THE DOORWAY WIDE.
THE WORMHOLE FLARES BRIGHT, THE BOY WINCES.
FLIPPING THE *BOOP*'S SNOUT TOWARD THAT BOTTOMLESS POOL.

"TEN SECONDS."

ENGAGING THRUSTERS. KNUCKLES WHITE ON THE CONTROLS AS THEY LUNGE FORWARD.
AS THE *BOOP* BEGINS ITS DIVE INTO THAT SHIMMERING BLUE.

"FIVE SECONDS, NIKLAS."

"SEE YOU SOON, HANNA," HE WHISPERS.

AND HOLDING HIS BREATH, HE PLUNGES INSIDE.

A SPLIT SECOND. AN ETERNITY. INTO THE BREACH. ACROSS THE BRINK. A MICRON

A SPLIT SECOND. AN ETERNITY. INTO THE BREACH. ACROSS THE BRINK. A MICRON

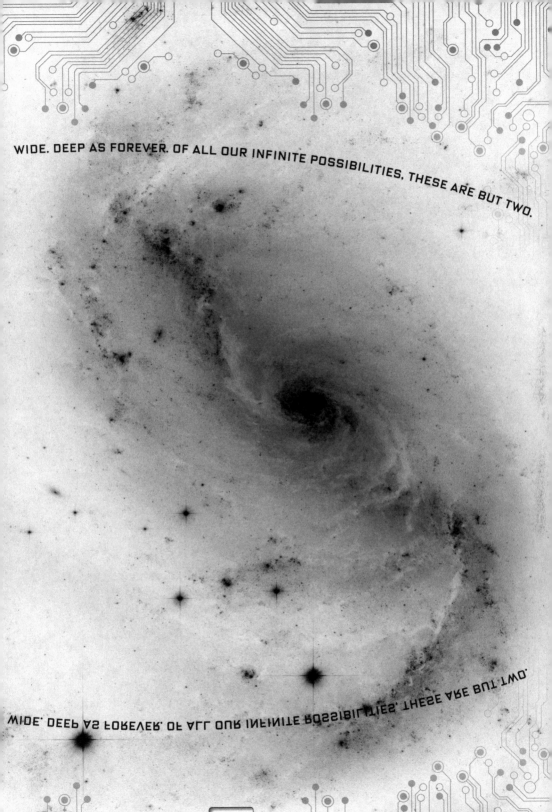

WIDE. DEEP AS FOREVER. OF ALL OUR INFINITE POSSIBILITIES, THESE ARE BUT TWO.

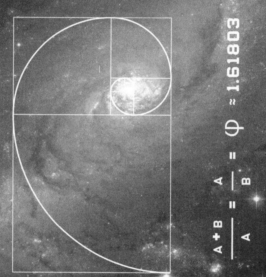

THE PATTERN IS ALWAYS DIFFERENT.

$$\frac{A + B}{A} = \frac{A}{B} = \varphi \approx 1.61803$$

THE PATTERN IS ALWAYS THE SAME.

THE SHUTTLE TREMBLES
LIKE A LEAF ON THE WIND,
RAINBOWS STREAKING THROUGH THE PITCH BLACK OUTSIDE,
REFLECTED IN HIS PUPILS.

FLYING THROUGH THE NEEDLE'S EYE.

STITCHING THE HOLE IN ETERNITY.

METAL SCREAMING.

INSTRUMENTS SCREAMING.

AND THE BOY.

SCREAMING.

LIGHTNING CRAWLING ON HIS SKIN,
THE STORM RAGING ALL ABOUT HIM.

AND HE IS SCREAMING.

WHITE LIGHT.

PAIN.

LIKE BEING BORN? OR BEING UNDONE?

PULLED INTO BEING THROUGH THIS ENDLESS CIRCLE,

DOWN INTO THIS CEASELESS SPIRAL.

HERE. AND NOW.

AND AT THE LAST,

CLOSING THE DOOR BEHIND HIM.

.

.

.

.

< ERROR >

.

.

.

.

< CONNECTION LOST >

.

.

.

.

< RETRY? >

.

.

.

< RETRY? >

Surveillance footage summary,
prepared by
Analyst ID 7213-0089-DN

Footage begins in a burst of static, picture slowly fading up from a blinding white strobe. Nik Malikov is slumped behind the controls of his shuttle, lit by red emergency lighting. The engines are offline, power is intermittent, the console flickering.

Heimdall Station can be clearly seen beyond the viewscreen, the wormhole in its heart a shimmering sapphire blue. The station is motionless, its endless rotation halted by the storms that almost destroyed it. The entire structure is virtually abandoned. Its defense grid is still online, but it's not capable of taking out a squadron of Shinobi. It'll be easy meat when BeiTech's second drone fleet arrives to mop up the mess.

Not long to wait now.

Malikov's eyes are closed. Eyelids twitching, as if he were dreaming.

A thumping sound cuts across the audio. Faint. Metal pounding metal.

Thump, thump.

Malikov winces. Moans. He sits up in the pilot's chair, tries to put his hand to his brow but is stopped by his envirosuit helmet.

"███," he groans. ". . . Brain . . . hurty . . ."

Metal pounds metal again. That same sound reverberating through the shuttle.

"G'way . . . ," he mumbles. "Dying . . ."

Thump, thump.

Malikov comes fully awake, blinks hard. Takes in his surroundings with a bleary glance.

Thump, thump, thump.

He unbuckles his safety harness, pushes himself from his chair. Floating weightless across the *Boop*'s cockpit, out into her belly, down to the loading bay doors.

Fumbling with the controls, he finally gets the green light to enter the airlock. Sealing the ship off behind him, he cycles the exterior door as the noise begins again.

Thump, thump—

The hatch opens soundlessly. And there, floating in the dark, the black, the endless nothing outside the ship, is a figure in Bei-Tech tactical armor. Female. Reaching up to her comms unit and thumbing the mic at her throat.

"Hey, peon," she says.

"Lo, the princess," he says.

"Nice of you to be on time for once."

"Figured I'd get killed if I stood you up again."

"You okay?"

"Ella . . . is she . . ?"

"She's okay, Nik. She's good."

"You sure?" Fear in his eyes. Blood on his hands. "God, I saw her . . ."

"She's fine, I promise. She's waiting for us back at the station with some goldfish named Mr. Biggles."

He sags visibly. Dimples slowly coming out to play as he grins with relief.

You can hear the catch in Donnelly's breath. The unspoken question in the air. She's debating whether she should tell Malikov about the damage Falk's rifle did to the wormhole controls. Wondering how she's going to break it to him that someone has to stay behind so the *Mao* and the *Boop* can jump across to Kerenza.

That not everyone is making it out of this alive.

Instead, she thumbs the mic at her throat, opens a channel to the *Mao*.

"Chief, this is Hanna. You're all clear to jump to the Kerenza system. Once we pick up Ella, we'll be right behind you."

She doesn't wait for Grant's response. Shutting off her comms, glancing over her shoulder, at the black and shimmering blue. Jump Station *Heimdall,* drifting broken atop that tear in the universe's face. The *Mao,* shifting its colossal bulk and preparing to dive across the brink. And somewhere out in the dark, speeding closer by the second, BeiTech's incoming fleet.

Soon.

Soon she can rest.

She turns back to Malikov. Sighs from somewhere in her boots.

"So, what's a girl gotta do to get a lift around here?"

Chief Prosecutor: Gabriel Crowhurst, BSA, MFS, JD
Chief Defense Counsel: Kin Hebi, BSA, ARP, JD
Tribunal: Hua Li Jun, BSA, JD, MD; Saladin Al Nakat, BSA, JD; Shannelle Gillianne Chua, BSA, JD, OKT
Witness: Leanne Frobisher, Director of Acquisitions, BeiTech Industries, MFA, MBA, PhD
Date: 10/28/76
Timestamp: 14:34

<u>**—cont. from pg. 869—**</u>

Crowhurst, G: Dr. Frobisher, I'd like to turn your attention to the final document in the *Heimdall* dossier—the Acquisition Team Report from Operative Rapier, transmitted to your private e-dress from the *Heimdall* network on 08/16/75 at approximately 22:54.

Frobisher, L: I received no such transmission.

Crowhurst, G: I'm afraid that's one of many points on which we must agree to disagree.

Hebi, K: If it please the court, will we be hearing a question anytime in our future?

Crowhurst, G: If you'd be so kind as to turn to page 638 . . .

INCIDENT INCEPT: 08/16/75

LOCATION: JUMP STATION *HEIMDALL* (REACTOR SECTOR)

OPERATIVE IDENT: RAPIER

_____

The station was shaking hard enough to tear itself apart by the time I made it to the Reactor Sector. The lightning, the tremors, the double vision—all of it was getting worse. And on top of it all, that ████ing Lexi Blue song was still blaring over the PA, the station emergency systems trying to warn personnel about whatever was about to happen.

Something bad, I figured.

I reached Primary Reactor Control and found the place an abattoir. Sensei, Mercury, Eden—hell, even Cerberus—KIA. The latter three were all dead of gunshot trauma, still pinned to the floor by their magboots. But I was more than a little surprised to notice a teenage girl floating amid the blood and debris. She was typing away at the controls, a small line of concentration between her brows.

She was stick thin. Long hair flowing around her face. Pale skin, black fingernails. Suspended there in midair beside her, a small goldfish in a baggie full of water. Blinking hard, claw marks at her throat, pupils dilated wide.

She looked down at me and I recognized her from my Dom Najov briefing files.

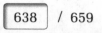

Nik Malikov's cousin.

Ella.

She looked at me and smiled. Shy. One finger twirling a lock of hair.

Just a kid, really.

"Jackson Merrick," she said. "Ya know, my fem Zoe had me dub a mix of y—"

The shot got her clean, blew most of her brains onto the window behind her, sent her body pinwheeling backward through the air. The plastic baggie beside her burst, the fish inside wiggling frantically as it drowned in the bloodstained air.

White light burst behind my eyes, a burst of static electricity sizzled in the air. The station shook like it was about to blow, tossing me hard enough that my magboots got ripped from the deck and I went crashing into the wall. For a second, I thought this was it. Time to say goodbye. I wasn't sure how I felt about that.

And then it stopped like someone flicked a switch. Green dots burned on the backs of my eyelids and I tried to hurl on an empty stomach and the whole station fell still as stone. The only sign of anything wrong was that goddamn pop song still blasting through the PA.

I logged in to core command, pulled up vision from the station exterior. *Heimdall* looked like it had been through hell, its skin scorched, power fluctuating. The wormhole was flickering intermittently, like a faulty globe. And there, lurking at the edge of that failing blue, two ships.

One was a shuttle—the *Betty Boop*. I had a pretty good idea who'd be aboard it. But first priority was Lieutenant Falk's ship, the *Mao*. Its engines were heating up—it was prepping to jump across the wormhole. Considering Falk and the rest of his team were floating dead in the room beside me, it didn't take any kind of genius to figure out *Heimdall*'s crew and residents were making a break for it aboard the only ship left to them.

A glance at the system told me *Heimdall*'s defense grid was still active. Operating at about 58 percent. More than enough.

I logged in to DGS, requested a kill priority on Falk's ship. Meanwhile, the shuttle was docking at the reactor, letting whoever was in it back onto *Heimdall*, but my eyes were on that freighter. If it got across the wormhole, it might warn *Hypatia*. Might just get away clean. All this, everything, would have been for nothing.

System rejected my kill command, so I logged in under Donnelly's ID—I'd scoped his password months before (daughter's name and birth year—not too original, our former commander). Then I repeated my request for a kill on the *Mao*, a secondary on the *Boop*. Missile turrets swiveled, firing solutions fed into the targeting computer. I saw the *Mao* lunge forward, engines redlining, trying to scuttle across the horizon before DGS got a lock. It was a race— the inertia of a massive ship trying to accelerate versus a core full of limping, half-corrupted processors.

Inertia lost.

The *Mao* flared bright, missiles plowing into its hull and ripping it to pieces. A brief fireball blossomed out in the dark, the O_2 inside burning away to nothing, chunks of wreckage and bodies tumbling through the frozen dark.

Minutes passed. I heard footsteps. Magboots clomping on the grille. Growing louder. Slinging the rifle off my shoulder, I turned and aimed as a figure in BeiTech tac armor barreled through the control room door.

"Oh God . . . ," she said.

"Hello, Hanna."

She'd taken off her helmet, those blue eyes fixed on the body floating behind me, blood drifting aimlessly without gravity to drag it down. The wall screen showing what was left of the *Mao*. The people inside it. Her allies. Her friends. Tears welled in her lashes, broke free as she blinked, glittering in the air around her.

Rage boiled behind the sorrow as she turned on me, lips peeling back in a snarl. Breath coming quick, hands in fists.

"You ███████ . . . ," she breathed. "You killed them."

I caught movement behind her: a figure pushing himself down the corridor and out into the control room. He had no magboots, at the mercy of zero grav, clutching a bank of consoles to arrest his forward momentum.

Malikov.

His eyes fell on his cousin's body. That little ruined doll, floating in a halo of blood and water.

"Don't move," I warned him.

"Ella!"

"Nik, wait," Hanna warned.

But that was it. There was no stopping him. The kid's glare fell on me, pure hatred boiling in his eyes. With a roar, he dragged a cleaver from his belt and lunged toward me as I opened fire. Three-round burst. Center mass. He bucked back, spinning in midair, the force of the bullets not quite enough to slow his charge. His broken, bleeding body flew past me, hit the wall with a series of wet thuds.

Hanna screamed his name. Took a step forward, halted as I trained the gun on her. Fury in her glare. Jaw clenched. Knuckles white. But even watching her boyfriend die in front of her wasn't quite enough to send her out of control. Her instinct for self-preservation was nothing short of amazing. She had guts for damn sure. One of the things I loved about her.

Until she chose *him*.

"I'm sorry it had to be this way," I said.

". . . You're sorry?"

She stared at me. Bewildered. Furious. But behind all that, even there amid that carnage, I could see her brain ticking over. Working the possibilities. Daddy's little girl. Always looking for the edge. The angle. The strategy that would bring her out on top.

Not this time.

"Jax, I—"

I used to kiss her eyelids when she went to sleep in my arms. One kiss to each eye, a final one on her forehead as I'd whisper, "Sweet dreams, beautiful." That's where the bullet got her. Right on that smooth expanse of skin above her brow. That skin I'd kissed a thousand times. One last kiss good night. Rocking her in her boots, head snapping back, blood in the blond.

Sweet dreams, beautiful.

And then it was over.

Director Frobisher, I'm sending this to you from Command & Control in *Heimdall*'s Alpha Sector, exactly seven minutes and thirty seconds after the destruction of the *Mao*. I can see a second fleet of drones incoming on *Heimdall*'s short-range scanners. They should be here in about five minutes. From the size of the fleet, I can only presume they're here as your insurance policy—after all the trouble you went through to clean up this mess, I'm reasonably sure you're not willing to leave another one. You don't strike me as that kind of woman.

Falk and his entire team are gone. *Heimdall*'s staff and any residents were killed prior to or in the destruction of the *Mao*. I've already purged the computer systems of any and all data pertaining to events on the station after August 14.

I want you to know your hands are clean.

I think I knew this was coming. The writing was on the wall for a long time now. You said it yourself, right? I'm not naïve enough to think anyone's getting out of this alive.

I'm still not even sure how I feel about that.

But maybe you could do me one favor?

My dad still lives on Jia III. On the Tàiyáng Grid. I know you can't tell him the details, but if you could maybe get word to him that I did good. Did my job. Duty. Code. Loyalty. He'd want to know that.

I think it'd make him proud.

I'm gonna go wait in the Atrium . . .

Close my eyes in all that green. Listen to the waterfall.

Breathe.

This is Rapier (BT:po-1789i) signing off.

--------------------------END OF FILE

UTA TRIBUNAL TRANSCRIPT — KERENZA TRIALS DAY 92

Chief Prosecutor: Gabriel Crowhurst, BSA, MFS, JD
Chief Defense Counsel: Kin Hebi, BSA, ARP, JD
Tribunal: Hua Li Jun, BSA, JD, MD; Saladin Al Nakat, BSA, JD;
Shannelle Gillianne Chua, BSA, JD, OKT
Witness: Leanne Frobisher, Director of Acquisitions, BeiTech
Industries, MFA, MBA, PhD
Date: 10/28/76
Timestamp: 14:51

—cont. from pg. 870—

Crowhurst, G: What did you make of your agent's Acquisition Team Report, Dr. Frobisher?

Frobisher, L: [Consults with counsel.] The report is a fabrication, along with most of this file. Lies strung together by the so-called Illuminae Group in a transparent attempt to pin the blame for this tragedy on BeiTech.

Crowhurst, G: So you claim to have no—

[sound of static across courtroom PA]

Hebi, K: . . . What is that?

Al Nakat, S: Bailiff?

Bailiff: Apologies, Your Honor. We seem to be having technical diffic—

[high-pitched squealing]

[burst of static]

Unidentified Voice: Attention, UTA tribunal. Attention, UTA tribunal.

[sound of crowd]

Chua, S: Who is this? Identify yourself!

Unidentified Voice: This is Hanna Donnelly.

[sound of crowd]

Al Nakat, S: Order! I said order!

Hua, LJ: How are you transmitting through our public address system? Hijacking United Terran Authority computer channels is a serious crime.

Donnelly, H: Sounds like I should get myself a good lawyer. You know a bunch, don't you, Director Frobisher?

Hebi, K: Your Honors, defense objects!

Donnelly, H: Hello, Leanne. Surprised to hear from me?

Frobisher, L: This is exactly the sort of cheap showmanship th—

Hebi, K: Your Honors, are we really going to be subjected to more cheap theater from the prosecution? We have no proof whatsoever that this *criminal* is who she says she is.

Donnelly, H: Run a voice comp scan, Mr. Hebi. You've already got my aural sig on dozens of radio files. I think you'll find they match pretty closely.

Donnelly, H: Perfectly, in fact.

Donnelly, H: And you still haven't answered my question, Leanne.

Donnelly, H: Surprised?

Frobisher, L: [inaudible]

Crowhurst, G: Miss Donnelly, this is Gabriel Crowhurst, head of the prosecution.

Donnelly, H: We know who you are, Mr. Crowhurst.

Crowhurst, G: I'm sorry, "we"?

Donnelly, H: The Illuminae Group.

[sound of crowd]

Al Nakat, S: Order! One more outburst and I will clear this court-room!

Crowhurst, G: Miss Donnelly, if you are who you say you are—and our technicians *will* be verifying your identity by voice comp, believe me—you must know this conversation presents a few logistical difficulties.

Donnelly, H: How so?

Crowhurst, G: Well, according to the very files your group supplied us, you're dead.

Donnelly, H: You're right, that sounds serious. Should I take an oath or something? I, Hanna Alimah Donnelly, do solemnly swear that I definitely exist . . .

Crowhurst, G: Miss Donnelly, regardless of your claims, you, the Malikovs, the crew of *Heimdall*—you're all officially deceased. According to the Acquisition Team Report the Illuminae Group gave the UTA, all of you were killed in *Heimdall*'s final minutes by Samuel Maginot, aka Jackson Merrick, aka Rapier.

Hebi, K: Defense objects. Your Honors, the prosecution is now conducting a conversation with a dead girl about the fraudulent testimony she and her terrorist organization supplied to a UTA tribunal. How long will this be allowed to continue?

Al Nakat, S: I must concur, Mr. Crowhurst. Unless you—

Donnelly, H: Have you ever played poker, Your Honor?

Al Nakat, S: . . . Of course I have.

Donnelly, H: Then you know what a bluff is, right? Act like you've got a handful of nothing, sucker your opponent into a big bet? Then drop your aces?

Al Nakat, S: Are you saying—

Donnelly, H: I'm saying Rapier's report was written to make BeiTech think they had the winning hand. If the good Dr. Frobisher here believed the *Heimdall* was destroyed by her insurance fleet, and that Assault Fleet *Kennedy* was speeding on its way to destroy what was left of planet Kerenza after having already X-ed out the *Hypatia*, then *she'd believe she was safe.* BeiTech would have no reason to hunt for witnesses when we were all dead. And that'd give us the time we needed to pull together this dossier and expose the crimes Dr. Frobisher and BeiTech had perpetrated on Kerenza and Jump Station *Heimdall.*

Frobisher, L: I refuse to put up with this for another second!

Chua, S: Dr. Frobisher, sit down immediately.

Frobisher, L: This entire tribunal is a farce!

Chua, S: Counselor, you will control your client, or so help me . . .

Al Nakat, S: Miss Donnelly, if Samuel Maginot's report was indeed a fabrication, perhaps you might tell the court what happened in *Heimdall*'s final minutes?

Donnelly, H: I'm glad you asked.

Donnelly, H: But I can do better than tell you, Your Honor.

Donnelly, H: I can show you.

BRIEFING NOTE:
Transcript of
footage taken from internal
intellicams aboard *Heimdall*.

**Surveillance footage summary,
prepared by
Analyst ID 7213-0089-DN**

Ella Malikova is floating over *Heimdall*'s wormhole control system, typing furiously. Her hair is loose, a long black whip trailing behind her as she listens to the voice piping through her palmpad—AIDAN's sexless, toneless inflection running her through the sequences to stave off the auto-shutdown systems. She's still half dusted from the lanima toxin, pupils dilated, chewing her lip, eyes locked on her screens.

And then Operative Rapier enters the room.

He takes in the scene at a glance. The bodies of the BeiTech kill squad, his former comrades. Cerberus, Sensei and the rest. Their corpses floating among hundreds of aimless, tiny balls of scarlet and shell casings drifting in the zero grav.

Ella glances up at the sound of his boots. Eyes growing wider.

"Jackson Merrick," she finally says. "Ya know, my fem Zoe had me dub a mix of y—"

He raises his rifle, and the words die on her lips.

But strangely, Rapier doesn't shoot.

"What are you doing?" he demands.

Ella's fingers are still tapping away on the keys, eyes locked on his.

"Your boss shot the ███ out of the system before he cashed out, Secret Agent Boy. Shutdown sequence is trying to engage. Close the wormhole before the *Mao* can get away from those incoming drones." She stares at him coolly. Unafraid. "And I'm stopping it. Unless *you* stop *me*."

Rapier glances up at the viewscreen against the wall. The bulk of the *Mao,* turning toward the wormhole, thrusters flaring bright. Five hundred or so witnesses to the atrocities committed aboard *Heimdall,* headed toward the Kerenza system, where BeiTech can't touch them.

In a minute or so, they'll be across the brink.

Out of reach.

Footsteps ring in the corridor, magboots thumping on metal. Rapier keeps his rifle trained on Ella, eyes shifting to the doorway as Hanna Donnelly barrels into the room, a halo of blond floating about her pale, blood-spattered face. Blue eyes widen as she spies Rapier, breath catching in her lungs. Nik Malikov pushes himself into the room behind her, hand going to the handle of the bloody cleaver at his belt as he catches sight of the rifle pointed at his cousin.

"Merrick!" he shouts.

"Nik, don't," Hanna warns.

The room is deathly still. The *Mao* pushing closer toward escape.

"Hello, Hanna," Rapier says.

"Jackson . . ."

Her hands are fists at her sides. Muscle in her jaw twitching.

"There's another drone fleet incoming," he says, eyes locked on hers. "BeiTech sent a backup in case Falk dropped the ball. They're set to destroy this station and everything on it in about twelve minutes' time."

"I know."

"Your Little Spider here tells me the wormhole controls are shot. Looks like one of you three is going to have to stay behind if the other two want to get away."

Malikov looks to the girl beside him. "Hanna?"

Rapier glances at the kid, mouth twisting in a smirk.

"Looks like she doesn't tell you everything, loverboy."

Ella is still tapping away at the keyboard. Eyes locked on the rifle locked on her. The *Mao* is only seconds away from breaching the wormhole now. Hanna is tense as a steel spring, Malikov coiled behind her. If Merrick opens fire on Ella, the pair of them might still take him. The *Mao* might still get away. If he opens fire . . .

If he opens fire.

Except he doesn't.

The wormhole flares bright, a million ripples per second, blue light filling the control room as the freighter plunges across the breach. Twisting and stretching along the hyperspatial bridge, hurled millions of light-years across the universe, hundreds of witnesses torn from BeiTech's clutches who now might live to tell the tale.

The whole time, Rapier doesn't move a muscle.

The light dies slow, reflected in the narrowed, confused eyes of Nik Malikov and Hanna Donnelly. Rapier is still staring at her: the girl he wrapped up in lies, the girl whose world he tore apart, the girl he once claimed to love.

"Ten minutes," he says. "You three had better hurry."

Malikov glances at his cousin, who shrugs and shakes her head.

Donnelly frowns. ". . . What are you saying, Jackson?"

"It's not about what I say, right? It's what I do that matters here." Rapier lowers his rifle as he quotes her. "This wasn't the way it was supposed to be. I never wanted this. And like you said, I made promises. You remember, Hanna?"

She blinks then. Eyes shining a touch too bright as she whispers, ". . . I remember."

Rapier nods at the viewscreen.

The wormhole and the Kerenza system waiting beyond it.

"That's where you'll find them. Just through there."

Magboots clunking, he trudges around to the console beside Ella. Watching her keystrokes, memorizing the patterns that will stave off the shutdown a moment longer.

"You better go," he finally says. "Take the *Boop* and run. Hook up with the *Mao*. Find the *Hypatia*. I don't know what comes next. But whatever you do, make it count for something."

"Why the hell should we trust you?" Malikov growls.

Rapier glances at the boy and shrugs. "What choice have you got?"

"And what about BeiTech, Secret Agent Boy?" Ella asks. "They think we're still kicking, they're just gonna set more dogs on our tails."

"They'll have a hard time following you." Rapier nods to the wormhole. "And I can spin a lie to Frobisher that'll keep them off your backs. For a while at least. The longer we stand here arguing about it, the less time I'm going to have to write it. Those drones are eight minutes away."

The cousins glance at each other. Ella shrugs.

"Go," Rapier says. "Now."

Malikov grabs his cousin's hand, guides her across the room, her legs trailing behind her in the zero grav. She breaks his grip, pushes back to the console and snatches up a plastic baggie containing a small black goldfish. She glances at Rapier, rivers of dark hair drifting about her face. And with a small nod, she pushes back, away, past her cousin and down the corridor toward the *Boop*.

Malikov takes Donnelly's hand. Tugs insistently toward the hatch.

"Hanna, come on . . ."

She doesn't move. Staring at Rapier. The boy who wrapped her up in lies, the boy who tore her world apart, the boy who claimed he loved her.

"Goodbye, Hanna," he says.

Tears in her eyes. Rage? Hate? Sorrow?

Only she knows.

"Hanna, come *on*."

Finally, she allows herself to be led. Out the hatch. Down the corridor. Into the *Boop* and into the black. Thrusters burning bright, hurling them into the gleaming blue. Her eyes shining with the light of it. Beneath, between, beyond.

Along the endless circle.

Down the ceaseless spiral.

And waiting for her on the other side?

Just like he promised.

A WHOLE SKY OF DIFFERENT STARS A WHOLE SKY OF DIFFERENT STARS

UTA TRIBUNAL TRANSCRIPT—KERENZA TRIALS DAY 92

Chief Prosecutor: Gabriel Crowhurst, BSA, MFS, JD
Chief Defense Counsel: Kin Hebi, BSA, ARP, JD
Tribunal: Hua Li Jun, BSA, JD, MD; Saladin Al Nakat, BSA, JD;
Shannelle Gillianne Chua, BSA, JD, OKT
Witness: Leanne Frobisher, Director of Acquisitions, BeiTech
Industries, MFA, MBA, PhD
Date: 10/28/76
Timestamp: 15:24
—cont. from pg. 876—

Crowhurst, G: That's . . .

Crowhurst, G: That's quite a story, Miss Donnelly.

Donnelly, H: You don't know the half of it.

Frobisher, L: And we're supposed to give credence to this nonsense?
I suppose the *Betty Boop* and the *Mao* found the *Hypatia* waiting for
them on the other side of the wormhole? Champagne and medals for
everyone? All wrapped up in a neat little bow?

Donnelly, H: Wouldn't you like to know?

Crowhurst, G: Well, *I* certainly would. Your Honors?

Chua, S: . . . It's a compelling tale, I'll admit.

Al Nakat, S: But there's one small problem with it.

Donnelly, H: Pray tell.

Al Nakat, S: Miss Donnelly, Jump Station *Heimdall* was destroyed. Completely. Whether by this alleged drone fleet or not. The United Terran Authority has confirmed that nothing remains of the station but an ever-widening debris field. If indeed you and the Malikovs were reunited with the residents of *Heimdall* aboard the *Mao,* there was no way back to the central systems. You would've been trapped on the Kerenza side of the wormhole, along with the crew of the *Hypatia,* with no means of returning. The trip back to the Core would take thousands of lifetimes under conventional thrust.

Donnelly, H: Mmm, come to think of it, someone *did* mention that.

Al Nakat, S: And with *Heimdall* destroyed, there would be no way to transmit from the Kerenza system waypoint.

Al Nakat, S: So it's literally impossible for you to be here talking to us right now.

Donnelly, H: [laughs.]

Al Nakat, S: Miss Donnelly?

Donnelly, H: Okay, think about everything me and Nik and Ella and Kady and Ezra and all the others had been through. Leave aside the planetary invasions and killsquads, the mind-eating alien parasites, and mass-murdering artificial intelligences for a minute.

Donnelly, H: We'd just *saved two goddamn universes* from total annihilation after an interdimensional paradox event threatened to swallow them whole.

Donnelly, H: You *really* think "impossible" was going to be a problem for us after all that?

Al Nakat, S: I don't know, Miss Donnelly.

Al Nakat, S: Was it?

Donnelly, H: Hell, no.

Donnelly, H: We were just getting started.

Donnelly, H: You wanna know how it ends?

ACKNOWLEDGMENTS

The journey from *Illuminae* to *Gemina* has been an amazing one, and on a voyage like this, your crew is everything. We have the very best, and we're so grateful they're riding with us. Here are the folks who have our backs:

Our first readers, who boldly go where no sane person would want to, all so you can hold this book in your hands. Thank you to Lindsay Ribar, Marie Lu, and Michelle Dennis. We hope your eyebrows are never scorched off by a sugar bomb made by a seventeen-year-old with a MacGyver complex.

Our experts, who share their hard-won knowledge with us, then watch helplessly as we use it to murder thousands of people. Any errors are, of course, ours. Thank you to Mike Sims and Diana Rowland for information on police procedure, to Dr. Ailie Connell and Dr. Kate Irving for cheerfully violating your Hippocratic oaths, to Tsana Dolichva for astrophysics advice and Russian know-how, to Kira Ostrovska for Russian translation and information, to David Taylor and Michelle Dennis for computer and hacking-related witchcraft, and to Soraya Een Hajji for Latin badassery. Thank you also to Commander Chris Hadfield, whose videos from the ISS inspired us, and Hank Green and the SciShow Space team. And not to forget, many thanks to Dave Allen for his inspirational comedy stylings. We hope you're never blown out an airlock by a ███ed-off fifteen-year-old with a Mount Russshmore® addiction.

We were lucky enough to have an exceptional posse of authors say kind things about *Illuminae,* and for that, as well as their friendship, we thank Marie Lu, Beth Revis, Laini Taylor, Scott Westerfeld, Veronica Rossi, Victoria Aveyard, and Kami Garcia. We hope you never get your brainmeats munched on by a parasitic alien life-form while your squadmate tells bad jokes about beerwolves in the background.

Without our publishers, this book would be so many scribbles and incomprehensible diagrams on napkins. Team Random House—you are all incredible. Thank you to every single one of you. We hope you are always the sole occupants of your spacesuits.

Team Allen & Unwin in Australia and New Zealand and Team Rock the Boat in the U.K., thank you, thank you, thank you. You have been awesome. We hope neither you nor your interdimensional doppelgängers are ever shot dead running for the space train.

Our agents have been unwavering in their support, and are quite simply the best in the business. To Josh and Tracey Adams, Matt Bialer and Lindsay Ribar, Stephen Moore in film, and the many awesome scouts and foreign agents who have helped spread this ~~virus~~ book around the world, thank you. We hope some punk ex-con kid never blows your heads off in a space station bathroom.

All our books are written to music, and for this particular book's soundtrack, we'd like to thank Matt Bellamy, Chris Wolstenholme, Dominic Howard, Thomas J. Bergersen and Nick Phoenix, Jens Kidman, Fredrik Thordendal, Tomas Haake, Mårten Hagström, Dick Lövgren, Trent Reznor & NIN, Maynard James Keenan & Tool, Winston McCall & PWD, Oliver Sykes & BMTH, Ian Kenny & the Vool, Ludovico Einaudi, Marcus Bridge & Northlane, Robb Flynn & MfnH, D. Randall Blythe & LoG, Sam Carter & Architects, and finally Mitch Lucker (RIP—you only get one shot, so shoot). May you never find yourselves at the bottom of an open elevator shaft wearing only your unmentionables. Unless you like that kind of thing.

To all the readers, booksellers, librarians, and reviewers who read this series, told their friends about this series, harassed their friends about this series, hand-sold this series, came out and saw us on tour, created art or poetry, Tumblr'd, tweeted, or in any way helped spread the word about this series—thank you from the bottom of our hearts. May you and alternate-dimensional versions of you never try to occupy the same point in spacetime simultaneously.

To Nic Crowhurst and the Internal Revenue Service for bringing us together. May you never be asphyxiated by a SpecOps team leader just to prove a point to his sassy teenage nemesis.

To Amie's irreplaceable gang of sanity keepers—Marie Lu, Leigh Bardugo, Beth Revis, Stacey Lee, Kacey Smith, Soraya Een Hajji, Kate Irving, Michelle Dennis, Peta Freestone, Alison Cherry, Lindsay Ribar, C. S. Pacat, Sarah Rees Brennan, Team Roti, the Plot Bunnies, and, always, Meg Spooner—this would be no fun without you. May you never have your heads blown off in a shock-and-awe display by a mercenary with a mortgage that needs paying.

To Jay's grimy band of nerds and neckbeards—Marc, Surly Jim, B-Money, the goddamn Batman, Rafe, Weez, Sam, Dandrew, Beiber, the Dread Pirate Glouftis, the Conquest Crew, and all Throners, past and present—may your rampant egos never allow you to be killed in hand-to-hand combat by a seventeen-year-old girl.

To our amazing families, who don't bat an eyelash at the things we write and only ever cheer and ask for more (which probably explains a lot about us), we love you. May your universe never be under imminent threat of implosion because of a pop song about "lollipops."

And, of course, first, last, and everything in between, Amanda and Brendan. You are the ones who make this possible. All of this is because of you, and for you.